MW01133851

LOKI'S SAGA

Loki's Saga

A Novel of the Norse Gods

J.D. Foslan

This novel is a work of fiction. Names, characters, places, and incidents are either the product of the author's imagination or are used fictitiously. Religious, spiritual, and mythological elements are used fictitiously and are not intended to represent the theological or philosophical views of the author.

Copyright © 2015 by J.D. Foslan. All rights reserved.

ISBN-13: 978-1519585479
ISBN-10: 1519585470

First Edition: August 2014
Second Edition: December 2015

10 9 8 7 6 5 4 3 2

acknowledgements

The author would like to thank E.L. Falls and E.B. Jones for their friendship, support, and encouragement over the years. Their thoughtful feedback helped make this book possible.

CONTENTS

"Kvað ek fyr asum,
kvað ek fyr asa sonum,
þats mik hvatti hugr..."

"Before gods
and sons of gods
I spoke the thoughts
that drove me on..."

- The Lokasenna

PRELUDE

Midgard Past

Steam lifted from the boiling oceans and the skies began to clear. In the seas, green scum gave way to more complex life. Soon, the new world was alive. Giant trees hoisted their thick branches to the golden rays, celebrating the eternal cycles. Their leaves rustled, casting dancing shadows, and all the shades of green that ever were sparkled like prisms, devouring the light of the bold, young sun.

One day, three gods strolled among the forests of this world, the world called Midgard. After a while, they came upon two ash trees growing side by side. The trees' trunks were dark and gnarled. When the wind whispered through their boughs, the ashes whispered back, almost forming words.

The three immortals considered this sight for a time. They decided that the two brave ashes should know the power of the gods.

Odin, the Father of All, stepped forward. His one eye was as brilliant and blue as the sky overhead.

"To you two trees, Ask and Embla, I give spirit," he said. Then he breathed upon their leaves. This was the first gift. Without it, there could be no others.

Next, Odin's friend and fellow god Honir approached the swaying branches. He shyly lifted his fingers to their leaves. His hazel eyes were full of doubt.

"To you two trees, Ask and Embla, I give will," he murmured uncertainly. The trees had little choice but to accept the god's gift as given. And so do mortals hesitate and know confusion in their hearts.

The third of the gods leapt forward. Lothurr, who was also named Loki, gazed upon the two ashes and grinned to himself. His dark eyes burned with amusement as he spoke.

"To you two trees, Ask and Embla, I give fire in the blood and the comeliness of flesh!" He laughed, and the trees took on new forms with his final blessing, becoming man and woman.

This was how mortals were made. They soon grew in number. They foraged into new lands and they crossed strange and savage seas.

Not all of them remembered the gods' words. Many only knew that their spirits sometimes soared and sometimes fell, that the best of their plans faltered, and that the burning of their hearts set them on dangerous and unpredictable paths. Others did not remember even that much. Nonetheless, they carried their gifts with them.

Throughout all of Midgard, prayers were uttered, songs were sung, and stories told. This was the inheritance of spirit.

In every corner, decisions were made or unmade, ideas considered, and endeavors pursued or abandoned. This was the inheritance of will.

And all across the world, sparks were struck and flames were lit. Some of these fed only on wood and staved off the night's cold. But others seared within the blood, stirring great passions and fueling great hates. The heat sustained life and the heat destroyed life.

This was the inheritance of fire.

CHAPTER ONE
THE CAVE

Midgard Past and Present

My bonds were loosening. I first realized it because I was thinking coherent thoughts again. My rage and the roaring grip of my madness slipped away. The High One's magic was slipping too. No accident that. Odin's spells never faltered unless he willed it.

Instinctively, I looked up. Pain came from above, but I could not remember why. Everything was black. I blinked, trying to focus on something. Anything. My breathing quickened as panic overtook me. I yearned for light. The darkness closed in around me like a suffocating force, and my mind almost flew back to those broken, howling worlds I had been trapped in for so long.

No. I was stronger than that. I would not lose myself again. I willed myself to focus on the present.

As my heart slowed, I finally picked out one sight. A pair of ruby pinpoints glinted down at me from the heights, sinister with their own magic. These were the pitiless, gloating eyes of a viper.

I remembered that its venom fell unpredictably. There were hours, days even, when I was left unmolested. At other times, the poison pattered down like the spring rains, swift and insistent.

I remembered too that I was a god. One of the Aesir.

An Aesir who had been wrenched back across three slabs of rough granite and bound tight. A god whose arms, legs, and waist were held fast by ropes woven from the sinews of his own murdered son.

It was all coming back to me now.

My pale skin was scratched and bruised, and my wrists were rubbed entirely raw.

What had I done to end up here? The memories returned, as sharp and clear as if I were reliving them. I had killed the God of Good. My own nephew, Baldur, was dead because of me.

So that was it. This was my punishment.

But a lot of time had passed since then. Surely, the other Aesir had made their point?

I knew much of magic, tricks, and shapeshifting. I knew how to find opportune ways out of the worst situations. I turned my head to one side and spoke an old and very powerful rune. Although my voice was weak and my lips were cracked, I could still cast it. The sound of its name echoed harshly off the stone walls, fading down dank tunnels and forgotten chambers.

Nothing happened.

I sighed to myself, not entirely surprised. As if Odin would leave me such an easy escape.

At least I had my mind back. That was something.

Later, I heard gentle, familiar footsteps. My wife, Sigyn, stepped up to me and dabbed a cloth to my lips. Refreshing moisture cooled my tongue.

"Thank you, my star," I murmured.

She jumped back, spilling the bowl. It clattered loudly as it hit the rock floor.

"Loki?" Shadow-gray eyes stared deeply into mine. She leaned in and put a soothing hand to my brow. Conflicting emotions flickered across her face like the ever-changing edges of a fire. Relief and fear. Sorrow and hope. She had been alone with a raving god far too long.

My wife was as lovely as ever. Her hair was the deep brown of the rich earth, draping over her shoulder like a veil, reaching to her slender waist. She wore an unadorned apron dress over her white linen gown. It was the warm color of cinnamon, tied off with a simple woven belt.

I managed a small smile for her. Sigyn exhaled softly, then brushed her fingertips against mine.

I started to speak again when a lone drop sizzled down from above, striking me full in the chest. Poisonous, slicing agony eroded through my divine flesh, devouring the squishy stuff of lungs and scratching away at my ribs, clawing me apart from the inside.

I threw back my head and screamed.

I was an immortal. The venom could not kill me. It could only bring pain. Dreadful, shuddering, cascading spirals of pain.

My wife acted with the quick instincts of a goddess. She snatched up another bowl, one wrought of enchanted iron, and held it over my helpless form.

Perhaps the snake was angry at me for regaining my senses. Perhaps it was too dull-minded to care. Either way, the venom streamed down in a torrent. Each time Sigyn turned away to empty the bowl, I was left writhing and shrieking, bound to the stones. The very earth shook and rumbled, sharing my agony.

Eventually, the worst passed. Eventually, we were left in peace.

Sigyn and I spoke of many things. Sometimes my wife trailed her fingers through my hair or held my hand. It was all the affection we could share. I loved her more than ever, more than always. Though our relationship was an odd one, even by Aesir standards, I cherished her in my strange way. Sigyn was my first love and perhaps would one day be my last love, but she was never my only love.

A god could be nothing but true to his own nature. I had once ruled over the wild flames and the joyous, primordial beatings of the heart. Faithfulness had never been an expectation in our marriage. Still, despite the poison—despite my imprisonment—some part of me treasured the chance to be alone with her, to be hidden away with my bright and shining star.

Outside, the seasons churned by. Decades and then centuries passed.

After an especially rough week when the venom had rained down non-stop, I felt another change. Sigyn was gone, getting us food. I waited for her. What else could I do?

When my wife returned, she paced briskly to my side, her hem sweeping along the clammy stone floor of the cave.

"I brought chicken and broth today," she said.

"Good. That's all I can handle." Same as every other day.

She fed me the moist tidbits, one at a time. When I was done, she walked the remnants of the meal over to the fire and set a cauldron of water on for her tea. The cave was cold, and tea was the surest way the goddess had to warm herself. My frigid and bleeding flesh could give her no comfort.

Later that evening, Sigyn ran the damp cloth over my wrists. Suddenly, she stopped and met my gaze.

"Loki, do you know that you have no scars now?"

"I know that my hands hurt less."

"I think your wrists are healed. What of the ankles?" With an efficient motion, my wife twisted around to examine my feet. "Also healed," she announced calmly. A stranger would have heard no excitement in her voice, but I could tell she was very happy.

"Try the bonds," I requested. She did, but they could not be moved.

Years later, when the poison hadn't fallen for some time and my wife sat beside her fire humming a quiet lullaby, a new set of footsteps echoed through the cave. They were not soft and measured like Sigyn's. No, these struck into the very stone, brutal and relentless. High above me, the serpent began to writhe. Its glittering crimson irises burned with hatred and, for the first time ever, it hissed.

I knew then that my imprisonment would end. Probably not that day. But a release was coming.

Wreathed by the orange light of the flame, the greatest god, the Father of All, strode toward me. His hair was the color of iron, frosted through with silver and white locks, and it fell past his shoulders. His beard was full and his cloak billowed out behind him. The immortal's single eye fixed on me, brightest blue and as hard as a diamond. Cold and implacable, it pierced the very soul.

"Leave this place, Sigyn," Odin ordered.

My wife left. No one disobeyed our lord, the ruler of all the gods, when he spoke in that voice.

Odin placed a large, calloused hand on my bare shoulder, then clenched down, his thick fingers curling like talons. The grip was not quite hard enough to really hurt, but it ensured that he had my undivided attention.

Then, just as he had once bent down over Baldur's funeral pyre and whispered secret words in the dead god's ear, so too did he bend down and whisper words in mine.

"Skoll and Hati will circle this world ten thousand more times ere you walk free."

I was the cleverest of the Aesir. I did the math in my head.

"That's over twenty-five more years of this torment!" I yelled.

He inclined his head to me grimly. "Strength to you, brother." With that, Odin straightened up, leveled me with one of his stormy frowns, and turned away. He didn't look back as his heavy boots hit the granite.

"You asked this of me!" I shouted after him, thrashing against my binds. "I'll pay you back some day! I swear to it, here and now! Father of cowards! Conjurer of rot! Lord of oath-breakers—pervert and monster!"

The other god halted, his cloak stirring in an unseen breeze. Its colors were those of lapis and steel, and they blended and shifted, each shade melding into the next. My heart fluttered in my breast, and bile rose in my throat. Perhaps I had gone too far.

His back still to me, the Father of the Gods slowly raised a hand. I cringed against my rock. The fickle light from Sigyn's fire gleamed off Odin's hair, turning it into a spool of glowing mirror threads.

His wrist twisted slightly. I hunkered down as well as I could, given my less-than-ennobling position, and muttered dark words to myself.

The wrist twisted again. His hand was so large: it was the hand of a warrior, as strong as the tide. That hand fell first to one side. It hovered, then fell at an angle to the other side. The All-Father took off again, whistling a tune lifted from an ancient and particularly coarse ballad.

He had waved at me.

I was trussed down to a wet, frigid stone for another quarter of a century, and that maggot-eyed, pus-sided bastard had just freaking *waved* at me.

I spent at least half that time screeching with white-hot fury, lost in my own ranting thoughts. Sigyn and I no longer talked like we had during the centuries before Odin's visit. My wife remained faithful to me and attended to my needs, but the closeness we had enjoyed was gone.

Nothing—no force in any world—could make us stop loving each other. But the knowledge of when I would be done with my punishment somehow changed its entire nature. I could no longer accept my captivity. I was impatient, fitful. Every drop of venom was now a personal insult. I was sure—so very sure—that the one-eyed God of War had known exactly what he was doing. He could have told me of my freedom the day it was upon me. Instead, he had gifted me with the corroding poison of anticipation.

As if the snake's poison were not enough.

At long last, my sentence ended. I'd just woken up from a dreary and bitter dream—something about traveling with Thor and getting outwitted by every enemy we encountered—when I felt a new sensation: a warm, springtime breeze caressed my skin. It was scented with growing things and promise, and whispered songs about wandering to new places for the sheer joy of it all. Never before had such a breeze found its way into that cave. I blinked a few times to clear my sight, then lifted my gaze to the serpent. I saw only darkness. No malicious, garnet eyes stared down at me from above. No boiling venom fell to dissolve my flesh.

I tried the bond on my right wrist first. It shifted with my tug. Emboldened, I pulled harder. The sinew binding lifted from the stone. It did not fall entirely away, but it was now slack. I easily slipped my hand through, then turned to the left bond. That one proved more difficult. Twisted half upright, I surveyed the cave. A few embers still burned in the fire pit, dull red and gray, but the chamber itself was empty. Sigyn was nowhere to be seen.

I was on my own.

Rocking and yanking, I finally managed to wriggle my left hand out. It was hard to get leverage, but I bided my time, pacing myself so I wouldn't succumb to exhaustion. I forced myself not to think of the end result. Twist, twist. Pull, pull.

My left wrist was bleeding again for the first time in many years by the time I got it loose. I sat up and grinned into the eerily silent blackness. The ankles were an easy matter. With both hands free, I could use every trick at my disposal.

I let myself slide from the granite. My bare feet hit the ground. I had pushed myself away from the slabs and had just found my balance when my legs tingled and trembled from the restored blood flow, then gave out all at once. I hit the cavern floor hard, scraping my hands against grainy rock.

"Screw this!" I yelled into the darkness. My jaw clenched impatiently as I stewed over my own impotence, waiting for the waves of pin-prickling agony to clear from my legs. Slowly, they did.

I began to feel more like myself. I pulled myself upright, then looked up to where the snake had hung.

The first edges of my Aesir power were manifesting again. If I squinted, I could truly *see* into that lightless space. Lodged in a glossy outcropping of water-worn calcite, the serpent lay at an unnatural angle. Its once-black scales were milky and flaky, as if it were close to shedding, and its eyes were clouded over with the pearl sheen of reptile death.

I should have enjoyed some sense of victory. Instead, bafflingly, I felt almost sorry for the creature. In its own way, it had been as much a victim as me. Then I shrugged to myself and spun away from the serpent, leaving it to its soaring, airy tomb.

My eyes fell on the stone, onto the dry, stretched-out intestines of my son.

At the sight, a red and pulsing hatred filled me, craving destruction. But I knew my powers would never fully return to me in the cave. No, I would leave the granite slabs as an altar to the All-Father's cruelty. Someday, I'd see him tied down there in the breath-stealing, sanity-tearing silence. Static and hallucinogenic blurs would pick at *his* one eye as he peered up hopelessly into the void. I would make sure no goddess eased his suffering.

The path to the world above was steep and treacherous. I had to tread carefully, alert for the slippery spots where groundwater coursed over glass-smooth limestone. In the distance, I heard steady plops and dripping. The cavern was always changing, evolving with the eons. The sound comforted me as I walked because it *was* sound. Glorious, normal, everyday sound.

Eventually, crystal-blue daylight cast aside the damp shadows of the underworld. I increased my pace and soon reached the mouth of the cave. Sunlit grasses bobbed in the wind, and a line of pristinely white clouds lumbered across the sky.

I tried to shout, but my throat closed on the noise. Instead, I ran. My feet hit the tangled grass, and stems and twigs crushed beneath me, cutting my uncalloused heels. Not caring about the blood, I threw my arms up, raising them to that brilliant, cerulean expanse.

No snakes there.

The shout welled up then, a primal roar, a resounding cry of celebration. I whooped and I capered. I jumped and leaped, exuberant, laughing. Unbound and free. Alive.

The sun moved down its arc and long shadows sliced over the field before I got myself under control. I planted my feet on the wonderful earth, then bowed my head, focusing.

Where was I?

Midgard. The knowledge came to me instantly.

I waited for the deeper parts of my mind to stir. At my will, they did so. The humming strength and power of godhood beat within my chest, still hesitating at the threshold. Building. Growing.

I lifted my chin proudly, my arms held easily at my sides. I looked up at the sun. Its cycles were as unstoppable as the serpent's venom had once been. I gave it a sardonic little smile.

I raised my voice again, this time forming coherent words.

"I am Loki, son of Farbauti and Laufey, blood-brother of the highest god! I am the Shapechanger and the Trickster! I am he who created the children of Midgard, who gave them blood and fire! Hear me now!"

All around me, the breezes quieted and grew somber in welcome. Birds crossing the sky on obscure flights suddenly took off in other directions, scattering. The grass rustled gently, hailing me.

And then—*then*—the eternal power of the Aesir flooded back into me, coursing through my veins and setting my consciousness ablaze. I plummeted into my own thoughts. Knowledge snapped to me, more obedient than any servant. I perceived the passage of centuries and immediately grasped the new technologies wielded by the heirs of Ask and Embla. Death, destruction, changing societies, and migrations all exploded across the sky of my mind. Hope, development, justice, honor, and hidden kindnesses also flashed through my understanding.

I who had once stood beside the All-Father and Honir to give life to the denizens of beautiful and terrible Midgard now knew the histories, loves, and hates of my creation. It was all there.

My lips curled up in a vicious grin.

This was going to be fun.

CHAPTER TWO
ABSENCE AND RETURN

Asgard Present

I went over my options. I had so many now. I decided to return back home to Asgard, to where the Aesir dwelt in everlasting splendor. I'd been imprisoned for over a thousand years and had been away from that realm far too long.

The memory of our divine mead swayed me. No other drink could compare. The mead of the gods was sweeter than a lover's embrace and its smallest sip could lift even the hardest heart. It danced on the tongue, as warm and pure as liquid sunshine. Suddenly, I realized that my throat was parched and that my stomach was rumbling.

With a flourish of my hand, I summoned my magic. My very substance fluttered, a shadow upon deeper shadows, and I launched myself into the azure skies. Glossy, sable wings drummed through the air, and my sharp claws gleamed. I cawed as I ascended from the heavy fold of Midgard. I was victorious and free. My body was as swift as the pathways between the worlds, and my thoughts were more cunning than an arrow that never misses its target.

When I reached the forests bordering Asgard, I carefully pulled in my wings and landed in an eternal grove. The golden beams of an endless morning streamed over me. Dew reflected the sun back, dazzling my eyes. Like pristine jewels, the drops trembled in the breeze, glittering off ferns and spider webs.

I considered myself. Any god could easily perceive his own appearance. While I had gone about as a crow many times before, the shape would no longer suit me. I wished to be myself again.

I concentrated my Aesir will. Another flickering of shadow and flesh changed me back to my normal form. With bold steps, I strode over to a mossy pool I had just called into existence and admired my admittedly unnecessary reflection. There was a certain charm, a ritual, to doing things the traditional way.

I wanted a more modern look for my hair. An instant later, feathery ebony bangs fluffed over my black brows, teasingly accenting even blacker eyes. I commanded the rest of my hair to be cut not more than a few inches from my scalp. It had grown far too long in the cavern, becoming weighty and unkempt. It was good to start afresh.

Gazing into my pool, I saw that my skin was pale. Too pale. I frowned and let the unceasing light tan it. I had no desire to look like the underbelly of a frog or an eyeless cavefish trapped forever in its midnight prison. A dash of sun and Aesir power soon corrected that problem.

I ran a hand over my clean-shaven face, turning my head one way and the other. My visage was most fair to gaze upon.

As usual, I clothed myself in my favorite crimson tunic, one I'd acquired at an ancient mortal market flush with expensive amber and furs. I had since enchanted the tunic, strengthening it for divine use. Nothing crafted on Midgard could last long in the higher realms. But the basic design was the same: it was as red as blood and trimmed with black fabric. Sigyn had embroidered the sleeves and hems with threads of shining gold. It was a handsome tunic, befitting a handsome god. I gave my reflection a self-satisfied wink and walked off into the forest, smirking to myself.

Naturally, I avoided Bifrost, the shimmering rainbow bridge that arched straight into Asgard. I had long since figured out many other ways into our realm. Though I would have taken Bifrost in a heartbeat, the catch was that it came with Heimdall. Pompous, rigid, all-seeing Heimdall. I really wasn't in the mood to make an accounting to him—not before I'd downed several horns of mead, anyways. And he always wanted a damned accounting, a report on our every coming and going.

As if these were any of his miserable business.

Soft paths winding through beds of pine needles soon gave way to open, sunlit meadows. I found I was enjoying the journey. My feet were now clad in luxurious lambskin boots. Those I had acquired at home. Mortals just couldn't make a good boot.

I stopped beside a stream, getting my bearings. I seemed to be somewhere outside Freya's hall. I struck off to the right. The temperature was perfect, and the skies were clear. It was a good day to be out and about.

Later, I heard the sounds of battle. Odin's chosen warred on their bloody field. I gave them a wide berth, staying out of sight. The drills, the maneuvering, the preparations: they were all so pointless. Surt the Flame-Giant would consume every world in fire someday. No one could stop him. The warriors might as well have sat inside their hall getting drunk off their mead. But Odin maddened them with war-lust and set them against each other to gash at each other's flesh.

The clanging of steel on steel grew fainter as I strolled past a stream. I passed through a grove of young saplings with silver, glittering leaves. They sang to me as I walked by: "Welcome home, Loki of the Aesir, cleverest of the gods!"

"And the handsomest!" I reminded them glibly. The young trees shivered, but didn't answer. I had only been the handsomest since Baldur had died.

The first sign I was almost to Valhalla was the smoke. Heady, woody scents mixed with the mouth-watering smells of roasting meat. The smoke hung in the fields and drifted among the trees outside Odin's hall, low and gray, a cindery fog that the Asgard sun could never quite dispel. I picked up my pace as the ashy tendrils embraced me, but I took care not to breathe in too deeply. Very soon, I would drink my fill of Valhalla's sweet mead.

I sauntered over to a side entrance. Gilded pillars of dark wood rose up before me, carved with spiraling knotwork and the heads of ferocious animals. Gems gleamed from the animals' eyes and from between their open jaws. I halted before these and frowned at them. The jewels seemed so very cold and sinister, like the eyes of the dead serpent. Or like the All-Father's merciless stare.

I curled my lip with disdain, then reached behind the arching ridge of one of the carved knots. With a flick of my wrist, I plucked a large ruby from the gaping maw of a fantastical dragon. The theft wouldn't be immediately obvious. Someone would have to peer around the pillar to see the empty socket where beige tree-flesh now flared as bright as a wound, a rending against the stained, gracefully crafted surface.

Humming a snatch of a forgotten ditty, I pocketed the jewel.

Naturally, Odin was expecting me. As soon as I entered his hall, his two wolves glided over, sniffing at me curiously. They were broad-shouldered and had iron fur frosted through with silver, just like their master's hair. Geri bumped against me with good humor, his shaggy coat cushioning the impact. But Freki just stared at me with his reserved yellow eyes, not quite sure if I still belonged there.

"Give it a rest, fur-face," I hissed at him, keeping my voice down so no one else could hear. The more suspicious of Odin's familiars laid his ears back and turned away, growling low in his throat. Geri, however, trailed along behind me, his tongue lolling.

The lord of all the Aesir sat on a wooden throne by a roaring hearth. His one eye impassively took in my every move. I'd calmed down since our last encounter. While I wasn't happy with him, I would still pay him homage, as was his due. I strode over to Odin's high seat and stopped in place, facing him. Then I bowed my head respectfully.

"Honor to you and your hall, Great One."

He rose to his feet. He was clad in a simple, fur-trimmed warrior's tunic of bluish gray, and his shadowy cloak hung off one shoulder. The Wisest of the Gods was a sight to behold. A silver lock fell over the gouged place where his second eye had once been. His nose was as aquiline and handsome as mine, but his brow was rough. The ruler of the Aesir stepped down, then clasped me on the arm. He did not smile, and there was no glimmer of emotion in his remaining eye.

"Hail to you, brother of my blood." The All-Father paused, then turned to one of the servants. "Gather the others. Let it be known that Loki is to be welcomed back among us." He scowled as his messenger fled. "There will be much talk tonight, and not all of it good. No matter. For now, come and enjoy the hospitality of Valhalla."

A horn was passed to me, brimming with the mead of the gods. I drank deeply, almost as gustily as Thor once had when he had tried to swig down an entire ocean. Finally feeling a bit sated, I wiped my sleeve across my lips. Neither Odin nor I spoke of my captivity. The god of war and magic took his own mead in measured gulps, still watching me.

"I require meat," I told another servant. I was brought steaming boar's flesh piled upon a steel plate. I ate heartily. Odin did not join me this time, for he subsisted on Asgard's mead alone.

I grunted as I pushed the emptied platter aside. "Valhalla is a fine place for a meal, brother, but I'd rather do my celebrating elsewhere."

Odin's hall never changed. The floors were plain, beaten-down wood. Thick pillars rose up to the shadowed, smoke-wisped roof. These were carved spear-shafts looted from vanquished giants. Far above, sullen glints of gold wavered in and out of sight. The whole place stank of rust. Mail tunics lay scattered across many of the benches, pinching seats for hardened warriors.

"No other hall will have you, old friend," the one-eyed god told me.

My lip curled again, but I said nothing.

Not much later, the other Aesir began to arrive. The first was Thor, which surprised me to no end. He was usually off fighting some horror or another, or out exploring strange and dangerous lands. Back in the old days, we had traveled all over the worlds together. I saw little trace of that friendship now. He was struggling to keep his expression neutral—and any sort of neutrality did not come easily to the Thunder God—but his cloud-gray eyes crackled with orange and white heat, a sure sign of his ire. He was dressed in brown leather mail worn over a plain tunic the color of summer oak leaves. His auburn beard was as big and bushy as ever.

Thor—the Slayer of Giants, the Thunderer, and the Protector of Midgard—wordlessly hefted Mjolnir, making sure I'd get a nice long look at it. The enchanted hammer, the most precious treasure of the gods, glowed and sparked with the plasma heat of lightning.

I rolled my eyes and ignored him. As if he could intimidate me that way. Hadn't I given him the damned thing myself?

Golden-haired Sif was not far behind her husband. She hesitated prettily by one of the hearths, her cheeks rosy and her green eyes shining. The other gods who had troubled themselves to show up found places to sit. Thor straddled a large bench, his hammer resting on his trunk-like thigh. Sif alone remained standing.

I took note of who hadn't come. Freyr was nowhere to be seen, but that wasn't unusual for him. He loved the woodlands and the crisp air too much to spend much time in any hall. Forseti—Baldur's only child—was missing too. Still brooding over his mom and dad, no doubt. With his dedication to the law, he was probably more aggravated about my failure to pay the wergeld than about the actual deaths.

My wife was not among the guests either. She had never enjoyed large assemblies. I gave her absence no more thought.

Skathi, the goddess of mountains, winters, and howling wolves, trailed in after the others. Her hair fell down her back in a loose braid, the honey-blonde and silver strands blending together like thin strata of rock. She wore a practical gown of unbleached wool, unembellished with any sort of decoration. She was not one for a lot of show, Skathi. Her girdle, though, was much fancier, with silver threads, green and white cloth, and a frosting of iridescent jewels. That was her idea of a joke, to adorn herself with just a hint of great beauty when she went about in such stark raiment.

The mountain goddess nodded to me distantly, the first of them to make any sort of less-than-hostile acknowledgement of my presence. Then, as if that small gesture had been a permission of sorts, beautiful Sif suddenly ran forward. She grasped me by the upper arms, squeezing them warmly, and planted a light kiss on each cheek. With a flush, she spun away, but her eyes were defiant.

Thor did not have the gentle or forgiving nature of his wife. With a snarl, he rumbled to his feet, his hard boots pounding the rough floor as he hefted his terrible hammer above his head, readying it for a strike. But he froze an instant later, caught underneath Odin's stabbing, single-eyed gaze.

"You did not hear wrong. Loki is welcome in Asgard once more. This is my will." The highest god's tresses blew about his shoulders, tossed up by a stray draft laden with orange embers from the hall's fires.

Everyone began talking at once. I lowered my head and kept track of who was objecting the loudest. I had a very good memory.

The gods had apparently grown complacent over the years. With my powers back, I perceived how they hadn't faced a real threat in ages. Thor the mighty Thunderer kept the giants far from their walls, and Heimdall the Sleepless guarded the bridge between the realms, ever vigilant. At the moment, Heimdall was saying something cutting about me. His light brown hair spilled over his rainbow cloak, and his white tunic gleamed like sunlight on diamonds. Odin watched him coolly, not interfering.

"Just wait, Heimdall, and I'll give you something to stick in your horn!" I whispered viciously. Although the interfering cur could hear a feather drop a hundred miles off, he did not hear me then. His own voice enamored him so.

Geri sensed that I was irritated and padded over. He laid his chunky head against the top of my leg, trying to soothe me in his wolfish way. I scratched him behind his ears and continued listening. He licked my hand.

Eventually, the gods realized that the All-Father was saying nothing. Silence gradually settled over the hall. Thor snatched himself a fresh horn of mead and guzzled it down aggressively.

"What say you, Great One?" he asked, slamming the empty drinking vessel on the table.

"I say you know my will if you have the ears to hear it. Or have the Aesir forgotten the laws of hospitality as surely as have the children of Midgard?"

They all blanched at that. Hospitality was a sacred duty.

Bragi struck up his lyre. Crafted in the old style, it was long and rectangular like a board. Its rounded corners were painted with bright colors, and a triangle of shimmering strings spilled down from the top of the instrument, thrumming at the god's touch. The Lord of Song played an optimistic tune, his fingers dancing, calling forth harmonies too beautiful to be heard in lesser realms.

I had to admit that I'd missed his music. Bragi himself didn't impress me much. He had a long beard and gold hair that fell down his back in soft ringlets. His deep blue tunic was nondescript, as was he. It was hard for a god to know where he stood with Bragi. The Giver of Music blended in and spoke neither favorably nor unfavorably when matters of concern arose. But he had been close to Baldur once. Not a mark in his favor.

As Bragi gifted the hall with his songs, the remaining Aesir trickled over to greet me.

Honir, of all of them, approached me first. His dull blonde hair was pulled back into a ponytail. With a hesitant frown, he clasped me on the arm. His grip was tepid and faltering, not unlike the god himself. Sometimes I pitied the mortals for receiving the gift of will from one such as him. I had tried to offset some of the harm with blazing passions, leaping blood, and the joys of the flesh. But all of that could only go so far. In the end, however, Honir had turned out to be a wise choice on the All-Father's part. The children of Midgard had swiftly proven they could handle neither Odin's spirit nor my fire without a steady, quenching balm of doubt. They sorely required the humility brought on by ceaseless questioning.

I had come to respect Honir despite all his dithering. He was my brother in creation and a good companion when the All-Father and I traveled the worlds. He was also too unsure of himself to hold me in any rancor for long. Like the other gods, he had cried out against me after Baldur's funeral. But the death was far behind us. He seemed willing enough to let bygones be bygones.

Regardless, I couldn't resist asking, "So, just how *are* you doing, old friend?"

"I... I—that is—" he stammered.

Skathi was next. Resolved as a snowstorm, she met my gaze boldly, and a tiny grin, meant just for me, flitted at the corner of her mouth. Her arm-clasp was hard, and I could feel the chill of her fingers through the cloth of my sleeve.

"Hail, Loki. Welcome home."

At least someone was finally showing me a measure of respect.

"Thank you, mighty goddess. You're too kind."

15

She snorted, not quite hiding her amusement. I had always been able to get a laugh out of the formidable Skathi, the great lady who ruled over the bleak and frozen lands of Thrymheim.

She stepped away, and Njord clasped my arm. The God of the Sea inclined his head gravely and gave me a reserved smile through his trimmed, slate-colored beard. Tyr followed him, obviously determined to make the best of things. The wise and quiet immortal—one of the very first of our number—did not speak. But he nodded to me formally, his golden hair brushing around his shoulders.

After him, Thor finally blustered up to me. He'd left his hammer on the table, his idea of meeting me halfway. The Thunder God's huge paw of a hand launched out and tousled my hair back to front and around again, leaving it thoroughly disheveled.

"Nice cut! Soft as a kitten's belly!" he declared to the assembly, his voice booming.

"Not as soft as your wife's arms!" I countered instinctively. Thor raised a heavy fist, noticed Odin frowning at him, then lowered it again, grumbling to himself.

I looked up at him. "We were once the best of friends, Lord Thunderer. Now you mock my manhood, and I can hardly still my tongue in response!" I gave him a nasty little smirk. "I think we should swear to a truce here and now, witnessed by the All-Father and the Aesir. What say you, Mighty One?" I held out my arm.

Thor glowered at me, but he couldn't refuse my offer without looking like a fool. As usual, I had outmaneuvered him.

"Truce," he grunted. Befuddled and unhappy, he clenched my arm.

The mead flowed and our voices rose in song. The more joyous tales of old were recounted, and cheerful talk filled the hall. We celebrated through the night and into the morning. Valhalla's golden shields hummed like bells above us, ringing with our laughter.

CHAPTER THREE
BLOOD BROTHERS

Jotunheim and Asgard Past

I was born before any mortal universe existed, in an ancient and terrible realm called Jotunheim. Jotunheim was the dwelling place of giants, and it was as a giant—not as a god—that I began my existence.

My father was Farbauti the Dreadful, who sired me among the brown blankets of pine needles. His form was like that of lightning. Farbauti was a Jotun, and he was not kind or given to affection. But one day he observed a comely young giantess swirling and singing among the groves, and even his hard heart was moved.

There was no childhood for one such as me. The two forces met, and from that instant on I thought quick thoughts.

I wandered my earliest home, entirely alone. Low, sooty clouds pressed down in every direction. Jotunheim soon bored me. At its most exciting, it offered storms and rocks, rolling grasslands, and raging rivers. There was no one to talk to. The few giants I met during my travels were simple in their thinking and pleasures, hungering only for the suffering and deaths of other beings. The air was always heavy, thick with frost and hard on the lungs. My heart too was heavy, for I was sick with loneliness. My awareness seemed to drift and circle upon itself, lost to the sheer dullness of my existence.

One day, I hiked treacherous cliffs overlooking a raging sea of flame. Difficult terrain was the only amusement available to me in that forlorn place. As I leaned over to brace my hand on a boulder, intent on pulling myself up a steep and challenging trail, a voice called down from above.

"Loki, son of Farbauti," it said, "come up here so we may meet." The voice was deep and rich, intelligent and wise. I had never heard such a voice before.

Afire with curiosity, I scrambled up the boulder and found myself facing a god. His hair was the healthy brown of the grass, and his eyes were as sharp and blue as the windswept skies.

"Who are you that you know my name?" I asked.

"Odin, son of Bor."

I considered his answer. "And who is this Bor to me, a child of Jotunheim?"

"Ask rather who his son is to you, Clever One."

"Who is he, then?"

"The one who would slay Ymir."

I flinched back. Waving my hands, I quickly shushed the bold god. "Let us journey together for a time, Odin."

"So be it."

After walking for nine days and nine nights, we finally crossed into the realm of the Alfar, the Light Elves. They were a strange and beautiful people, but even we had difficulty seeing them clearly. Their home was full of the highest magic and their speech was a kenning song. The Light Elves knew the first charms and had danced among the very earliest worlds, for they were almost as old as Yggdrasil, the Great Tree that encompassed all the realms and was the Source of all being.

"We may speak freely here," I told Odin.

His eyes met mine, taking measure. "Will you stand with me, Loki? Will you fight against Ymir?"

I hated Ymir, but I was not an idiot.

"What's in it for me, son of Bor?"

The god nodded sagely, as if he had fully expected my question. "What would you have?"

I hesitated. "In truth, I don't know, Mighty One. I only know that I'm tired of Jotunheim."

His sapphire eyes lit up like cheerful young stars. "Then we have our deal! Fight at my side and join my company in Asgard!"

I shook my head. "No. I have heard much of your kind, even on the storming plains. The gods would never welcome me. My blood is the blood of your enemies."

Odin fell silent. The gales tore at his chestnut locks, and his lapis-blue cape soared and flapped like a banner. At last, he held out his hand.

"Then let your blood be blood of mine," he declared. The warrior god drew a knife from his belt and slashed it across his broad palm. He passed the knife to me, hilt-first. I cut deep into my own flesh, and we pressed our hands together. The crimson ebbs and pulses soaked into our skin and mingled. My heart burst to life, filling my being with the joy of battle and all the cunning of the Aesir.

"And so we are brothers. Let none gainsay it." Odin smiled at me, showing his teeth. I saw that a new sort of grimness had settled on his lips. His hair had turned the harsh iron color of Jotunheim stone, laced with the frost of our winters. His cloak was now tinged with duller, grayer shades.

Bound to Odin's cause, I approached Ymir in his lair. He was a creature of death, ice, and the void, and his home reflected his nature. No hearth burned, and the only speech inside those walls was the whispered agony of suicide and despair. Vicious words of self-doubt settled over my mind, a denial of all beauty and all purpose. I spoke hurriedly, eager to leave that dreadful hall.

"Lord of Giants, I bring you a gift."

"Nothing you bring could ever interest me. You seek only your own death."

"Perhaps later. One of the goddesses has heard of your strength and valor. She wishes to meet you."

"Is she fair?"

"The very fairest. Freya, they call her."

Ymir was not immune to flattery. He followed me willingly, and we journeyed across lifeless, shifting sands while reeking steam poured from gashes in the earth. I bent my head down and hunched my shoulders, miserable in the other Jotun's presence. Ymir's impatience grew with each step.

"Enough," he ordered. "It is time for you to die. As I devoured your mother, so will I swallow you. Whole and screaming."

My dark eyes narrowed. I had often wondered what had become of Laufey, my father's consort.

Freya emerged from the twirling steam. Her long, blonde hair was sunlight after the rain, and her smile was welcoming. She cast an admiring glance at the giant. With a victorious roar, he lunged for her. A heartbeat later, the Aesir gods raged out of the sulfurous mists, howling war cries.

The first of them was Tyr with his razor-edged spear. His golden hair streamed behind him as he leapt up and struck true, driving the point into the giant's exposed side.

Next, slight Freya joined the battle. As blood-crazed as any male, she whipped a dagger from her gown and hacked at Ymir's thigh. The giant had no time to beat her off, for he was already locked in close combat with Tyr. I thought I saw two fuzzy blurs thrash into being beside her, wailing unearthly wails.

Freya's brother, Freyr, ran forward with his sword held high, his amber eyes burning with disgust for our enemy. Another god, armed with a bow and arrow, took to the fight. A fourth joined them an instant later: his brown hair and beard shimmered with refracted light, with all the colors of the rainbow.

The most depraved of all the giants towered above us, dreadful in his immensity. His shoulders were so wide that they scraped against the frozen skies, throwing suns from their courses and hurling galaxies to entropic deaths. His shriek carried up the Great Tree, rattling all its leaves. Ymir's face was the face of each creature's most secret and most perverse fear, and his fists were the stark grave with no promise of rebirth.

Odin entered the fray. He did not own his magic spear yet, but he was still the most formidable of the gods. He carried an axe with practiced ease. He gorged its blade along Ymir's limbs, following the paths of arteries. The giant's blood gushed forth, wetting the ground beneath us. I lost my footing and scrambled about in the muck. When I looked up again, I saw that Freya had been tossed from her perch on top of Ymir's leg. I pulled myself up and dashed over to help her. Waving off my outstretched hand, she snarled savage curses in a dozen languages.

"He'll have us! Do something, Jotun!"

"I know a charm, but it requires three wills."

She nodded sharply. "Odin!" shouted the warrior goddess. "We need you! Join us!"

The Father of the Gods glared at us. The fire of combat coursed through him, but he was never one to lose his wits. Grudgingly, he lowered his axe and trudged over to us.

The three of us—Odin, Freya, and I—stood back to back and shoulder to shoulder. Blood and dirt boiled around our knees. We were all strong in the ways of magic. On that day, we shared our powers freely, without any thought of our own interests.

I spoke a Word, and flame burned through Ymir like a fever.

Freya said another Word, and hope began to drip through the void that held his being together, corroding him from the inside.

Odin whispered the final Word, an enduring truth that can never be lost. Ymir fell.

The World Tree groaned and creaked. Deep among its roots, the dragon Nidhogg cried out, spouting flame. His moan reverberated up through the branches, shaking Yggdrasil's highest realms.

When the battle was over, we scattered the giant's wispy brains across the skies. Poisonous, bright, and burning, they would birth new stars. In turn, those stars would give rise to new worlds. We ordered Ymir's bones to circle and coalesce around a fresh sun we called forth at the very site where we had defeated him. Those bones would soon become a host to life. This was the greatest insult we could give him, for Ymir had once been the fiercest enemy of all that might ever live.

Our newly created universe was a shining tribute to our victory, and we looked after it closely. But the children of Jotunheim also took a special interest in the place. Our desecration of Ymir was an affront to them and all they stood for. And so, that universe—and that one world in particular—grew into a field of war, a disputed middle realm locked between the strongholds of gods and giants. That was how Midgard came to be.

At the time, however, my thoughts were on my own future. Soon, I would travel to Asgard. Odin had promised me a home among the Aesir. A god always kept his oath.

My first glimpse of Bifrost stole my breath away. I had known only the brown fields and stormy skies of Jotunheim. The sight was incomparable. I could only stand at Odin's side, staring at that luminous pathway of smoldering scarlet and vibrant yellow, of burning green and richest violet. Silent tears welled up in my eyes, and I was not ashamed of them. For all my power with fire, I had never seen such color or beauty.

My blood-brother gently took my elbow and guided me forward toward that bridge of purest light. He seemed to understand. His expression was serious, but very approving.

Before I could set one foot on Bifrost, a broad-shouldered god crossed in front of me, blocking the way. I blinked and found myself looking upon another Aesir, the chestnut-haired god who had helped us defeat Ymir. Up close, he was exceedingly handsome. His tunic was woven from the softest white wool, and dazzling rainbows streaked along its hems. Despite his splendor, the other immortal did not seem happy. His lips were compressed into a tight frown, and his multihued eyes blazed with wrath.

"Stand aside, Heimdall," Odin said. "Loki is with us."

"He's a Jotun," Heimdall countered.

My blood-brother slowly shook his head. "He is also an Aesir. I'll say it again. Stand aside. Let us pass."

That was the first time I ever heard that edge of command that sometimes crept into Odin's voice. I shivered away from it, though I was not the one who had brought it on. Heimdall curled his lip, but immediately backed off, bowing to his lord. Who could disobey that tone? Who could match his will against the will of the very highest god?

Fear sliced through my gut. I was to live with these beings. I, who was already very much used to walking my own paths, to thinking my own shrewd thoughts. Was I to lose all that? Was I to lose myself?

"Come on, Loki," Odin said quietly. His blue eyes were compassionate. It was time to go home.

I swallowed, but forced myself to meet his gaze, to keep my movements steady and calm. Anything had to be better than Jotunheim. I followed my blood-brother up the rainbow bridge, up to eternal Asgard.

Heimdall was not the only one who distrusted me. The other gods were less outspoken, but their hostility was no less obvious. As I sat by Odin's throne supposedly celebrating my first night among the Aesir, chilly eyes tracked my every move. There was a tension in the hall, like that of a very close-knit family waiting, with folded arms and tapping feet, for a stranger to finally grab up his cloak and be on his way. I was poured mead and offered food, but I knew I was not welcome. They merely followed the rules of hospitality. Because they had to.

I didn't touch the meat or drink. How could I enjoy anything of Asgard's when everyone was staring at me like that?

After a while, Odin rose to his feet. "Our numbers grow," he proclaimed. His words carried throughout the hall. "We now have a God of Fire."

Freya lifted a beautiful eyebrow. "Lord of All," she said, "I'll be the first to admit he did well by us in the fight. But surely he can't live here? We of the Vanir came to you as gods. A giant, though? Is Asgard any place for one born of Jotunkind?"

Odin nodded soberly. "A fair question from the fairest of goddesses. But Loki and I took an oath. Know that you question the right of my own blood-brother to dine with me here in my hall."

Freya's amethyst eyes widened, and the other gods began murmuring among themselves. If anything, their scowls turned more foreboding. I hunkered down in my seat. At that moment, I felt more alone than I had ever felt in my all-too-lonesome life. I was surrounded by immortals and seated near a warm hearth, but none of that mattered now.

A male Aesir stood up. His golden hair flowed over his shoulders, matching his gold-spun tunic. His bearing was that of one who preferred silence, of one who was very old and very wise. Tyr gave me a curt head-dip, then lifted his mead horn to the assembly.

"I drink in honor of you, All-Father. And I drink in honor of your new brother—our new brother. Welcome, Loki. Welcome to the company of the Aesir." Tyr's voice was as clear and bright as a cloudless night sky, and it rang with an ancient sort of authority.

Many long looks were exchanged, but the others slowly took up their horns. One by one, they raised their drinks in a salute, first to Odin, then to me.

My blood-brother smiled at them all, well pleased. "So shall it be from this night forward. If you drink to me, drink to Loki as well."

chapter four
the vanir war

I learned much about my new family as I settled in. Some, like Freya, had not originally been Aesir at all. Asgard had a sister realm, one equal to it in beauty. Its gods, the Vanir, were gifted in the oldest magics. They called their realm Vanaheim.

From the start, the two sets of gods could not get along. They had very different ideas about what should be. The Vanir stood for ceaseless prosperity, for light and peace. They wished to rule over a stable and placid cosmos in which each universe would shine on, brilliant and static, until it finally ended in fire. The Aesir, however, thirsted for struggle and change, for the tempering of spirits against adversity. They embraced conflict and the soaring cacophony of life they knew would surely follow.

Eventually, the Aesir and Vanir went to war. When both sides finally tired of their struggle, they exchanged hostages. Heimdall was one, as were Freya and her brother, Freyr. The two siblings' father, Njord, lived in Asgard as well.

Odin told me of these things as we strolled through the gleaming fields of Asgard. My new blood-brother clearly enjoyed my company. His eyes would light up each time I discovered a new sight or when I capered off to examine a particularly lovely tree. He'd chuckle deeply and follow a ways behind me, his stride controlled and steady. Everything was new to me. Every breath was full of joy.

"You have the innocence of a child about you," he said. "You delight in all things."

I smiled softly from where I had crouched down to tease a dandelion between my nimble fingers. Its tiny, narrow petals intrigued me. There had been nothing like it in Jotunheim. I had not known the All-Father for long back in those days, but I did know him well enough to take his words as a compliment.

Odin sighed all of a sudden. I jumped to my feet and faced him, letting my head to fall to one side in concern. A strand of shoulder-length black hair trailed over my cheek. I had already discarded my dull Jotun clothing and wore a simple tunic of red, for bright colors ever fascinated me.

"What's wrong, my brother?" I asked.

"You're a good companion, Loki, but I miss my friend Mimir."

I nodded, saddened on the other god's behalf. Mimir lived in Vanaheim as a hostage. Many years had passed since Odin had last seen him.

"The Vanir are lucky to have him," I told him consolingly. "Truly, you gave them the greatest gift. Even Freya cannot compare."

My brother made an approving noise in his throat. "Spoken as an Aesir. You understand us well."

"Of course I do. I share your blood!" I grinned impishly and Odin could only laugh.

All too soon, no one in Asgard had anything to laugh about. We gathered in Valhalla to hear about Mimir's death. One of the Alfar—the Light Elves—brought us the bad news along with the god's severed head. An Aesir's eternal life was ended. We all wondered how such a thing could happen.

Tyr and I joined Odin after the others left, soundlessly offering him the comfort of our presence. The God of War was hunched over on his throne, his great hands clenched into solid, shaking fists. His friend's head was nestled in the crook of his arm.

We waited, unmoving. The All-Father needed us.

Finally, my blood-brother looked up. His eyes were glazed and his breath was short. "There is more to this," he told us in a steely whisper. "I feel it."

"Who can kill an immortal but another immortal?" Tyr asked.

Odin suddenly grew very alert. "Yes, who? I will take on a new form and journey into Vanaheim. The truth is best found at its source."

He stood, his face dark with suspicion. Mimir had died surrounded by other gods, by other immortals. We all knew the Vanir could be subtle and strange. The head was proof enough of that: an Aesir would have sent back the entire body or nothing at all.

My blood-brother returned swiftly, and we quailed in his wake. He told us of how Mimir had been slain in cold blood. The gods of Vanaheim had not been pleased with their hostages. His closest friend's death was a murder, a personal message to him as Asgard's ruler.

When Odin finished his tale, Freyr nervously rose to his feet. The All-Father took in the other god's every move with a baleful expression, already reaching for his axe. There were many Vanir in our midst, and Freyr was the first among them. They could do us much harm if they struck at that moment, while we were still in shock. But Freya's brother only exhaled sorrowfully, blinking back tears. His red-gold beard flickered like treasure in the light of Valhalla's fires.

"Lord of All," he said, "my people have returned your good faith with cowardice and violence. I'll swear myself fully to the Aesir if you'll have me."

His sister spoke next. "I too would give you my oath." Her voice was like a fine blade being unbound from a silk sheath.

That night was one of the few times I ever saw Odin truly taken by surprise. He actually paled before he moved his arm away from his weapon.

"I give you my word as well," Njord declared. He nodded to his two children, his handsome face concerned.

"I swear it too!" Heimdall growled, hefting up his bright sword. "Better to defend holy Asgard than to mix with oath-breakers! Blood-kin or no!"

Shuddering with emotion, my blood-brother bowed his great head to them. His face was mottled with the rawest pain, but his eyes shone with the profoundest gratitude.

"I'll have you all," he said simply. "I'll have you all, and with gladness."

The twisting branches of Yggdrasil were our warpath, and its glittering leaves were our guiding stars. We marched across the World Tree, seeking our vengeance. Our boots thunked, echoing against its eternal wood.

Our journey was a long one, and I had plenty of time to take in the scenery. Each of Yggdrasil's leaves was an entire universe brimming with living, swirling worlds. Every once in awhile, I'd spot a leaf falling away—a dying universe. It would flare for a moment, an explosion of light against the soothing, fractal wholeness of the Great Tree. Then, the leaf would vanish, consumed by fire.

The sight was disturbing, for it was a reminder that all things were finite and that only Yggdrasil itself would endure. Surt the flame giant, a being of chaos and total annihilation, raged out there among the boughs. He swept onto each leaf as it trembled and separated from its Source. His sword was keen and remorseless. With that sword, he could slice through every last subatomic fiber of a doomed universe. All its worlds and suns fell before him, morsels to feed his insatiable hunger.

A wormy feeling of self-loathing trickled through me. I too ruled the fires. But what did I leave behind when the burning was done?

Eventually, we reached Vanaheim's golden gates. Odin opened them with a single, ferocious kick. The gates broke into a billion glinting pieces and blew away like scattered stardust carried off on snarling gales of fury. Our enemies' realm would never again be inviolate, would never again know complacency. Our arrival had already changed its very nature.

We put the Vanir's highest lords to death and retrieved Honir from their halls. He too had been one of their hostages. The god that would one day join me in creating mortals stood beside me as I wove fire among Vanaheim's bejeweled pillars, incinerated emptied council chambers, and set achingly lovely meadows ablaze. Soon enough, I'd learn that Honir almost never had a firm opinion about anything. But on that day, his face was as hard—as committed and resolved—as any other Aesir's.

One morning long after our invasion of our sister realm, I entered a forest I'd never been in before. The clean light of Asgard was more subdued there, and the trees were all aspens with thin, papery trunks and quaking leaves. I paused, listening. Hissing winds blew through the groves, and the slender trees rustled accusingly, warning me to turn back. I ignored them.

I had to speak with my blood-brother immediately, before he left home again to collect souls for Valhalla. After the Vanir war, Asgard had flourished and many of the gods had taken wives. I was already an uncle and a great-uncle many times over. I too had finally decided to marry, but there was a problem. My bride and I were planning to bypass certain venerable Aesir traditions. I knew that at least one of my fellow immortals would speak out against our betrothal. I also knew that a few words from the All-Father would still his tongue.

Further up a disused path, I rounded a bend. A large structure built entirely of silver towered above the treetops and flashed over the hills. This was Valskalf, Odin's forbidden hall. I had been a god for many centuries by then, but even I felt a tremor of unease as I approached its knotworked doors.

Valskalf's doors clanged open, metal ringing against metal. The lord of all the Aesir greeted me, his one eye glittering enigmatically. I lifted my chin and followed him inside.

We did not enter into Hliskalf, the secret chamber from which all the worlds and realms could be seen. No one but Odin and his wife Frigg were allowed in that room. Instead, he offered me a chair at a small silver table. A tafl board covered most of its surface, and delicate game pieces were already laid out for play. He took the seat across from mine.

"A game, Loki?"

"I'm not here for games, brother."

The All-Father fixed me with his lone, burning eye. He had torn out the other to win a drink from the Well of Wisdom. Soon after that, he had sacrificed himself to himself on Yggdrasil—had hung there, pierced and bleeding, for nine anguished nights—to learn the magic of the runes.

His gaze was truly fearsome now. I returned it measure for measure.

"Then tell me why you are here." The other god was curious, but he also seemed distracted. As if he had other things on his mind.

"I've come to discuss Sigyn. I want to marry her."

Odin knew me better than anyone. He nodded, unsurprised. "So marry her."

"The others won't like it. I'd have you bless us and welcome her to Asgard yourself."

The All-Father's gray brows drew together as he considered my request. I spun one of the metal tafl pieces between my fingers, watching it twinkle.

After a while, my brother spoke again. "I might do that for you, Loki. But a gift requires a gift."

I rolled my eyes. "So you always say. What do you want this time?"

Odin's response was immediate. "Stand with me again in Midgard. You gave mortals the fire in their blood. You must think of another blessing to add onto your first. If you would have me on your side, you must be on mine."

So that was what was troubling him. Midgard. The influence of giants had been growing as of late. The Jotuns gorged themselves on human minds and hearts. We could not let them prevail.

"I'll come up with something," I promised.

I always did.

The next morning dawned clear and bright, but deep cloudbanks hung off the western horizon. These promised storms in the afternoon, for we Aesir were passionate gods, and too much fair weather would have burdened our spirits.

I stood before the Well of Urd where we immortals held council each morning, gazing into its shimmering white depths. Flawless quartz crystals surrounded the small, round pool. Each stone was pressed against the next, glowing with its own iridescent light. Shifting reflections played against the red fabric of the unembellished tunic I wore back then. My dark hair stirred in the moist breeze, brushing about my shoulders.

For a while, I waited alone. Odin finally appeared at my side.

"What have you decided, Loki?" he asked, resuming the previous day's conversation without preamble. "The children of Ask and Embla are weakening. What gift will you give them?"

He waited on my answer, hulking and brooding. The well's churning waters tossed up drafts, ruffling his gray beard. I toyed with the end of my belt and bided my time.

"The mortals share stories and laughter around their fires," I said at last. "Stories and laughter shall be my gifts." I grinned unpleasantly, my expression turning feral. "Those two blessings, and the wisdom of blisters and seared skin besides! Never say I'm not generous!"

My blood-brother frowned at me, less than pleased with my answer. "Nothing is ever simple with you, Loki."

The other gods arrived at the well. Sigyn took a place beside me, her dark brown hair cascading down her back. Her cheeks were pink with the flush of youth. My lovely goddess slipped her hand into mine. She wore an unpretentious gown the color of fresh earth, draped over a long woman's shirt of light gray. A sparkle—the light of Alfheim—followed her as she moved, casting traces of a fey magic entirely unlike the powers of the Aesir.

I squeezed her fingers. I could have had any shining goddess or giantess for my own, milky of skin and bright of hair. Instead, I raised our two clasped hands above the well. Flickering streams of light bounced off the pool, creating rippling bands under our interlocked fingers.

"Today I announce my betrothal. Sigyn and I shall stand on the pinewood platform and be joined."

I waited for my blood-brother's blessing. The All-Father's face was distant and unreadable as he gave it, but his tone left no room for argument. Our marriage would take place within the month. The other gods congratulated us enthusiastically enough.

When the initial well-wishing trickled down, I found myself facing Baldur, Odin's son and my nephew. His brow was white and his pale hair gleamed in rivalry to a sun. He wore his beard trimmed, and his garments were of the finest snowy silk, embroidered with gold. Wherever he stepped, sweet-smelling flowers soon bloomed. Rare songbirds often alighted nearby him, warbling rapturous songs.

I could see that Baldur did not share in my joy.

"Uncle," he said in his warm, honeyed voice. "This is sudden news. Why would you wish to marry... Sigyn?"

I tried to keep my tongue civil. My betrothed was some distance off, chatting with Frigg, and I would do nothing to disturb her happiness.

"Why would I not, Baldur?"

He sighed, his clear blue eyes full of some sort of weird sympathy. "Come, look around you, uncle. Are not the truest daughters of the Aesir fair? Stalwart Thrud and sweetest Hnoss, attentive Fulla and ever-loyal Var? Do not all of these seek a husband?" He paused meaningfully. "You have already brought much grief to our realm. I am very concerned for you. One of those goddesses could temper your flame and bring us peace. Sigyn, alas, will not."

I barked out a laugh. "Temper *my* flame? I've never heard you joke before, nephew! What a time to start!"

The handsome god's eyes flickered reprovingly. I raised my dark brows at him. Gentle Baldur, the God of Good, had really been getting on my last nerve lately.

"I do not jest, uncle. Listen to my words. Heed my counsel. My judgments are the fairest and wisest in all the realms."

I snorted at that. "Your own son, Forseti, pronounces fairer verdicts. And he's certainly wiser than you!"

Baldur's only child looked up sharply when I mentioned him. Forseti was a very young god with the mannerisms of an academic. His jaw, however, was firm and strong, a twin to his father's. His hair was of the purest spun silver, as thick and wavy as Baldur's, but cooler than distant moonbeams. Those locks fit his personality well. My nephew's son was the God of Law and ever dispassionate.

Gray eyes locked on mine. Forseti's mouth twisted down. "Kindly leave me out of this discussion, Loki." When he spoke, his voice was low and ponderous.

28

I winked at the younger god, knowing how it would irk him. We'd had dealings before, him and I. He always took himself so seriously.

"I meant no offense, Forseti! I'm just noting how the son surpasses the father!"

He turned on his heel and stalked away, his movements tense.

Baldur was shaking his head. "See? You stir up strife yet again. Heed my wisdom, Mischief-Maker. Seek another wife."

That was the final straw. I had already indulged my nephew's insolence far too long. It would end there, that very day.

"Enough, Baldur! I hear no wisdom! I hear the empty baying of a mongrel! Go find a boot to chew on, if you must worry at something."

My nephew's eyes widened in disbelief. "Uncle?"

I rounded on him, barely inches away, my own gaze pure fire. "Oh, stop playing the innocent, God of Curs! You've done more damage to Asgard than I ever have! Even Odin knows it. When's the last time he spoke to you? Can you even remember?"

"You go too far!"

"You haven't gone far enough. Didn't I tell you to find a tasty boot?"

Baldur's fair lips pressed into a line. That was about as much of a reaction as I could expect to get from him. In his own mind, the God of Good never looked to his interests, only to those of others. I was just being ungrateful.

I forgot about him as soon as he left. I had better things to think about.

After all, I was to be wed.

CHAPTER FIVE
A CRIMINAL HISTORY

Asgard and Midgard Present

The evening was turning oppressive. Heat sizzled between the mounting thunderclouds and the slender birches fretted under the humid gusts. I was quickly recovering from the worst of the cave, but my freedom felt almost confusing at times. I couldn't figure out what I was supposed to *do* with myself.

I paced about Valhalla for lack of anyplace better to be. I was restless and I was bored. Geri followed on my heels as my boots pattered out senseless, disorganized beats. Meanwhile, the All-Father surveyed his warriors with a bleak, introspective smile. Their spirits were high after fighting. The crude former-mortals guzzled down horn after horn of mead and sang raucous songs, oblivious to the building pressure in the air, to the suffocating anticipation of a storm that wouldn't come.

I curled my lip up at them. My blood-brother's two crows could have carried a tune better, and to more effect.

Odin suddenly caught my eye. His smile vanished. "Loki, your moods sour my hall. Take them somewhere else."

I inclined my head to him. "As you say, brother."

Geri scampered behind me as I ambled over to one of Valhalla's many exits. The wolf stopped at the threshold, peering out into the night. He would go no further. I ran my fingers through the soft fur on the crown of his head and whispered runes of knowledge in his ear.

That done, I struck off for Midgard.

I clad my feet in fine leather shoes that slapped against the asphalt. My pants were dark silk and my crimson shirt was precisely tailored. I refused to look anything less than my best when I appeared among mortals.

I paused under an electric street lamp and sniffed curiously at the exhaust-tainted air. The smell wasn't as bad as it had been in the old days. At least the place no longer stank of manure.

A haze of conflicting perceptions seemed to spin over my brain like cobwebs, dragging it down. The wisdom of the Aesir still burned within me, but caught between so many humdrum mortal thoughts, that wisdom came to me unpredictably, flickering like a candle.

I waited on the corner. I knew the confusion would clear if I gave it time. Still, I'd never felt so many human minds in one space at once. Their world really had changed.

Gradually, I adapted to Midgard. I found a shop that was open late.

Fluorescent lights bleached my skin as I made a bee-line for the spirits and plucked a bottle of rum off the shelf. I sauntered back outside without paying. A security camera recorded my passing, but I willed the tape to static and muttered a glamour over the one human who had noticed me.

Outside, the moon hung white and remorseless in their light-saturated sky. Most of the stars were lost to sight, but the night was pleasant. The dead leaves of another season crackled under my feet, and the air was alive with earthy songs. It was the end of the week and many people were happy. They feasted and celebrated, making merry.

I drank lustily from the bottle as I walked, enjoying the rum's strange taste. Feeling very pleased with my adventure, I cut onto a sidewalk paralleling a major road and laughed out loud as cars whished by me. All too soon, most of the rum was gone.

I was just starting to wonder what I'd do next when erratically flashing lights stabbed into my eyes. A large man got out of his car. He was broad of shoulder and sure of step. To my Aesir sight, he glowed with the blessing of Thor the Protector. The mortal's thoughts were structured and dutiful, those of a sworn warrior with high ideals.

"Good evening, sir," he told me.

My first instinct was to turn tail and run, but my legs were weakened from the drink. I also sensed that the human would give chase.

"Good evening," I slurred, my voice cautious under the alcohol.

"May I see your identification?"

"I don't have any," I hiccupped.

"Okay. What's your name?"

"Lothurr Laufeyarson," I replied.

Swaying slightly, I looked him in the face, waiting to see if recognition would hit him. It was under the name of Lothurr, after all, that I had given life to his kind, quickening them so their blood drummed songs through their hearts. Odin had been at my side, as well as irresolute Honir. But that had been too long ago. We three gods were lost to his consciousness. The mortal warrior did not fall to his knees to worship me, nor did he raise his voice in my praise.

"Sir, you're under arrest for being drunk in public," he said instead.

"I'm not drunk," I countered immediately.

The warrior ignored me. "Sir, place your hands behind your back."

Unsure of myself, I followed the order. He stepped behind me and cold metal snapped around my wrists. In that instant, all my sanity flew away. I knew only the ripping binds, the agony of my own son's guts slicing into my flesh. I screamed the scream of a god, enraged. With a fury born of panic, I lashed out, kicking and spitting. A gob of saliva hit the mortal in the chest.

For one ecstatic moment, I thought I was free, even though my arms were still wrenched and strung behind me.

I started forward. The warrior slammed into me, taking me to the pavement. For the second time in so many days, my skin scraped and bled, and grainy pain shot through me.

Enough was enough. I spoke a rune of magic, fully expecting the son of Ask to back off.

My charm flared and sizzled into nothingness. Lightning crackled in a scathing reply, visible only to me.

I had been found in violation of a mortal law and bested by a mortal authority who unwittingly enjoyed Thor's favor. Apparently, I would have to deal with this on Midgard terms. Recognizing the futility of any further struggle, I bowed my head. The human was trained for combat, and he was very fit. I, however, had always relied on my wits and spells, not the vigor of my strikes.

"Attacking a police officer. That was *real* smart, buddy," he said as he forced me into his car.

"I'm sorry," I told him.

We drove for a while. There was a soundproof sheet of glass between us. It was inlaid with metal and crisscrossed like a tall board. I couldn't see where we were going; more metal blocked the view.

Finally, we stopped. The warrior helped me out, gracious in his victory.

"I really am sorry," I repeated.

He made a noncommittal noise.

We were in a vast indoor port of some kind, locked in on all sides by, again, metal. I was led to a heavy door. The warrior of Thor halted in front of it. A camera took measure of us, and the door clanged open.

We waited in a smaller chamber, caught between the first door and a second. The other opened only when the first had closed, blocking any escape.

A stench hit me. I was surrounded by cement block walls painted over in ugly hues. The acidic tang of a nasty cleaning solution prickled up into my sinuses, and the odors of stale alcohol and vomit enveloped me. The steady, golden power of Tyr, who championed order, flowed through the building.

I was herded past a sign and over to another crisscrossed sheet of glass. A man in a suit was seated behind the pane. Tyr's general consecration gave way to a stronger, silvery white light. Forseti had many servants of his own in Midgard, and the official we now faced was one of them. The God of Law's serene energy glittered off him, illuminating his desk, books, and computer.

"Do you swear?" the man in the suit asked. He spoke to the warrior, not me.

"I so swear," proclaimed my captor. Thor's blessing—vigorous, cascading sheaths of green and orange flame—blazed to life around the warrior. He would speak truthfully, this man.

I looked around. One of the other warriors barely had any light on him at all. He growled provocative words to his prisoner, then shoved the man against the concrete wall. The mortal in handcuffs had done much to earn such treatment, but his vanquisher only diminished himself with his actions. Perhaps I had been lucky in my way. On the other hand, my magic might have prevailed against that lesser, gray-shrouded child of Ask.

The warrior who had caught me was finishing up his account of our battle when I finally turned my attention back to my present circumstances.

"Do you understand the charges, Mister Luf—Lar—um, yarson?" The servant of Forseti peered at me with tired eyes. From the two men's minds, I gathered that it was either very late or very early. If they had lived normal lives, they would have been asleep by now.

"I am to be charged with being drunk in public, honored lord," I said respectfully. Their thoughts warned me to be careful of my tone.

The official in the suit moved forward in his chair, closer to the glass that separated us. His brow furrowed. "Do you think this is some sort of joke, sir?" he demanded.

"No. It's no joke."

"Where did you say you're from?"

I thought quickly. The name of a nation sprang to my lips. "Iceland, sir." I copied the title he had used on me, for he clearly preferred it.

Forseti's man looked over at his computer. "Do you understand you're also charged with felony assault and battery? For attacking a police officer in the course of his duties?"

"No, sir." But I did, when I pulled the knowledge from his open, human brain. I had challenged a guardian of the local mortal law. Now the interpreter of those same laws was taking stock of my behavior. To them, the crime was a serious one.

"I said I'm sorry."

The Thunderer's consecrated warrior actually sighed. "You'll have to deal with it in court," he told me, not entirely unsympathetically. "This guy must be new to the country," he added for the other mortal's benefit. "He was really cooperative once I got him down."

The official nodded, then started asking me questions.

"How long have you been here?"

"Only the evening."

"Fresh off the plane?"

"The plane of Asgard, yes, sir." They both thought I was talking about one of their flying vessels marked with its fleet's colors.

"And you really don't have any identification?" The question was an important one. I knew that much now.

"Of course I do." As long as I didn't conjure against the men directly, I had some power left to me.

"He didn't tell *me* that!" Thor's warrior was angry with me. I'd just lost all of his good will. He rooted through my pockets while I stood there with my hands bound behind me. A few moments later, he pulled out an Icelandic passport. He slid it through a slot in the window, to the silver-lit man in the suit.

The servant of the God of Law grunted, examining the birthday and photo. Then he looked me over. I'd put myself down as exactly thirty, born that same day. "Happy birthday, I guess," he said in a flat voice.

"Thank you, sir."

The interrogation resumed. "How long are you staying here?"

"Not long," I replied unwisely. The singing penumbras of the other gods were tripping up my tongue, making it very difficult to craft a plausible lie. A phrase as devastating as wildfire screeched through the minds of both mortals: *flight risk.*

The man in the suit stood up and came back with a sheaf of papers as tall as his hand was wide. He was frowning deeply. Forseti's blessing seemed to glare around him, painful to my Aesir gaze. "I've been here a long time," he said, "and I've never seen a history this thick!"

"History?" I asked.

"Your criminal record."

"Oh." I felt as I had when I'd shapeshifted into a salmon, only to find myself snared in a cruel net. All my deeds were recorded in black ink. The God of Law's dedicated servant could read them as surely as Forseti himself could have read them, far off in his gold-pillared hall.

The official flipped through the papers, and his frown became confused. "These dates are all messed up."

"Can I see?" asked the warrior.

"Sure." They had to split the stack into two parts to get it through the glass.

My captor was baffled too. "This is—what—three hundred pages of larceny?"

The man in the suit stiffened, staring down at where he had broken up the sheaf. His thoughts turned to steel then. "Officer, this man was convicted of murder. See, right there."

A pity for me that my interactions with Baldur were in the record along with everything else. Even more of a pity that these had come to the mortals' attention.

Forseti's Midgard representative pushed the damning sheet through the slot. The warrior's expression was cold as he skimmed it.

"I've done my time on that," I told them, not denying anything. "It was a misunderstanding." Neither man answered.

"What is *up* with these dates?" groused the mortal in the suit again.

"Probably a computer error." The Thunder God's chosen shrugged dismissively and jotted down a note in a little book he carried. There were other people in line. Both the sons of Ask were sure of my fate by then anyways.

Bending close to the opening in the glass, the God of Law's servant addressed me for the final time. "I'm holding you without bond. You'll see a judge Monday morning."

I found myself in a Midgard holding cell. Choking on the stench of the place, I settled into a greasy chair, one of many bolted down in a long row. The seats faced a TV suspended near the ceiling. A game flicked on the screen, bright with attention-catching colors, but the jail announcements scrolling across the bottom blocked part of the view. Some of my fellow captives, with eyes only for the loud box above, hooted or made cat-calls as they watched. I was reminded of Odin's hosts and their futile battles.

I leaned back in the uncomfortable chair and tried to doze off. I had something of my Midgard form about me now, and it was tired. The game droned on, so much rising and falling background noise. The shouts and talking of the other detainees jolted me back to wakefulness every time I started to fall asleep.

Ridiculous. I muttered a word of magic, and silence fell around me. I'd have spoken another charm, but there were more warriors outside the room, and they too were strengthened with Thor's gifts. My spells would only reach so far.

I slept as well as I could, with my arms folded up against my chest. Compared to the cave, the padded and bolted-down seats were pure luxury. Still, I would have preferred a bed in Asgard.

A few hours later, a man took a seat beside me. I stirred awake and allowed my silencing rune to fall away. Alcohol wafted from the mortal's very pores. He wore a beaten T-shirt, an old padded jacket, and jeans that had seen much work. His hands were calloused, and his face was round and friendly.

"*Disculpe, señor,*" he told me with a smile. He looked about here and there, as if ending up in a drunk tank were a pleasant surprise of some sort.

I shrugged and mumbled back a reassuring response in his native tongue. I was one of the Aesir; I could speak any language from any of Yggdrasil's innumerable worlds.

My new companion was very pleased. He flashed me an inebriated grin and began chattering about something that would have made no sense to anyone but him. I easily read his story between his words. He'd come from another continent to the south, and his father had given him his first drink when he was fourteen. He had a wife, and she'd be in tears—at her wit's end, furious, and despairing all at once—when she found out he was here. They rented a small home and had young children. He worked random construction jobs, sometimes every day of the week, but his bosses often cheated him out of his pay. The alcohol blurred his reason and made him very easy to exploit.

He knew the drink was killing him and his family, but he couldn't seem to stop. The addiction had set in all too quickly.

I didn't like what I saw. It wasn't fair. I perceived that the thoroughly intoxicated fellow sitting next to me was honorable enough in his way. Unlike some of the others incarcerated with us, he had never raised a hand to his wife or children.

I spoke up, interrupting the man's drunken monologue. "*Te preparare algo.*"

I cast another rune, and a styrofoam cup appeared in my hand. I held it out to him. With a trusting smile, he downed the liquid I'd offered him, licked his lips, and then laughed heartily. The mortal murmured a word of thanks and promptly slumped over to one side, falling into a deep sleep.

I crumpled up the cup and ordered its destruction. Obligingly, it fell away into fitful quarks.

Not that it really mattered, though. A vessel that had contained even a few fallen drops of Asgard mead could not hold up long in that world anyways.

My new friend would never again thirst for the alcohol of Midgard. I copied him and went back to sleep.

cɦap꓄εr six
fREya

L ate in the morning of the day named for the waxing and waning moon, I stood before the servants of Forseti again. This time, they had paperwork for me to sign. The judge had given me a bond.

I paused over the sheet, curious. My benefactor's choice of name was even less creative than my own. Apparently, I owed my liberty to one Freya Njordsdottir.

As I lifted the primitive pen from the page, my full Aesir strength surged back to me. By Midgard reckoning, I was truly free to go. As soon as I moved away from the window, I reached out with my will. Here, a lonesome file stored on a network vanished. I cast a longer-acting charm on the paperwork. Its ink would slowly begin to fade and then, overnight, bleach away to nothingness.

Lothurr Laufeyarson had never been through their system.

The most beautiful of all the goddesses was waiting for me outside, flexing her fingers impatiently. Freya's sleek and shining blonde hair was pulled back, held from her brow with a handsome clip. She wore an expensive navy-blue suit with a lace blouse underneath. The chemise peeked out from under the collar of the suit, every bit as striking as foam against deep waves. A simple chain of gold hung at her throat and a tastefully understated diamond watch graced her wrist.

I stared at her. Something was wrong.

Brisingamen, her divine necklace, should have flashed about her neck like a thousand galaxies, obscured from mortal sight but visible to mine. But the gold chain was from Midgard, just like the rest of her clothing.

Freya brushed a stray bit of cat fur from her sleeve. "Really, Loki, only *you* could end up in one of their jails," she said by way of greeting. Her coral lips pursed, and she looked me up and down. "You're a mess," she told me.

"I'll deal with it in a moment," I growled, waving a hand at the mortals swarming by around us.

"Well, come on then." She was off. Her gait was quick and sure despite her exorbitantly priced high heels. Muttering to myself, I followed her at a half-run.

We entered the bottom level of a parking deck, chilly with shadows. No one else was around. I willed myself clean and—just to be contrary to Freya and her ever-so-professional look—changed my pants over to a simple pair of cotton khakis.

The goddess reached into her purse, and a chirp and click sounded from nearby. At her gesture, I slid into a leather passenger seat and peered at the bright controls.

"Don't touch anything," she ordered. She turned the key. The Midgard vehicle roared to life, then settled into a smooth purr that very much reminded me of her two cats.

Freya navigated the roads with ease. This time, I could see everything I was passing. Garish signs and grimy buildings littered the landscape like corpses left after a war.

"Have you eaten yet?" she asked me, ever practical.

"Not much. Their food was wretched."

"Let's get brunch then."

"Thank you for looking out for me, Freya."

"Don't think you don't owe me," she responded immediately. Her soft hands clutched the wheel firmly.

"Entirely fair," I agreed.

An instant later, her head shot up and she cursed viciously as she spotted something in the mirror.

"A tailgater! I'd show him right now if I had my blade on me!" She slashed her hand to her left and the insulating pane of glass slid down at her command. Cool, damp air hit me. "I'll spill your guts and the guts of all your children, you bastard spawn of Ask!" Freya shouted out the window. The other driver gave her the middle finger as he blew by, and she shook her fist at him.

"Is this some sort of Midgard custom?" I questioned innocently. "A rite of greeting, perhaps?" But my voice dripped with amusement.

"Just shut the fuck up, Loki!"

I grinned at her.

We pulled into a small parking lot outside a low building sheathed in blue and silver tin. Parts of it were constructed of square blocks of glass, each as clear as ice.

"Best diner around," she told me. We found a table in a corner, where the cube-glass wall curved around us, fiery with liquid sunlight. It was a small place that had been built from a trailer, and it was old by local standards.

Freya tapped her foot and pored over the menu. After a minute, she slapped it down onto the table. A server came up to us bearing cups of coffee instead of horns of mead. After my weekend, the coffee seemed more appealing than alcohol.

"I'll get the waffles," Freya said, "and an order of fries. He'll have the eggs and potatoes. Side of bacon."

"I haven't even had a chance to decide yet!"

"I'm in a rush. Besides, I got you something you'll like. And I'm paying."

I rolled my eyes, but didn't object further.

We drank our coffee. Freya's gaze shot up hopefully toward the door every time someone entered. After a while, she sighed moodily.

"Loki, tell me something."

"Ask it."

The soft lips of the goddess trembled and her glorious eyes, the crystalline purple of the twilight sky, misted over. Her thin shoulders hunched under the fancy, tailored lines of her suit. She suddenly seemed very vulnerable.

"Tell me, have you heard any news of Od?"

I paled at her words. The bane of every single Aesir was to be asked that question by the fierce and lovely immortal who now searched my face imploringly from the booth opposite mine.

"I haven't been free long, Freya," I said very carefully. "From the cave, that is," I added. She nodded, and I went on. "I *did* see some sign in Odin's hall that he is doing well. Such news as that is."

The poor goddess had no idea Odin *was* her husband. It was a terrible thing, to be joined forever to the mightiest of gods. The All-Father could not have had just any wife. My blood-brother had married a goddess very wise in all the ways of magic. To protect something of herself, she had separated from herself. I was a shapechanger of no small ability, but even I could not fully understand what she had done. The younger goddess—independent and willful, gorgeous and urbane, swift with a sword and swifter still with a spell— remembered that she was wed. But the details always escaped her. And so she searched the worlds, looking for her lost husband.

We all knew of the tragedy that was Freya's marriage, and even I would never make light of it. She took lovers and cherished them deeply, but her greatest love was for the one she could never remember.

The beautiful immortal reached out and held my hand in hers, squeezing it for solace. Her touch was very warm.

The food arrived and we ate. Freya doused her waffles in a disgusting syrup and plunged into her meal like a ravenous wolf falling upon a deer. I smiled at her vigor. A hearty meal would give her some of her spirit back. I hated to see the goddess lose her fire for long.

"Where are you off too?" I asked when she slowed down.

"I have to get my necklace."

"A worthy goal. Surely you know I didn't steal it? Not this time, anyways."

"Of course I know that. I gave it away, Trickster!"

My black eyes widened.

"Oh, stop it. Look, why don't you come with me? Do you have anything better to do?"

I thought about Asgard and Odin's ultimatum to take my moping elsewhere. "No. Not really."

In the parking lot, she paused beside her car with her keys in one hand

and frowned at it critically. "This is going to take too long. I still have to feed my cats."

She motioned me forward, then chanted a word of power over us. It was a strange one, twisting on the tongue. I had never heard the charm before and I could not recall it when she was done, though I was the most intelligent of the gods.

We appeared in another parking lot. Her vehicle stood next to us, unscathed. I looked about, arching an eyebrow dubiously. "Apartments? You live here?"

"I have a nice place, Loki. Don't judge it until you see it."

We rode an elevator to the top floor of the building. I disliked the awkward technology intensely. The bronzed mirrors and polished woods did nothing to set my mind at ease. The space was confined and the floor heaved underneath us. The lack of control did not suit me at all.

We walked across plush white carpeting, passing down a long hallway. Finally, we approached a door that looked exactly the same as every other door there. Gentle magic spilled from the threshold. Freya rattled a key in the lock and gestured for me to enter.

The same elegant, classic taste that informed Freya's choice in clothing was reflected in her apartment's decor: black leather couches faced a brass and marble fireplace, and original oil paintings hung from the walls, depicting pastoral scenes. Each landscape was illuminated by its own electric light, displaying the artwork to its greatest effect. Near the entrance, an indoor bar of maple wood and glass took up an entire wall, glowing with more lights. The goddess had stocked the bar with award-winning wines and bottles of pricey, single-malt scotch. A state-of-the-art sound system poured soothing music through the room.

With my Aesir gaze, I also saw the place's ambient spells and charms. The apartment could follow its mistress anywhere and appear in any Midgard city.

I danced aside as two cats darted forward, attempting to slip out the open door. Freya easily pushed them back in with her foot.

"I suppose the mortal realm could be worse," I conceded.

She flashed me a smile, then glided into her kitchen. The goddess took a bag from a high shelf and began filling her pets' bowls. Both animals had the striped, shaggy gray fur of forest cats and looked identical, even to most Aesir eyes. The cats twitched their ears, uninterested, as the goddess placed the bag of dry food back on the shelf.

"They're used to better fare," I noted.

One began purring, then ambled over and knocked her head against my shin. I crouched down and stroked her behind the ears. The purr grew louder. The other cat padded over and rubbed against my bent knee.

"They've always liked you, Loki."

"That's because I can tell them apart. Hello, Buthlungr, furry lord," I said to the male. "Greetings, fair Mennskurth, lady of all the cats."

Freya clapped, a sound like silver coins pattering. "Well done!" Her face became more serious then. "We need to go. My necklace will be in the shop any minute now." She held out her arms critically, examining the navy sleeves. "And this won't do at all!"

With a whisper of divine will, her blazer changed to a looser, gauzy shirt of cobalt, threaded with real gold. The lacy top remained underneath it, creating a layered effect. Her businesslike skirt became an elaborate sarong, dyed in many shades of blue. It reached to her ankles. Expensive pumps turned into expensive sandals, and her fair skin darkened to the color of the creamed coffee we had drunk.

I made an appreciative noise in my throat, much liking what I saw. The goddess was attractive in any form.

"Your turn. I'll not go about as a foreigner in any mortal land. Neither will you if you're coming with me."

"Just where are we off to?"

"Indonesia."

"Ah." The name gave me the knowledge I needed. I created a loose cotton shirt of crimson for myself and gave it a mandarin neckline embroidered with stylized flames. I tanned my skin and changed the features of my face slightly, but left my haircut alone even though my bangs were too long for that country. It was not in my nature to ever entirely blend in.

"Very handsome," declared Freya. "You'll brighten the evening of many a Midgard woman now."

"I'd much rather brighten yours," I leered.

She ignored that, lifted her small chin, and held out her hand to me. I took it, grasping her fingers harder than necessary as she boldly pronounced a travelling rune.

Night was quickly settling over the land. A warm breeze stirred my shirt, bearing the invigorating scents of incense, tropical plants, and roasting meats. I sensed an undercurrent in the air, and my shoulders unknotted little by little. My breathing felt a bit freer in that place. Not far away, I noticed a weathered shrine of volcanic stone wrapped up in a checkered, black-and-white cloth. A meal meant for gods lay on it. Fine portions of rice were arranged in palm leaf bowls and decorated with flowers.

"They're polytheists," I said.

"Yes. On this island, anyways. You don't think about it when you're down here, but it always comes as something of a relief, doesn't it? I stop by quite often."

We walked along a dusty road. The walls of housing enclaves rose up on either side, blocking any view of the families within. We could hear the barking of their dogs, though.

We entered a tiny shop. Plastic water bottles were on display in one corner, and the counter was stacked with colorful fabrics, patterned with paisley swirls. A set of shelves held jewelry and other treasures. I picked up a wood carving, beguiling in its detail.

"That's Saraswati," Freya told me. "One of their goddesses."

I shrugged and put the statue back down.

She turned away and greeted an old woman. The two of them began haggling over bracelets, each enjoying the battle of wits.

"How about this one? The blue is perfect for you!" the wrinkled mortal exclaimed in her native language. Freya pretended to consider it, but I could tell she was biding her time.

Not much later, a young woman came into the shop, smiling widely. Her canine teeth had been polished down flat, as was the custom on that island. Freya folded her hands in front of her chest and gave the mortal a respectful bow. The Midgard woman returned the gesture. Her bow was deeper, as was appropriate. She was dressed in a gauzy, long-sleeved shirt over a tighter top of pink lace, and wore a matching sarong. The mortal reached behind her neck and unclasped a tool-worked chain, then lifted a delicate necklace from the soft brown skin above her breasts. To me, that necklace seemed to be woven of eternal suns stolen from the heavens.

The young woman handed Brisingamen back to Freya. The goddess nodded and placed it around her own neck. After the pretty mortal had left, she purchased an exquisite bracelet from the old woman. A daughter of the Vanir would never buy anything less than the very best.

We strolled out into the night, now taking our time. Freya slipped her arm peaceably into mine. The islanders were not given to showing physical affection in public, but we didn't care. The air was too heady, the sky too dark and vast above. Both of us could feel the pulse of life around us. Asgard, for all its glory, sometimes did not seem as sweet.

"I love a story," I reminded her. "I know there's one here!"

"It's a story *about* love," she replied, her voice becoming very serious. "The families are strict here. A woman loved a man, and a man loved her back, but they could not be together. Until, one day, a stranger gave the woman a necklace."

"Brisingamen," I said. "No mortal would be able to stop their union."

"Exactly."

"Lucky for you she gave it back!"

"That was the condition. Some can still be trusted here, Loki."

For a change, I stilled my tongue and did not mock the goddess about how she had acquired the necklace in the first place. It was a good night, and Freya seemed pleased with my company.

We walked until the morning, our steps light on the beaches. Although fires burned in some of the temples, most of the island slept. In the land we'd left behind, electric lights flooded the skies and illuminated the streets until dawn. But here, something remained of the dark's true power.

We watched a sunrise together, our arms still linked.

"I'm tired," Freya said at last, "and I must check on my cats soon."

It was strange to travel from one night into another. The goddess swept over to her bar and put a bottle of white wine on ice. I sat near the fire and scratched Buthlungr under the chin. The cat had made himself at home on the sofa's leather armrest. He leaned over to nip my hand when he thought I was ignoring him for too long.

Freya poured me some wine, as smooth and pale as shimmering platinum. She took a seat nearby, and I grinned at her. We'd resumed our regular forms, but we kept the comfortable island clothing. Freya's silky blonde hair, loosened and falling to her waist, was striking against the many blues she wore.

"You understand Midgard more than most," she said quietly.

"I do. I understand what a night like this could mean, should you and I desire it!"

I hadn't guessed wrong. She smiled invitingly, sidled closer to me, then reached up and ran her perfect fingers through my feathery black hair. My blood sang and tingled, and a hungry sort of hush settled around my mind. I shot an arm out and grabbed her by the waist, drawing her close.

Our lips brushed. Freya's tongue teased the corner of my mouth. Then she leaned down and began to gently draw a line of kisses along my neck, following the line of the cotton collar. Her fingertips pressed against my chest, then glided up. They pulled insistently at the top of my shirt, moving cloth aside. My breathing quickened.

I had a few glorious seconds of enraptured anticipation before the ice hit the bare skin of my chest. The weight of the cubes rippled down and struck my stomach in one shocking instant, stinging me with cold.

I yelped and pushed the beautiful goddess away.

Freya found her balance again in a moment.

"Cool yourself, God of Fire!" she exclaimed, her voice ringing with laughter. Giggling maniacally, the loveliest of the immortals flung herself to the other end of the couch. She beat on the leather as if it were a drum, thoroughly consumed by her mirth. The cats disappeared into another room, frightened off by the noise.

"Well, shit," I said. I reached out, grasped the half-full bottle of wine by the neck, and helped myself to what was left. She was too busy laughing at me to complain.

The feisty warrior goddess could be as much of a jerk as I was some days.

CHAPTER SEVEN
THE QUEEN OF THE DEAD

Niflheim Present

Niflheim was one of the oldest realms and was also the home of the dead. Its borders were the gnarled and ancient roots of Yggdrasil. Journeying to Niflheim was always an ordeal. For many days and nights, I traveled snaking paths worn deep into the living wood of the Great Tree. My only company was the void and my only comfort was the fading light of the stars.

Down in the misty pits, a few lost leaves clung to Yggdrasil. It was a strange universe indeed that unfolded itself into existence in those depths. I thought the leaves must surely lose color and die, for they were sickly and perpetually veiled in darkness. But they grew all the same. The fearsome dragon Nidhogg skittered about nearby, endlessly spitting poison as he gnawed and tore at the Great Tree's roots. I did not envy any life born to those murky worlds.

I was still rankling over Freya. I also wanted to keep away from the Aesir a while longer, and I had another family outside Asgard.

My first child was the serpent Jormungand, whose mother was the giantess Angrboda. He encircled the universe containing Midgard, forever gnashing at his own tail as he sheltered our favored realm within his coils. I never bothered to visit him. Jormungand was mighty, but he was incapable of speech.

Then there was Fenrir the wolf. The worst of all my children, Fenrir was black of fur and slathering of jaw. He had inherited much of my intelligence and a Jotun's own hungers. Bound by the gods with threads spun from the sound of a cat's footfall and the saliva of birds, he gibbered and raged in a cave hidden in the icy depths between far-flung galaxies. That was Fenrir's prison, and even I avoided the place. I was his father, but he'd devour me as quickly as he would devour anyone else.

That left my third child, Hel. I was off to see my daughter, the very Queen of the Dead.

Hel's realm was populous. Many souls rested there before they found their way back up to the mortal worlds, always subtly changed by their passing. More confident spirits journeyed straight up Yggdrasil without entering her realm at all; those could always find a sure branch to traverse, and new lives awaited them. But a few souls crawled between the worlds, wallowing in their own evil. After a while, even my daughter could not help them. They eventually sank into the darkness outside her hall and languished away in the mists until, all starving, they ripped away the very last morsels of their own forms and ended their existence.

I was careful to leave Niflheim's deeper corners undisturbed. Still, sometimes—just out of the corner of my eye—I'd notice a sooty shade trapped in its own wispy web, radiating malevolence as it turned upon itself to feed. They were the doomed, those beyond any hope of redemption.

I finally reached my daughter's hall. Her home was chilly and grim, a vast and brooding island lost in a sea of fog and ghosts. Hissing voices echoed around me. Their words were indistinguishable, but it was never a good idea to listen more closely. Niflheim's dead were confused. They could offer no wisdom.

As I stepped inside, the spirit of a fallen mortal brushed against me, attracted to my warmth.

"I did what I was supposed to do," she said, her speech as distant and thin as an untangling string.

I was not in any mood to humor a ghost. They all sounded alike after a while.

"I was a good person," the spirit prattled on. "Why am I here? I didn't hurt anyone."

Fed up, I turned on her, my god's eyes condemning.

"Your son dwells broken on Midgard because you let your husband rain hard words on him each night! Did you ever intervene? Did you ever seek help? Or did you let your silence do your talking?"

"I took care of my family," said the spirit. "His father never hit him."

"The words were blows enough, you coward!"

"I did nothing wrong," she insisted.

It was pointless to speak with Niflheim's dead. They had all refused to face the battles they were supposed to have fought in life. I curled my lip up in disgust. How did my daughter ever keep her patience about her?

Hel was in her hall as always, ministering to her guests. Empty plates were laid out on frigid stone tables, and liquidless goblets gleamed among winding piles of pearls. There was no food or drink that I could see, but for the ghosts, it was a feast. The living could never dine on the offerings of Niflheim.

My daughter slowly and gently stacked pewter plates, murmuring soothing words to beings only she could perceive. Long, silver-white hair spilled over her shoulder. The pale skin of her jawline glistened as she worked, and her red eye gleamed in the shadows.

She started suddenly, hearing the noise of someone living in her dead domain. She turned her face towards me, and I could see her other half, with its coal-black skin and a single, glittering eye, dark like my own. Ebony tresses fell from that side, stark and straight.

Hel wore a simple, undecorated gray dress and no jewelry. Although her hall was full of buried wealth—jewels and brooches, armbands and crowns—she took none of these riches for herself. She did not feel the need.

Her mouth fell open, surprised, small, and cute.

"Father!" she exclaimed. She rushed forward. I took her in my arms and stroked her hair. There was something of a child's innocence about Hel. Many saw only the disfigurement of her body. I saw her gentle gaze and the strong lift of her chin. She was a young woman of great beauty and greater resolve. I had always been very proud of her.

My daughter sobbed against my shoulder for a time. Her duties wore her down.

"I thought I'd never see you again until Midgard fell!" she whimpered into my tunic.

"Nonsense," I told her, my tone cheerful. "Who could trap the Trickster for so long?"

"Odin, perhaps."

I didn't answer that. As usual, she knew a bit too much of the truth.

I followed her to her throne and pulled up a seat for myself. It screeched and wailed against the flagstone floor as I moved it.

"How have you been, child of mine?"

"As I always have been, father. I take some comfort when a soul finds its way from here."

"Most do if they spend enough time with you, lovely one."

She nodded, her adorable face sober. "Thank you. I hear so few kind words."

I bristled at that. "The Aesir cast you down here, all alone! I'm sick of it! I have my powers back, Hel. Name what you would have. I'll do anything you ask!"

She shook her head quietly. "Nothing can be done, father."

"What you need is a companion. A true friend in this place."

"I have you."

"Poor comfort when I can never stay for long." Niflheim was no home for even a bold spirit, much less a god. "No, there is another solution to this if we put our minds to it."

My daughter watched me intently, scared. I spoke of hope in the realm of the dead. It brought her no joy, only terror.

"A pet," I said after some thought. "Even Odin has his crows and wolves. What shall you chose?"

"No pet could survive here," Hel replied in her hollow voice. Her eyes, one like onyx and the other like garnet, stared back at me, empty of all emotion.

I would not be swayed. "An Aesir pet could. Perhaps Geri might—" I stopped in the middle of the thought, then smiled widely. Deviously. "No, I have a much better idea! Why settle for one pet when two could bring so much more joy?"

"I don't know what you mean, father."

I stood up, walked over to my daughter, and took her by the shoulders. I kissed each cheek: one damp and cold, and pale as a maggot, the other swarthy and dry like scabs and stone.

"Wait here, my darling. Soon, I will have a gift for you. A gift to make even the Queen of the Dead smile!"

This time, I abstained from drinking and made sure that no mortal authorities were about. I had already wasted enough time in Midgard's odious jails.

I knew when Freya would be gone. Unlike me, she was dutiful about attending the morning councils at the Well of Urd. I spoke a word to break the warding runes over her apartment and sauntered inside. The infuriating goddess had set up an excellent line of defenses against local threats, but she hadn't thought to worry about divine incursions.

Her mistake. Especially after our little date.

I stopped at the bar and snatched up a bottle of single-malt scotch that could have paid for Freya's car, with coin left over. I walked into the kitchen and turned on an ostentatiously aerodynamic can opener. It buzzed invitingly.

The cats—as cats do—ran straight for me, almost bowling themselves over in their haste.

"Hello, friends," I said. I murmured honeyed words in their pointed ears and scratched their necks. I was no fool. I knew Buthlungr and Mennskurth were fearsome when they were angry. They were utterly devoted to their mistress and would react badly when they realized I was taking them away.

My voice eased into a peaceful melody and I sang a spell over them. Within moments, both cats drifted off. Mennskurth even snored softly. I searched the apartment with my Aesir perceptions and found their carrying case. Apparently, it hadn't gotten much use. The carrier's only purpose was to slip the cats past mortal eyes.

I plopped both felines inside and fastened the latches. Then I tucked my bottle of scotch under my other arm and fled the scene.

Hel's eyes were wide as I set the cage down on her cold floor. A faint, molten-yellow light already beamed from within, warming her realm of gray. The cats had their own power about them and they had begun stirring outside the gate, before I'd made it into the hall. They were groggy and disoriented, but were rapidly regaining consciousness.

My daughter stepped forward tentatively, like a little girl examining a present at Yule, unsure if she were allowed to open it yet. She looked up at me and, at my nod, crouched down and unlocked the mortal-made carrying case.

The two cats burst out. They immediately began pacing about and sniffing.

"The great hunter under your table is Buthlungr," I said. "The fair lady slinking along the walls is named Mennskurth."

"They are lovely, father." Hel walked over to the female cat. Mennskurth glided forward and sniffed at my daughter's ebony fingers, then rubbed herself against the offered hand. A happy purr rumbled through the Hall of the Dead.

"Won't they suit you better than the whining of spirits?"

But Hel frowned uneasily.

I set out the scotch and called forth drinking vessels that were not of that realm. We both sipped from our goblets, keeping watch over the cats. Eventually, they decided their new home would do. Golden sunlight spilled down from nowhere. The forest cats curled up together in the rays. Their eyes closed, and their whiskers drifted back and forth, tracking dreams.

"So beautiful," murmured my daughter wistfully. Her expression hardened an instant later. "I know you stole them, father. It was cruel to bring them here. Cruel to them, and to me."

"Would they rest so peacefully if they had been abducted by force?" I protested. She didn't answer, but she also didn't believe me.

"Fine," I sighed. "They were Freya's."

Hel considered that, her black and white hair falling about her shoulders. The attractive goddess had been quick to condemn her to Niflheim, just like everyone else. Freya, like all the others, had seen only a monster birthed of a giantess.

"They seem to like it here," she said quietly.

"They do," I assured her.

"Freya will be angry, though. Will she come here seeking them?"

"Calm yourself. Who of the gods but I ever comes to Niflheim?"

"Baldur once, and sometimes the All-Father too."

I shook my head. "I'll go among the Aesir and make sure the trail is hidden."

Hel said nothing. She stood up and plodded over to the cats dozing in the ambient golden rays. She reached down and stroked Mennskurth's brow. When her finger lifted, a white blaze shone from between the cat's contentedly closed eyes. With her other hand, she touched Buthlungr. A midnight streak blotched his forehead. He stirred and stretched, his curling claws flexing in a relaxed way. He meowed up at my daughter.

"No, father," said Hel. "You must take them with you. Look at my hall. Do you see any ghosts?"

I followed her gaze. "None, sweet child." The hall was empty and entirely silent. No whispering spirits disturbed our conversation.

"They cannot abide the cats, and I must fulfill my obligations. Please, go now, and take them away."

Frustrated, I clenched my teeth. "I'll visit more often," I promised her. "I can do that much for you."

My daughter put her arms around me in another hug, this time one of farewell. She was already sneaking looks at the table, planning ahead. Her shoulders were tense under my hands, for she was ready to be about her tasks.

48

I gathered up Freya's cats and headed off for Asgard. But I left Hel the scotch.

CHAPTER EIGHT
home again

Asgard Present

Light danced through the trees and shimmered off the dew. I leaned against a
tall maple tree by the Well of Urd, waiting on the other gods. I had
propped myself up on one leg and jauntily angled the other against the trunk,
letting my boot scrape the bark. My arms were folded across my chest and my
tunic gleamed vibrantly red in the morning sun. A tiny, superior smirk hovered
on my lips.

Freya arrived with everyone else, dressed in a stunning blue Aesir gown.
She spotted me immediately, reclining indolently against the tree, and her eyes
flashed with rage. The beautiful goddess pounded forward, her fists clenched
at her sides.

"Where are they, Loki?!"

"Where are what, fairest of the fair?"

"You know damned well what, god of thieves and lies! I'll have my cats
back or I'll have your spleen!"

I made a show of glancing down to examine the gold threading on my
sleeve. "Sigyn, the embroidery is unraveling again. Would you take care of it
for me later?"

As usual, my wife kept herself off to one side, some distance from the
crowd. Skathi stood with her, and their faces were solemn. Sigyn looked up at
me, nodded once, and then went back to her discussion with the icy mountain
goddess.

Freya was spitting curses. She spun away and quickly returned, dragging
Forseti by the arm.

I hadn't been anywhere near Baldur's only son since I'd escaped the cave.
I searched his eternally young and clean-shaven face, but I saw only confusion
as he tried to disengage himself from Freya's grip. When he met my gaze, his
expression was entirely impassive. Neutral.

I noted that Forseti, the God of Law and Justice, was no longer in the
snowy white, silver-trimmed shirt he had once preferred. Now he garbed
himself in a long tunic of the deepest black, the same color worn by so many
of the judges of Midgard.

Or the color of mourning. Which of those impulses had inspired his
change?

"I'll have your judgment on this now, Forseti!" Freya snapped. "My cats
are missing, and Loki is guilty!"

"You know this how?"

"They are gone from my apartment, and only Loki could have entered!"

Thor strode up to us, red of beard and broad of shoulder. His stormy eyes were amused. "Hey, now wait a minute. Just how did Loki know where you live, Freya?" The Thunderer was all false innocence. Such a theft might have bothered him normally, but he was no one's idea of a cat person.

"A valid question," Forseti contributed.

My smirk turned into an outright grin. I was enjoying this.

Freya looked over her shoulder, to the trees shading Sigyn and Skathi. She pursed her lips and said nothing.

"I think your cats will be back soon," I told her.

"Liar!"

"Perhaps even now," I added, pointing to the well. Buthlungr crouched between the quartz stones, his tongue flipping and curling against the surface of the pool. His gold-green eyes were half closed, and droplets flecked around his whiskers.

Freya rushed forward, knelt beside him, and began stroking his thick fur.

"Where's Mennskurth?" she demanded, looking straight at me.

"How the hell should I know?"

"And who really cares?" added Thor. He folded his arms across his chest, then winked at me. Almost like old times.

We spoke of other topics. The second cat trailed in eventually, bearing a drooping vole in her jaws. She placed her catch at Freya's feet and mewed up at her questioningly.

"Thank you," Freya murmured. She shot a glare at me. Then she bent down to rub the cat's head and her face paled. "What is this? My cat is marked!" She spun around to Buthlungr. "And the other too!"

I kept my mouth shut and pretended to be as surprised as everyone else. Some of them, like Thor, couldn't muster up even a semblance of interest in the matter.

Forseti refused to hear any further talk of the cats. Odin remained on the sidelines, drawing silence to himself as he observed us all. The morning meeting of the gods ended, and I turned to leave.

Baldur's son stepped over. "Walk with me, Loki." His gray eyes were unreadable. I frowned at him, suspicious. But I could not well refuse him.

We followed a dirt path for some time, not speaking. Beech trees rustled around us and songbirds flitted about like airborne gems. We were heading in the direction of Glitnir, I realized. I had no desire to go to Forseti's hall, to where he judged the deeds of mortals and gods.

"Stop," I said. "What's this all about?"

Forseti peered one way, then the other. He seemed to be confirming that we were alone. I didn't like it.

I made the subtlest of gestures with my left hand, furtively preparing to defend myself from an attack. Forseti carried no weapon, but he had many friends. I, on the contrary, was not always so well regarded in Asgard.

"I know my father died at Odin's order," he said, completely taking me by surprise. We regarded each other for long moments. My fingers relaxed and my spell melted away.

"You found this out how?" I asked at last.

"Every case is recorded in the books of Glitnir." The younger god's expression turned chilly. "Nonetheless, you were a willing principal to the murder if I don't miss my mark. Which I almost never do. Your hatred of Baldur ran deeper than I'd have thought possible."

I lifted my head up, focusing my gaze on the treetops so that I would no longer have to endure his stare. "What happens now, Forseti?"

The other Aesir sighed. I looked at him again. He seemed very tired.

"I see what remains of fact, but little glimmer of motive. So much has been lost. I'd have the full story of why my own grandfather would condemn my father to death." His tone did not change, but he watched me intently.

"No way!" I exclaimed, suddenly frightened. "Odin swore me to silence! I won't say another word unless *he* agrees to it!"

Forseti sighed again. "Then I shall consult with him. Perhaps he will relent."

"Good luck with that."

We went our separate ways. I let my feet guide me closer and closer to our border with Alfheim. The air became tingly and electric, and strange, darting lights danced at the corners of my vision. I heard a pan-flute playing far off. Its liquid notes rose and fell and spiraled back on themselves, primal and unpredictable.

I trusted my Aesir instincts, but I traveled cautiously. At certain points, two small holly trees might grow side by side, and where their prickling leaves interlocked, a gateway to another dimension would form. Or the long branch of an ancient tree might arch over an inviting pathway, gracing a nearby stream with its touch. There too a portal could arise. My divine sight took in much, but I struggled to pick out the shifting doorways favored by the Light Elves. The landscape was ever a trap.

Typical of the Alfar. And Odin said *I* couldn't keep anything simple.

My wife adored the place, however. She had no trouble navigating Alfheim, and she strolled through those forests and meadows every day, sometimes speaking with fey and magical beings. We'd built our home in the borderlands where Asgard crossed over into the realm of elves.

I passed a familiar river, followed a trail up a gentle incline, and at last arrived at a longhouse constructed from dark logs. The deep and shadowy greens of the forest enfolded it like a cloak. Laced ferns clustered around our home and velvety moss grew over much of its wood. Our roof was cluttered with acorns and fallen leaves, and two intersecting beams carved with open-mouthed dragons' heads jutted up off the main structure. Valuable topazes glinted from their eyes, yellow and bright.

Next to the heavy maple door, an adolescent fox dozed in a patch of sunshine. Its leg was wrapped in a linen bandage, and the acrid scents of medicinal herbs wafted off its coat. We hadn't been back for long, but my wife had already managed to find an animal in need of care. I smiled to myself and gave the fox a welcoming pat. It felt very good to be home.

The inside of our longhouse was hardly any match for the dwellings of the other Aesir. A plain, wood-and-stone table stretched along one wall under a broad, open window that offered a view of the dappled forest. A cutting board was already set out, and a golden knife that had once been used for sacrificing mortals to the sun lay beside it, ready for chopping vegetables. Iron pots and pans dangled from above, next to dried bunches of rosemary and sage.

There were signs that the house was mine as well as Sigyn's. A tall vase of pure gold sparkled at one end the kitchen table, filled to the brim with cut emeralds. Further in, a tapestry woven in every shade of red hung from the rough beams. I'd stolen it from a fire temple long ago. Our simple shelves held a variety of coins plucked from the mighty rulers of fallen kingdoms. These were scattered among interesting branches and half-opened milkweed pods, water-smoothed stones and banded feathers. Sigyn's natural treasures rested alongside my more exotic acquisitions of jewels and drinking vessels, trinkets and pouches—anything I could easily conceal. The other shelves were thick with scrolls. Midgard's ancient libraries had known my attentions as well.

Higher up in the dimness near the rafters, a line of icons expropriated from bygone emperors gleamed in a row. Each was illuminated with thin sheets of gold. Their subjects' large, soulful eyes followed the comings and goings of an Aesir. The monks who had painted them so many centuries ago would not have approved of their current location.

I paced over to our hearth and started up the fire with a god's will. A home was not a home unless flames warmed it. That done, I waited for Sigyn.

She appeared later, carrying wildflowers in one hand. My wife wore a sleeveless brown dress trimmed with gold. Her brow furrowed slightly as she noticed the fire. She stepped inside, out of the blinding sun, and spotted me sitting by the hearth.

Sigyn paused, half hidden in shadows.

"Greetings, husband," she said. Her tone was unsure.

Our last few decades in the cave had been especially tense and unpleasant. When I had regained my freedom, both of us had sensed a need for time apart, a need to put some distance between ourselves and the torture we'd endured. We had each suffered greatly in our own way. If I knew my Sigyn at all, I knew that she had longed for the open skies and the elven forests even as she had dedicated her every hour to catching the serpent's poison in a bowl.

"Hail, wife," I said respectfully.

She went to the kitchen and started preparing lunch. Meanwhile, I got up and contemplated my appearance in a mirror that had once reflected the image of a king. Better for it now that it held the reflection of a god.

"Forseti looked striking in black, did he not?" I asked. The chopping stopped. My wife peered up at me and her shoulders hunched nervously.

"If he did, I didn't notice," she replied.

I sighed with exasperation. "Am I like Thor, to be jealous of every stupid thing? Look if you want. Do more if you want. He is not unhandsome. You could do far worse for some entertainment."

"As you say, Loki," she murmured. She went back to her cutting.

I raised my hand to my chin and gazed at my image. I was sure I could pull off black to far more effect than the God of Law. My tunic changed and darkened. Not bad. But I seemed terribly grim with both midnight hair and a midnight shirt. I willed my fluffy bangs to a brilliant auburn shade. It was hardly the first time I'd gone about like that.

"What do you think, my star?" I spun around with my arms extended to give Sigyn a chance to admire me from all angles.

"Very nice, husband of mine."

We ate by the fire, both soothed by what had once been routine.

"The cave was not bad in every way," I told Sigyn when we were done with our meal. "I feel I know more of you now."

"And I of you," she agreed, reaching for my hand.

"What shall we do with our afternoon?"

My wife smiled at me impishly, as full of light and joy as the Alfar woodlands she loved.

I took her in my arms. For a time, we forgot all the worlds.

The skies of Asgard were not always fair. The next morning, I wandered through a grassy field whipped by fierce gales. In the outlying groves, the leaves flipped over, their silver undersides heralding a coming storm. The clouds were heavy and low, and the air smelled of heat. I looked up as the entire sky blazed to life, flaring yellow from a diffused, sourceless lightning.

A sound like a mountain hitting a rock-giant boomed nearby, repeating itself every so many minutes. Too slow to be a drum. Too quick to be coincidence.

I was not surprised to find Thor outside on such a day. The other immortal braced himself, one leg behind the other, and hurled his great hammer, Mjolnir, off into the distance. It was lost to the gathering storm and the horizon. The Thunder God bowed his head and waited, his lips moving as he counted.

Perhaps fifty counts in, the hammer came spinning back, flashing orange and white. He lifted a brawny hand and caught it with ease. Seconds later, a boom echoed across the green fields.

"What do you want, Loki?" Thor asked. He hardly spared me a glance. His gaze was locked on his target, too far off in the distance for me to perceive.

"A god can walk, can he not? How goes your practice?"

"Well, until now." He shook out his auburn beard, then considered me. The winds tossed about my legs and tugged at my cloak.

"Lose the hair," he told me.

"What?"

"Someone might think we're related with those red locks of yours. Lose it and you can stay."

"Fine," I grumbled. I changed back to my former self, with jet-black hair and a crimson tunic.

"Better," said the Thunderer.

"I was pulling the look off."

Thor didn't reply. He flung his arm back and then snapped it forward, sending Mjolnir flying again. He waited. Another bang shook through Asgard. This time, the ground beneath our boots trembled as if from an earthquake.

"Throw that thing any harder and you'll take down Yggdrasil itself," I commented.

The other god's honest eyes widened. "You really think I could do that?" he asked. The Thunderer's deep voice held entirely too much enthusiasm.

"Certainly, Mighty One. Let's make a sport of it, you and I—you with your hammer and me with my fire! Between the two of us, we'll have the World Tree fallen by dinnertime!"

Thor growled into his beard, catching onto my sarcasm. He turned away from me with a threatening rumble. "That's exactly what I missed the most about you, Loki! These damned smart-ass conversations you always insist on having!"

Hearing something over the wind, the Thunderer lifted his hand again. This time, Mjolnir slammed into his palm with so much force that he actually winced.

"Now *that* was a throw," he told me.

"It was indeed."

"Well, come on then," he said, slipping Mjolnir into his belt. "I need a drink after all that work. You can keep me company."

"Careful, Thor. Someone might think that you actually liked me again."

The other god shrugged. "The past is the past. I've got better things to do than sweat over it. No, I don't approve of everything you've done. Not by half. But the All-Father says you're to live here again, and that's good enough for me."

I bowed my head to him. "Thank you." For once, my tone was not light nor my words mocking.

The Thunder God grunted, his ruddy cheeks flushing. "Yeah. Whatever. Look, dragging our feet isn't going to make my ale any tastier. Could we pick up the pace here?"

Thor's stride was wide and swift. He carried himself about the worlds on legs like tree trunks. But I was swift too, and we arrived at his forge in little time. He poured a bready, amber brew into two horns and offered one to me. Where many of the gods took mead, Thor often preferred beer--the thicker and foamier the better.

He watched his forge fire critically as he drank. "Balance that out for me, will you, Loki? I have to deal with Sleipnir today."

I did as he asked, well used to flames and their tricks. "There. The perfect temperature for your horseshoes."

The other Aesir gulped more ale from his horn, then nodded.

"I'm not in any mood to face that beast," he told me. He never was, but Odin's steed always needed new shoes. Sleipnir, with his eight long legs, was the quickest horse in all the realms. He could go anywhere, jump any wall, and keep up with any bird in its flight. He was Odin's joy, the Ruler of the Gods' greatest treasure. The All-Father rode him through many worlds; the iron protecting Sleipnir's feet never lasted long.

We waited on my blood-brother and his steed. After we'd polished off another round or two of ale, the war god and his horse finally barreled down from the clouds. Odin's eye flashed like a mad star and Sleipnir's flanks were steaming. The battle stallion threw back his head in a furious cry.

My blood-brother laughed as he swung himself down from his mount. "A grand morning!"

"It is indeed!" Thor agreed. "Let's see the damage."

Sleipnir strode forward, his legs arching high. The horse towered above me; I barely reached the base of his chest. His gray fur was as thick as hoarfrost and seemed almost luminescent under the sheet lightning. The steed's nostrils flared, and I fell back, giving him and Thor plenty of room.

The Thunderer cradled a hoof in his strong hand, then went to the forge. Patiently, he held his tongs over the fire, readying a shoe.

"Forseti visited my hall last night," Odin told me. I didn't answer. There seemed to be nothing to say.

"He sought knowledge not available to him in Glitnir," continued my blood-brother.

"Yes. I know."

"I thought you might. Our agreement still stands, Loki."

"I know that too."

The mightiest of the gods nodded bleakly, his one eye as implacable as a siege. "Good."

"That's five today!" Thor exclaimed when he had finished the hot farrier work. "And I'll need five more drinks to soothe my throat from the cinders!"

Odin laughed and clasped his red-bearded son on the arm. "We ride again! Luck against the giants, Thunderer!"

I was just as happy to see the Lord of All go.

"Well," muttered the Storm God. "Now I have the rest of the day off. What say you, Trickster?"

"I say I'm not going to sit here drinking beer all day if that's what you have in mind."

His brows fell. "It isn't! No, let's find ourselves some amusement and work up a thirst worthy of Valhalla! A day's adventure makes the night's feast jolly!"

I smiled into my horn. "Truly spoken, old friend."

We ambled over to another area off the forge where Thor sometimes parked his golden chariot. Its knotwork crackled with old magic, glowing under the deepening cloud-cover. Two goats grazed nearby. Their coats were shaggy and brown, and their strange, horizontal-pupilled eyes burned with insane goat thoughts.

"Where should we go?" Thor asked.

"The ladies of Jotunheim always enjoy company," I mused with a suggestive grin.

"Forget it. Sif and I are getting on well lately. I'm not going anywhere near the giantesses."

"Well, fine then. Spoil my fun."

"How about Nidavellir? It's been ages since I've pissed off the dwarves."

I mulled the idea over. The realm of dwarves was dense with caves, and I had no wish to travel underground. On the other hand, Nidavellir was also full of gold. My fingers itched as I remembered the place.

"Do Brokk and Eitri still live there? After all these years?" I asked him.

"They do."

"I've owed them a visit a long time now," I said in an ominous voice.

Thor shrugged good-naturedly. "I just want to beat someone up. If you have a target in mind, that's all right by me."

The two dwarf brothers I spoke of had once gifted Mjolnir itself to the gods so they could win a bet against me. But those days were long past. Since then, Brokk and Eitri had struck off on their own and refused to have any further dealings with Asgard. Thor wouldn't trouble himself on their account now.

We set off for Nidavellir as the first raindrops hit the ripe pastures.

chapter nine

The Realm of Dwarves

Nidavellir Present

Nidavellir was a gloomy realm shrouded in an eternal murky twilight. Stagnant pools peered up into the overcast skies like dead eyes, and the ground was littered with sharp stones. Thor and I trekked across a sodden field, our heads bowed against the wind. We were careful to avoid the rocks. A false step could send us flying.

Thor had left his chariot at the border, and I had made my own way to the realm of dwarves. I could cross the span between worlds more swiftly than any goat.

After a while, we reached the entrance to a cave. I stared at it a long time, not liking what I saw.

"Let me guess," Thor said. "You've got a phobia now, don't you?"

I bridled at his words. "Hear me, Thunderer! I am no white-livered mortal to be so easily devoured by one experience!"

"Well, stop standing there like a wuss then. I didn't come here for the scenery."

We marched into the cave with me in the lead. Roots scraggled along the pebbly walls and clusters of mica glittered from the dirt. We heard drumming. It was soft at first, but grew louder as we trod deeper into the earth. The rhythms drifted around us in complex, enchanting patterns, quickening the heart. The reedy sound of some sort of bizarre instrument melded with the beats, whining in our ears.

"Place never changes," my companion grumbled.

"The dwarves can only create in gems and metal. Nidavellir shall always remain the same."

"No, it won't. The population's about to drop," said Thor, ever the philosopher.

We continued down the damp passages. Eventually, we found the hall I was looking for.

"Hail, Brokk! Hail, Eitri!" I exclaimed gleefully as I walked in. I raised my hand in a lively greeting. The golden threads on my sleeve twinkled like stars as they caught the light from the dwarves' forge.

"Loki!" yelped Eitri, the second and more intelligent of the brothers. He was only as tall as my waist, and his sharp face and gnarled limbs were entirely colorless. The dwarf's hair was swarthy and his skin was spotted with grime.

His brother looked similar except for the solid gold chains he had woven through his beard. They rattled as Brokk lifted his head to gaze up at me. Both the dwarves' eyes glinted like obsidian, scared and unhappy. Thor curled his lip and showed his teeth.

"Hardly a welcome like last time!" I told them. "Where are the horns of fine mead? My friend and I had a thirsty journey down your tunnels!"

"You'd have us serve you before you slay us? Where's the honor in that?"

I cocked my head, then addressed myself to Thor. "Well, darn. They know why we're here."

"You, Lord Thunderer!" shouted Eitri. "You carry the hammer we made for you! Surely you would not kill us in cold blood?"

Odin's son frowned. "Yeah, perhaps that would be hasty. Tell you what. Bring me the mead, and I'll let Loki kill you instead."

"My magic offers them a quicker death than your beatings," I said. "Thor, you truly disappoint me today."

"They sewed your lips shut, not mine."

I began chanting a rune, one that would tear through the two dwarves just as their needle had once torn through me. The brothers were not immortal. They would not survive as I had.

"No, stop!" yelled Eitri. His sibling cowered behind him. "We can make it up to you, Loki!"

I paused in the middle of my spell and regarded the ugly creatures. My dark bangs ruffled in the hot winds of the dwarves' fire, and the hem of my tunic fluttered about the tops of my legs, distracting me with its movement.

"Just kill them already," Thor contributed from nearby. He was squinting at a row of stoppered gold vases, no doubt hoping to find mead. His expression was just a touch bored.

"I'd hear their offer first, Thunderer." I faced the dwarves. "How would you appease a god who rightly seeks your blood?"

"Is there not blood you seek more than ours, Loki?" whined Eitri, desperate.

There was. There was at that. My eyes narrowed thoughtfully, but I could hardly strike the deal I suddenly had in mind with Thor standing right next to me. Instead I said, "Enough. You'd die too easily in this place. I'll change your forms and take my revenge at my leisure."

I twisted the words of my spell, bending my shapechanger's magic against my enemies. The brothers cringed, hunkering down to the dirt floor. They began to pull in upon themselves, becoming smaller and smaller. Their hair fell away and their disgusting white flesh hardened into carapaces.

Two pill bugs wriggled in the soil, their many legs struggling and their fragile gray antennae twitching. I scooped them up, and they curled themselves into tiny spheres.

"I'll have words with you later," I promised them as I secured them in one of my pouches.

Thor was shaking his head. "Magic is for goddesses," he told me for about the ten-thousandth time. Immortality was burdensome that way.

"I'll not allow these two a quick end."

We set off down the passages again seeking the main hall. It too was just as I remembered it. The roof was lost to the obscurity of wet mist, and its stone pillars trickled incessantly. We strode inside with our heads held high, as if we had an invitation to be there. The dwarves looked up from their gold. Their bellows slowed and their hammering stopped. As they realized who we were, they began hefting their swords and readying their crossbows.

"Is this how you welcome your gods?" Thor inquired expansively.

"You only come to slay us. The very earth speaks of it."

The Thunderer shook out his auburn beard. "They catch on fast, don't they?"

"Truly," I replied. I pulled a gleaming sword from one of their stockpiles and twirled it about, getting a feel for the balance. The blade sang with their spells. The weapon could have been made for me.

"Let's cull a few maggots born of Ymir!" my companion growled. He raised his hammer.

"Wait!" a dwarf interrupted for the second time that day.

"Oh, for crying out loud," I muttered, rolling my eyes.

"We have the hand for you, as promised to your sister! Allow us to pay our debt so we may live!"

I stalked forward, my new sword at the ready.

"What's he talking about?" asked Thor.

"How would I know? We're not here to chat!" But I did know. The speaker was Bombor, and I was going to slice his throat wide open before he got out another word.

Lightning flared in front of me. Super-heated plasma blocked my path. "Not so fast, Loki. I think we're missing something important here."

Bombor exhaled with relief and addressed his kin. "The Thunderer will hear us. Bring him mead. Show him the hospitality of Nidavellir."

A drinking horn of the purest gold was offered to Thor. It was worked with innumerable blue diamonds more glorious than any sea. He accepted the horn and took a long swig from it. The Thunder God smacked his lips.

"Not bad," he admitted.

"Fuck," I cursed under my breath. I lowered my sword.

Two other dwarves, Dain and Iri, shuffled forward. They carried a severed metal hand woven entirely of lustrous gold. Its shining fingers stretched toward the fire, though the hand itself was connected to nothing.

"What's that?" demanded my traveling companion.

"The hand of Tyr, as sworn to you."

"I've never heard of this," Thor confessed.

Iri scratched his head. "One of your goddesses bought it of her own flesh.

60

Surely you know?"

"Freya!" Thor growled. He slung back more of the mead, angered at the thought of the dishonor that had been brought upon us all. Again.

"No, another, almost as fair."

I sidled away, pretending to be very interested in one of the forges.

Thor shot me a suspicious look. "Loki, do you know anything about this?"

I clamped my lips shut.

"It's a fine hand," declared the Protector of Midgard, spinning it around in the dim orange light. The limb sparkled and gleamed, alive with the oldest dwarven magics. "Tyr will be well pleased. Mjolnir can wait for Jotun blood."

"We're relieved to hear it!" exclaimed Bombor.

"Still, I would hate to have traveled all this way only to leave so quickly. Who's the best storyteller among you? I'll have this tale."

Jari the dwarf stepped forward and bowed low to the Thunder God.

I groaned and took a seat by a forge, wishing that the crackling of the flames and the ceaseless pounding of the drums would swallow up the dwarf-skald's words.

"Ages ago," began Jari, "when the mortals above us were much wiser, and the mighty and holy name of the Thor the Thunderer was rightly extolled in many of their lands—"

"Good start!" the God of Storms approved, raising his horn in a salute.

Jari nodded back graciously.

"It was in those days that one of your number, a goddess, first visited our caves. Fenrir the wolf, the vile and gruesome child of Loki, was but recently bound." Hundreds of onyx eyes fixed on me. I tapped my foot impatiently.

The storyteller continued his tale. "We dwarves had been recently summoned to Asgard to solve the problem the Trickster had brought upon you—"

I sprang to my feet. "Enough!" I snapped.

Jari blinked at me. "Do I speak any words that are not true?"

"I am a god! You will speak of me with respect!"

Thor held up his empty horn and waved it about a few times to get our hosts' attention. "Can we just get on with this?" he rumbled.

Jari coughed. "It shall be as you say, my lords. Certain events transpired, and mistakes may or may not have been made by hereinto unnamed parties. We dwarves crafted a magic cord to bind Fenrir until the end of days. Bombor, whom you have met, was one of those skilled spinners, and it was he who caught the breath of a fish for Fenrir's cord. But the huge wolf, being ever crafty just like his—that is... never mind—would not permit himself to be bound unless the great god Tyr lay his own right hand between his jaws. When Fenrir realized he had fallen into a trap—"

"Yeah, yeah," Thor interrupted. "I know. I was *there*."

"Of course, Mighty One. I only seek to create the scene."

"Months later, a fair goddess appeared in Nidavellir, speaking gentle words. We soon learned that she had come on Tyr's account, for Loki was her dear friend and she wished the Aesir to forgive him."

"Couldn't have been Skathi," muttered the Thunderer, mostly to himself. "Before her time."

Jari shook his head, making the chains in his dark beard jiggle. "Truly spoken, my lord. No, this was no goddess of ice, but one of fire. Her hair was long, the dancing reds and oranges of our forges. Her eyes were full of light and brighter than any treasure. Her skin was soft, and she wore long raiments of spun gold. Precious jewels glittered like stars from her fingers and neck. Many of us felt our hearts stir that day."

I had known exactly how to get the dwarves' attention.

"At first, she would not tell us of her purpose. She cooked finer meals than we've ever had before or will ever have again, looked after our cows, and told us wondrous tales by the hearths at night.

"In time, she took some interest in Nainn, the dwarf who had done the most to forge Fenrir's binds. With many beguiling words, she asked him to craft the hand you now have in your possession. But Nainn had heard much from the former guardians of Brisingamen. Those four were the most hideous dwarves among us, but they had known the embrace of the fairest goddess and were ever wont to brag of it."

Thor scowled into the drinking horn.

"Inspired by the unsightly brothers' tale, Nainn would accept only one form of payment. He himself was of noble birth, and he thought to found a dynasty upon the flesh of the Aesir woman. The goddess bore him twin sons. Meanwhile, Nainn sabotaged any progress he made on the hand. For some time, things went his way.

"But the Aesir lady was wise. She figured out that the work was taking too long. When she discovered Nainn's treachery, she punished him for his oath-breaking. He now lies buried under the dripping wall in the back. We put up no stone in his memory. His sons work among us, and their skill with the forge is incomparable. Their father's dream is dead. They live as equals to every other dwarf in this hall. Understand, we will have no king."

Two dwarves peered up from their bellows. Their hair was red and was tied back with solid gold bands, and their eyes were like the night sky above a burning forest. They did not seem displeased by the tale. I looked away, not giving them a single twitch of acknowledgment.

Jari bowed again. "The goddess left hurriedly on other business, but her threats were clear enough—indeed, they blistered our ears and made our hearts skip in their places for terror. She never came back for the hand, but I am certain that you, fearsome Thunderer, will deliver it safely to Asgard, as was always intended."

Thor pondered what he had heard. His shaggy beard was flecked with dwarven mead. Finally, he nodded and thanked the skald for his story.

We got up and left. I noticed that I had never been offered a drink. The children of Nidavellir owed me a great deal already, and they had only added to their debt that day. I smiled evilly and touched the pouch where two of their finest artisans now languished as pill bugs. Brokk and Eitri were only the beginning. I had many plans in mind.

When we reached the chariot, Thor set our treasure in a secure place, then slowly turned to look at me. A moment passed. I thought he might not have figured out the truth. But a few seconds later, he started beating his broad hand against the carriage, roaring with laughter.

"Nice—try!" he gasped, leaning heavily against its golden side. His mirth and the mead made it difficult for him to stand straight. "Oh, the halls of Valhalla will be lively tonight!"

"You won't tell a soul!" I hissed.

"I think I will!" Thor doubled over, his laughter booming through the drizzly fields.

I thought quickly. Blackmail wouldn't work on him. Thor had been through troubles of his own in the giants' hall of Utgard, but his struggles were common knowledge. The story was still told among gods and mortals. In the end, he had proven himself the strongest of all the Aesir.

I was not so fortunate in my dealings with the dwarves. Odin had alluded to my time with Nainn once before, right before he had ordered me bound. Nothing was entirely hidden from my brother—not when he could sit on his throne in Valskalf and survey all the realms. But no one else had known any of the details. Until now.

In the cave, I'd had nothing but time for self-reflection. I decided on an approach I never would have dreamt up before my imprisonment.

I let my shoulders slump. My dark eyes sought out the dying yellow grass that marked the border between Midgard and Nidavellir. Worms spun among the blades, fleeing the watery reflections of the mortal world's sun.

"I'll tell you a secret, Thor. I felt very bad about Fenrir. A father's shame. Tyr was never unfair to me. He'd always been a friend to everyone. Myself too, I had hoped." With a forlorn sigh, I examined my own boots.

I was lying, of course. I had been scared. I liked Tyr, but I never would have endured Nidavellir—much less Nainn's attentions—for his sake. No, I had thought I'd finally gone too far and that my fellow Aesir would send me back to Jotunheim. Back then, I could imagine no worse fate.

"What's this?" demanded Thor. His voice was suspicious.

"I of all the gods felt sorry," I said. "Is that so hard to imagine? I sought to make amends. By any means necessary."

He stopped laughing and his warrior's eyes grew troubled. "You, Loki?"

"Indeed, old friend. I took much hardship on myself. But that's all in the past." I forced a morose frown onto my lips and met his gaze squarely. "Thor, tell the other gods whatever you want. The important thing is that our brother will be made whole. I have waited a long time for this day."

He grunted, considering my words. Fitful breezes, confused by the outlands between realms, ruffled at his beard.

"I guess we don't need to share the *entire* tale of how you came by such a wonder." Thor's tone was thick with respect.

I stepped over to him, allowing my stride to falter a few times with false humility. I reached out and clasped the other Aesir on the arm. The cloth of his tunic was rough and scratchy under my hand. He returned my grasp, inclining his head gravely.

"You are truly the most honorable of gods," I told him.

He huffed his breath out and shrugged. "Let's get the hand back."

"I think I'll ride with you... if you'd permit me?"

Thor was pleased by my request, as I had intended. He welcomed any chance to show off his chariot, but I almost always journeyed with my own magic, under my own power. I clambered in beside him. The carriage's golden sides were as high as my chest. When I looked forward, I could see only the hindsides of the goats. How could any god stand to travel so?

"To Asgard!" my friend shouted. The animals took off, showering sparks from their hooves as the Thunderer spurred them into the skies.

Thor's chariot wasn't as bad once it was in motion. The Midgard steppes sped by below us, and the sky darkened with our passing as if an early sunset were blanketing the mortal world. Lightning flared in our wake, leaping from cloud to cloud before it crashed to the ground. The air was tinged with a brassy luminosity, alive with an energy that prickled our scalps.

The mortals could not see us, but they sensed that the storm was unusual. Some of them crossed themselves, murmuring prayers that were not directed to us. Peasant women in embroidered shirts whispered of bad spirits.

My hair lashed against my brow, and rain struck my face. Something else danced on the edges of my Aesir perceptions. I frowned thoughtfully and turned my full attention to the lands below. They were vast and wild. Fire, not electricity, lit up a fair number of the homes.

"Some of them remember you!" I called to Thor. "They speak another name, but the image is of you!"

"Yes, that's why I fly this route!" He shook out the reins, urging his goats to make greater haste as they pounded along the skyways. They responded with terrible shrieks and redoubled their efforts, straining against their leads.

We reached the rainbow leading to Asgard. Ages had passed since I'd last traveled up the bridge of the gods. Bifrost was as solid and as beautiful as ever, and my heart sang as we crested its arc. Midgard faded into a wash of brilliant cloud tops and white sky, and was lost to our view. Ahead, chalky cliffs rose from an opalescent haze. As we drew closer, I could see blindingly green grass rippling under a steady breeze.

I hadn't realized just how much I'd missed coming in over Bifrost. But I had not missed the god who awaited us at its end.

Thor pulled his golden chariot to a halt and raised a hand in salute. "Well met, Heimdall, guardian of sacred Asgard!"

"Well met, Lord Thunderer, protector of Midgard!" The other god did not smile as he spoke. His tawny hair and full beard were alight with tiny rainbows.

It took Heimdall a moment to notice that Thor had a passenger. His azure eyes went hard, and his hand automatically drifted toward his scabbard.

Heimdall and I had never been friends. The god who defended borders and kept all things at a proper distance was no companion for the god of wits and tricks, who brought the close burning of the flames.

"Loki," he said. "Taking the main road in? For a change?"

I curled my lip in a contemptuous snarl. "That's my business, Heimdall. Why don't you mind yours? For a change?"

The chilly Vanir unsheathed his sparkling sword.

"Your exploits concern us all, child of Jotunheim! What evil do you visit upon us today?"

No, we had never been friends, Heimdall and I.

"Oh, calm down already," Thor interrupted over the insistent bleating of his goats. The animals were eager to return to their stable. "We won a treasure today, Lord Heimdall."

"A treasure? What is it?"

Even the good-natured Thunderer lost his temper at that point. His auburn brows sunk and his mouth twisted. "Come with us to Valhalla if you'd have the story. I'm not going to give it to you here."

Heimdall's all-seeing eyes narrowed and sought me out, as if Thor's refusal to answer his question were somehow my fault. But he put his glinting sword away and followed us into Asgard.

CHAPTER TEN
TYR'S NEW HAND

Asgard Present

Thor had always been one for making a dramatic entrance. Valhalla had hundreds upon hundreds of doors for all of Odin's hosts. But the Thunderer chose the grandest set, the ones at the very front of the hall where the golden shields peaked like the prow of a great ship.

The pale form of a stag clicked along the roof, searching for moss to nibble on. His antlers were covered with white velvet and dripped a steady stream of divine mead. The enchanted creature peered down at us and his liquid brown eyes widened with astonishment. Entire ages had passed since Thor and I had last returned together from an adventure.

The Thunder God's heavy chain mail did not slow him. He strode boldly into Odin's hall, moving with confident ease. Thor had donned his battle helmet for the occasion, a plain headpiece of unadorned leather and iron, crafted for the practicalities of war.

"HAIL THE AESIR!" he boomed. The victorious shout shook the rafters and carried throughout all of Asgard. Odin looked up from his throne, his one eye calm. Little took the All-Father by surprise. His two crows, Huginn and Muninn, shifted about on his shoulders. Their beady eyes were alert.

Many of the gods had already gathered in Valhalla that evening, seeking the warm companionship of the hall. Any who weren't present would hear Thor's call. The Thunderer stomped up to his father's high seat. I hesitated, then trailed after him. I caught the others' expressions on the sly. They could try to hide their frowns and the distrust in their eyes, but I was no fool. I saw their real faces.

Thor had secreted our prize in a velvet bag. Closed-lipped, with his broad arms folded over his chest, he waited for everyone to arrive. After a bit, even Sigyn and Freyr straggled in. They had both traveled a long way, from the borderlands next to Alfheim. The two of them sat next to each other, apparently wrapped up in a discussion of some sort. Knowing them, it probably concerned Light Elf magic. Freyr's red-gold head was bowed very close to my wife's deep brown one. Both of them looked amused. Sigyn put her delicate hand to her lips. Her eyes danced with laughter.

Freyr's father, Njord, was not far off. The God of the Sea was stately in appearance, with a trimmed beard and straight, glossy hair of deep gray. The Aesir who blessed ocean voyages and brought fair breezes to the shores wore a rich tunic of greenish blue. It was trimmed with pearls in many shades: rose and black, cream and silver, gold and cobalt.

Skathi, of course, sat as far away from Njord as possible. They had been married briefly, but the relationship had not ended well. She caught my gaze and nodded once, then focused her attention back on Thor. Her intelligent eyes were bright with curiosity.

Freya was as beautiful and striking as ever. She wore her usual sapphire-blue gown under a lush scarlet cloak threaded with gold. The goddess balanced her favorite dagger in one hand. It could cut into meat or into an enemy with equal vigor. Her two cats had stretched themselves out on the hearth next to her. Their furry bellies were turned up and their front paws were curled to their chests, for they knew Valhalla was safe.

Idunn sat by Freya, alongside Sif with her dwarf-made gold hair—one of the innumerable gifts I'd won for Asgard back in the early days. Honir was near the goddesses, his expression vague and confused. Heimdall had taken a place up front, close to Odin and Thor, and his face was intent. Even in the smoky hall, his hair and beard shimmered faintly with all the spectrum's colors. Forseti stood further off, his silver hair contrasting with his long black tunic. He held a mead horn in one hand and sipped from it sparingly. His gray eyes were reserved, ever distant and impartial.

Tyr himself was off to one side, speaking quietly with Bragi. His honey-blonde hair caught the firelight. As always, he wore his beard trimmed short. Since he was not out on the field, he had garbed himself in the gold-spun tunic he wore to peaceful assemblies. I had thought of that shirt long ago when I had first sought out the hand. His tunic and armor were all of gold. It was fitting that his new hand be of gold as well.

Thor raised his gargantuan drinking horn to the gathered gods.

"Friends, I bring you the best of news tonight! I have traveled with Loki to Nidavellir, where we seized a great treasure for the Aesir! Its like has not been seen since I took up Mjolnir!"

There were cheers and calls of "What is it?" and "Show us, Thor!"

The burly Thunderer grinned, thoroughly enjoying himself. He wasn't about to let his moment slip by. I sighed, resigned to standing up there in front of everybody while he dragged things out.

"First the story, then I'll show you our prize!" Spoken like a returned warrior, all right.

Thor spun a good tale, leaving out any mention of the goddess. To hear his account, the dwarves had crafted the hand for their own ends and we had wrangled it from them by force.

Against my will, I found myself catching Odin's eye. His thin lips curled up ever so slightly when I met his gaze, and he leveled me with a cold, knowing smirk. Even his crows seemed to be in on the joke.

I looked away again, clenching my hands and silently fuming. Odin could be such a *bastard* sometimes.

Finally, Thor got around to pulling the hand out of the sack. A profound hush immediately fell over the hall. Everyone stared at the golden hand and then at Tyr. No one wanted to speak, to destroy to magic of the moment. The brave and beloved god slowly rose to his feet. He held his left arm at his side, but the right ended in a vicious, blunt stump. He started to say something, then choked on the words.

The Thunderer moved forward and gravely held out the dwarven treasure. His stormy eyes were compassionate.

Tyr lowered his head respectfully and received the hand. Its intricate golden fibers began to shine with a soft, white light. The injured god touched our gift to his gnawed right arm. The light flared once and died to a flicker, and the metal suddenly blended directly into Tyr's flesh. He winced, then relaxed again and nodded to us all with a reassuring smile.

For the first time since the earliest days of Asgard, Tyr lifted his right hand and wriggled his fingers. His honest eyes brimmed with unshed tears, and he bowed low to Thor, then to me.

"Bold Thor. Clever Loki. I... I am grateful. I cannot express how much so. Thank you. Thank you, both." His lip shivered and he fell silent.

"Thank Thor, certainly!" complained a nasty voice from the front. "Loki only makes some small recompense and deserves no praise! Too little, too late!" Heimdall bared his teeth in a snarl.

Odin leaned forward, his mighty fingers digging into the carved and gilded wood of the armrests. His crows flapped their wings and readjusted themselves on his shoulders.

"Hard words for such a happy occasion," he said. The All-Father's expression was as unreadable as Forseti's. He seemed to be waiting for something.

"I only voice what many here leave unspoken, guarded in their hearts."

"Perhaps," acknowledged Odin. I may have been his blood-brother, but I could not expect him to back me up in all things.

Heimdall looked about the hall and then nodded to himself. "Congratulations, Tyr." His voice was strong. He seemed to want everyone to hear him. "Now I must return to my duties." He came forward to clasp Thor's arm and solemnly thank him for bringing the gods a wondrous treasure indeed. I was not far from my traveling companion. Heimdall turned away from the Thunderer and started for one of Valhalla's hundreds of doors. His steps were fast and sure, and his focus was intense.

I was caught entirely unprepared when his muscled shoulder slammed into my thinner one. I stumbled back, flailing, then regained my footing with an Aesir's speed.

"Oops! Sorry, Loki!" he exclaimed in a snide, sing-song voice.

"Screw you!" I pounced at him, slamming a palm hard into his side. The blow itself lacked much force, but I had already called up fire. The nearly translucent, blue-purple center of the very hottest part of a flame seared forth from my palm, burning into his shirt and skin. Crackling orange tongues lashed out from where I'd struck, eating at the cloth of his lovely tunic.

Heimdall yelped and spoke a protective rune. The fires immediately died. We both backed up, watching each other closely, our eyes full of hate.

"You little cur!" he hissed. "No *warrior* fights with magic!"

"Pretentious bully! What do you know of honor in a fight? I'll spill your blood long before Ragnarok, Heimdall!"

"Enough," interrupted Odin. His voice was soft, but it carried through the entire hall. Even the popping logs in the hearths suddenly grew still.

My old enemy and I fell silent.

"Forseti, what say you?" asked the wisest and the mightiest of all immortals.

The God of Law regarded us coolly. "Strife has no place here. Not now. If they must fight, let them do it elsewhere."

Odin grinned, showing his teeth. Never a good sign, that. His smile reminded me of the laughing gleam of a killing sword, of the giggling white of bones scattered across a blooded field.

"I will give you two a choice," he declared, dreadful in the ecstasy he was taking from our division. Heimdall and I both swallowed audibly.

"The first choice is that you abandon your fight until the end of all things is upon us. Clasp arms and swear to peace before myself, Forseti, and all the gods." His cold blue eye glittered with a pitiless sort of amusement. The All-Father knew exactly how likely we were to accept that deal.

"And the second?" I asked, my voice nervous with fear.

"You shall have your war."

Heimdall spoke up immediately. "I will swear no peace with evil! Let us take up our blades! Freyr, I'm glad you're sitting with Sigyn! She'll soon be a widow and will need a friend!"

"Wait a minute," I snapped at my enemy. "Hear what the Hanged God would have of us first, you fool!" Trust Heimdall not to think things through. I knew my blood-brother better than that. There would be conditions to the fight.

Odin's smile widened. "You remain shrewd, Loki, and ask the right questions." Huginn and Muninn cawed, the harsh noise echoing off the shields above. They took to the air in a burst of ebony feathers, circling the tables and sounding their coarse cries.

"Heimdall, Loki is no match for you in strength. He would lose any contest of arms between you. Brother of my blood, Heimdall is no match for you in wits. Your battle may not be one of the mind."

My enemy clenched his jaw. "Then what would you have of us, Odin?" he grated.

"A simple thing. A test of wills." Honir looked up, blinked a few times dazedly, and went back to his mead.

I nodded thoughtfully and ran my hand along my smooth-shaven chin.

"A fair idea, Lord of All," I said with great care. "But I suspect there must be more to this? Your crows would not screech with such bloodlust if it were otherwise."

Odin nodded once and his demeanor turned very serious. "If you will not swear to peace, you will take on mortal forms entirely. The first who cries 'no more!' loses to the other."

I snorted derisively. "Wonderful! I've been mortal more times than I can count! Let's see Heimdall keep up with me!"

"You miss my meaning, Loki. I speak not of appearances, Shapechanger and Trickster. You will have no Aesir knowledge, no magic to command. You will be a true son of Ask until you relent."

My smug grin vanished. Even Heimdall's expression became alarmed.

"You've got to be shitting me!" I exclaimed, throwing my arms in the air.

"We could die," my old enemy agreed. "That's a fine end for Loki, but Asgard cannot afford to lose me."

Odin glowered at the Watcher, his single eye flashing dangerously. "Asgard cannot afford to lose either one of you," he said. "Did I not sacrifice myself to myself on the Tree, hung out and bleeding for nine nights? I know the fate of all the realms." His hair and beard flickered silver in the smoldering light. "I will allow each of you a second, an immortal to watch over you until the other breaks. There shall be no death. A sworn peace or singing battle: chose now. I'd have you resolve this war between you, one way or another."

Forseti folded his arms across his chest and inclined his head grimly, first to Heimdall, then to me. We were out of time.

"I am no coward," said Heimdall. "I guard us from the giants and I can guard my own will. I choose war."

"And you, Loki?" Odin's voice dripped with that appalling, battle-mad glee of his.

"Oh, war, definitely! I'm already looking forward to it!" I quipped.

The Hanged God seemed pleased by our choice. "Heimdall struck the first blow, here among friends," he said. "Loki shall have the first choice of which god stands beside him when he becomes a true mortal."

Freya darted to her feet, her amethyst eyes blazing. "Excuse me?!"

"Or goddess," murmured the All-Father, raising a placating hand.

But I had already made my decision. "I'd have Thor watching my back."

"No fair!" Heimdall shouted. "He's the very Protector of Midgard!"

"Loki's choice will be honored," declared the God of War. "A clever pick, for a clever god. Take as much care in yours, Watcher, and you might know the victory!"

My enemy put his hand to his beard, stroking it as he surveyed the assembled Aesir. I frowned as he lingered on Freya. She knew a great deal about Midgard and could be a tremendous ally to him. I was also on her bad side at the moment. The others hadn't paid her concerns much mind, but she had no doubts that I had made off with her cats. Freya would delight in getting revenge on me if she could.

But Heimdall moved on after some contemplation. Odin regarded him with a steady patience, his visage calm and expectant.

A vindictive smile lit up the Guardian of Bifrost's face. "Odin, if Loki can have Thor, then at least order it so that I will not be a thrall among mortals. Allow me some status, some measure of wealth. Is this acceptable to you?"

"It is."

"Then I chose Forseti as my second."

The vast hall turned lively as the Aesir murmured among themselves and exchanged many questioning looks. To the very best of our knowledge, the God of Law had only taken form in Midgard once, and quite briefly at that. Although he could hold his own in a fight, Forseti was not a committed warrior like my own guardian.

Heimdall was straightening the sleeves of his ivory tunic in a satisfied way, clearly well pleased with himself.

Odin settled back into his chair, his lips curling up in approval. "Wisely named, shining Heimdall! This will truly be a battle worthy of the Aesir!"

Huginn and Muninn let out raucous shrieks. The two crows spiraled down from above and landed on each of our shoulders. It was Huginn, of course, who sought me out. Muninn pressed himself up against Heimdall's neck. Memory ever favored the God of Boundaries.

The other gods laughed and applauded, looking forward to the diversion. Only Forseti seemed displeased. He held himself stiffly, his scholarly fingers clenching his arms so tightly that he was probably leaving bruises.

When the mead began to flow again, he turned his gray eyes on Odin. "Grandfather, it would be better if I were not involved in this." But the mightiest of us shook his head, unwilling to entertain his objection. The God of Law was stuck with his charge.

We celebrated the upcoming conflict, as was our nature. Heimdall and I kept to the far sides of Valhalla, him with a put-upon Forseti, a laughing Njord, and a cackling Freya. I drank my mead with Sigyn and Freyr, and Thor and Sif. Tyr joined us briefly, but soon drifted off again. It was not his way to take sides. He was brave and wise, a friend to all who lived in Asgard. He found his way to Odin, and they were soon lost in their own conversation.

The hours of the night shortened, the fires blazed less brightly, and the shadows deepened. I nuzzled up against Sigyn and laid my hand on her knee.

"Take this, my wife," I whispered in her ear, handing her my pouch. "Take good care of the contents for me while I'm gone. You always have such a way with natural things."

She smiled at me and leaned in, letting her hair brush my cheek. "What's in here, husband?"

"Pill bugs. Very important pill bugs."

Sigyn giggled at that. "I'll give them lettuce," she promised.

I kissed her near the base of her throat and then returned to my mead, the sweetest drink in any realm. I knew I would not enjoy it again for some time.

ChapTeR eLeVeN
a BaTTLe of WiLLS

Midgard Present

I woke up to a piercing, grating noise, repeating itself over and over again. There was a disgusting, sour taste in my mouth and my skin was crawling. Struggling with the tangled blankets, I pulled myself up on my cot and hit the snooze button on the alarm. The jarring cacophony ceased.

I stood up, caught in a morning fog, and began to get dressed. Jeans, undershirt, red cardigan. My room didn't have a sink of its own, but there was a mirror on one wall. I ran a brush through my black hair and got rid of the worst of the rumples.

Mindlessly, I started to reach for my toothbrush when it suddenly occurred to me that something was horribly, horribly wrong.

The crawling across my skin intensified. Cells were dying, decaying. My heart fluttered, the blood washing back on itself with an unwholesome murmur. Neurons fired, slow and inefficient. These too were careening toward death. Even now, I could feel a connection lost, an unraveling haze settling over one tiny part of my brain. My breath stank of rotting bits of food, too many to ever be cleansed.

I myself was rotting. Time slithered through me, devouring and destroying me.

With a hasty, jerking motion, I flew to my knees and grasped a trash bin. Discarded receipts stuck to the grime at the bottom. My stomach quivered, then heaved. Clammy and shaking, I felt my new body come under control. I slowly got to my feet, staggered down to the shared washroom, and cleaned myself up as best as I could.

Still, everything that I was continued trickling along toward its inexorable end.

I wondered if mortals could feel themselves dying. Probably not, I concluded. How would they be able to function? The perception must have been an Aesir one.

My memories blurred and jumbled. Acting on a dim echo of an instinct, I tried to reach out with my will to get a true sense of where I was. There was only the murky space within, the clinging vapors of my own limited thoughts. I was truly cut off and alone.

I wasn't surprised. It was exactly Odin's style to allow me a god's view of my own mortality and nothing else. I walked back up the hall, my head hanging and hurting.

"You missed breakfast, you idiot. The dining hall's closed now."

"Bugger off, Rich," I said to my brother. Resentment flared within me just at the sound of his voice. Always the golden son. He was taller and stronger than me, with appealing curls of light brown hair and a strong, freckled face. His room was right across the hall from mine. The fates were cruel.

"Prat," he told me. Another memory stirred. I was talking to Heimdall, who had called himself by the name Rig when he had last traveled through Midgard—not Rich. He had been a Vanir originally, a god of wealth.

We stared at each other for long moments, struggling with our recollections of a shared mortal childhood. Of being fraternal twins and the worst of rivals. The bitterness was real. The memories were not. Between one breath and the next, I found it very hard to believe that everything I knew of Rich was an illusion. My human consciousness clung to the familiar, false history, as if many layers of cobwebs had been spun over my mind and woven through my being.

"Had enough yet, Luther?" he asked with a cold smile.

"Are you nuts? We're just getting started."

My brother laughed, a mocking sound. "Then enjoy taking your first class on an empty stomach." I remembered then that I was doing a course in computer science and had only five minutes to get to another building.

I dashed into my room, grabbed a book, and scrabbled down flights upon flights of stairs. We lived at the very top of the student residence, my hated brother and I.

I slid into a seat just before the professor arrived. He clutched a small, plastic mug of cafeteria coffee in his hand. The room had a high ceiling and was nearly freezing so early in the morning. Oil portraits of important people lined one wall. The professor ambled up to a whiteboard and began his lecture, occasionally drawing on the board to illustrate or emphasize a point.

I followed most of the class with ease. I had sat the requisite mathematics exam and scored very well. Another counterfeit memory. I told myself that it didn't matter and tried to pay attention.

When the lecture was done, I filed down the stairs with the other students. My hand began itching like mad. I scratched at it. Tiny cells of skin flaked off, falling, dust to the ground.

Dust. What I was becoming with every cursed mortal breath.

I put my hand to my mouth, then slumped heavily onto the stairs. I felt bone cold, but I was sweating profusely. I wrapped my arms around my knees and bowed my head, shivering. Other mortals stepped around me, leaving me to my misery. I shook all the harder and tried to keep my gorge from rising again. What an embarrassment that would be.

"Are you quite all right?"

The voice was compassionate. I found myself staring into the eyes of a human woman. She was a tad plump and very young, with straight, honey-blonde hair. She wore a blue and pink rugby shirt over her jeans, and no make-up. A simple gold cross hung from her neck.

"Not really," I told her. Tears welled in my eyes, unbidden. I couldn't do anything to stop them.

She reached into her handbag and pulled out a tissue, then silently gave it to me.

Strange emotions raged and churned through me, all out of control. I held onto my knees as if they were my lifeline, trembling and sniffling.

The mortal waited, her eyes soft and patient.

"It's only the first day," she said. "Things will get better. You'll see."

I shook my head despairingly. "I... I really don't belong here."

"Don't be daft," she told me with no rancor. "This professor is tough. You just need to keep reading, and you'll do fine in the course."

"Not the course," I muttered. "The course is easy." I straightened up. Some of the fire of my nature was starting to resurface, even through my mortality. I grinned at her arrogantly. "So very, very easy!"

Odin had once gifted the sons and daughters of Ask and Embla with spirit. Through that first blessing, they had received unquantifiable hunches, gut instincts, and dreams of far-off places and possible futures. The confusing atmosphere of Midgard and the sinister influence of the giants constantly worked against their inheritance, but it was always with them nonetheless.

The young woman had sensed something. She pulled back, and her face twisted worriedly before it shadowed over with outright revulsion. The kind-hearted mortal did not like the vibe she was getting off me. Not at all.

"I have to go! Good luck!" my classmate exclaimed. She practically fled my presence. I shrugged to myself and stood up.

Attending a class on an empty stomach hadn't been any fun. Rich had been right about that much. I went off in search of food.

The dining hall's walls were painted in pastel colors and accented with frilly baroque molding. Tall windows overlooked well-kept tea gardens, and more oil paintings graced the walls. The place was very crowded. Student voices boomed from the high ceiling, creating a roar like the sea's. I found an open seat at one of the long wooden tables that stretched from one side of the room to the other. As I sat down, I realized they were similar to the hewn tables back in Valhalla. I did not pursue the thought. It was too painful.

Rich plunked himself down across from me. Although we couldn't stand each other, we each apparently felt an undeniable compulsion to seek out one another's company.

"How was tort law?" I asked him around a mouthful of uninspiring meat.

"Great. Everything I'd imagined it would be. And computer science?"

"An insult to my intelligence, brother."

He looked disappointed and I smirked. It seemed our studies would not be what broke us, here at a Midgard university.

We ate in an aggressive sort of silence until Rich spotted a group of young men walking by. "Excuse me. They're from my class."

My brother was off, eager to cultivate new friends of status. Even if they were wealthier and better looking than him, they'd quickly accept him as one of their own. He had always had that effect on people.

No, he hadn't, I reminded myself viciously. Not the way I was remembering it. In fact, he spent most of his time off by himself, watching for invaders. But my human brain pushed back. Mere tales, it told me. Pure fantasy.

My afternoon lab was a relief. For a time my dying consciousness could forget it was dying while I analyzed lines of code. The complexities of object-oriented programming were a welcome distraction.

The next day, I left the college grounds. A porter sat in a booth reading a newspaper. He didn't even look up as I passed. I found myself facing a very busy street with a sidewalk swarming with people and bikes. The walled colleges were a sanctuary from the chaos of a bustling university city, but I needed more books. The professor had suggested we get started with the supplementary reading. I had my pride, if little else. I would outshine the other students.

I made my way through town as well as I could. The bikes buzzing by were annoying—even more so when their riders took it upon themselves to shout invectives at a disoriented pedestrian like me.

I found a large bookstore, brightly lit and clean. Bookstores of all sorts were everywhere, though places for drinking were even more common. I made my selections and started for the front, intent on paying for my new acquisitions.

Strangely, I had no desire to steal the texts. Mortal existence truly was a bane.

Before I reached the till, my eyes fell on the history section. Some whispered impulse drove me toward those books. I picked up a volume and began leafing through it. At first, it was simply interesting, a mere diversion. Stone Age artifacts, the legacy of the Celts. But then I spotted a photograph of a runestone.

My breathing stopped. I couldn't read it. I should have been able to read those letters, but I couldn't. The loss surged through my being like an engulfing void. Suddenly, understanding those sharp markings again was the most important thing in the entire world.

I tried to get a grip on myself. It was just a language. One language among hundreds, and a dead one at that.

The last, lost Aesir bit of me wasn't buying my excuses. Not for an instant. If I weren't human, I'd know that tongue again. I'd know the runes and the magic they offered a god.

I curled my lip up angrily. There was no way I was going to let Heimdall win our war so easily. No, there was another way to take care of the compulsion that now consumed me.

My fleshy mortal brow furrowed with my resolve. I sought out the linguistics section and snatched a guide to Old Norse off the shelf. I paid for all my books, the ones for class and the one that kept me glancing down into the bag every few seconds, just to make sure it was still in there with the others.

I returned to the walled college, to my residence. By the time I'd reached my floor, I was panting from the climb. Too many stairs. My human self apparently preferred intellectual pursuits to physical activity. Another difference between me and my brother, who kept himself in good shape.

I waved off the illusive memories.

Once I was in my room, I hunched at my desk, mercilessly pushing my sleep-deprived brain through runic writing exercises. My new computer science books lay in a stack by my elbow, forgotten.

Much later, a familiar pounding jolted me back to the present. I opened the door on my brother.

"There's a group for the pub tonight. You might want to come, Luther." Rich leveled me with a nasty smile. "Unless you'd rather hide in here? Like a coward?"

"I'm no coward, Rich."

He peered over my shoulder, his eyes turning curious despite himself.

"Old Norse? What does that have to do with anything?"

"Come in and I'll show you." It was my turn to smile maliciously. Predictably, as soon as he opened the book I had so gleefully placed in his strong hands, the blood drained from his face.

"Now do you see the allure?" I sniggered at him.

Tears wetted his eyes and spilled down his ruddy, peeling cheeks.

"It—it doesn't matter. I'll still win this, Luther."

"I can already read the runes and form basic sentences. Don't you wish you remembered even that much?"

He began shaking, his jaw clenching with rage. In one motion, he hurled the volume at the wall. It struck with a heavy thud, then crashed to the ground in a disheveled heap, bending the pages and cracking the binding.

I sniggered all the louder, entirely gratified by his violent reaction.

He eventually got a hold of himself again, and we went the pub. It was built in the traditional style, with dark stained beams and pale plaster walls. The inside was clean, but poorly lit. Rock music played over the speakers.

A dozen students from our residence had taken over a corner. We joined them. I sipped at a stout, enjoying the earthy taste and the alcohol as I idly watched the other mortals interact. Many presented assured, outgoing faces, but even without my powers, I could pick up on their uncertainty and fear. They were young creatures trying to find a path in their world.

Rich drank with his new friends. I noticed that he downed three beers in little time and was already moving on to his fourth.

I smirked to myself, amused all over again. He was still thinking like an Aesir, forgetting the limits of a human body. I pretended that I hadn't seen his empty glasses, basking in my imminent victory. The full brunt of a hangover would force Heimdall to concede the battle to me. My win had come almost too easily, but that was his doing, not mine.

The next morning, as I was dropping off notes from my morning lecture, I heard the violent sounds of my brother being sick in his room. He had missed all of his classes and had failed to show for breakfast.

A curious emotion stirred in me. We were at war, but I actually felt sorry for him.

At lunch, I wrapped a few bananas and loaves in serviettes and brought them upstairs with me. I knocked at Rich's door. He opened it, stooping painfully, like he had been on the losing end of a dreadful fight.

The room stank. I opened a window to air the place out. Searing light spilled in, making my brother groan. Outside, the sun was high over the city's towers and spires. The sounds of rumbling buses and the smells of fumes wafted in with the infusion of outside air.

Rich sat down on his cot, squinting. He ate in silence. His brown hair was a mess, and his skin was distinctly gray.

"The bananas will help," I told him. "They have potassium."

"Why are you doing this?"

"Doing what?"

"Helping me. We're enemies, Loki."

I stared at him. He had just used my true name. No surge of recognition coursed through me. It was like hearing the dimly remembered name of a stranger. An icy horror gripped me, curdling through my mortal intestines and making my throat ache with tension.

"We don't belong here, Heimdall," I said at last, very deliberately.

I realized that had been why I had brought him food, though his agony could spell my triumph. Compassion. Compassion for a foe who was also a fellow exile.

The other young man's face paled at my words, from a torture far more profound than the hangover. I had named him as well and, like me, he had just as clearly felt nothing.

We took measure of each other. Him, disheveled and foul on the cot. Me, thin and trembling in jeans and another cardigan—orange today.

"You'll break before I do," he said in a rough voice. "I've already been through the worst." He gestured at the bin, full of his liquid sickness.

I shook my head. "You know little of mortals, then."

"And you do?"

I didn't bother answering that. "Go take a shower, brother. No one's using it right now, and you stink."

He shot me a nasty look, gathered up his towel, and headed off.

By evening, I was restless. I was tired of studying and I wanted to be in motion. I didn't need anything outside the college, but I set off on a walk, determined to explore more of the city I was forced to live in. Odin had promised me Thor's protection. At least I could be certain that nothing I encountered would kill me.

I found a gently flowing river. Long, flat punts rocked on the water, tied up and secure. Martins twittered and careened above, their calls high and eerily lovely. The sunset lit up wisps of cloud, turning them a deep pink.

It was a beautiful night, but I was used to perceiving so much more. I felt like gray sand blocked my vision. A part of me wished I could concede the fight. But I was so very close to winning. I was sure of it.

I strolled beside a wooden fence near the river, watching the sky fade to purple. A crow descended from a nearby tree and landed only an arm's length away. Hardly normal behavior, that. The diurnal bird should have been seeking its roost.

"Huginn?" I asked, keeping my voice low.

The bird twisted its head over its shoulder and cawed. Another crow joined it. Although my mortal memories were lies, I almost fell over my own feet when the second crow opened its sharply pointed beak and actually *spoke* to me.

"*I'm* Huginn, little godling. You really *have* lost all your sense!"

I raised a finger to my lips. "Hush! Someone will hear you!"

"Oh, no. We're quite alone here. Do you give up, *Luther?*"

"Of course not!"

Muninn hopped closer to me, cocking his head to one side.

"You should take a nap," he said. "It's late. You must be tired. Doesn't the grass look soft? We'll both watch over you, have no fear."

I frowned at him suspiciously. "Why would you want me to sleep here, Muninn? I have a room, you know."

"Well... you're truly a mortal now, Loki. Sometimes mortals don't wake up. And I'm really, really hungry." His eyes flickered, turning white and filmy as he shifted even closer to me, steadying himself with half-raised wings.

"You're a sick bastard, Muninn. Just like your master."

"Come on, brother," rasped Huginn. "Let's see if Heimdall's ready to back down."

"Leave your window open," Muninn advised me, scuffling about on his clawed feet. "It would be a shame to waste eyeballs as lovely as yours, should you die here."

They took off as I went through the feeble curses available to me in the mortal language that now pervaded my thoughts and speech.

As I made my way back to my college, I found a store that was still open at that late hour. It was cluttered with all sorts of offerings for tourists:

postcards and shirts, calendars and cups. I peered about, uncertain why I had come in.

I spotted a short, black metal rack with souvenir jewelry. Simple, mass-produced silver pieces hung from cheap cords. Something about them was calling out to me.

I carefully spun the display around and immediately understood why it had attracted me. In one swift motion, I snatched up a replica Thor's hammer. I shuffled impatiently at the counter as I waited for the cashier to ring up my find, then swiped the amulet back from her the instant it was paid for, ripped off the cardboard label, and hastily bound my purchase around my neck.

It wasn't much. But I felt just a little better.

CHaPTER TWELVE
MORTAL ENEMIES

Midgard Present

a soundless, chilly drizzle collected against the closed panes, obscuring any view of the outside world. When a certain critical mass was reached, a winding stream of water would mournfully course down the glass like a single gray teardrop.

I had been human for a month. As a god, I'd once thought I'd known something of the eternal. But one month trapped in my decomposing body had taught me otherwise.

Mortality was the ultimate monotony. It was a thousand inane chores, pointless tasks, and exhausting exchanges, each stacking up on each other like lead weights over the heart and mind. At least once a week, I had to walk my laundry across the college, over to the basement of another building. With each new day, I had to find time to shower when it wasn't in use by another student. Eating was duller than I ever could have imagined. But the circle of torment didn't end there. Every night, I had no choice but to descend into the strange, clinging darkness of human sleep, where my severely limited brain churned through unresolved imagery from its fictional Midgard childhood.

I knew I was depressed. As far as mortals went, I was a well-read and highly intelligent young man. I recognized the signs readily enough.

If I had truly been human, I might have sought help. But what good would it do me? There was no drug to cure lost godhood. No therapist could talk an Aesir through his pain. I'd simply have to suffer and bide my time. Like I hadn't done *that* before.

With a sigh, I put my textbook aside, then reached over to switch off my fluorescent lamp. I had to go to my afternoon lecture. I didn't want to leave my room. I never did lately.

The lecture was in an echoey hall with sterile carpets and bad lighting. I found a seat up front and set out my laptop. We were working our way through introductory probability theory, a particularly idiotic subject if ever there was one. Likelihoods meant nothing to gods.

As always, I stifled my yawns and flipped my hand up whenever we were asked to solve an especially complex problem.

Today was different, though.

"You're wrong, Luther." The professor gave me an odd look. I had never missed a question before.

I immediately snapped awake. A few of the other students tried to conceal their smirks. I was brighter than any of them and took no pains to hide my abilities. My failure pleased them.

The rest of the lecture moved by at a trickle as the instructor discussed the finer uses of the variable that I'd forgotten to mention in my answer. I tried to stay focused, tried to keep my mistake in perspective. But my human brain argued back, offering up biting recriminations. My dim memories of Asgard only reinforced my sense of despondency. Everything I did was a hollow pretense, an empty series of rote motions. Everything I did was meaningless.

How could I have missed something so *obvious*?

Finally—another eternity later—the lecture ended. I shuffled my way back to my residence. The drizzle had let up, and moist golden light spilled over the pathways, soothing and warm. But I had no eyes for such sights. My thoughts and emotions were caught in a poisonous feedback loop, cutting me off from the world around me.

With heavy steps, I passed the chapel and the dining hall, then entered a small courtyard. I spotted a human couple sequestered behind tall rose bushes, whispering vapid nothings to each other.

It took me a moment to realize that the male was my own brother. Rich was dressed in a casual gray workout shirt that showed off his well-muscled arms, and his wide back was pressed against a centuries-old brick wall. He cradled a mortal woman against his chest, locking her in his embrace. She didn't seem to mind. Not in the slightest.

My brother didn't notice me. Rich was thoroughly lost in the depths of a kiss. His eyes were closed, and his head was tilted forward with ecstasy.

I snarled to myself. *I* had given mortals that gift. Back in Asgard, Heimdall passed his days and nights in solitude, watching over Bifrost. But here he was a young man. Something about him appealed to the Midgard women. Somehow, he came across as open and guileless, as gentle and warmhearted. It was disgusting.

I shared none of his interest in human lovemaking. What was the point, when I couldn't feel the soaring spark of another's mind or perceive the deepest longings of the blood? I might as well take a bag of meat in my arms or press my lips against a statue. There was no passion to be had in my present form.

I still had to get past them. More than ever, I longed for the sanctuary of my room. Lifting my chin disdainfully, I strode up the path.

"I could have sworn you had a test tomorrow!" I said loudly as I went by.

Rich looked up with a frown, holding his mortal to his breast. But his face quickly eased back into a smile. "Remember who watches over me! I'll be just *fine*."

The young woman's brow furrowed with confusion, but Heimdall leaned in again, distracting her with another one of those intense kisses.

Truly disgusting.

Later that night, I set my books aside and tapped on Rich's door. He opened it without a word. His face was grim.

As soon as I was inside, my rival handed me a cold bottle of beer. I accepted it and plunked myself down in an uncomfortable dormitory chair. He took a seat on his cot, cross-legged. The mournful strains of a saxophone poured through the small room, and after a minute, he closed his eyes, nodding in time to the music.

I noticed that Rich had rearranged his prisms again. Cut triangles of glass occupied all the flat surfaces by the windows and were spread out across his desk. Small, faceted globes and stars dangled from rough pins in the ceiling, twisting on their strings. He was always determined to catch the morning light, to fill his dreary room with rainbows for those few short minutes when the rising sun streamed in at just the right angle.

None of his mortal lovers would have understood. But I, his most hated enemy, did.

We always met at the same time every night. Usually, we had nothing to say to each other. We'd just drink, our every movement tense with a profound mutual loathing. Rich and I couldn't stand one another, but we had no better reminder of Asgard than each other.

This night, though, my rival moodily swished his beer around in its bottle, then slowly shook his head.

"I miss Himinbjorg," he told me. "I miss the cliffs and sky. I miss drinking mead in my hall and the view of my waterfalls."

"I think I miss Sigyn the most," I whispered back. "But I'm not sure. It's so hard to *remember*."

We didn't speak of our lost Aesir powers. That would have been too much.

I took a long drink of the crisp, pale lager that Rich always bought for us. Tomorrow, we'd meet in my room and have a few porters while the heavy beats of electronic music thudded in the background. Such was our routine.

The very thought of another twenty-four hours in Midgard stabbed me to the very core of my being. I downed the rest of my beer in a few quick swallows, fighting the agony burning through my lungs. When I raised my arm to wipe my sleeve against damp eyes, Rich said nothing insulting.

My brother silently handed me another lager, my last for that evening. It would have been so easy—too easy—to drown our sorrows in a fog of alcohol. And that was why at the end of each cursed mortal day, my sworn foe and I drank together. We each allowed ourselves two beers, always in one another's company.

Finally, I stood up to leave. I gave Rich a brief nod, which he returned.

Neither of us spoke as I left.

A few days later when we had a break from our classes, we sprawled on the short grass beside a duck pond. Summer clouds teased their way across the sky, casting the world into shadow, then easing it back into light.

My brother idly tossed stale bread to a moorhen and her chicks while I watched him with narrowed eyes.

"How long can this go on?" I asked abruptly.

He shrugged his broad shoulders.

"I'm losing my mind," I told him seriously. "One of us has to back down."

"Go ahead then."

"You first."

I heard a soft, all-too-familiar tsk-tsk-ing from behind us. I clambered to my feet while Rich arched around awkwardly to peer up at the matronly woman who had apparently been able to find us with no trouble at all, though we were but two humans in a city with over a hundred thousand people.

"Mother," I said quietly, my voice thickening with fear. Technically, Odin's wife—the goddess Frigg—was not my mother. But my deluded mortal brain remembered it otherwise.

Unlike us, Frigg was entirely Aesir. Her magic was strong and her form was simply a disguise. She stretched out her arms to me, demanding a familial hug. Reluctantly, I plodded forward. I had to bend down slightly to return her embrace, as I was taller than her. Her gray and blonde hair was pinned up into an elegant knot, and she wore a suit of cornflower blue. The neckline and skirt were trimmed with creamy white, and the cut was modern, almost severe. Somehow, she made the suit look more elegant than relentlessly professional. A matching satin scarf circled her neck. It was whimsically patterned with keys.

Another dim recollection stirred--the design was not nearly as whimsical as it first seemed. I fuzzily recalled that Frigg held the keys to every hall in Asgard. There was no place she could not enter, no lock she could not open.

"What are you doing here?" I asked the goddess.

"What sort of question is that, Luther? I missed my boys."

I swallowed nervously at her tone and backed up so Rich could receive his hug. Frigg had once arranged to have her own husband tortured over a fire for eight nights so she could win a wager against him. A god—or a mortal—took her lightly at his own peril.

My brother accepted her embrace with beaming confidence. He gave me a smug wink as he stepped away. Rich had always been the favorite.

"Come, walk with me," Frigg ordered. Obediently, we followed her, making our way past weathered, moss-grown brick fences. Soon, we were strolling through a secluded garden. Only a few flowers were in bloom. A strange breeze sighed through the trees, smelling of iron. Of blood.

"Loki," the goddess said, "Heimdall's clearly doing better than you. You might as well concede. To be blunt, Odin expected this to be over by now."

I halted, staring at her. My mortal mind struggled with her words, for they ran entirely counter to all my memories of her. Grudgingly, the pieces fell together long enough for me to understand what she was asking.

"No. That's not going to happen," I said in a low voice. It shook as I spoke. I had none of the authority of a god. I sounded lost and pathetic.

"You're a mess," she continued relentlessly. "The giants may not recognize you, but they feed off your depression. You only help Asgard's foes by dragging this out."

"Oh, leave him alone!" Rich spat. "This is our fight, not yours. Stay out of it!"

Odin's wife slowly lifted a perfectly manicured brow at my enemy. He met her gaze steadily. There was something incongruous about the sight: he, a freckle-faced young man in a university T-shirt and jeans, facing off against the most powerful of goddesses.

Frigg leveled him with a mysterious smile, the sort of smile that reminded me of well-fed predators indulgently watching deer grazing under a bright sky. Heimdall only frowned back and folded his arms across his chest. Even in his human form, he refused to be cowed.

After a bit, the goddess chuckled with deceptive mildness. The sun caught the blonde highlights in her hair, making them shine like newly spun flax.

"Have it your way," she told us. "But know that your father grows impatient." With that, she was gone. Not a single pebble on the garden pathway rattled against another to mark her passing. There had been no flashes of light, no sound. Nothing to indicate that an Aesir had stood before us only a moment before.

My brother gave me a long look. "'Father grows impatient,'" he repeated in a sarcastic falsetto. "Can't they just mind their own business?"

I snorted at that. "Of course not. You know how gods are."

For several heartbeats, we both just stared at each other, hesitating over our blasphemy. Then, a jolt seemed to pass between us. As if we'd been freed from some compulsion, we both started laughing. Soon, we were laughing so hard that we lost our balance. My brother and I collapsed onto the grass, still caught up in the hilarity of it all.

As I leaned forward, nearly doubled over and barely holding myself off the ground on a propped-up knee, I was swept away by the sort of raw joy I hadn't felt since I'd first woken up in a mortal body. I wondered if this was what it meant to be a child of Ask and Embla.

I was a powerless thing, a dying thing. I was a single speck of dust in an infinitely dangerous cosmos. But for all that, defiance burned in my heart.

I wouldn't back down.

I wouldn't live on someone else's terms.
Not even the gods'.

Our newfound spirit of camaraderie lasted through dinner. As we stood outside the dining hall under a purpling sky, Rich turned to face me, raising his eyebrows questioningly.

"I want to do something different tonight. Have you ever been to a club, Luther?"

"You mean dancing?" My skepticism must have shown on my face.

"Yeah. It's fun."

I shrugged awkwardly. I knew my brother often went out after we took our beer together. Now I knew where. But my mortal self was not at all pleased with the idea. I wasn't popular like Rich, and I'd only embarrass myself if I accepted his invitation.

"They have that electronic music you like," he added.

I reminded myself that all of my human memories were falsehoods, a shroud of smoke and magic spun by Odin. I forced down the panic coursing through my body and gave Heimdall a determined nod. I was sick of playing by Midgard's rules. It was time to choose as an Aesir would.

My brother seemed to know everyone at the club even though he'd only been mortal for a month. A security guard waved at him as we descended a flight of stairs. The place was busy, with many people entering and exiting. The nauseating odors of beer and sweat closed over my nose and mouth like a muffling hand. I found myself balking at the door. The wildly thumping beats accosting my ears were terrifying. They left no room for any sort of measured thought. But the sight of what awaited us within was too much. Pulsating lights in dim shades of red and blue stabbed through a miasma of hanging smoke. In between the flashes, I saw the crowds, a surging ocean of humanity.

Instinctively, I backed up, almost running into the people behind us. My brother sighed and leaned in close to me, speaking into my ear. "It's *fine*. Just give it a chance."

A nasty suspicion hit me. "You're just trying to win, aren't you?" I hissed from between clenched teeth.

"No, I'm *trying* to have a night out. Come on. You'd have loved this sort of thing when you were a god."

He was right. I would have, and the realization filled me with both fury and despair. Before I could say anything else, Rich dragged me inside.

I found myself in a world of stark, unfinished concrete. Apparently, someone had decided that warehouses were the wave of the future. There were no decorations, and the interior lacked any warmth. The tables and chairs were solid metal, lined with pretentious-looking rivets. The curving, stainless-steel bar matched the soulless furniture.

I followed Rich, pushing through the hordes. I felt better once I had a pint in my hand. The alcohol took the worst of the edge off, and even my Midgard-bound mind wondered what it had been so afraid of.

"This isn't too bad," I conceded.

My brother gave me a sage little smile, then refocused on something behind me. His face lit up an instant later.

"Wait here. I'll be back," he promised. Before I could object, he was gone. I saw where he was rushing off to, even before he joined the group of young women clustered around one of the tiny tables. He swept one of them up a vigorous hug and introduced himself to the others.

Typical. We were supposed to be keeping an eye on each other while we drank, but he just *had* to skip off and flirt with the locals.

A weird surge of emotion hit me, leaving the acrid taste of bile in my mouth. Wasn't that something *I* would have done? My mortal brain couldn't fathom the thought, but my anemic memories of Asgard told a far different tale.

My brother lifted his arm and gestured to me. Grudgingly, I dragged myself over to the group. I was all too conscious of my rough jeans and plain black T-shirt. The women were better dressed. Their jeans were fashionably cut and their chemises were sleek and stylish. Meanwhile, my brother carried himself with so much confidence that his clothes didn't matter. His own jeans and workout shirt seemed like the perfect attire.

One of his young friends was looking me over. I immediately pulled my eyes away from hers and fixed my gaze off on some random point on a featureless wall.

"Luther, right?" she asked, talking loudly so I could hear her. "You're into that Viking stuff, aren't you?"

I grunted noncommittally, still staring into the distance.

"He is," Rich put in with an easy laugh. "Runs in the family!" The mortal woman quickly lost interest in me. Their moronic conversation droned on, but no one else tried to include me in it.

Eventually, after my second and last beer, I split off from the group and found an unoccupied corner in the shadows, out of range of the flaring beams. Standing with my head bowed, I closed my eyes and listened for the beat. My pulse was fluttering erratically. I wasn't sure if I'd be able to feel the music—really and truly feel it. So many of my own gifts had been lost to me in human form. Did I dare to hope this one would be any different?

The pounding rhythms and the swifter melodies of a keyboard poured through me. Suddenly, something clicked. I lifted a hand and took a step to one side. I could sense the flow of the music. I cut an elaborate twist and swirled my arms up with sharp grace. My dance wasn't like anyone else's, but that wasn't important. Everything around me fell away. I was caught in the rise and fall of the drums, swept up in my movements. Sticky sweat collected along my spine, pooling unpleasantly at my waist. My skin—the gruesome shell that confined me, that separated me from my own divine nature—flushed, growing hotter with each beat of my doomed human heart. But a part of me was free. A part of me soared on the undulating notes and was lifted up by the quickening vibrations, the transcendence of sound.

And then—then, just as I was truly beginning to immerse myself in my dance—the electricity went out. At once, I was plunged into darkness. Seconds later, a few people yelled, and a rising tide of concerned chatter filled the lightless club.

I stopped in place, the hairs along my arms prickling. Some instinct warned me that the outage was not natural. The air felt heavy—clingy and viscous, like fresh tar sweltering under a merciless sun. If I hadn't known better, I would have dismissed the noise I heard next as a product of my imagination. But I did know better. A subtle laugh dribbled through my brain. It was cruel and keening, and brittle with madness.

I knew exactly what that laughter meant. The giants had found us. They had figured out who and what we really were, and they were coming for us.

With a swooshing roar, the emergency systems clicked on and the frantic music started up again. The mortals around me relaxed. As far as they were concerned, everything was back to normal.

I was shaking with fear. What a prize two Aesir would be, caught in mortal form! How easy it would be to devour us when we were human! Heimdall and I only had two protectors in Midgard. An onslaught of Jotuns could over-whelm our guardians. Even Thor had his limits.

I flew toward Rich's table, barreling my way through the crowds. He was soothing one of the young women, speaking words of comfort into her ear. I noticed that she didn't seem particularly frightened, but she was enjoying the way he was touching her, the way his fingers brushed her wrist.

When I finally reached him, I could only stand beside his chair panting. My throat felt swollen and sore, and my tongue was like a wad of cloth in my mouth. The manic gleam in my eyes warned my brother that something was wrong. Rich gently removed his hand from the pretty mortal's arm.

"What's the matter, Luther?"

"Can't—can't you feel it?" I managed to choke out.

He peered about, saw nothing, and shrugged. An instant later, a crash of thunder rattled the building. Glasses trembled on their tables. A number of them slipped to the cement floor, scattering jagged splinters in their wake.

I didn't mention Thor, though that last strike had clearly been his. Speaking an Aesir name would only allow the giants to pinpoint us in the crowd. Instead, I tugged at Rich's sleeve.

"Come on! We need to get out of here!"

"You're letting your mental problems get to you again."

I started to reply, but as the full meaning of his words sank in, something deep within my chest broke apart, shattering just like the glass.

"*What* did you just say to me?!" I shrieked.

"You heard me. You're just being paranoid. Go on if you want. I'm not babysitting you anymore."

Every memory of a childhood filled with rivalry and torment flooded through me. I might as well have been eight again. I threw myself at Rich, too far gone to think about what I was doing.

I would have been content to shove him a few times, but he dodged my attack and sprang to his feet, sending his chair clattering to the ground. My hated sibling lashed out, snagged me by the ear, and gave it a hard twist.

Enough was enough. I'd been at his mercy too many times, suffered too many taunts and blows when our father had been away. The liquid-hot need for revenge screamed through my being, and I was delighted to obey its call.

I flailed wildly and managed to land a punch. I wasn't sure where I'd hit until Rich abruptly released me and stumbled back a few steps. I looked up. Blood was gushing from his busted lip, splattering onto his shirt.

My mouth fell open. I simply stared at him, not quite believing what I'd just done. A few moments went by in dead silence.

Then he got a hold of himself again. "You fucking psycho!" he roared. For all his bulk, my brother could move quickly when he wanted to. Before I could recover, he slammed me against the nearby wall and wrestled me into a headlock. Dirty fingernails raked against my skin, burning and painful.

I made an incoherent noise, faltering under the weighty sense of my own helplessness. I tried to lift a knee to strike back, but my panic was too great. My leg wouldn't respond.

I scraped about futilely, trying to escape. Rich's broad hand closed around my pendant. He yanked down on it sharply, using the cord to pitch me onto the beer-stained cement. I didn't even have a chance to get my hands under me to break the fall. I thudded against the floor chest-first

I lay still. Sparks seared at the edge of my vision like clusters of purplish stars. I rested my cheek against the cool surface of the floor, willing them to go away. As soon as I could see properly, I launched myself back to my feet.

Rich's expression had changed, but I was too consumed with rage to wonder why. I flung myself at him again. My heart slammed in my ears and my skin tingled as if someone had pierced it with a thousand hot needles.

"This isn't real!" he yelled over the music.

The words infuriated me all the more. The bastard was so eager to discount everything he'd ever put me through. Still, something felt wrong. I hesitated over my next blow.

My brother was watching me with wide, frightened eyes. He backed away from me, as if I were the more powerful of us. He was scared. I couldn't for the life of me think why, but he was actually scared.

I wasn't anyone's idea of a fool. I was already having second thoughts about what we were doing. The college would not look kindly on our behavior if word of it got out. I had dreams. Plans. And every last one of them involved excelling in my course and graduating. No, I wouldn't let him take that from me.

I clenched my fists at my sides, but didn't attack him again. I just stood in place, panting for breath and glaring at my despicable brother, looking him straight in the eye.

"Loki," he said softly.

I shook my head impatiently at the nonsensical word.

"Loki!" he repeated. "Stop thinking like a mortal!"

I didn't know why, but I began trembling. Contradictory thoughts swirled through my mind, rending at each other, tearing through my head. An instant later, I blacked out.

Not much time could have passed. When I came to, my brother was holding me upright, supporting most of my weight on his broad shoulder. His hand clutched my arm to keep me from falling.

Rich bent his head close to mine, his hot breath blowing on my neck. "We're gods, damn it!"

Everything snapped back into place. I heard thunder rumbling again far off in the distance and recognized its significance. Thor had everything under control. The giants were retreating.

"We'd better go," he told me quietly.

I trailed him outside. Once we were on the streets, we could see that there wasn't a cloud in the night sky and no storm in sight. A few stars twinkled above, bright enough to pierce the city's ambient light.

We paused, taking stock of one another. I had some idea of how I must have looked, tousled and pale, with my mouth still half open in soundless terror. My throat was raw and dry, and it pinched as if I had swallowed grit.

Heimdall stared back at me with haunted eyes. "We almost forgot," he whispered. "We almost *truly* forgot."

"You recovered first," I pointed out. "You could have let me go on forgetting.

His face contorted with revulsion. "No, Loki, I couldn't! I couldn't let anyone get that lost!" He paused before adding, "Not even you." Heimdall turned away from me. He seemed to be trying to convince himself of something. "Besides," he muttered, almost to himself, "if you went mortal, you'd win, right?"

I didn't answer immediately. "If you could call that winning." My voice faltered as I spoke. The idea of it was simply too vile, too appalling.

My enemy hunched his shoulders. He was still in shock, just as I was. "I would never do that to you. Never."

I sighed and nodded at him grudgingly. I knew he spoke the truth.

90

"You're not all bad, Heimdall," I admitted.

"Neither are you, Loki. Neither are you."

The following morning, my body still ached. I had hardly slept at all, but—exhausted or not—I needed to get outside. I skipped breakfast and took off for the footpaths surrounding town. Poplars arched up to the skies and free-ranging cows grazed placidly in the fields. I was comforted by the luxurious scents of the soil, the woodsy air, and the sun-drenched grass.

Out in the countryside, there were moments when I could almost imagine I was my true self again. But they were only moments. They disappeared again as quickly as they came.

I lifted a hand to my mouth, yawning as I walked, then stopped, looking up at the treetops. Light sifted down through dark oak leaves, creating dappling patterns that beguiled my weary mortal eyes. I thought of Asgard. Of my own realm and its light.

I finally made my choice.

It wasn't the scratching and decaying flesh, the clouded thoughts, or the ongoing, gut-gnawing sense of purposelessness that decided me. Not even the threat of losing my Aesir memories could sway me. But roaming among the trees, feeling that golden light on my face, recalling what it had been like to be a god... that, and that alone, finally allowed me to swallow the last of my pride. Heimdall could have his stupid victory.

When I got back to our residence, I charged up the last flights of stairs and pounded on my brother's door. It flew open.

"Loki! I've been looking for you all morning!"

"I was out walking. And thinking."

His brows lowered. My brother looked almost as bad as he had with the hangover. His eyes were red and dry, and there were purple circles underneath them. He obviously hadn't been able to sleep either. I wouldn't let that change my mind now.

"Listen, Heimdall," I told him, "I've made my decision. You win. Your will is stronger than mine."

The other god-turned-mortal was shaking his head emphatically. "No! No, it isn't, Loki! I wanted to tell you the same thing."

"Oh."

We both stared at each other. The world seemed to freeze in place around us. Then, moving with respectful deliberation, I held out my arm to be clasped in the Aesir fashion.

"Peace?" I asked.

His hand was a slab of warm, limp meat squishing around my arm. "Peace. I swear to it, Loki. My word is my bond."

"I swear to it too, Heimdall. Let us be as brothers until Surt comes for us with his sword."

He grinned at me wryly. We waited with our mortal flesh still bundled around us, as suffocating and useless as wool coats on a hot summer day.

Nothing was happening.

Heimdall's expression grew alarmed. "We both concede the fight!" he shouted into the air. "What more could Odin want of us?!"

"He's a twisted son of a bitch!" My voice was no less hysterical than his. "Could be anything!"

"Shut up, Loki! You'll only make it worse! May the All-Father forgive me!"

The door to Heimdall's room swung open from the outside even though it was designed to automatically lock itself each time it was closed. No one should have been able to join us.

"By Mjolnir, calm down already!"

Thor, resplendent in his usual oak-green shirt and with his hammer at his side, regarded us with easy amusement.

"Odin told me to tell you two hotheads that it takes *time* for mortality to lift. Maybe more for you, Loki, after what you just said." He shook out his beard.

Heimdall started laughing with relief. The noise cut off abruptly as something occurred to him. "Wait. You have your protector, Loki. Where's mine?"

"Downstairs, waiting for us. He's not happy with you, Heimdall. Something about hiding the Poetic Edda in your law books or some such nonsense. Doesn't take much to get his tunic in a twist, let me tell you."

I winked at the god who had shared true mortality with me. Then, a surge of joy lifted through my being. I recognized it. It was the energy of godhood.

I concentrated. A instant later, I triumphantly held up the guide to runes that I'd left laying on the desk across the hall, in that cramped, pathetic space that had once served as my room.

"Sweet, sweet power," I crooned as I willed the book away again. Using Aesir magic had been something of a strain, even across such a short distance. But I could feel how, with each heartbeat, I was coming back to myself.

I untied the hammer I'd bought and offered it to Thor. "Yours, I believe."

He grunted and accepted it. "Want to know something, Loki? You were never really one of them. You too, Heimdall. You both looked different, no matter what Odin was pulling on you. Like pyrite mixed with gold."

"That's hardly a flattering comparison!" I objected.

He gave a mighty shrug of his shoulders. "Gods shouldn't play at being mortals. It's bad for everyone."

Heimdall and I exchanged a knowing look. I realized he was again clothed in his white tunic, and his light brown hair was long, as it had been before we had agreed to our ordeal. He now wore a cloak of pearly gray that was slowly brightening, separating into different sheens and hues.

I willed my own outfit to change and felt a warm tingling through my fingertips as the last vestiges of mortality evaporated. My skin was smooth, unchanging. Eternal. My mind was as sharp as dwarf-crafted needles, and the city lay wide open before it. The computers I had once worked on—that had been hailed as marvels of Midgard technology—now moved with tectonic slowness.

We joined Forseti. The God of Law was waiting for us outside the steep stone walls of the college. His arms were folded against his long black tunic. He watched the humans crossing by in front of him, his gray eyes reserved as always. Forseti didn't meet Heimdall's gaze immediately, but his mouth pressed down into a hard line as the other god approached him.

"Poorly done, Heimdall," he said in the tone of one pronouncing a judgment.

"What do you mean, Forseti?"

"You did the bare minimum required of you. You snuck your own reading material into your classes and failed to take the lectures seriously."

"I'm an Aesir, not a mortal."

"You were a mortal at the time and sworn to my service. The same obligations applied."

"Wait. You're serious? I didn't *study* enough for you?!"

Forseti raised his strong chin and returned the other god's disbelieving stare with a frigid one of his own. "Indeed I am. The law is not a kind mistress, Heimdall. It is fortunate for us all that you are ultimately charged with protecting Asgard and not the local jurisprudence."

My former enemy could only sputter at that. Then his expression changed. "Hey, what about Loki? He was pretty distracted too!"

"Loki was not my assignee." Forseti frowned up at the sky, his silver hair fluttering about his shoulders. "If we're quite done here? I miss Glitnir."

"Of course," replied the god who watched over Bifrost. Between one moment and the next, they were off. The blue expanse above me flared and a rainbow sliced over the entire city, pointing vaguely north. Its colors were pure, living light. No rain or drizzle accompanied it. It simply was.

Many of the mortals glanced up, saw the most perfect rainbow that Midgard had known or ever would know, then lowered their heads and kept right on going. Smaller numbers stopped, lifted their wondering eyes to the heavens, and fell silent, awed by what they were seeing.

I stared up at it too, taking in more with my Aesir gaze than anyone in that city could have hoped to comprehend. Thor stood beside me. I had no inclination to follow that bridge back to Asgard. Not yet. My chosen second still seemed to have some sense of loyalty about him. He waited on me, his coppery hair tossing in the breeze.

The sky eventually returned to normal, and people went back to their tasks and thoughts, to their own internal, muddling worlds.

"I thought you'd beat us all back to Asgard," the Thunder God told me. "Yet here you are."

"This city gave me a great deal to think about. I just might return the favor." My eyes gleamed dangerously, and orange sparks crackled across my fingertips.

With a menacing scowl, Thor slowly wrapped his thick right hand around the short handle of Mjolnir. The hammer flashed then, like wildfire. "Or you might not," he suggested in a rumbling voice.

"It was a joke! Nothing more!"

"Why don't you move along, Loki? Surely you've had enough of this place?"

"No. I need to see it afresh, as an Aesir. My mortal memories will plague my dreams if I don't."

"Stay out of trouble. I mean it."

The corner of my mouth lifted sardonically. "But of course, Lord Thunderer."

CHAPTER THIRTEEN
THE FATHER OF ALL

Midgard and Asgard Present

I whistled to myself as I strolled through an artisans' market. As a god, I could read the stories behind each painting. Every piece of jewelry was a tale of mined stone and processed metals. When no one was looking, I pocketed a few trinkets. The horror of mortal existence was already fading.

Nonetheless, I instinctively avoided all the places I had ever visited as a Midgard student. Though the colleges were open for weekend tours, I would not go back to the one I had attended. I kept away from the pub where my rotting tongue had tasted mortal beer, the busy street with the bookstore, and the paths I had once wandered beside the river.

I kicked at the pavement, for I had a feeling I was being manipulated. When I tried to strike off for the curio shop where I'd bought the pendant, my own feet refused to take me there.

Perhaps Thor was right. Perhaps there really was nothing left for me in that city.

I set off in a new direction with success. I passed an immense cathedral of pale gray stone. Its turrets looked like barbs, tiered and elaborately carved. In the fields, I came upon the footpath I had walked just that morning when I had decided to let Heimdall win. I could travel it without interference.

Leaving the university town behind, I hiked off into the trees, past fens and pastures. The movement felt good. I didn't care where I was going, but I avoided Midgard's dull, ugly housing developments and its major roads.

Many hours later, when the sun was sinking into a cloudbank, I felt the wind pick up. I drew in a deep breath, taking in the acidic, bracken aroma of fallen leaves and the sharper odors of an approaching storm. Caws—hundreds of caws—sounded from the woods bordering the fields. With an explosion of black wings, a murder of crows warped and spun over me, an undulating tapestry of carrion birds. I increased my pace, alert now.

I wasn't entirely surprised when I heard another set of boots and spotted the shifting edge of a gray cloak in my peripheral vision. I paused on the dusty trail and faced the other god.

Odin carried a heavy walking stick and wore the wide-brimmed hat he favored when he was about in Midgard. Like Thor and I, he often roamed this world. An admonishing squawk sounded from the branch above. Huginn was not impressed with how I had conducted myself as a mortal. Next to him, Muninn preened his glossy feathers with his formidable beak. He didn't bother to apologize for hungering after my eyes.

"You have no idea what it was like!" I snapped at Huginn. The All-Father watched me, inscrutable. The crow cawed back something rude, then launched himself into the air. Muninn followed a heartbeat later.

"Hail, Wise Lord," I said.

"Hail, brother of my blood."

We continued on in silence. I was certain that Odin had joined me for some purpose, but I could not rush him anymore than I could stop Yggdrasil from shedding its leaves.

Perhaps he picked up on my mood, on my ponderings over endings and inevitabilities.

"You may have changed Ragnarok, Loki," he said. His voice bore hints of flint and steel, of storms and forgotten war-songs.

"No one can change Ragnarok. Not even you."

"Perhaps. Perhaps not. The wise women of old, the prophetesses and the witches of the seithr, sang to me of Tyr facing the wolf with one hand. So tell me, has that not changed with your gift?"

I shrugged. "Ragnarok is a long way off. Any treasure can be lost."

"Or stolen," Odin agreed.

I frowned at him, and he lifted his silvery brows in response.

"If you have plans," I said, "keep me out of them. I'm done taking falls for you."

"What had to be, had to be. You knew that. And you went willingly to the kill." He referred, of course, to Baldur's murder.

"I did. Just as you say. But I'll still have vengeance on you long before Surt consumes us all." I spoke bluntly, one Aesir to another, not hiding my intentions. As if he didn't know them already.

Odin's thin lips curled back in a dreadful smile. "I'd expect nothing less. Try me, Loki. I welcome the challenge." I might as well have been talking about a tafl match, not the debt I owed him for my time in the cave.

I shook my head viciously. "You won't grin like that when it's upon you!"

Odin threw back his head and laughed, a terrible sound. "Come, let us speak of other things," he said, unperturbed by any threat. Such was his way.

"As you wish," I agreed.

We roved beside a gurgling stream winding among moss-covered stones. Drizzle misted the air, making no sound as it fell.

"Do you remember Otter?" asked the Father of All.

"I certainly remember his family. The self-indulgent wretches."

"Yes," Odin said. "Even I don't know where their spirits have gone, but they will never find rest in fair Asgard."

Once, when Odin and I had been exploring Midgard with our friend Honir, I slew a man by accident. The mortal Otter had been a shapechanger like myself and had taken on the form of the animal that shared his name. My two companions and I had been hungry, and I killed him when I saw him, thinking that an otter would make a fine meal. His father and brothers had demanded gold in repayment for the death. Brazenly, they'd held my friends hostage while I journeyed off to Nidavellir to win them their wergeld.

Otter's family had asked for one treasure too many, though. I gave them a golden ring cursed by the dwarven sorcerer Andvari. Mortals had sought to blackmail gods, to make Aesir their captives. I'd ensured they paid the price for their folly.

I regarded my blood-brother, my dark eyes thoughtful. "What about Otter?" I asked him. "What does he matter now?"

"He doesn't, Loki. It's Andvari's ring I'm after. I have a purpose in mind for it."

"I told you to leave me out of your plans. Besides, the ring destroys anyone who holds it. You know that."

He shrugged. "You turned back the dwarf's magic once. You deflected his curse onto Otter's family when it should have fallen on you."

"I did. With ease, my brother."

"It was no simple trick. I think you could do it again."

With an immortal's grace, I jumped onto a fallen log. Crouching down, I regarded the other god with a dubious little smile.

"Maybe. But even if I could, Odin... even if I could, why would I want to?"

"Because you're an Aesir, and I'm striking at Jotunheim."

I shook out my black bangs. The All-Father was right. I'd help him in any battle against the giants.

"Fine. But I won't make you any promises this time. My magic is my own."

"As you say." The mightiest of the gods inclined his head to me soberly, then struck off down another path. His two crows dropped from the treetops, each darker than a starless night, and circled him as he left.

I smiled to myself as I watched him vanish into the murky forest.

I finally knew how I would get my revenge on Odin.

The heath was almost entirely barren. A spiny gorse bush with yellow flowers clung to the rough soil, and its blossoms were the only real color in a world of mist and soggy dead grass.

I stood in the borderlands outside Asgard, close enough to Jotunheim for the sun not to shine and the wind to moan with soft despair. It was a good place to speak with dwarves. They could not abide sunlight when they had their own forms.

I set my pill bugs down on a flat rock, then stepped back, murmuring runes of power.

"Brokk and Eitri, foul creatures, hear the words of your god."

The stupider of the brothers, Brokk, staggered to his feet. He seemed befuddled at having only two legs all of a sudden. "You're no god of ours, Loki," he declared. I motioned with my hand, and he popped back into the shape of a pill bug.

"Hail, Loki, my lord!" Eitri exclaimed quickly, raising his arms in a warrior's salute.

My mouth twisted with pleasure. "See? I always tell everyone you're the smart one."

"Please," he whimpered, "I'm tired of being a pill bug. What would you have of me?"

I chortled at him. "A bug of the soil grows weary of being a bug of the soil?"

"Please, my lord." He sank to his knees, his soot-colored hair falling over bone-white cheeks. I gloated at his distress.

Eitri had helped Brokk sew my lips shut after I'd lost the wager I'd made with them. The other gods had looked on and laughed, so smug and secure— as if the treasures I'd just won for them had always been theirs. My wounds had healed with divine speed, but the sting of the brothers' needle had lasted far longer. It was lovely, so very lovely, to have the two dwarves in my clutches now.

I let him grovel for a bit. Eventually, I said, "Arise, worm. I do have a use for you."

"Anything, my lord."

"Brokk wielded your needle against me many ages ago. He's an idiot and of no further use to me. You will crush him under your boot. Then we shall speak of other things."

Eitri somehow managed to turn even paler than he had been before.

"I... I can't. He's my brother."

"Do I look like I care, little worm?"

"No, my lord... but...."

"Do it, or share the same fate."

Tears formed in his onyx eyes. Slowly, the dwarf lifted his iron-clad boot, his face screwed up with pain. I watched him, smiling pitilessly. I kept silent, waiting to see if he'd really complete the task I'd laid out for him.

"I'm sorry, Brokk," he whimpered. Then he brought his foot down upon the stone. It hit with a clang, the metal shedding sparks.

I allowed him to huddle there blubbering for a while. "Eitri, look," I said. I held out my hand and unfurled my fingers. He tentatively lifted his head. A pill bug rested in the center of my palm, curled into a tiny gray ball.

With another spoken rune, I restored Brokk to his true shape. The gold chains in his beard clinked loudly as he whipped around to face Eitri. The vaporous air so close to the realm of giants bounced the sound around in odd ways, adding to the dismal feel of the place.

"I can't believe you!" he yelled. "After everything we've—"

"Shut up, Brokk," I interrupted him. "You'll both listen to me and no other. Look on the bright side, my sun-cursed slugs. Now you know exactly where you stand with each other! And with your god!" I favored them with an evil grin.

Eitri was trembling. He shrank away from Brokk, his eyes seeking the ground. I gave them a few minutes to settle down. I felt no mercy for them, but I needed their attention.

"Heed my words, Brokk and Eitri. You asked once whose blood I desire more than yours?"

Eitri nodded, his face lost in despair, while Brokk glowered at me.

I sighed. "Brokk, you try me. Show some respect or start a new life as a worm lost on the border of Jotunheim."

With great reluctance, the dwarf struggled against his own expression, forcing it into an impassive mask. His jet-chip eyes burned with silent fury, however.

"Better. Know this, ugly creatures. I would have Odin's blood on my hands. Or rather, on yours."

"No one can hurt the All-Father but the All-Father," intoned Eitri listlessly.

"Precisely."

"I don't understand your meaning, my lord."

Brokk snorted at his brother's tone, and I fixed him with a baleful stare. He straightened up and tried to look attentive.

"Of course you don't, Eitri. The two of you have the dullest minds in all the realms."

"Yes, my lord."

"The Father of All shares his power each morning. Huginn and Muninn, his two crows, carry his will and his sight. He fears for their return every day. I trust you follow my meaning now?"

"Strike at the crows, strike at the god," Eitri said immediately.

"Very good. Perhaps there is some hope for you after all."

He swallowed with apprehension.

"You brothers make such wondrous treasures—so fine that they almost cost me my head! Now you shall craft a wonder for me: chains to stop Thought and binds to halt Memory."

Brokk grumbled into his beard. "And then you'll let us go?"

"Your debt to me will be repaid, yes. You shall live, and not as pill bugs."

The two hideous dwarves traded a long look. At first they thought they were getting off easily. But then the import of what I was asking sank in. It was Eitri who caught onto the one potentially fatal flaw to my plan.

"And the All-Father?" he said. "He'll know our work as surely as he once owned the magic ring Draupnir. He'll hunt us down and kill us."

"Eitri, Eitri," I murmured, shaking my head.

"Where shall we make these chains? There is no forge here," protested Brokk. "We'll need to go back to Nidavellir to forge you such a treasure." His face was merry with poorly concealed slyness. The predictable insect actually thought he could escape me in the tunnels of his home realm.

"You'll do your crafting here on the forge that I, the God of Fire, provide you," I told him. I leveled Brokk with a deathly smile, letting him know that I had seen into his heart.

It was no difficult thing for me, an Aesir born of the Jotuns, to call up what they needed on that desolate border. Soon the two dwarves were sweating over a fire so hot that it burned white and purple, not orange. I summoned up a chair, a footrest, and a horn of mead for myself, then stretched back to watch them work. I needed to be absolutely sure they would not betray me. Everything hinged on the quality of the chains. More, it was great fun to take my leisure there beside them while their arms rose and fell, growing sorer and sorer with each strike. The skin along their faces and arms soon darkened to an angry red, blistered from the steady heat of the flames.

Nine days went by as I sipped my mead. On the ninth evening, Brokk pulled two sets of chains from the dousing barrel. Each one shined with its own light.

I sauntered over and cradled the bright fetters in my hands, examining the workmanship closely. Gems glittered from delicate bands meant for the twig-like legs of birds. The golden links swirled about like the tentacles of one of Njord's sea-dwelling predators. The chains' prey called to them from across the realms.

"Oh, these will do. These will do nicely," I whispered.

"Can we go now?" demanded Brokk, always one to interrupt a moment.

"You may! Eitri, you have managed to show some respect." I sang a rune over him. "You have the Trickster's protection: Odin will not see your hand in this." I spun on Brokk, my eyes smoldering with distaste. "You, though! You must face your own consequences! You've made it abundantly clear that I am not your god and you shall have no blessing from me, Brokk of Nidavellir. This is my curse: you will stand alone before the All-Father! You will know his judgment and his fury!"

The two dwarves cowered away from me, then turned tail as suddenly as startled deer and dashed off into the night. Their moans and whines echoed from the foggy blackness long after they were lost to sight.

I slipped my newly crafted treasure into my pouch and willed the forge to nothingness. The night was young and Odin slept in Valhalla.

My blood-brother's hall was very still in the early hours before sunrise. A number of his chosen warriors dozed at the tables, warmed by the perpetually blazing hearths. Low shadows danced among the strong shafts supporting the roof. Their knotwork seemed especially sharp and sinister, as menacing as exposed blades.

I crept past the sleeping former mortals and entered a dim corridor. The musty scents of aged wood and fresh smoke tickled at my nose. At one point, I paused to suppress a cough.

I had snuck into a few bedrooms in my time, as Thor's wife, Sif, could attest to. But the All-Father's bedroom was a different matter entirely.

Bending down, I spoke the rune I had laid on Geri. The wolf woke up and treaded over to me, his muzzle opening in a huge, pink-tongued yawn.

"You fight for me tonight," I told him. Odin's familiar gazed up at me with calm yellow eyes, then perked his ears forward agreeably.

With my ally at my side, I slinked into the room.

Frigg's breathing was deep, and her husband's strangely quiet. Odin was a light sleeper, I remembered from our journeys together. Not like Thor, who could dream of ale and welcoming feminine arms through one of his own storms. I would have to be very careful.

On a perch directly above the All-Father's bed, the two crows slept the sleep of creatures who thought themselves safe. Their heads were tucked contentedly under their wings. I eyed them greedily.

I'd have only one chance to capture them before their master awoke. The warrior god's enchanted spear, Gungnir, was propped within easy reach. A battle axe lay not far off. Its blade was sharp, ready to dispatch any trespasser.

My movements were deliberate and precise as I gently loosed my pouch and brought out the ensorcelled gold chains. They writhed eagerly in my grip. I tossed them forward and in no time at all, the small gold bands clamped shut around each bird's heel. Glittering, tiny links twined themselves around their glossy black bills and their sleek, midnight wings.

The crows were mine. Huginn and Muninn didn't get out so much as a caw before they snapped into my waiting hands.

With Geri on my heels, I tiptoed out of the room and disappeared into the warm Asgard night. Eerie cries and chitters echoed back to me from the trees. Many sounds that had been lost to other realms could still be heard in ours.

I finally stopped beside an ancient yew tree, a favorite hiding spot of mine far from any hall. Its trunk was a curtain of warped, living wood surrounding an airy cavity—the tree grew around its own hollowed interior. Conveniently, one of its gnarly roots arched within its rough chamber, forming a rough bench. I bent down to gain entry to the yew. Thick limbs draped down over the hole. Stubby needles and clusters of waxy red berries screened me from hostile eyes.

I smirked at my captives as I took my seat. Their beady eyes darted about, frightened.

"Soothe yourselves, brothers. I mean you no harm. Odin's the one who will suffer this day."

The crows ignored me and continued struggling against their chains. A sharp feeling of pity stabbed through my chest. Their plight reminded me too much of my own.

"I'll unbind you, Huginn and Muninn, but you must stay in this tree until the sun sets. Will you promise me that?"

Huginn's thought, bright and angry, dashed across my mind. He would do as I said, but he was very displeased with me.

Muninn's response was slower. He recalled a time, long ago, when we had flown together through Midgard. His brother had been ill, but he could not make his daily journey alone. I had shapeshifted into a crow and gone with him. At his urging, I remembered careening over the sea together as the waves dashed below us and hot sunlight sparkled off the rolling swells.

Yes, he would remain. But would I be so kind as to find him an eye or two to nibble on?

I carefully unfastened the binds and put them back in my pouch. The crows shook out their wings. Huginn's eyes were cold and hard, and Munnin's were hungry and hopeful. They fluffed up their feathers and inched away from me until they found a comfortable perch, side by side, further up the root.

"Geri," I said to the wolf, "my honored guests require food." The wolf licked my hand and bounded off.

"What will come of this?" I asked the crows. Neither one answered.

I waited. The molten light of morning streamed into my refuge. Dew twinkled from the yew needles, and songbirds took up liquid melodies. The start of the day seemed normal enough.

Geri scurried back inside with a sizable hare in his jaws. He dropped it at my feet, and Muninn immediately swept down and began stabbing at its head. Huginn, however, made a rawking noise of disgust. He was not interested in any gift from me.

The sun rose higher, and I began to feel strange. There was a tingling on my brow and a pressure over my ears. Almost imperceptibly, the forest shuddered. The tremor built up gradually, then all at once exploded into a full quake.

"FOOL!" The thought tore into my mind, and I spun on Huginn.

"What?" I snarled at him.

Images deluged their way through my Aesir consciousness. Even I was hard-pressed to keep up with them.

Yggdrasil itself was shaking with the All-Father's loss.

"I don't care," I told the crow. "Did the Great Tree mourn for me when I was bound in the cave?"

Huginn returned my look, cool and steady, then inclined his head very somberly. I curled my lip and turned away. Outside, the sky grew shadowy and cheerless, as if an eclipse had blocked all the light from our realm. Such things did not happen in Asgard.

The Cosmos Herself was growing dim.

Odin's wolf, Geri, whimpered uneasily and bumped his head against my leg.

"Just a little longer, old friend. I think I've about made my point."

All the sounds in every universe and every realm choked off, extinguished. I could no longer hear my own breathing. Muninn peered down at me then and opened his beak in a silent caw.

Suddenly, I was afraid. How could I release the crows if I couldn't speak my runes? The last thing I saw as everything faded into blackness was Huginn's burning, reproachful gaze locked on me. His eyes were as hard as the grave.

An infinity passed.

No time at all passed.

I took a ragged breath. Damp air filled my lungs. Twilight had fallen on Asgard, and the crows were gone. I stretched languidly, feeling my strained muscles loosen.

A part of me longed to return to Valhalla and see how much trouble I'd caused. But things had gone a bit further than I'd intended, as they sometimes did. My fellow Aesir always turned against me on such occasions. I decided that I'd better leave them alone for a while.

I ducked out of the hollow yew trunk and murmured a spell to myself, then unfurled my new dappled brown wings. The falcon was the swiftest of all animals, the perfect shape for evading angry gods. My scaly toes had just lifted off the ground when a voice called out from the forest.

"Halt right there, Loki!"

I shrieked once, indignantly, then blurred back into my own form.

Ullr, the god of skiing and winter hunts, had an arrow trained on me. But not just any arrow. His bolts never, ever missed.

"How did you find me?" I demanded.

"Yew trees and I go way back. You know that."

I raised my eyebrows and made a face at the bow. "I don't suppose you'd consider pointing that thing somewhere else?"

"Not a chance. The All-Father wants to see you. He's not happy."

I sighed. "Ullr, I'm sure I don't know what you're talking about." I kept my hands spread, showing him I wasn't about to try anything. Not when he had me within his sights, anyways.

"Thought and Memory themselves speak against you. Or so Odin says. All I heard was peeved cawing." He held himself in a relaxed stance, his unerring weapon at the ready.

Little phased Ullr. He had honey-blonde hair that grazed the middle of his neck and a neatly trimmed beard and moustache. The other god wore a multicolored jerkin of thick wool—red, blue, and green—over a crisp white tunic. Though he preferred skis, Ullr was very quick on his feet as well. He was one of the few gods who could almost keep up with me when he was of a mind.

"Come on, Loki. The hunt is up and the lord of us all is waiting on you. I understand that he just can't wait to hear your tale."

"I'm in no mood to share stories!"

Ullr laughed, a delighted, heart-stirring peal that brought to mind light refracting through the powdered glitter of dry snow. He was the God of Joy, and his laughter sang through my heart. But the dreadful arrow still tracked me, not wavering in the slightest.

Valhalla was empty when we arrived. I held myself tall, my expression proud and unapologetic. When I looked over my shoulder, I could see Ullr's amused smile.

Odin nodded to the other Aesir, then took his seat. My escort kicked his boots up on a bench, plucked up a waiting horn of mead, and guzzled it down with friendly cheer.

I faced my blood-brother. "Here I am, lord," I said sarcastically. "What would you have of me?"

The one-eyed god made no response. The All-Father loomed in his high seat, his iron and silver beard hanging down over his metal chainmail. I stalked over to a nearby bench and helped myself to some of the mead that had been left out for guests. Even the servants were gone. Only Odin, Ullr, and I remained.

Soon, I grew uncomfortable in the lingering silence. I glanced up at my blood-brother now and then, expecting him to speak. But he said nothing.

All at once, Odin thundered to his feet. The sound of his iron-soled boots striking the floor boomed throughout Valhalla. I didn't have time to react. Like the side of a mountain that—all in a single instant—breaks into sheets of rock and crashes down into the sea, he was upon me, twisting my tunic and lifting me up toward the ceiling of shields above. I choked, unable to breathe. His arm did not twitch. It might as well have been stone.

He held me fast as my feet futilely scraped for purchase against the empty air. I dangled helplessly until black sparks rushed across my vision.

Then I found myself standing again, gasping. I pressed my hands to the base of my throat, feeling the scraped and bruised flesh, tender under my fingers.

Odin still did not speak. The one blue eye was filmy with an emotion that went beyond anything as simple as fury. The highest god's presence coursed through the hall. Ullr stood up and quietly backed away until he was at the far end of a space built to host thousands of the slain.

I, however, did not dare move. Slowly, I sank to my knees. I knew better than to offer any apology. There was no place for words. The mightiest of the gods reached out and slammed a hand down onto my shoulder. Just as he had in the cave.

I remained motionless, though his touch burned worse than my own. It crackled with a cold, primal fire, with the yawning void of the deep nights before any star was spun or any world formed.

Again, an infinity passed,

Again, no time at all passed.

The hand lifted. Odin mutely turned his back on me and strode out one of the side doors, his blue-gray cloak spiraling and slashing behind him like a gale full of daggers.

I swallowed and pulled myself to my feet, looking around the nearly empty hall. Every last fire had died in its hearth. I could only see with my Aesir sight.

Ullr appeared at my side. The God of Joy took me by the arm, guiding me from Valhalla. He led me outside, back under the twinkling, living stars.

We did not speak either. But I was grateful for his company.

CHAPTER FOURTEEN
ANDVARI'S RING

Asgard and Jotunheim Present

The next morning, the All-Father greeted me as if nothing had happened. As if I hadn't hurt him more than anyone had ever hurt him before. I bowed my head to him, lower than usual, and his single eye glittered briefly in acknowledgement.

We both knew our contest was over. Another would arise in its time, less serious than yesterday's. That was his way and mine. For now, we were at peace.

I had not slept at all the previous night. Ullr had finally left me, satisfied that I would be all right, and I had wandered through the forests alone. Stifling a yawn, I watched the other Aesir gather by the Well. No one spoke of what I had done.

Ullr rested under a pine tree, his head bent close to Skathi's. The joyful lord of the wilds—the god who loved skiing and the freedom of flying over the snow—was a good one for keeping secrets. I was certain that Odin had picked him out for that reason and that, by the High One's will, no other immortal would recall the dark time when Memory had been lost and Thought obliterated.

Heimdall walked up to me and offered me an arm-clasp. I returned it in silence. The gaze we exchanged was laden with significance and was deeply respectful.

Another enmity gone. It was all a bit cloying, really.

My blood-brother brought us to order. "Our power grows," he said. "Let us move our council to Gladsheim and plan for war against the giants."

Many of the faces around me lit up. Freya fell to her knees and stroked her cats, whispering blandishments into their tufted ears. Thor made slashing motions with his great hammer. It left crackling streaks in its wake with each arch, utterly destroying the serene atmosphere around the Well. Tyr also looked excited. He flexed his new hand, then lifted his wicked, blade-edged spear in a salute.

The corners of Odin's mouth curled up almost imperceptibly. Their enthusiastic response pleased him. He gave us a formal nod, indicating that the meeting was over. As the others drifted away—some boasting and eager to fight and others, like Bragi, less so—my blood-brother approached me. His blue eye was afire with anticipation.

"Loki, remember how we spoke of Andvari's ring?"

"I do."

"Go to Forseti's hall. Maybe he can find it for us."

The God of Law had not attended the assembly at Well of Urd that morning. I pursed my lips, realizing too late that he of all the Aesir would notice a gap in yesterday's records.

Odin squeezed my arm. Perhaps he had read my thoughts. Then again, perhaps not. Either way, he meant that I was to be off.

Glitnir, the hall where gray-eyed Forseti read of every deed ever done and judged each one in turn, seemed unchanged. As always, it towered above an uneven plain of the lushest green, shining like a beacon. I kept to a dirt trail, avoiding the sodden fields. A mighty river gashed through the wild land, gurgling and singing. Weathered gray cliffs enclosed the surging waters, forming a dropping chasm that directed the river on a straight and true course past the hall. Some ways upstream, a great waterfall eternally roared and frothed, brewing white foam. Snow-capped mountains peaked further off in the distance, often merging with the low clouds, forming layers of cool color.

A fence crafted of the purest silver ever smelted encircled the hall, shining as brilliantly as its lord's hair. The posts were worked with oath-rings, and runes pronouncing the authority of the Aesir were carved into the mirror-bright metal. Their bold, ordered lines caught the sunlight.

A keen-eyed hawk stared down at me condemningly from the gate, then opened its beak in a warning screech. I made a rude gesture at it as I entered the courtyard.

Glitnir itself was thatched with silver. Its pillars were all of red-tinged gold, a reminder that order was sometimes bought with blood. With Odin's instructions still burning in my ears, I passed between wide metal doors that would only close in the final moments before Ragnarok. Justice did not sleep— not until the very end.

I stopped abruptly once I was inside. I barely recognized the place. Glitnir's walls were now blocked up with gleaming shelves, from marble floor to shining ceiling. These were neatly stacked with books from every world. A humming bank of computers stood on the far side of the hall, their soft blue lights illuminating everything nearby, including Forseti's expansive desk. Its polished onyx was trimmed with dignified sterling insets.

I grinned when my eyes fell on the device he had set up on one corner of his massive workspace. It would have looked terribly out of place in any other hall, but in this one, it was entirely appropriate.

The other immortal kept a coffeemaker within easy reach. It was made of filigreed silver, with a carafe of cut and sparking crystal. The pot was still half full, and the bitterly aromatic smell of an entirely Midgard beverage wafted through the God of Law's domain.

Sitting as straight as a birch in his heavy chair, Forseti drank from his steaming glass. He seemed to be enmeshed in a thick tome, but his eyes—

neither notably dark nor light, and ever reserved—rose to meet mine almost as soon as I crossed his threshold.

"Loki, welcome," he said in his ponderous voice. He set down the coffee. His movements were solemn.

"Hail, Forseti. It's odd to be welcomed here when I'm not on trial!"

The other Aesir's lips actually twitched up slightly. "You'll recall that my servants in Midgard welcomed you too, and quite recently. I am certain you found their judgments fair."

"Yes, fair indeed—and their information entirely too accurate!"

The other god nodded, choosing to take my response as a compliment.

"I like the new decor," I told him. I gestured expansively, then walked over to the computers, getting a sense of them. They looked like they could have come from Midgard, but they ran at Aesir speeds.

"I'll thank you to leave my systems alone."

"I didn't do anything!"

"You're curious, Loki. Trouble enough, that."

I raised my eyebrows at him and didn't deign to reply to such a comment.

"The library is new," I said instead, an unspoken question in my tone.

Forseti got up. With unhurried decorum, he paced over to one of the shelves.

"Aesir law," he explained, indicating the books next to him. They glowed silvery-white and hummed with runes. "The laws of ethics and of higher justice," he continued, pointing down a corridor that stretched away into a pewter-colored haze. "And the legal heritage of all the worlds." He included the remainder of his hall with a swoop of his arm. Wide arches patterned with luminous metals opened onto new rooms, and odd patches of light shimmered like entrapping Alfar portals.

"Truly? All the worlds, born of every leaf on Yggdrasil?"

"Every last one." Forseti's eyes turned very cold and bored into me. "Of every last leaf of the Eternal Tree that was so recently disturbed, as a matter of fact. Know that few deeds are lost to this hall."

Each word was the hit of a hammer. I flinched, then by instinct sought to defend myself, to ameliorate his judgment.

"Was it truly so bad, Forseti?"

The God of Law stalked forward, every muscle tensed under his black tunic. The other immortal was about my height. He held me under the full weight of his glare, almost nose to nose, before he spoke.

"No thought? No memory? No consciousness? Does that sound at all right to you? Is that what we Aesir stand for?"

I squirmed at his pronouncement.

"The giants rejoiced," he continued relentlessly. "All the mortals in Midgard and beyond would have fallen if they had only perceived the death that came upon them yesterday."

I stepped back and managed to continue looking him in the eye. "It won't happen again."

"I know. I know, Loki." The other god lost his intensity between one heartbeat and the next, then sighed like an exasperated older sibling. "Come, have some coffee with me. What brings you to noble Glitnir?"

"Odin seeks Otter's cursed ring, the one the dwarf Andvari gave me long ago." I picked up a glass and took a skeptical sip from it. The brew wasn't bad, for all that it lacked alcohol. The God of Law knew his way around coffee, it seemed.

"Ah." Forseti's head fell to one side, his silvery hair brushing his stark tunic. "Yes. Of course."

He considered the problem. I watched him expectantly, drumming my long fingers against the stone of his desk. I was not always a patient guest.

"Well?" I demanded after a bit.

"Property records," he said with gravity.

"Right. So where's the ring?"

"These things take time, God of Fire." He got to his feet again, leaving the crystal cup behind, and set off down one of the corridors.

I saw no point in following him. I tilted my chair back and threw my booted feet up on his desk with a mischievous little smile. Leaning back precariously, I began humming a tune that had once been popular among men condemned to the noose. I rested my hands against the back of my head, elbows spread. I was sure my irreverent pose would piss him off.

Forseti came back bearing a heavy volume bound in leather. He glanced at me and didn't so much as tweak an eyebrow. The God of Law sedately returned to his seat, opened the volume, and began working his way through the pages.

"Anything?" I asked after a bit.

Without lifting his head, he waved a hand, a forestalling gesture. He would not be rushed.

I rocked gently in place, then moved on to another song. It also involved convicts.

Eventually, he found what he was after. "Here it is." The other Aesir's voice was as collected as always, but it rang with triumph. "Oh, and get your damned feet off my desk, Loki," he added, the faintest touch of humor showing in his gray eyes.

I laughed and complied.

"The trail ends in Jotunheim," Forseti told me. "There has been no owner for centuries. Here, look." He handed me the tome.

I scanned the runes, then shook my head.

"Bring this to Gladsheim," I told him. "I'm sure Odin will want to see the bad news for himself."

The God of Law winced. "I suppose you're right," he replied without any enthusiasm.

Gladsheim was located in the meadows off Valhalla. It was the oldest and most sacred of groves, the holy site where we gods held our most serious councils.

Forseti and I walked through a gentle radiance that hugged the fields like a mist spun of sunlight. Unlike mist, however, the light neither dimmed the land nor obscured sight. We stepped respectfully among the white-trunked trees. A sense of peace, of inviolability, pervaded everything around us.

Beneath the graceful branches, twelve square chairs of Alfar gold were arranged in a perfect circle. These were strictly reserved for the Aesir. However, another ring of chairs surrounded our high seats. There a visitor might rest for a while and listen to the open assemblies of the gods.

Ullr moved about the very center of the grove, where the light was almost unbearably bright. He was busy examining the oath-rings for any sign of blemish. After a while, he smiled with satisfaction and took the chair directly across from mine.

I sat down too. Naturally, my seat had the crackling traces of fire about it. It was immediately to the left of Odin's, for I was one of the three creator gods who had given life to mortals.

We waited on the others, knowing that one space would never again be filled. Baldur's empty seat shone like an ineffably beautiful memorial. I looked away, fidgeting.

Njord came into the circle and greeted Ullr. The God of the Seas wore his usual pearl-trimmed tunic, and his eyes sparkled with merriment as he took his spot next to the other Aesir. It was impossible to not feel better when the God of Joy was near.

Red-bearded Thor treaded over next and sat off to my left. He left one empty chair between us, for Heimdall. All of our disagreements were laid aside in Gladsheim. Ullr, who loved the lonely wilds and the solitude of snow, sat beside Njord, who looked to the warm ocean winds and the bustle of commerce. Generous, kind-hearted Freyr took his place at the left hand of precise and deliberate Forseti. And I, the Trickster who crossed all boundaries, sat within easy reach of Heimdall, the Watcher who guarded all boundaries.

Odin was the last of us to arrive. He wore a blood-stained mail tunic and a plain steel helmet with a peaked, onion-domed crown. His gray hair draped over his vast shoulders. His crows and his wolves never followed him into Gladsheim. Neither he nor any other god ever carried a weapon into the holy grove.

The All-Father immediately walked over to the oath-ring and murmured a blessing over it. It flared like a sun, sanctified by his will.

"Hail the Aesir!" Odin declared. We all watched him expectantly. Me, relaxed, one leg stretched out impertinently. Tyr, intent and frowning. Bragi sat between Freyr and Ullr, looking faintly uncomfortable. While he loved to sing of wars, he had little interest in actually fighting them.

"The Jotuns grow bolder," said the wisest of the gods. "Midgard trembles under their assaults. Human minds turn to despair and their hearts are lost in shadow. Their spirits, which I myself made eternal, descend to Niflheim to be tortured by Jotun thoughts even after death."

Thor growled low in his throat and clenched his right hand into a fist.

"I see much with my magic," Odin continued. "Andvari's ring could be a great boon to us. One way or another, we must claim it for ourselves."

I raised my eyebrows at Forseti, indicating that he could have the honor of delivering our news. He gave me a tiny nod back, dignified as always.

Odin missed nothing. His unsettling gaze fell on the God of Law. "You found the ring?" my blood-brother asked.

"With ease, grandfather," he replied calmly. "Recovery of the asset may prove to be a more rigorous undertaking, however. The records indicate that it was last seen in Jotunheim itself."

"No matter," rumbled the Lord of All. Forseti and I exchanged a relieved look. The one-eyed god addressed his son then. "Thor, you'll retrieve the ring for us?"

The auburn-haired Aesir bared his teeth in a fierce grin. "I will! The giants won't know what hit them!" He leapt to his feet, and Odin held out the oath-ring. The Thunder God gripped it tightly, swearing himself to the charge.

The Father of All turned to me. "Loki, you're with Thor. I want you both gone before noon."

Jotunheim was not a welcoming place. The sky was perpetually shrouded in ash. When red lightning wasn't booming in a random cacophony, throwing up streamers of incinerating lava, icy winds shrieked in my ears promising the rending of all creation.

I had journeyed back to my home realm many times since I'd shared blood with Odin, always searching for my birth-field out near the pine groves. I could never find it. Jotunheim had changed through the eons, responding to the pitiless, maddened thoughts of the immense beings who dwelt there. Many of my past haunts were long gone.

Thor and I rested on top of a stony rise, leaning against our walking sticks as we watched sulfuric cinders whirl over a barren gully. We had traveled far and still had not encountered a single giant.

"This is almost too easy," grumbled my companion. He wore studded leather over his leaf-green shirt, and his bearing was restless. "We should have had a scrape or three by now."

"You've been through here a lot, friend Thor. You don't think you've killed them all, do you?"

"Rabbits breed with more discretion and less speed. No, something's afoot. Make no mistake."

We scrambled down a gritty incline and landed, with the sure skill of the Aesir, beside a stinking yellow pool.

"This is it, Thor. The last place the ring was ever owned."

"Do you see it?"

"No."

"Great. Can we get out of here now? I'd have better hunting in Midgard!"

My expression turned sly. "Certainly, Lord Thunderer! Let's be off at once, and you yourself can tell Odin the tale of how we made absolutely no attempt to find the treasure he's after!"

Thor growled something rude into his beard.

We circled the steaming, sulfuric water, then picked through the rock-strewn crevices surrounding the pool. Our Aesir perceptions did us little good in that bleak realm. Neither one of us could figure out where Andvari's cursed ring might have gone.

"Everything involving Otter has always been more trouble than it's worth!" Thor complained. His voice was heated.

"Truly spoken," I agreed. I sighed, then sat down on a warm stone to rest for a bit. "We're missing something, old friend. I feel it."

"Well, figure it out fast. I'm hungry and I could really use a beer."

Something about his words caught my interest.

"Well, then. Here's a riddle for you: who owns the barley from which your beer is brewed, once it's mashed and strained, and the drink is ready for your thirsty throat?"

"He who grew it, of course."

"No, he owns the coin he was given for the barley. Try again."

"This is stupid, Loki."

"Just answer my question. If you can."

"Fine. The brewer, then."

"Wrong again, Mighty One. There is no barley. There is only your ale."

"It had better be dark and frothy if I have to listen to any more of this nonsense!"

I held up an appeasing hand. "What if the cursed ring were transformed? It was but gold, after all."

Thor folded his thick arms across his chest and frowned at me, considering the possibility. "You think that's what happened?"

"What else, if not? If someone had hidden it or carried it away from here, surely we would sense that?"

"We would." The Thunderer peered into the sky, and his eyes narrowed.

"Dangerous weather coming," he commented. "I should know."

"Give me a moment. Perhaps a hint of the ring's fate remains." I walked over to the sulfur pool, singing softly. A line of flaring runes began to etch their way across the surface, drawing themselves at a painful crawl. They were bright and yellow-white against the duller yellow of the sulfur.

"Loki," Thor interrupted, his deep voice agitated. "You need to stop what you're doing. Now."

"The spell's almost done. We'll have our trail and Odin's prize too."

A second later, the ground buckled underneath me and a bellow resounded from the ashy clouds. Smoke poured down on us, as if the dragon Nidhogg had flown up the trunk of Yggdrasil to personally involve himself in divine affairs. I could no longer see. Swearing profusely, I pulled myself closer to the pool, trying to get a glimpse of the last runes. They still burned, but I couldn't make them out through the smoke.

"I *told* you!" Thor yelled. Mjolnir thrummed to life, scattering incandescent light everywhere. I concentrated on my runes. There was a crack of metal on something that might have been stone, and another shake that seemed to arise from the ground itself. A giant wailed close by.

"We've got company!" the Thunderer shouted. He did not sound entirely unhappy about it.

"Tell them I'm busy!" I snarled. And then the base of a small mountain slammed down in front of me, taking out the sulfur pool and the rocky crevices and slopes around it. I cursed again, this time far more explicitly.

The giant's foot lifted. My world dimmed to smoke and shadow. The next step would crush me if I didn't move.

I threw myself into the shape of a martin and barreled away, chittering with rage. Darting through the ash, I could hear Mjolnir striking true. The giant screamed, a noise like every thousand-year-old tree in a thousand-year-old forest creaking in the same gale at the same time.

"Hear me now, sons of Jotunheim!" Thor called into the howling winds. "Don't fuck with the Aesir!" My friend was the bravest of gods, but his battle cries sometimes lacked a certain finesse.

"Too late! They already have, brother!" I twittered darkly. I was missing the last few runes. A battleground was no place to try to reason my way through what I had read. There might be enough to go on later. Or maybe not.

Flipping and diving, I blurred and hit the ground running, back in my own form again. My chest was tight with fury, feeding my flames. I called wildfire to my hands and hurled it at our enemy.

The giant yelped and then yelped again as Thor's hammer struck it directly between its malevolent, black and orange eyes. Weakened by my magic and the Thunderer's blows, it finally began to topple. That created an entirely new threat. What our enemy had failed to accomplish through purpose he might yet accomplish through accident.

"Over here!" ordered my companion. An instant later, I stood at his side. I took a prudent step back, placing myself behind the larger Aesir.

The giant's shadowy form blocked out the sky as it fell toward us. I made a face and closed my eyes. When I opened them again, the corpse lay to our left. The space between the dead Jotun and us was no greater than the length of sword.

I gave Thor a horrified look.

"Relax," he grunted. "I know giants."

Later, when we were closer to the border of Asgard and had made our camp for the night, I took a scrap of paper from my pouch and sketched out the runes I'd seen in the pool. We were both tired, and rock surrounded us on every side. Our fire burned only by my magic. There was no tinder anywhere on that stony plain.

"Any luck?" Thor asked grumpily. We were out of ale and stuck in a wasteland. The Thunderer did not approve of our situation.

"Not really. The ring isn't in Jotunheim anymore. I'm sure of that much."

"Fantastic. Eight realms and an infinite number of universes to go."

"I think we might be forgiven for letting this quest slide," I told him.

He huffed and moved closer to the warmth of the flame. But a moment later, my friend stiffened. I heard something too: a chaotic pounding off in the distance, as if an entire world's drums were all being played at the same time, to entirely different beats.

"Oh, screw it all," Thor muttered. He rose to his feet, as strong and steadfast as ever. But he kept shooting looks over his shoulder, over to where the noise was coming from.

"What's going on?" I asked, managing to keep my voice reasonable. Something was scaring the Thunder God. I was certain, then, that we were in deep trouble. He grabbed up his cloak and tossed mine over to me. I caught it with quick ease.

"You know that giant we just killed?"

"Not personally, no."

"Yeah, well, it might have been a chieftain." A low bellowing noise reverberated from behind us. The Jotuns were sounding their battle horns.

"And you're mentioning this just now, friend Thor?"

"It's hard to tell with giants. I didn't want you to worry if I was wrong."

"Thank you so much for that!"

We sped off for Asgard, pressing through our fatigue. I hunched down in my cloak as dry winds sliced at me. My feet were numb, and I wanted sleep more than any treasure. Even the rock outcroppings were beguiling. A bed of sharp pebbles and brittle flint was still a bed.

But the cacophony of drums and marching feet urged us on. The giants had raised an army in little time, and we knew where their forces were heading.

Two Aesir had slain a Jotun chief.

All the Aesir would pay.

chapter fifteen
the giants invade

Asgard Present

O din's lips curved up in an unnerving smile. We were back in Gladsheim readying ourselves for war. The goddesses had found seats on the benches outside the central ring. We carried no weapons into the holy place, but many fingers were already twitching with anticipation.

Freya shuffled behind Njord, her hand grasping for a whetstone that was not there. She wore a deep blue tunic under her leather mail, and her hair was pulled into a tight, rope-like braid. Her hawk-feather cloak hung from her narrow shoulders, and it shimmered with its own magic.

Heimdall stirred next to me. He had given the alarm before rushing straight to the war council. He was clearly eager to be off.

I listened to the talk and frowned to myself, running my hand over my chin. A great deal had changed since I'd been condemned to the cave. Asgard's walls would no longer hold off the giants. We'd have to meet them in combat.

My blood-brother could not have been more pleased. His single eye glittered with battle lust. It had been ages since the Aesir had last fought together. I was sure, then, that the All-Father had known exactly what he had been doing when he had ordered us into Jotunheim. Thor and I had been sent there to provoke our enemies, nothing more. This clash had been brewing for centuries, but the giants had needed a push before they'd invade our realm.

"VICTORY TO THE AESIR!" Odin roared. The Hanged God's tremendous voice filled the sanctified grove, and every last one of the hallowed trees rustled back its support for our cause.

"Victory!" we shouted back. Some of the gods and goddesses stomped their feet rapidly, hooting with exhilaration. Our meeting was ended.

I followed Honir out. After our eons of adventuring together, it was still second nature to help him gird for battle. In the sunlit fields beyond Gladsheim, stone longhouses lay tucked away in sunken hollows, and these were stocked with every sort of weapon and every kind of armor. Honir and I had always favored the same repository. We ducked under a low lintel and descended worn granite stairs.

The interior of the longhouse was plain, all whitewashed fieldstone walls and rows upon rows of dark-stained racks. I eyed their offerings dubiously. Everything looked so bulky and clumsy.

Honir caught on to my thoughts immediately. "I know how you dislike armor, Loki, but you should at least wear leather." The other god's expression was curiously peaceful. He ambled over to a mail tunic and ran his hand down it contemplatively. He seemed to be in no hurry, though Jotunheim's armies approached our borders.

"No," I said. "It would just slow me down."

The other Aesir shook his head. His dull, brown-blonde hair brushed about his shoulders. "Well, help me get this on."

I stepped over and lifted up the chain mail, holding it out as he fought to get his arms into the sleeves. After some struggling, Honir pulled the suit over his head and began adjusting his belt.

"Are you entirely sure this is what you want to wear?" I joked.

The other god's face went hard.

"Enough, Loki," he said abruptly.

I blinked at him, taken aback. We hadn't been alone together since I'd been freed. I was suddenly very conscious of the packed dirt under our feet, of the gleaming instruments of war lined up to the ceiling, and of the dusty scent of straw. I was even more conscious of the strange, severe glint in Honir's hazel eyes and of all the time that had passed since I had last journeyed with him.

"What do you mean?" I asked, moving away from my fellow god. I flushed and took a seat on one of the bales, watching him closely.

"We've traveled so much, seen so many things. And yet... you still don't get me at all, do you?"

"What of it?" I said heatedly. "We're about to go to war! Do you really want to have a heart-to-heart now?"

"I do. There's no better time, really. Nothing is set, you know. No victory is secure."

I shrugged, managing to get my temper back under control, and nodded at him. I could not easily refuse my brother in creation. If he wished to talk, we'd talk.

"Fine, Honir. I'll listen. But don't you think we'll win today? The same as always?"

"There is no 'same as always.'" He paused and then exhaled slowly, a serene smile lighting up his face. "Think about it, old friend. Isn't it a wonderful thing, to not know?"

I scraped my feet on the floor, trying to be patient. Heimdall's horn blared outside, urging us to the war field. The battle was not yet on us, but it drew close. The other Aesir's gaze flickered toward the door, but he gave no other indication he had heard the summons.

"The Vanir always knew, or thought they did, at any rate," he continued. "They wanted all things to be set. You pick on me, Loki, yet Odin named me second creator. Me. Not you, his own blood-brother. Maybe you should ask why."

My mouth twisted into a snarl. "Kept this bottled up a while now, have you?"

He paid my words no mind.

"Loki, you of all the gods should honor my words. If everything were set, if there were no doubts—no mystery—where would you be right now?"

Honir's eyes locked onto mine, holding me. The world seemed to be suspended. I saw the truth of things in that moment. I swallowed heavily.

The other god gave me a relaxed nod, satisfied that I understood him at last.

"Uncertainty is beauty," he murmured. "Uncertainty is joy. Without it, we are all but prisoners. Now, tell me, what do you think of this atgeir?"

My brother in creation took up a long-poled weapon from the nearest rack. It had an axe-like blade for slicing set opposite a rounded mallet for crunching bone, and it was tipped with a wicked spear that could pierce any armor. The weapon offered its wielder many options.

"An excellent choice, friend Honir," I said in a quiet voice.

He beamed at me, then went to another rack. He handed me a jerkin of buttery black leather. "Try this on. It was made for you. From... before."

I leapt to my feet and slipped the tunic over my head. I could have been wearing no armor at all; it was entirely weightless. Red runes glowed along its hems, and warding power flowed around me.

"Well, well!" I exclaimed. I spun around thoughtfully and stretched my arms out, then fell into a fighting pose, as if ready to strike. I straightened up again and grinned at my fellow Aesir. "This will do nicely!"

We headed off for the plains. The sky was a sheet of deepest gray, smooth and unvaried. It was only along the horizon that the leaden cloud cover finally broke, giving way to an ambient yellow half-light that whispered of storms and blood-soaked earth. Odin, the mightiest of all the gods, blessed the day. He preferred to battle under shrouded skies.

Honir walked over to the other warriors. Njord held himself at the ready, his face tranquil. He carried a golden sword shimmering with encrusted pearls and rubies. Freyr was nearby, clutching an unadorned sword of his own. I saluted them and glided over to Skathi and Freya.

Skathi was smirking to herself. She wore a tunic of white leather trimmed with silvery fur, and her hair was bound under a simple helmet of steel. The wintry goddess waved me over, her pale eyes glittering with fervor. Skathi adored the intricacies of combat.

"I have an idea, Loki. When the time's right, follow my lead and try to keep up." She gave me a chilly little smile.

I grinned back. We both knew much of magic, and we knew how to coordinate our attacks. The giants were in for a very bad time.

The others filed onto the field. Heimdall was wearing heavy chain mail over his snowy tunic, and Tyr was in his usual gold. The taciturn warrior god held his razor-edged spear in his new hand. Ullr paced over to them, readying his crossbow. He wore reindeer-hide armor over his wool clothing.

I started in surprise as Forseti joined them, clad in a mail coat that reached his knees. The scholarly God of Law gripped a golden axe. I recognized it, of course. It was the same axe he used to execute those he found guilty of the most atrocious crimes. Its single, holy blade was set close to a filigreed shaft. The weapon of judgment hummed with its own power, ringing like a struck bell.

It was easy to forget that Forseti could hold his own in a skirmish. Although he wasn't as burly as Thor, Heimdall, or Njord, the younger Aesir carried himself with a quiet strength. He moved as if all his weighty mail were the softest muslin.

Odin nodded at him approvingly. Then the All-Father lifted his gaze, taking us all in. Mounted on gray Sleipnir, he loomed above the plain.

"No arms will be raised, nor a single spear thrown, until the war is declared. We fight with honor this day. I'd have no Jotun gainsay our triumph." His one eye burned with his words.

Forseti inclined his head. "I'll declare it, grandfather. When the time is right."

"Good."

I arched my eyebrows and exchanged a look with Skathi. She shrugged at me. Somewhere along the way, the clash had turned into a formal affair. I wouldn't let that change my strategy, however. Incineration did not lend itself to the finer proprieties.

We waited, and the gales tore at our hair and tunics. The goddesses who weren't fighting—my Sigyn among them—began a steady, measured beat on their drums and took up a chant against our foes. They were Aesir to the core: they'd cheer us on and rain spells upon those who dared cross us.

A chaotic, discordant force swelled beneath the more immediate rhythm the goddesses were keeping. Soon, I could hear the noxious blasts of Jotun horns and the stomach-churning rumble of their drums.

The giants were nearly at our walls.

A black shape, unimaginably vast, cut itself out from the clouds. Its pupilless eyes smoldered with gray fire, and it bore a club the size of one of Yggdrasil's branches in its enormous, taloned hands. The Jotun was a dreadful sight by itself. Even more dreadful were the hosts thundering in behind it: every sort of frost giant, with burning blue and white eyes; giants of the rocks and giants of the mountains; nameless giants spun of the void who sought to drown all of creation in despair; and, of course, giants of the flame, the allies of Surt himself. These last were the worst, for they knew that if they did not have their victory this day, they would surely have it on another.

Thor cursed into his beard and hefted Mjolnir. Odin shared a secretive smile with him.

"Hold yourself, my son. The time comes."

The Jotun in the lead swung its gargantuan leg over our walls. The vile being moved with fluid ease. A heartbeat later, it stood entirely on our soil. It let forth a screeching bellow that cut through the air and shivered through our souls.

"—crimes of trespass and profaning the sacred grounds of Asgard," Forseti was saying under the tumult, "I now find you in violation of Aesir law. The sentence for your blasphemy is death, and judgment will hereby be rendered upon you and all others who enter this holy realm with invidious intent." He lifted his golden axe above his head, supporting it with both hands. "To war!" he shouted.

Thor had been gritting his teeth from the strain of waiting. The All-Father raised his hand, and Huginn and Muninn cawed loudly from his shoulders.

"Now, my son," Odin said in a deceptively quiet voice.

At my blood-brother's order, white and orange lightning sizzled across the wind-blown expanse. That crackling trail was the only way we could track Mjolnir's swift flight. The immense Jotun roared and quavered, then launched itself toward us. Behind it, the other giants were pulling themselves over the wall in thrashing, sickly waves, like nesting insects squirming to reach a dropped piece of bread.

Insects, I reflected, did have one redeeming trait: they were highly combustible.

I willed up flame, a nearly transparent plasma that hovered at my fingertips and danced across my palms. Beside me, Skathi spoke a rune and an invisible, icy shield formed over us, as thick and immovable as a glacier. Sleipnir reared up, screaming a horse's scream, and Odin barked out his own spell, runes known only to him, meant to grant our safe return from the battle.

Before I could draw in another breath, they were upon us. I found myself slinging rapid curses at a pack of rock giants. They howled like wolves as they fell. But like wolves, they were viciously clever. As I spiraled flame through the lungs of one of the invaders, its smaller companion darted behind me and took a slash at my hamstrings. I cried out as its claws cut into my flesh and careened off to one side. Anger fueled my spell; my attacker burst apart, splattering hot lava onto its allies. They shook and groaned as the steaming drops dissolved their stony hides.

I jumped up and whirled about in a mocking little dance, then threw back my head and laughed at them. What was the point of a fight if a god didn't have some fun at his enemies' expense?

Thor's daughter, Thrud, charged by me, her auburn braid streaming behind her and her muscled legs pumping. Her face was very intent and uncharacteristically worried. I broke off from my rock giants and followed her.

Her father was still locked in combat with the single Jotun who had led the attack, and a gang of frost giants now encircled him. Thrud and I fell upon them. She sliced their guts wide open with her shining steel glaive, and I sent fire through them, melting their throats and turning their grasping hands into useless, dribbling mush. Their weapons clattered to the ground.

That threat taken care of, Thrud leapt into the fray with her father, slashing and stabbing. Thor grinned at her as he slung his hammer against their foe. Overwhelmed by the double attack, the towering monster finally staggered to its knees, its putrid voice lifted in a wail.

Thrud's spear-tip found its jugular vein, and black, viscous blood poured out onto the tangled grass.

"That's my girl!" Thor crowed.

I turned from them, looking for another battle.

Freya had shapeshifted into hawk form, and the clouds around her flashed with rosy white light as she sung runes over a troop of fire giants. She seemed to be doing just fine on her own.

Ullr's arrows pattered down among the Jotuns, swift as the undulating torrents of a storm. He moved with unfathomable speed, and his expression was serious for a change. Meanwhile, Honir tore through their ranks with his atgeir, switching attacks as he went. I smiled to see him at his work. My fellow creator could certainly fight. There was no hesitation, no equivocation, in him as he took down Asgard's enemies.

And then laughter—gray and deep and full of unspoken wisdom—lofted over the battlefield. The sound was frightening, but it had nothing of the giants about it. My heart soared in response. Odin, the Lord of All, was with us.

Astride great Sleipnir, my blood-brother stampeded over our attackers. His spear hacked through Jotun flesh as fast as the quickest thought. I muttered words of power and added the blessing of fire to his killing hits. Giants gnashed their gravelly teeth with pain, and the stench of their burning wounds filled the air.

Odin laughed all the louder, well pleased with my magic.

"Loki!" called a female voice. "Get over here!"

I was at Skathi's side in an instant.

She lowered her head, enunciating cold runes and drawing up their ancient magic. The clouds spun above us, turning as white as hoarfrost. She spoke another rune, and blue light flared. With a crash that shook through all of Asgard, terrible ice pillars dropped from the thunderclouds, smashing down upon the giants and crushing many of them before they could comprehend the threat.

I surveyed the lines of corpses, awed.

"I left space between those columns for a reason!" she growled at me.

I understood her meaning immediately. With a smirk, I wove pure sheets of orange flame between the frozen towers, scorching our remaining foes. Living bands of fire and ice, the primordial dooms, arched between the sky and earth like a gate fallen shut. The Jotuns' pounded and broken bodies spoke of their error, of the gods' judgment.

The giants nearest the wall exchanged panicked looks. Several moments passed. Suddenly, they gave flight all at once, pushing and gouging at each other as they frantically sought an escape from our realm. Thor took off after them with a roar. Mjolnir flared and boomed again and again as the Thunder God hurled his weapon with a simple, rapid brutality, his face darkened with fury.

Closer in, the last of the Jotuns were meeting their end. Forseti bent down and almost lovingly drew his axe across the pulsing throat of one of the void giants, intoning words of condemnation all the while. A blazing golden line gashed through its neck, and it fell back with a rattling sigh. The God of Law rose to his feet, his gray eyes stern.

Tyr launched his spear into a fleeing frost giant and smiled as it crumbled to the ground. Its flailing fingers scratched at the earth, killing tussocks of grass with its touch. Njord lobbed off the head of a smoldering fire giant. He too smiled to himself, his perfect teeth gleaming, as its head bounced against the soil. With calm decorum, the God of the Seas pulled a square of linen from his pouch and began wiping down his sword.

Freyr was weaving and dancing between two rock giants, his blade seeming to flow with its own grace. The god of the Alfar realms crouched and spun around, slicing off one Jotun's leg before he pounced up like a cat to run his sword through the base of its companion's chin. Gritty, sickly gray fluid pumped onto the plain as both intruders bled out. He raised his sword to Njord, bowing his red-gold head respectfully. His father returned the salute.

I sensed someone approaching behind me and whirled around, fire springing to my fingertips. But it was only Heimdall. The other Aesir gave me a tired nod. His white tunic was ripped and stained, but his eyes sparkled with triumph. He had ranged out and fought the giants straggling at the battle's edges, cutting them down before they could foray deeper into Asgard. His blazing sword hung from his belt, its diamonds shimmering.

"Nice fight, Loki," he said.

"It sure was, my friend."

Heimdall, the guardian of our realm, surveyed the damage. Strewn limbs and wrecked, stinking corpses littered the plain. Above, the slate-gray clouds slowly parted, and molten rays tumbled down over the battlefield, illuminating our vanquished enemies in grisly detail. Open, bloody wounds and loosened intestines gleamed like moist copper, and dead Jotun eyes stared into the uncaring sky, reflecting back its stark light. Golden flame traced the outlines of jagged bones, and vicious, curving teeth glinted from permanently open mouths, shining as bright as needles under the Asgard sun.

Odin reined in Sleipnir and looked out over the defeated armies and slain hosts. He had placed himself just outside the light. Caught in shadow, the God of War drank in his works. He said nothing and moved no muscle. Humid gusts stirred at his horse's mane. Though he was as silent as a burial mound lost beneath winter trees, I knew my blood-brother was well satisfied with everything we'd wrought.

The gods had won the war.

The Aesir stood strong.

chapter sixteen
VINGOLF

Asgard Present

There were two places in Asgard I was never supposed to enter. One was the forbidden chamber of Hliskalf in Odin's silver hall. The other was Vingolf whenever the goddesses met for one of their secret councils.

Vingolf was a bright and joyous place, a soothing home to many of the righteous dead. It was also the site of a great hall where the Aesir gathered to drink and feast. But some days, Vingolf was off-limits. The goddesses convened there to discuss important matters just as we gods sometimes convened in Gladsheim. Unlike us, they did not deliberate openly. Another woman might hear their words, but no male, whether god or mortal, could go into the hall during their sessions. Even my wife would not tell me what they spoke of.

My curiosity gnawed at me. Vingolf's hospitality and fine wines were not enough. I wanted to know what happened there behind closed doors.

I had been a Goddess of Fire once and could become a goddess again. The very afternoon before Yule, I set off for their council on silk-slippered feet.

Winter gripped much of Asgard, but Vingolf's seasons were unchanging. The air was as fresh and pure as Gladsheim's, and rich with the perfumes of growing things. Flowers glowed like sunlit stained glass, and the leaves of every tree were afire. I passed through vineyards too beautiful for any mortal world. I gently took a grape between my soft fingers and bit into it. Its juice was as sweet as any mead ever served in Valhalla.

The hall itself rose over the land like a sharp-peaked mountain. Tiers of dark wood adorned with gold and gleaming gems embraced the cloudless sky. The path to its gate was rose quartz, and Vingolf's steps were of the loveliest amber. I treaded lightly up the stairs, my movements smooth and pretty.

The goddess Syn waited by the door. She raised a hand in warning, her palm out to me.

"I don't recognize you, shining sister. Tell me your name."

"I would rather keep that to myself for now, noble defender. Know that I am a goddess of the flames. I have but recently found my way here to Asgard and would seek the Aesir goddesses' company. And their wisdom."

The other immortal's dark eyes narrowed with suspicion. Syn's hair reached to her waist and was every bit as black as mine in my preferred form. She was the guardian of those who stood accused and the keen supporter of a refusal rightfully given. It was natural that she should root out unwelcome guests and stop intruders from entering the hall.

"Fair words," Syn replied, "and from a fairer goddess. I find it difficult to trust a stranger, however."

"Is there any way I can prove myself to you?"

"Perhaps. Come, and I will introduce you to the others before we begin our meet. If they decide in your favor, you can stay. If they decide against you, you must serve as our handmaiden for a year and a day. Do you accept these terms?" She smiled at me shrewdly, expecting that her hard condition would turn me away.

I paid it no mind.

"Yes. I do."

Syn led me indoors, to a circle of cushioned wooden chairs. Her jet-dark hair swished with each step. As she paused at my side, ten pairs of eyes—those of the seated goddesses—took measure of us. Twelve of them had once gathered in that space, but Nanna was dead. Her seat in Vingolf was empty just as Baldur's was in Gladsheim.

"This visitor, a goddess of the fire, seeks to attend our council. And now perhaps you will favor us with your name?"

"If it is so important, know that I am called Raudfifa"

Skathi was watching me with cold, intelligent eyes. Of all of them, she was my greatest threat. My gentle, playful Sigyn was already clapping her hands together with delight, ready to welcome a new sister into their midst.

Freya frowned, skeptical. "I've wandered many worlds, but I have never heard of you."

"I fear that I dwelt in darkness for some time, remembered only by the dwarves."

"Poor worshippers for a goddess," Thrud put in sympathetically. Thor's daughter was dressed in green and orange, and a band of beaten bronze held back her auburn hair. She was the very strength of good leaders, the protector of honorable chieftains.

I bowed to her, my long lashes fluttering prettily.

"Quite so, mighty daughter of the Thunder Lord."

She grinned at the honorific, her smile as wide and as vigorous as her sire's.

"Flowery words and flattery count for little here," interrupted another of the immortals. "Tell us of your deeds, Goddess of Flame." Ran, the Goddess of the Sea, was assessing me with steady, reserved eyes. Her wavy, foam-white hair flowed down her shoulder like an endless breaker. She was married to the sea-giant Aegir who had once owned a grand hall. My curse of fire had long since torn their home apart. Aegir and Ran lived in humbler dwellings now. It would be best if she never realized who I was.

My voice was clear as I answered her. "I keep the fires of the forges even

125

and I know much of crafted treasure. I speak all the languages of men and gods, and can twist an evil spell back on the one who throws it. I have power over runes as well—and over dreams."

Var, the goddess of oaths, lifted a contemplative eyebrow. Her hair too was very dark, a deep walnut brown that nicely complimented her piercing blue-green eyes and amethyst-colored gown.

"Swear to what you have just said," she instructed.

"As you wish. I swear."

She nodded to the others. "Our guest tells us the truth."

A sigh of relief went through the chamber.

Kind and welcoming Sif—Thor's wife and Thrud's mother—stepped forward, her gold-spun hair glittering as she moved. She handed me a cut crystal glass, full of the shining wine of Vingolf. My lips curled up in an ironic smile as I accepted it. In the dark months after Baldur's death, Sif had once offered me mead in a glass that was not dissimilar to the one I now held. When I had taken it, she had begged me to speak well of her before the other Aesir. But I had not.

I raised the glass to them in thanks, then took a sip.

"A wondrous drink, sisters! Long have I wished to see Vingolf. Its hospitality is greater than I could have ever imagined, bound as I was in the darkness of Nidavellir."

Lofn inclined her head to me gracefully. She was a goddess of love and could arrange even a forbidden marriage. She was also very close to Odin and Frigg, and—like them—preferred blue. Her apron dress was the color of the sky, embroidered with flowers and ivy. She wore a gown of snowy lace underneath it. Her light brown hair spilled down her back, loose as always.

Beautiful Idunn, with her golden tresses and sparkling eyes, gently squeezed my free hand. "Be welcome among us," she said in a musical voice. She had always been especially trusting.

"You honor me, lovely goddess," I told her. I squeezed her hand back, and she started. A puzzled crease flitted over her brow.

"There is much fire in you," she murmured as she hastily backed away. I hoped she had not recognized my touch. I had taken her by the hand once before when I'd guided her down Bifrost into the waiting clutches of a giant.

"My apologies, fair Idunn," I said contritely.

Syn and Skathi were eying me warily, even though Var herself had vouchsafed my oath. Sigyn skipped over and also clasped my hand briefly in hers. Without any self-consciousness, she gave me a light kiss on the cheek, then danced away again. I couldn't help but let my eyes follow her. My wife was the most beautiful of them all, so happy and joyous, with her lustrous brown hair tumbling down to her belt.

Perhaps I watched her a bit too long. Gerd, Freyr's wife, nudged me and motioned to a seat outside the ring of twelve chairs. Born a Jotun like me, she shone as a beacon, her loveliness that of the moon and stars. Her voice was lilting and filled with power.

"Please do not think us rude that we ask you to sit to the side. The twelfth place in our council must always stay open. One of our sisters is gone forever. Nanna followed her bright Baldur to the grave. Her grief was her death."

"How horrible!" I exclaimed, as if I knew nothing of those events.

"It was." Gerd's eyes were flecked with every shade of blue and violet, and hard as jewels. "Her murderer drinks in Valhalla once more. I'll not have anything to do with the place, these days."

My wife quickly looked at her feet, her cheeks reddening.

"Shut up, Gerd," growled Skathi. "We all know what you think, yet you drag it out again and again with our own Sigyn sitting right in front of you."

Freyr's dazzling wife turned her back on them. She busied herself lighting incense. Soon, heady scents drifted through the hall. I took a seat outside the circle and waited to see what would happen next.

When Gerd was finished, she sat down. Their ring of chairs surrounded a small wooden table bearing a single, gold-encrusted bowl. The vessel started to glow warmly from within. Amber light rippled over its edges, falling to a point just outside their circle, illuminating their radiant forms.

The council began.

I wasn't entirely surprised to see that Freya and Skathi were the unspoken leaders of their little gathering. We gods all bowed to Odin's will in the end, but the two goddesses seemed to be equal in authority. Thrud was obviously their champion, quick to offer her hearty voice in their support.

I soon grew bored. They talked of the smaller concerns of Midgard: love, childbirth, crops, and protection. Freya quietly rolled her eyes during the worst of it and fingered her dagger. Thrud and Skathi sometimes yawned, though they tried their best to hide their apathy. Ran and my Sigyn said the least. Both of them listened respectfully, but neither had much to add.

I sighed to myself and trailed my feminine hand over the golden folds of my dress. The hall was warm and the wine was going to my head. Although I was a trespasser and would suffer the fullness of their divine wrath if they caught me off guard, I almost dozed off a few times.

The monotonous meeting continued.

Suddenly, I heard my false name. I stiffened in my chair.

"Yes? You spoke of me?"

"We were curious about your plans, Raudfifa," Lofn said. "Some of the gods seek a wife." Trust the goddess who arranged marriages to drop that on a stranger she had just met.

"I don't know if I shall stay in Asgard," I replied carefully. "I did wish to see it, though. Just once."

"Lofn speaks wisely," contributed Var, who was also far too quick to think of weddings. "Why rush off? One as lovely as you might find happiness in an

Aesir's strong embrace."

"I couldn't presume, fair sisters."

But they were focused on me now. Matchmaking, it seemed, was an appealing diversion. My own Sigyn beamed at me gaily, then dashed over to take a seat beside me. She ran her fingers through my lengthy flame-colored locks, brushing the tips where they ended at my waist. Her touch tingled, and I shivered, wishing we were alone back home in our longhouse.

"Let's see," she said. "Heimdall and Njord have no wife, nor do Honir, Forseti, or Ullr— "

"Leave Ullr out of this!" snapped Skathi.

Lofn sighed loudly. "So you finally admit to your love, Skathi?"

"That's his business and mine, and no one else's."

Var and Lofn exchanged a smug look. "Let us know when you change your mind, Ice Goddess," said Var. "I'll hear your oath and sanctify your vows."

Skathi lifted her chin coolly and remained silent.

"Four gods then," continued Sigyn, as lighthearted as ever. "Which is the handsomest, do you think?"

I favored her with a lady's modest smile. "Loki is the handsomest, of course. But, alas, he's already taken!" I patted her hand as if we were sisters. "You are most lucky!" My wife flushed happily and didn't disagree with me. Her response pleased me.

Gerd spoke up. "You'll be lucky, Raudfifa, if Odin takes no notice of you. Perhaps moving on with due speed is a good idea." Her lips straightened into a bitter line.

The other goddesses were quiet for an awkward moment. Then Sigyn shook her head with annoyance. "You went to him willingly, Gerd. And now you're distracting me."

"He sang runes. My heart was always Freyr's and Freyr's alone."

"So you've said," muttered night-haired Syn. "Yet even I could find no refusal."

Gerd stood, her eyes flashing with barely contained rage. "You go too far!"

"Enough!" Freya was on her feet too, her blonde hair a curtain catching the gold light from the bowl. "Is this the hospitality of Vingolf? Do we show our visitor only dissension?"

Murmuring apologies, Gerd and Syn both backed down.

"Get Raudfifa more wine," Freya ordered. Her tone was brisk.

Meanwhile, wintry Skathi, somber in her gray dress, studied me with an arched brow. "Never have such heated words been exchanged in this holy council. Can it be coincidence that they're heard now, when a goddess of fire is among us?"

"I did not seek this, honored lady," I told her, bowing my head reverently.

"Maybe. Maybe not." Her voice was as cold as a world without a sun.

"I think Sigyn brought up a good question earlier," Thrud interjected. Her honest eyes were thoughtful. They were the color of the spring's first buds and as pretty as her mother's. "Of all the gods, which is handsomest? I for one can think of worse subjects to ponder!" She gave us all a wolfish grin. No blushing maid was Thrud.

She turned to me. "We have one opinion. Who else would have a say?"

Gerd looked up sulkily. "Freyr, obviously. Any goddess who is not blind can see it."

"Ah, the dear prejudices of love!" replied Lofn. "I am glad you have them. But, no, I would have to say that Njord is the god most worth gazing upon."

Var shifted in her chair. "If we must speak the truth among sisters, I'll admit that I find Forseti easy on my eyes."

Thrud was guffawing and slapping her knee, thoroughly enjoying the turn their discussion had taken. "How about you, Sigyn? Would you agree with our visitor?"

I was shocked when my wife hesitated for long moments. "I may be married," she said, "but I can still be objective. Freyr has his own charms, and Tyr is always striking. Bright Heimdall is not an unpleasant sight either, nor is Ullr on his skis."

The others seemed almost as startled as I was—except for Thrud, who laughed all the harder.

"No one would say I have the handsomest husband," Sif told us as she resolutely folded her arms across her chest, "but I hardly think it matters!"

"Od was the handsomest god of all," Freya whispered sadly, "for all that I can scarcely recall his face most days."

"And you, Skathi?" asked Thrud, her tone light and bantering.

"You know I'm not answering that."

"Ran then?"

"Njord, if I must pick from the Aesir."

"And lastly, Idunn. What say you?"

"My Bragi is ever the handsomest of gods," she declared, all innocence and loyalty.

"The goddesses have spoken. Well, more or less. Njord has two definite votes and carries." Thrud chuckled and poured herself some more wine.

"Hold on," said Freya, shaking herself out of her melancholy. "You never voted, Thrud."

"I'm not going to, either. My fancies are my own."

"That's hardly fair after you've heard our answers to your question!"

"Too bad," she smirked, very much reminding me of her father when he was in one of his moods.

But I had other concerns just then.

"Njord?" I objected disbelievingly. My voice cracked and became a screech. "Njord is your pick?!" I felt heat rising to my cheeks. "Sigyn, take back what you said! Then we'll have the truth!"

Syn strode up to me and clamped a hard hand down on my shoulder. "Quiet! Skathi was right! You bring only discord, Raudfifa. I think you should leave this peaceful hall and never come back!"

The others soberly nodded their agreement.

"Foolish goddesses!" I spat.

In a blink, I was on my feet, releasing my spell. A male Aesir again, I stood before them in my crimson tunic, my black hair fluffing over my brows. They gasped at the sight of me. "See how carelessly you let the cleverest—and the handsomest!—of the gods slip into your midst? What will you do now, fair ladies? A man knows all your secrets!" I paused, then sniggered caustically. "Yes, you're a fine sisterhood indeed! I count myself as very impressed!"

Sigyn slashed around the others, her chin held high and her adorable gray eyes burning with defiance. "You know nothing of us, husband! Nothing at all!" She shoved me in the chest. I stumbled back a step and waggled my eyebrows at her.

"Calm yourself, wife! Perhaps Skathi will share Ullr with you if you need some soothing? What say you, goddess?"

Skathi's gaze was pure ice. "Get out of here, Loki. Now."

"Aw, jealousy. Isn't that cute?" I leered at her mockingly.

Thrud's face had turned to stone. She stepped in close to me, lifting a heavy, threatening fist. Freya glided forward with her dagger drawn, and Syn already had a spear lowered to my chest.

"We'll have the last laugh, Trickster!" Thor's daughter snarled. "I'll pummel all your insults right out of you!"

"And I'll dissolve your bones when she's done!" Ran added viciously.

"So much for the vaulted hospitality of Vingolf! I can tell when I'm no longer welcome!"

I ducked under Thrud's arm and easily danced out of their reach. I could move faster than any of them and was already through the vineyards by the time they made it to the door.

The fires and the flowing mead of Valhalla awaited me. I had a tale to tell indeed.

chapter seventeen
The Oath

Asgard Present

Honir was perched on a nearby bench. The light of the raging hearths transformed his dull, washed-out hair to a coppery orange. "I don't get it," he confessed. "Why deceive them? Why all the bother?" His expression was confused.

I drolly toasted him with my golden mead horn. I had kicked my boots up next to me and now leaned against the table, propping myself up on my elbow. I was entirely at ease. Like Freya's two cats, I could make myself comfortable just about anywhere.

"Why, Honir? Because it was funny! That's why!"

"Sigyn won't speak to you for a month," he predicted with an uncharacteristic measure of certainty.

"That's her choice," I shrugged. "I made mine."

Thor sauntered over and topped off my horn.

"Bragi!" he bellowed. "Get to work on a song! Don't leave out how my Sif was loyal and my Thrud was strong! Why, my own daughter would have beaten you to a pulp if you had only stayed another minute!"

"You're missing the point entirely, friend Thor."

"Oh, no. I don't think I am. And I know damned well you're leaving things out. It couldn't have all gone your way!"

I waved him off with a snort. "Who was there? You or me?"

"You, obviously. I don't make a habit of going around dressed like a woman."

I laughed derisively, sloshing my mead. "You made a fine enough woman when Mjolnir was on the line!" I always enjoyed picking on him about the time he had worn bridal clothes to get his hammer back from a giant named Thrym. I had accompanied him to the thieving Jotun's hall, disguised as his handmaiden. Unlike him, I felt no shame about our ruse. We had recovered what was ours and had no small amount of fun doing it.

Thor's bristling brows sunk dangerously. He did not appreciate any reminder of *that* particular adventure.

Forseti had positioned himself some distance away from us as usual, but he could hardly hide his interest. "Loki, it is my advised opinion that you trespassed," he said seriously. The God of Law held up his sterling mead horn to me. "It is also my advised opinion that it was entirely worth it!"

I saluted him back with my own drink. "You know, you had one vote for handsomest god yourself. Would you like to know who cast it?"

"No." Forseti's tone immediately turned severe. "I would not." I prudently dropped the subject. I'd met dwarves who were more easygoing about their gold than he was about his privacy.

"It's a good evening for stories," Freyr said. He sat nearby, looking cheery in his woven tunic of red, gold, and green. It was difficult to believe that he was married to such an unpleasant goddess as Gerd. "Do you have another?"

I shook my head and pulled myself upright on the bench. "Nothing like sneaking into Vingolf, no," I told him respectfully. We usually got on well, Freyr and I. My flames renewed the forests he held in his care, spiraling them through their cycles of death and rebirth.

The other immortal eyed me thoughtfully. After a moment, he stood and walked over to Odin's empty throne. Yule would soon be upon us, and the All-Father journeyed through the worlds, calling forth the untamed magics of the longest nights. The gods fell silent as Freyr took a place next to one of the carved armrests and planted a strong hand against the side of the ancient wooden seat. His red-gold locks glowed in the firelight like the promise of summer.

"Now's as good a time for this as any," the former Vanir announced mysteriously. With the one exception of Forseti, everyone else nodded, their faces expectant.

The nature god's amber eyes bored into mine. "Loki, we'd have another tale from you this night." The others were all twisting around in their seats to look at me.

"What's this all about?" I demanded. But I was smarter than any of them, and I already had my suspicions.

"Baldur," Freyr answered immediately. "We want to know what happened between you and Baldur."

I snorted and shook out my bangs. "Of course you do!"

"His oath binds him," Forseti said tightly. "You're only wasting your time. And mine."

Thor held up a heavy hand. "Not so fast," he rumbled. "We've got nine gods here tonight. Let's put our heads together. How'd the oath go, Loki? Tell us that much. Maybe there's a way around it."

The God of Thunder could be brutally clever when he wanted to be. He usually solved his problems with enthusiastic blows, but Thor's mind was sharp. He would have been a poor friend to me otherwise.

I couldn't think of our friendship now, however. I pressed my lips together and scowled off into one of the roaring fires.

"Answer the question!" The red-bearded Thunderer was rapidly losing patience with me.

"It's an oath of *silence*, Thor. Do you really think I can get into the details?" My voice dripped with sarcasm.

"You might want to *try*," he countered ominously.

"Yes, Loki, it's—" Njord began in a more reasonable tone. Whatever he had wanted to say was lost as the others started talking all at once. They were much louder than him, and their words were an excruciating cacophony pounding into my skull and raining down on me like hailstones. My shoulders tightened under my tunic. I felt bruised. Exposed.

"Enough!" Forseti's voice cut through Valhalla, restoring immediate order. He set his drinking horn down with no small amount of force and pulled himself to his feet, looking more than a little incensed. Like myself, he had probably wished only to relax, to enjoy a free and pleasant evening.

"Odin administered the oath," he told the now silent gods. "Only Odin can lift it. Surely you realize I've pursued this line of inquiry already, and to no avail?" Forseti did his best to keep his voice even, but repressed fury and betrayal edged every word.

I understood the pain he was trying to hide. I understood it better than anyone else there could have. My blood-brother was keeping truths from the very god who was supposed to be able see every deed, to know every fact. It was no small thing, to forbid an Aesir that which made up his very nature. I'd been cut off from my own fire and magic for over a thousand years. I could relate to the God of Law's suffering in the most personal of ways.

The hall was as still as an endless summer's hot, muffled skies. No one knew what to say next. I waited for someone else to stir, then gave up and took a long drink from my mead horn.

Njord rose to his feet, the pearl hems of his tunic glimmering red with the flames. He was usually a gentle, contemplative god. Now, he walked over to Forseti, put an almost fatherly hand on the God of Law's shoulder, and murmured something in his ear. Then he strode over to me, majestic and tall. His face was the very storm clouds over his seas.

"You always say you're the cleverest of us, Loki." Njord's voice was hushed, but within it I heard the relentless power of waves eating the shore. "Show us some of that cleverness tonight! Find a way to give us the tale!"

A dark mist fell over my vision. The God of the Seas had no idea what he was asking of me. A heartbeat later, something slipped inside of me, tilting further and further off-balance until what I thought of as "myself" careened away and disappeared over some nightmare horizon.

I realized, then, just how astoundingly offensive Njord really was.

I said nothing to the other god. Rather, I let my magic answer for me. Deep shadows slithered through Valhalla like grimy shrouds of silk, wrapping the pillars in murk as they climbed toward the rafters. Within moments, no gold shone or gems gleamed within the hall. The fires closest to me soundlessly hurled themselves to new heights, burning orange and coughing out blistering, unbearable heat.

Thor jumped away from our table with a curse.

I was perfectly comfortable, of course. I basked in the glow of my own maddened flames. An eerie smirk ghosted along my lips.

I let them take in my power, delighting in the fear I saw on their faces. Finally, I spoke. "I see how it is with you! All of you!" I laughed an empty laugh, devoid of any humor. "You'll take my jokes and stories, but when I won't give you what you want... well, here we are! Stupid, selfish gods!"

Shaking my head, I helped myself to some more mead. By then, it was boiling in the horn and went down my throat like molten gold. No one else there could have swallowed such a drink.

Njord—brave, insane Njord—actually moved a step closer to me. The God of the Seas seemed to be immune to my darling fires. I didn't like that, not one bit. My face contorted, and I bared my teeth up at him in a feral snarl.

The former Vanir regarded me with quiet dignity, ruddy light dancing along his belt and shimmering over his tunic. "Trickster," he said simply, "you owe Forseti a great debt. None of us welcomed you back on Odin's account. Baldur's own son spoke in your favor."

I giggled at him, then twisted my arm and sloshed the rest of my steaming mead into the closest hearth. My point was clear. Why would *I* need any of *them*?

Tyr was reaching for his sword. He had a warrior's instincts, and he knew when things were turning ugly.

I paid the golden-haired immortal no mind. I could melt his sword and his arm too if I but willed it. Instead, I drew myself to my feet and poured all my vicious attention onto the God of Law.

"Oh, so that's what happened? *You* spoke for *me*, Forseti?" I chortled, and the sound of it was discordant even to my own ears. "A whelp put in a good word for one of the creators?" I tilted my head to one side, pretending to consider the matter. A slow, deranged smile spread across my face. Some tiny, trapped part of me knew full well that I was in the grip of the cave and was absolutely horrified by everything I was doing. But that part had no say now.

"You pretend to deal in the truth, son of Baldur," I murmured. "So tell me truly, where were you at the beginning of time, when I spun universes from the flame? Where were you when Ymir fell? When we set Midgard's sun in its sky?" I paused meaningfully, then stomped my boot against the worn planks for emphasis. "Nonexistent! That's where! Speak to that, God of Law!"

The younger Aesir didn't flinch. Firelight shivered through his silver hair as he inclined his head ever so slightly. He was actually acknowledging my point.

Fresh rage swept through me. How could he remain so... so... *calm*?

I hissed the name of a rune, summoning fire to my open palm. In no time at all, I cradled the very heart of a star in my narrow hand, and it pulsed with its own fury. "You know," I continued in a soft voice, "I think I liked things better the old way. You've presumed to judge *me* so many—"

Light fingers tentatively brushed my shoulder. The hesitant touch was electric; I could only shudder as it arched through my very being. After it lifted, I paused for long moments, trying to remember what I'd been so angry about. The flame I'd been holding puffed out, forgotten. The hearths settled back down to normal and the gloomy shadows coiling against the ceiling retreated.

I blinked.

Honir's hazel eyes searched my face. "Are you all right?" he asked, his voice full of concern. I might as well have tripped over a stray root, not flown into a tirade and threatened to annihilate a fellow god.

I gave him a shaky nod and whispered back my thanks. I couldn't bring myself to look at Forseti, so I addressed Freyr instead.

Freyr, the god who sheltered sleeping seeds and brought renewal to the spent earth, had asked me to tell them about Baldur. He deserved to know what had really happened. He deserved the full story. They all did. And perhaps—just perhaps—sharing the tale would put that frothing, hate-driven part of my mind to rest.

"I'll ask Odin to lift the oath," I promised. I turned away from the former Vanir and gazed deeply into the flames. I tried to fight down the churning revulsion I felt for myself, for what I was capable of.

"Do it tomorrow at my hall," Thor instructed.

I shook myself out of my dark reverie and nodded back shortly. The Aesir always celebrated the first night of Yule under the Thunder God's roof, drinking hearty ales and feasting on fine foods. My blood-brother would be there with everyone else, and he would be in a generous mood.

My old friend gave me a conspiratorial wink. "Hey, it'll be just like old times, Loki. Right down to most of the goddesses wanting to cut out your liver and serve it up with the roasts!" The Thunderer's booming laugh echoed throughout Valhalla. The other gods finally relaxed.

"You'd better get going," Thor added more somberly. "You can't leave Sigyn alone, not on Yule. You'll have to talk fast to make things right by tomorrow."

He spoke the truth, of course. I sighed and left Valhalla. The winter sun clung to the horizon, its light weak and watery, barely showing through the stark gray branches. My teeth chattered as a frigid breeze brushed against my cheek. The pungent scents of woodsmoke mixed unpleasantly with the sharp, iron tang of freshly spilled blood. The All-Father's chosen had fought hard.

Disquieted, I hurried past the battle fields, seeking the paths to the Alfar lands. I was already having second thoughts about my promise. What was I going to say to Odin? What could begin to sway the Wisest God? I was the craftiest of all the Aesir, the very quickest with wiles and tricks. But even I was at a loss.

I found Sigyn sitting outside our home, bundled in a wool blanket with her knees pulled up under her arms. She watched the winter stars, waiting for the swift lines of light that traced falling meteors. I treaded up beside her and frowned into the sky. The magics of darkness and yearning, of slicing blades—of the hunter and the chase—already coursed unseen through the air. Odin's shadowy power loomed over all the worlds.

"Come inside, my light."

My wife hunched her shoulders. "I'm not happy with you, Loki."

"I know. But *you* know I could hardly resist the challenge."

She shook her head and started to get to her feet. Sigyn was just forgiving enough to accept my hand when I offered it to her. She stood in front of me, her long hair ruffling in the chilly winds. Her perfect lips curved down, delightfully serious. I didn't dare lean in and kiss them just then.

"You were quite pretty," she conceded after a long and significant pause. "And we'll certainly remember *that* meeting."

"As you say, my star."

She slipped her arm into mine.

Honir had been wrong. Our love ran deep, ran eternal. Even the cave could not shake it. What was one little prank between us?

Thor's hall, Bilskirnir, was at the top of a rocky tor. Mighty oaks dominated a landscape in which the sky was never entirely clear, never entirely at rest. Standing side by side, my wife and I considered the path leading up to the hall. The trail looked steep and uninviting, and it was hedged in with spiny bushes.

I intertwined my fingers around Sigyn's. "Shall we do this the easy way, love?"

She laughed, a sound like chimes on the breeze, and squeezed my hand tenderly. "Of course, husband."

I spoke a rune. An instant later, we were overlooking the ancient, rolling forests from atop the tor. The racing storm clouds now seemed close enough to touch.

Still holding hands, we approached Bilskirnir's entrance. My wife and I were dressed for feasting. My tunic would have been the envy of any bygone Midgard king with its thick layers of gold embroidery and overlays of rich black velvet. Sigyn was breathtaking in a silk gown of silver and white. A tooled circlet of argent ivy leaves crowned her head. We Aesir did not garb ourselves poorly at the worst of times. At Yule, we were splendid.

Thor's hall towered up like a mountain, but its highest tiers were cloaked by the storm, lost to a world of inky cloudbanks and rolling thunder. Bilskirnir was very old, and it was built entirely of oak. Carvings detailing the Thunderer's many deeds covered its vast walls. Captured flags of every color—the spoils of battle—drummed in the crossing winds. Some had been taken from Midgard or other mortal worlds, but many were of Jotun make.

I spotted Odin brooding alone beneath one of the snapping flags. His hair streamed under the woven steel headband he wore only at Yule, and his cloak flared in the gusts. Diamond-encrusted broaches glittered from his shoulders. His holiday tunic was of the deepest blue.

"Go on," I told Sigyn. "I'll only be a moment."

She nodded and stepped lightly over to Sif, who looked resplendent in a dress of brocaded gold. Thor's wife caught her in a warm hug and beckoned her inside.

"Joyous Yule," I said to Odin.

His one-eyed gaze fell on me. "Joyous Yule, brother."

I stood beside him. Odin surveyed the lands below as a chieftain might survey his warriors before a battle. Gray, leafless branches scratched at the sky. A murder of crows took flight all at once, cawing, as the gale picked up, roaring a warning. A deepening gloom engulfed the forests and settled between the valleys.

"Freyr asked me to talk with you," I told him.

The other god made no indication he had heard me, but I knew he was listening.

"Everyone wants you to unbind me from my oath, to allow me to speak of Baldur."

The mightiest of the Aesir lowered his head ever so slightly. I started to back away, but my blood-brother suddenly lashed out and clutched me by the wrist. His broad fingers grinded into my skin and for a fearsome moment, I thought I had truly angered him again. But he only gestured toward the groves below with his free hand.

A dreamy, golden light twinkled from afar, barely visible between the trees. It seemed familiar somehow. I smiled at the sight of it, though I could not have said why.

The light grew in intensity, flaring like a sun pulled to the ground. It blazed toward us as night fell over the land. In its wake, a singing radiance spread through the forests, leaving every twig and limb sparkling. It looked as if the world had been frosted by warm, gleaming crystals, as joyous as morning rays. The sleeping oaks shimmered with countless pinpoints of light. I was reminded of a summer field filled with fireflies or a new universe bursting into life.

I laughed as the memory returned. "Gullinbursti!" I exclaimed. "I haven't seen him in ages!"

My blood-brother nodded enigmatically and finally released my arm.

Freyr's huge riding-boar flew up the pathway Sigyn and I had shunned, his hooves clinking and striking up sparks as they hit stone. The God of the Feast reined Gullinbursti in near the flags and waved a greeting to Odin. His gold-bristled mount was huffing loudly from the run, his breath steaming in the chilly air. Dancing beams spilled around us, smelling of pine needles and growth.

"Hail the Aesir," Freyr said solemnly.

"Hail the Yule," Odin responded. As the other god dismounted, I strode up to the boar. I crooned soothing words, then reached up to stroke one of the soft, tufted ears.

"It's been a long time, old friend," I murmured. Gullinbursti was another of the prizes I'd once won for the gods long ago; the dwarves had forged him from magic and brought him to life deep within their realm. With a good-natured grunt, the golden boar dug his snout into my shoulder, dribbling saliva all over my fine tunic. I didn't really mind. I gave his ear a vigorous scritching, and the huge animal leaned into my chest, the better to enjoy the attention.

Freyr was watching me with gentle amusement. "He missed you too, Loki."

With a final pat, I left Gullinbursti to his own amusements and followed the other two gods inside.

Bilskirnir was a comfortable hall. Thor was fond of wide, fur-padded chairs and roaring hearths. The oak-beamed ceiling was high and vaulted, and the columned walls were hung with round shields. Off to one side, intricately carved archways opened up onto a stone balcony, offering expansive views of the stormy skies. But within the hall, hundreds of festive candles flickered in the drafts, and garlands of spruce and holly decorated every surface. The hearths were at full blaze. Fine ales and meads gleamed like amber in their horns and goblets.

I strode up to Thor and clasped him on the arm. "Joyous Yule."

"Joyous Yule." The God of Thunder wore his usual green, but his tunic was embroidered with copper and gold oak leaves in honor of the holidays. My friend's eyes widened in mock alarm as he returned my grip. "Loki, your hand is empty! No god may remain sober in my hall!" He pressed a frothing drinking horn on me.

I enjoyed my mead as I drifted among the others. Ullr smiled wordlessly in greeting. He was clad in a snowy white shirt trimmed with silver fur, and seemed to be in a particularly reflective mood that evening. Skathi approached us and gave me a reserved dip of the head before she tapped the God of Joy on the arm. He was laughing heartily by the time she'd led him off to dance with her.

Sigyn found me not much later, and we joined the dancing as well, weaving through complex steps with quick flair and unspeakable elegance. None of the others could match our grace. Who could hope to keep up with us, the God of Fire and his enchanting wife?

When the song ended, a curious despondence settled over me. Despite all the revelry, I could not forget the previous evening.

I took leave of Sigyn and restlessly paced the wide hall, avoiding all conversation. It had been a while since I'd explored Bilskirnir. Before the cave, I had passed many a night under its vaulted ceiling, drinking with Thor. The place hadn't changed much over the years. My friend's home still echoed with laughter and friendly talk, and ready flames still brightened every hearth.

I noticed a couple of treasures I'd never seen before hanging on the walls next to the exit onto the balcony. With a contemplative little smirk, I sidled toward them. A filigreed shield-mount grabbed my attention. It looked quite valuable, and the craftsmanship was superb. Moreover, it was small enough to fit inside my pouch.

As I mentally weighed Thor's fierce temper against the simple joys of an opportune theft, I felt someone's eyes on me. I spun around and made a frustrated noise in my throat.

With a nod, the God of Law deliberately lifted a crystal cup to his lips and took a single sip of white wine, watching me closely. The younger Aesir was garbed in a brilliant red tunic for the holidays. Predictably, it was trimmed with silver.

"Happy Yule," I told him. I didn't even try to hide my irritation.

"And to you." The cool gray eyes never left me.

I fidgeted impatiently, hoping he'd go away. Forseti was having none of that, however.

"Come, enjoy the view with me. The crowds grow tiresome, do they not?"

Grumbling under my breath, I accompanied him out onto the balcony. The sky was dark and all stars were hidden from view, but the sunken valleys and hidden spaces between the trees still glittered with a billion tiny lights. There was a timeless beauty to it all—a quiet, enduring strength. Above, grisly winds moaned, calling for blood. Joy and horror, and life and death: these all met when the sun was at its weakest and the nights at their longest.

Forseti and I stood together, lost in our own thoughts. My time in the cave had changed me more than I had realized. Strangely, I found the silence a relief.

The other god lingered over his wine as if he'd be content to spend most of his night on the balcony. After a while, my usual restiveness caught up with me. My horn was empty and my throat felt dry. The sweet aromas of roasting meat wafted out on the wintry air, reminding me that the Yule feast would begin soon. Succulent hams and crackling trout awaited me, perfectly seasoned to go with the mead. Honeyed sweets and divine fruits would make the tables groan. My mouth watered at the thought of it all. I decided that I'd indulged the God of Law long enough.

"Nice talking to you," I told him with an ironic bow.

Forseti lifted an eyebrow at me. Then his gaze grew distant and changed, becoming closed and defensive.

Odin had appeared at my shoulder. Even now, the God of War carried himself with a certain tension, a readiness to spring to battle. But I saw that something more was going on. The two gods took measure of each other. Their every movement was fraught with suspicion, with unbending Aesir resolve. The family resemblance was uncanny.

I eyed the open doors. Whatever lay between them, I wanted no part of it.

"Loki, stay," my blood-brother ordered. He turned to his grandson. The storm picked up all of a sudden, setting our tunics to flapping, and tugging at our hair. A sharp gust peeled back his long iron locks, revealing the scarred and gorged tissue that disfigured one side of his face.

"The others have asked me to allow Loki to speak of your father." Odin's eye glinted like the merry edge of knife. "Everyone wants me to lift his oath. So, what say you now?"

The younger immortal lowered his head, but there was nothing submissive in the gesture. "I say you already have my answer, Odin."

"Truly? Your decision need not be so... final." A weird howling bubbled up from below, from among the blackened hills and valleys. Wolves were out on the hunt, scourging across Thor's wild lands.

With a reproving grimace, Forseti placed his wineglass down on the stone wall. The rising winds plastered his crimson sleeves against his arms and whipped his gleaming hair about his shoulders.

"What is mine is *mine*," he stated in the coldest of tones. "How many times do I have to I repeat myself, grandfather?"

My blood-brother nodded, then indicated to me that I was to follow him.

Back inside Thor's hall, the other gods were still laughing and celebrating, waiting on the main feast. Many of them had gathered around Bragi to hear his Yule songs.

"What was that all about?" I asked as we made our way toward the mead.

"I'll tell you in a moment."

I stepped to one side to pass Heimdall, who was chatting blithely with Thrud. Thor's auburn-haired daughter was dressed in shimmering gold silk, and she'd replaced her bronze headband with one of gold. Its knotwork was exquisite, and it was set with a single green topaz that sparkled like a dawn star at her brow.

Heimdall's eyes were sparkling as well. He looked especially handsome that night in a snowy Yuletide tunic dusted with crushed gems of every color. I winked at him as I went by, and his grin widened in response.

Odin and I took up fresh horns and headed for a fire pit in the far corner. Deep shadows flicked along the walls and heavy smoke tickled the backs of our throats. My blood-brother stared into the flames as if he could read the future in their writhing depths.

I waited on him, saying nothing. Something about his presence, the presence of another creator god, comforted me. I craved that solace more than any mead.

After a while, he finally spoke. "If bargaining won't work, I'll have to rely on deception," he told me. "The God of Law is stubborn."

I shrugged, not quite following his meaning. "I could have told you that much."

Odin smirked at me without parting his lips—that dangerous, meditative grin he'd so often given me during our adventures together. My blood-brother could stir up at least as much trouble as I could when he was of a mind. He shifted closer to me, speaking with hushed intensity.

"I need a book, Loki. One forgotten tome from Glitner's vast halls."

"Really, Odin?" I sighed. "And that's how you thought to get it? That's... hard. Even for you."

"A book is but a small price to pay for wisdom. I of all of the gods should know."

I couldn't argue with him there.

"Fine." I said. "But where does that leave the rest of us? Forseti's not one to change his mind."

"There are alternatives in any fight. You yourself have snuck into Glitnir before."

I backed up, recoiling at the memory. "Only once! And I won't try it again!"

Honir wandered over to us then, carrying a foamy tankard of Thor's ale. The God of Uncertainty wore a milky tunic trimmed with pewter embroidery. He blinked at us a few times, then coughed and addressed himself to Odin.

"My friend, I've been thinking a great deal the past day."

The mightiest of the gods immediately gave him his full attention.

"Yes, Honir?" he said, very respectfully.

"Well, after what we saw last night...." Honir trailed off, then frowned at me nervously. I waved a hand at him, urging him to continue.

"It's all right. I won't take offense."

Honir coughed again. "I'd just like to say that ambiguity does not suit us. It's all right for me, but it's not good for the gods." The corner of his mouth twitched up in a self-effacing smile. "I think we need to know what really happened with Baldur. We need closure. And consider who's asking, old friend."

My blood-brother nodded slowly. He regarded the two of us for what felt like a very long time. Then he lifted his gaze, taking in the hall.

Sif and Thor bent over the table together, their shoulders almost brushing as they laid the final garnishes on a spit-roasted ham. They were laughing at some shared joke, in high spirits. Further off, my Sigyn tossed back her head with cheerful abandon, her hands linked with Freyr's and Gerd's as the three of them swirled to a jubilant Yule melody. Bragi gave them an indulgent smile, his fingers flying over the strings of his lyre. Idunn had pulled a stool next to his and was snuggled in comfortably against his shoulder. Further off, Thrud nudged Heimdall, and he leaned in to catch something she whispered in his ear.

Standing next to Odin, I sensed something of his thoughts. I saw what he saw: a family. A family that was missing something of itself. A family that had already been through its darkest hour together and then forgotten everything. I knew what my blood-brother's answer would be before he even gave it.

I knew I'd finally be allowed to tell my tale.

The last edges of the storm had vanished. The sky of Thrudheim, Thor's realm, was clear. Bands of stars were strewn across the endless vault, nearer and brighter than any I'd ever seen over Asgard.

We had gathered around a bonfire under that wide sky. The mead and the ale still flowed, but our Aesir instincts had called us out into the open air. Winter breezes pushed against our cloaks, carrying the brittle scents of dead leaves, frosted earth, and burning wood.

Everyone had gathered to hear my story, the story of why a god—a god known for his goodness, forgiveness, and light—had needed to die.

I rested on a log near the fire, one leg stretched out irreverently. I wetted my throat and looked to Odin for permission to begin. Forseti sat next to me, his hands planted on his knees and his face grave. Of all of them, he deserved to be the closest, to hear me the most clearly. When I moved, my elbow sometimes touched his. Side-by-side like that, I couldn't help but feel the gentle, silver-white edge of his power. It was oddly soothing in its way.

The All-Father spoke, his deep voice reverberating over the soft hisses and snaps of the fire.

"Tonight there will be no storms over Thrudheim," he pronounced. "This is both the first and last night of its kind. By my will, much was forgotten. By my will, memory returns to us. The time is right. We must be made whole again."

The eyes of the other immortals shone like jewels in the firelight. Odin paused, and his tone changed, taking on its own power, thrumming with ancient magic.

"Brother of my divine blood, brother in creation, God of Fire and Trickster...." Bizarre energies surged through me as the High One named me, for Odin was the lord of inspiration as well as war.

The All-Father's gaze locked on mine, and much passed between us in those few moments.

"Loki, tell us about Baldur. I release you from your oath."

I began my story.

CHAPTER EIGHTEEN
BALDUR

Asgard Past

Baldur was a newborn the first time I met him. I had not lived among the Aesir long, as gods count the ages. Ymir was but recently slain, and Midgard was still young.

The sun had set over Valhalla and thunder rumbled outside. Great hail stones smacked against the golden shields above, filling the great hall with bings and clangs. I hunched over a table by the All-Father's empty high seat. Every once in a while, Thor would look up and try to include me in a conversation.

The other gods were still reserved, though I shared the highest god's blood and had helped them defeat Ymir. It was not easy for them to warm up to someone born of Jotunheim. I kept my distance. I had accepted Thor's invitations before, and it always ended the same way. The others would grow very quiet and their lively talk trickle off to nothing. Then they would find reasons to be elsewhere. Plausible, sensible reasons all, but ones that had entirely slipped their minds until I'd joined them. I was in no mood to go through the same tired dance again. I drank my mead alone.

Frigg had been in labor for some time, and everyone was feeling tense. The fires of Valhalla smoldered fitfully, kicking up cinders that seemed to burn the lungs. Geri, who was already my friend, lay beside the All-Father's throne, his muzzle pillowed across his paws and his yellow eyes rolling with worry. Every once in a while, he whimpered. Huginn, Muninn, and Freki were nowhere to be seen. Perhaps they kept Odin company or guarded Frigg in her labor.

I drank some more and the others chatted. Eventually, we heard the tread of iron-clad boots drawing closer and closer, audible over the hail.

Thor was up in a flash. He darted to his father's side. Odin wore his steel battle helmet and a full shirt of chain mail. The brooding God of War cradled a linen-wrapped bundle in his arms. It neither stirred nor cried, and we all feared the worst, seeing him standing there with that motionless child.

"Hail the Aesir." The All-Father's voice was subdued, but it carried over the storm. "I present my son, Baldur, to you this night. Thor, bring me a bowl of water so I may finish his naming." The red-bearded warrior thudded away and was back in little time. Odin sprinkled glittering waters over his son. "I name you Baldur," he said formally, completing the ritual.

He looked at me. "Loki, come forward. It is proper that a male child learn from his uncle. Pledge yourself to guiding him."

I pulled myself to my feet, leaving my horn behind. I stepped forward proudly and laid my hand on the newborn's head.

"I pledge it, my lord."

That night, I actually felt grateful. My blood-brother was making much of me in front of the other gods. Little did I know how that baby would seal my fate.

The child still did not cry. I leaned in, peering at the small creature, my eyes dark and curious. His skin shone intensely, like sunlight on snow, and his hair was spun gold.

Baldur grew up swiftly, as was a god's nature. We often took long walks together through the forests. Tyr taught him the ways of the sword and Ullr led him on the hunt, but there was much that I was bound to impart to him, the more so when his father was off at war or away delving into the affairs of mortals.

My nephew soon began acting strangely around me. His fair lips often pursed, and his flawless blue eyes glinted with disapproval.

As we made our way along, we were stalked by every kind of bird. The air was thick with clouds of butterflies seeking proximity to the boy. Tree limbs dipped low, hoping to touch their leaves to his cheek, and flowers sprang up eagerly wherever his feet fell, bending to honor his passing.

"Today we'll try you on rune spells," I told the beautiful child. "See that stone, alone in the field? What if it were a giant? What would you cast at it?"

"The others say *you're* a giant, Uncle Loki." Baldur barely reached my waist, but he spoke to me as boldly as any adult.

"Yes. I was, long ago. Your father and I shared blood, and I'm an Aesir now as surely as you are."

"No, you're still a giant," he told me coldly. I stiffened at his words. My nephew's clear blue eyes were cutting into me, seeming to chip away at my very soul. "You're not really one of us, are you?" he continued relentlessly. "You're different. The others have light hair, but yours is as dark as a crow's wing. And when trouble comes, it's *always* because of you!"

"You'll show me respect, Baldur, or I'll make you show it!" I raised my hand, ready to slap the little brat right across his perfect, curving jaw. He only laughed. My blood twisted upon itself and froze in my veins.

"Just what will you do to me? All my father's creation protects me! See, like this!" The butterflies rushed forward in a blinding wave, the twittering birdsong changed into a roar, and furry shapes surged out of the woods like a tide. I screamed in pain as a thousand tiny beaks stabbed into my flesh and a thousand more flashing teeth sank into my legs. It was too much, even for an Aesir. I turned on my heel and fled. Baldur's giggles echoed cruelly behind me.

I stormed up to Odin's throne that night, my mouth pressed into an angry line. My blood-brother watched me closely. His eye reflected back the hearth light, showing nothing of his thoughts. He frowned at me.

"Something disturbs you, God of Fire?"

I held out my arm and pulled back the red sleeve of my tunic, revealing my many scars. "Your son set his animals on me! See, I'm still bleeding!"

"Did you not raise your hand to him?"

"I did. He was being insolent."

The Hanged God just stared at me, not twitching a muscle. I waited, not moving either.

"You cannot handle a child?" he asked at last.

"I'll handle him, all right!"

"Enough. I'll speak with Baldur. The bond between a child and his uncle must not be broken. You will take him out tomorrow, and he will heed your lessons."

"As you say, my lord."

"Do not try to hit my son again, Loki," Odin added, his voice turning as cold and fierce as a wintry field of slaughter. "I myself will pay you in kind for every blow dealt."

Prophetic words, though I didn't know it at the time.

I licked my lips and backed away nervously. The God of War never voiced an idle threat.

Baldur danced over to me the next day, an open smile lighting up his face. He jumped up, performed a spin in the air, then flew forward and wrapped his smaller hand around my agile fingers.

"I'm sorry, Uncle Loki," he apologized. I blinked at him, surprised by the complete turn-around. I listened for any hint of sarcasm, but as he continued speaking, there was nothing but sincerity in his tone. "I was mistaken. I shouldn't have listened to the others." The warm, bright hand squeezed mine hopefully. "Do you forgive me?"

"Of course I forgive you," I replied, remembering Odin's orders. But something fluttered within my breast—an unpleasant premonition. I ignored the feeling and told my nephew which runes he might use to soften another's heart, to cajole an enemy to lay down his sword. His crystal-blue eyes were wide and attentive.

From then on, Baldur was good company. Soon enough, his beard came in, as golden as his hair. Our training was done. He knew much of magic and the blade, and he went off on journeys with Tyr to fight the giants. With my mornings free, I explored the strange and beautiful lands along the borders of Asgard, wandering further afield than I ever had before.

One day, I found myself near the realm of the Light Elves. I grinned to myself as I dodged around a stone trapped with fey magic, enjoying the challenge to my wits. Gentle singing seemed to tickle at my ears just below the range of hearing. Honeyed rays streamed between the tree trunks, and the shimmying leaves glowed with ancient charms. I sensed many presences around me: some curious, others ambivalent, and some hostile. All had a very peculiar feel to them. They were neither gods nor mortals, and they hid themselves from view.

I discovered an entangling web of thin, innocuous-looking roots and leapt out of the way before they could snare me.

"Well spotted!" exclaimed a happy feminine voice. The pitter-patter of clapping sounded from nearby. I straightened up quickly and looked about, but I saw nothing.

"Are you an Alfar?" I asked the rustling leaves and tossing silver grasses. "I am a god, yet I do not see you!"

"Up here!" the voice giggled.

I stepped over to a vast oak tree. A goddess had nestled herself into the secure crook where a large bough parted from the trunk. She kicked her bare feet back and forth merrily. Her hair was a deep, chestnut brown, and she wore a dress that was almost the same color. It was embroidered with gold.

I thought she was quite pretty. The day was beginning to show some real promise.

"Fairly met, lovely one," I said. I raised a hand in greeting.

"Well met," she agreed. Her gray eyes sparkled, full of mirth. "Who are you?" she asked after a bit. "I've never seen you in these fields."

"Loki son of Farbauti, blood-brother to the highest god himself!"

She touched her fingers to her mouth. "An Aesir!" she exclaimed. "Hail and welcome!"

"I'd feel more welcome if you'd come down from that tree," I suggested with a grin. The beautiful goddess nodded and landed next me, as sure-footed as any cat. Up close, I could feel the Alfar energies on her. The sense of them was intoxicating. Beguiling.

"I'm Sigyn," she told me, holding out a pretty hand. I took it, raised it to my lips, and let the kiss linger just a tad longer than was strictly appropriate. Her responding laugh was sweeter than any music.

"I've heard of you, Loki son of Farbauti" she told me. "You're a god of fire."

"You heard correctly. And you, my shining star, what is your story?"

"I live in these lands, and I bring joy and victory to the earth—and to the Alfar." She let her head fall to one side charmingly. "I've met only one Aesir before. A god named Freyr. He often comes to our realm."

"What did you think of him?" Before that moment, I'd never disliked Freyr. But jealousy suddenly blazed through my chest.

Sigyn shrugged indifferently. "I think you're more interesting, God of Fire. I can tell that you know the ways of magic as well as the dance of the flames."

"Yes, I do. We should walk together, you and I, and discuss these things." My tone was light, but my eyes burned. The goddess was very attractive.

I held out an arm to her and she took it. She skipped as we made our way along, sometimes disengaging from me long enough to twirl about before she ran back over to lock her arm in mine once more. At one point, she pressed her cheek against my shoulder. Her smile was unaffected and content.

As the sun dropped behind the hills, I raised her hand to my breast and placed it against my heart. "I'd very much like to see you again, Sigyn."

"I'd like that too."

"Tomorrow, then?"

"Yes. Can you find your way back to the tree?"

"For you, dear one, I could find my way through the eternal and featureless flames of Muspelheim."

Her modest giggle was an enchantment, and it made my blood sing.

Back in Valhalla, I helped myself to a large horn of mead and started a throwing game with Geri, tossing him a heavy bone which he'd tirelessly fetch and return to me. I was practically falling over myself for the good mood I was in.

Thor finally couldn't take it anymore. He excused himself from the other gods and stomped over to me. "You're in a rare humor, Loki," he noted.

"Quite right." I flipped the bone into the air, and Geri launched himself up on his hind legs to snatch it between his heavy fangs. With a satisfied growl, he hit the floor and brought it back to my waiting hand.

Thor stared at me expectantly. "Well?" he said at last.

"Well what?"

His eyes narrowed, flashing with the quick, darting heat of lightning. "Just spit it out, already!"

I gave him a mischievous little smile. "As you say, friend Thunderer. If you must know, I met a goddess today. She was very smart and was not a strain on the eyes either."

The mighty warrior's face lit up and his expression became very approving. "Who was she?"

"Sigyn."

"Never heard of her."

"She lives near the Alfar lands."

Thor coughed at that, looking somewhat uncomfortable. He had never been much for the tricks and intrigues of the Light Elves.

"Come, take your mead with us," he said. "I want the full tale." I lifted my eyebrows, but I knew better than to argue with the Thunder God.

"Keep the bone, Geri," I told Odin's wolf. He panted at me cheerfully.

With the towering bulk of Thor to my right, I wetted my throat and began to speak of Sigyn. I soon warmed to my topic. Freyr regarded me with even more interest than the others. I met his gaze and my mouth curved down with displeasure.

"God of the Feast, she did say she knows *you*."

Freyr shrugged. "It's true. We're friends."

I didn't like that at all. Those were still the days before Freyr had snuck into Odin's forbidden hall, peered through the realms, and fallen madly in love with Gerd. Later on, his heart would belong entirely to her. Back then, he'd had no goddess or giantess of his own.

"What sort of friends?" I demanded.

"Loki, shut up," interrupted Thor. "That's his business. You just met her."

But Freyr's amber eyes were tranquil. "No, Lord Thunderer. The first love is always the hardest. I have no designs on your goddess." He tipped his golden mead horn to me. "Fortune to you, God of Fire."

I settled back down, mollified. Freyr had been one of the Vanir, the gods of success and prosperity. His blessing carried much weight.

"That's right," mused Thor. "This is your first time smitten, isn't it, Loki?"

"I think it's your turn to shut up."

He guffawed loudly and gave me what he considered a companionable pat on the back. I barely kept my seat from his demonstration of friendly solidarity.

"Speaking of young love," murmured Tyr, looking past us.

Baldur had entered with gentle Nanna, his new wife, on his arm. Her blonde hair fell down her back, woven into a braid as thick as her wrist, and her mid-section was already filling out with her swift pregnancy. My nephew nodded to us, then led her over to the table. He sat down and Nanna poured him his mead, though we had plenty of servants in that hall. Odin's bright-haired son thanked her, then slipped his cloak off and folded it with great care. He placed it over the bench beside him to soften her seat. A pink blush rose to Nanna's cheeks. She took her place at his side, her sky-blue eyes shining with happiness.

The other gods were determined to fill Baldur in on my day. I noticed that my nephew's flawless lips pursed whenever a mention of the Alfar realm was made. But he said nothing untoward.

Sigyn and I met the next morning, and the morning after. The years flew by, a mere blink to us gods. I ventured to Midgard, sometimes with Thor, and sometimes with Odin and Honir. It was back in those days that we found the ash trees on the shore and created mortals.

I had just returned home to Asgard one evening when Baldur's son approached me, entirely alone. I was making fast headway through the pine groves, my mind already on flowing horns of mead, when I came up short. A teenaged Aesir stood in my way. His wavy, silver locks gleamed in the frail light, and his gray eyes were cold and grim. He was dressed in a dazzling white tunic threaded with silver to match his hair.

"Hail, Forseti. It's been some time. What do you want?"

He didn't answer immediately. He just hung there in the middle of the trail, blocking my path.

I started to get angry. "Speak or move. Pick one."

The young Aesir lowered his head, his strong jaw clenched. "They say you can break any bond." His voice was liquid and somber.

I stared at him. "You're thinking of Odin, not me," I said at last. "The All-Father has that magic."

His eyes flickered, full of shadows. "How about shapechanging?" he asked.

"That I can do. As can Odin."

"Then turn me into something." He sounded every bit as imperious as his father.

"Like what?" I snapped, exasperated. My journey had been tiring, and I was in no mood for adolescent games.

"Anything. I—I don't care... I...." Silent, unshed tears brimmed in the other god's eyes. I paused, then stepped forward and began to reach out a hand. But my perceptions told me not to touch him. A touch would only bring him greater injury. Pain flowed around and through him. I sensed the edges of it, circling and hopeless. I could have been standing before a giant, not a god. There wasn't the slightest trace of Aesir joy left in him.

"Forseti," I said in a very quiet voice. "What's this all about?"

He lashed his head back and forth, saying nothing. For a heartbeat or so, he remained in the middle of the path, shaking, his fists balled up so hard that a drop of blood, and then another, trickled from between his fingers, falling to strike the dirt. With an inhuman sound, half sob and half scream, he set one foot after the other and fled into the trees.

I considered following him and thought better of it. I'd only hurt his pride when I caught up with him.

The young god had grown quickly, I reflected. I had only been in Midgard a little while, and he was already on the cusp of manhood. My thoughts were sour by the time I arrived at Odin's hall. Asgard was eternal, yet time marched on.

I guzzled down my mead without tasting it. After a few horns, I took to drinking the dark, rib-tickling beer that Thor preferred. It better suited my gloomy disposition.

The next morning, I sat by Sigyn in her tree, my agile legs dangling over the coarse bark. I was still in a foul temper. Rippling waves of ensorcelled light teased their way through the grasses below us, humming weird melodies.

"What wrong, Loki?" asked the goddess I cherished.

"Everything is changing," I told her.

"You're born of the storm's fire. Surely change does not scare you?"

"It doesn't as long as I bring it." I exhaled heavily. "We should get married, you and I."

She had the good sense not to laugh, but her gray eyes danced. "You're just being silly because you've been away too long."

"I mean my own words. Don't take them so lightly."

"Who will be our witness? Var? We both know you'll keep no wedding vow." She snuggled in and kissed me on the cheek. Sigyn was no more troubled by my nature than she was by the nature of anything else around us. She did not expect the tree to bury its branches in the ground and arch its roots to the sky; she did not expect the God of Fire to be a faithful mate.

I lifted her palm to my lips. "You're right, and I won't. But love is something, is it not? Even without loyalty?"

The intelligent, fey goddess considered my words, her perfect brow furrowing. "Would you ask me to give what you cannot?"

"What does that mean?"

"You were jealous of Freyr. Even when there was nothing to be jealous of."

"I had just met you, Sigyn. Things were different then. Your will is your own, and no god can take it from you. Not even one you might marry?" I let the question linger between us.

Delicate fingers finally brushed my own, tentative and unsure. I leaned over and whispered words meant only for her into her ear. Her fingers tightened around mine until there was no longer any doubt left in her glorious eyes.

Months later, I paid Forseti a visit. The weather was dreary, and damp gusts blew at my cloak. The God of Law was standing on a high stone overlooking the sodden green meadows surrounding Glitnir. The river raged in its course, swollen from the rains.

With an easy bound, I landed beside the other Aesir, then did a double take. For all our powers, his tunic was soaked through, his pale skin glistening under the cloth. His hair was lank and wet, and his expression was every bit as bleak as Odin's had ever been. It was not a natural look on one so young.

I eyed him for some injury, but saw none. I did, however, observe goose bumps where one sleeve had pulled back a bit from the wrist.

"Loki," he said in an uninflected, sepulchral voice.

"You're cold, Forseti." I murmured a rune, and the air around him warmed. His face didn't change.

"Do the others know what you're going through?" I asked.

"Less than you do. And you know next to nothing."

"So tell me. Maybe I can help."

"Even Grandfather can't help. My burden is my own." His shoulders fell, just a little, and the hardest of the hard lines lifted from his visage. He was still a grim and serious young god, but he no longer seemed entirely lost. "What do you want, Trickster?"

"Legal advice."

His eyes locked onto mine. "You're a criminal by almost any code from any world. How's that for legal advice?" His tone was curiously bitter.

"Accurate enough. But that's not what I'm after. I seek to be married without swearing it before Var."

"Ah, yes. Why stop with petty theft when adultery is so alluring?"

"Just answer my question, Forseti."

He frowned. "Fine. It would hardly be right for you to be denied what any other may have on the mere account of your nature. I can't abide unfairness. I myself will conduct your wedding—if Odin approves of it, of course."

"You, Forseti?"

"Why not me?"

I shook my head, amazed. "Your own father has no use for Sigyn. He says so little, and yet I so hear much."

"This is my hall, not his."

"You'd go against his wishes? For me?" The drizzly winds beat at my face.

The other immortal's gray eyes bore the gallows in them. "No, Loki, not for you. For justice. I'd stand against the All-Father himself if I had to, for justice."

I made a face. Still, I held out my hand to Forseti and he reluctantly clasped my arm, sealing his promise. Although he was a scholar, his grip was iron, almost painful. I didn't mind.

CHAPTER NINETEEN
THE APPLES

Asgard Past

It was the golden age of the gods, the dawnlike times before harsher epochs fell upon us. The massive walls of Asgard had been rebuilt, and we possessed the dwarven treasures I had so craftily won for us. Thor had his hammer, Odin his fearsome spear, and Freyr his golden boar. Not that anyone had been noticeably grateful. My lips still ached from Brokk and Eitri's needle some nights.

Our realm was finally secure. Odin traveled far and wide, riding eight-legged Sleipnir—another of my gifts to him—through all the worlds. But even the mightiest of the Aesir occasionally yearned for home. When he returned, we'd hold council among the bright trees of Gladsheim.

My nephew had many opinions, and he always wanted to share them with the rest of us. I was actually grateful for my blood-brother's wanderings. Thanks to Odin, we did not meet in the grove often. When we did, our gatherings dragged on longer than they ever had before and accomplished far less.

I drummed my fingers on my armrest as Baldur approached the oath-ring yet again. His snowy tunic was almost blinding in that holy place, and his voice was like honey or a welcome from a cherished friend.

"Power is dangerous," the handsome Aesir announced. His blue eyes were practically on fire. "I ask all of you here, who has power like unto us, the true gods?"

Ullr and Bragi listened attentively. Thor grunted, jiggling his keys on his knee. The Thunderer clearly longed to be off on his own adventures, Mjolnir back in hand. I wished I were somewhere else too.

My nephew continued on with his pompous droning while I made a show of letting my eyes wander and yawning hugely.

"I propose that we henceforth mete out our power with greater care," Baldur finally concluded. "Every god must answer to all the others. We will then have a lasting peace."

The All-Father stirred. His cloak was draped over his knee and the top of his tunic was untied. He had made himself comfortable, settling deep into his own enchanted chair. His patience with Baldur seemed nearly infinite.

"We've been at peace some time now," Odin said. "What truly worries you, my son?"

"Ragnarok. It may come at any time."

"You seek to stop it?" My blood-brother's tone was genuinely curious.

"I do. Moreover, I have a plan. Ask yourselves this, wise gods: how could we ever take up arms against each other if we were required to turn to our brothers for our very lives?"

My nephew did not look at me, but I felt his thoughts aimed in my direction like ready arrows.

We Aesir had powers with dreams and prophecies. Even back then, there were hints that I would one day fight against Asgard, that I would betray the gods and stand beside the flame-giant Surt at the very end.

Fire to fire.

"How would this plan of yours work?" Honir asked. He shifted forward, his mousy blonde hair falling against his shoulders. For once, he sounded more reserved than Odin. His plain beige tunic glowed warmly in the sacred grove, taking on the beauty of sunlit wheat. Nothing remained untouched in Gladsheim.

Baldur inclined his head to the other Aesir. "We shall transfer all our power to a vessel and draw from it together each morning."

I flinched, thinking of my magic.

"Your plan is too dangerous," I said. "What if your... vessel gets lost, Baldur? What then? Thor over there would be as weak as a mortal. I bet Jotunheim would thank you, though!"

My friend grunted, not liking the turn our discussion had taken.

Baldur made a dismissive gesture. "I know of only one thief in Asgard." The God of Good raised his voice, addressing the others. "I trust no one *else* opposes my idea?"

Forseti sat three chairs to my left. He hunched his shoulders miserably, but didn't object. The silver-haired Aesir had only recently come of age and joined our assembly. His youth made him hesitant. He almost never spoke up unless a matter of law was involved.

In too little time, Baldur's motion carried. All our might was willed into a few dozen shining apples chosen from one of our loveliest orchards. The fruit was of gold, as beautiful as any treasure, but I was not impressed. Our loss was too great. The sacrifice was too profound.

Odin asked the goddess Idunn to watch over the apples. Bragi's wife was as gracious as her husband. Like him, she was loathe to take sides in any dispute. She was also focused, attentive, and precise. She would be as careful with our power as the God of Song himself was with his stringed instruments.

My nephew was surprised by Odin's decision.

"Idunn?" he asked. "You'd have Idunn protect the fruit?" His fair brows lowered in consternation.

"My choice troubles you?"

"No, father. Only... Idunn lacks neither skill nor concentration." Here, he nodded to Bragi. "But she is an innocent. I would suggest that we find a more worldly guardian for our apples."

Even Idunn's husband could not argue with his logic. Bragi smiled thoughtfully into his curly beard. "Baldur does have a point," he admitted to us. "My Idunn is the sweetest of all the sweet goddesses. She believes everyone to be as good as she is."

Odin moved his fingers only slightly, but he immediately caught our attention. "The decision is mine, and it is made."

Months passed by. With each new sunrise, I rankled at how I had to stand in line with the others beside the Well of Urd, waiting for the gentle goddess to dole out my power.

Was I an Aesir, or was I one of Freya's cats mewing for its breakfast?

I decided that they all needed a sharp lesson. I hadn't settled on one idea or another when, out of the blue, I fell into the clutches of a Jotun named Thiazi.

Thiazi was viciously clever, and he had a ready mind for magic. Normally, he would never have been able to capture me, but thanks to Baldur, I was hardly at my best. One anemic fruit per day was a sorry replacement for godhood.

The giant shapechanged himself into an enormous eagle and dragged me all about the realms until he had beaten me within an inch of my life. Battered and bruised, I finally agreed to make a deal with him.

I delivered trusting Idunn straight to him, along with the wooden box holding our golden apples. For the first time ever, the gods aged. Immortality itself was a divine power, we soon learned.

All was not lost. I borrowed Freya's hawk-feather cloak and easily recovered the goddess and her fruit. A frustrated Thiazi chased me all the way back to Asgard and flew straight over our walls in his eagle form. We lit bonfires under him, killing him on the spot.

The morning after I'd saved Idunn from the giant, I strode up to accept my pittance. My lips were curled up in a scornful sneer, and my dark eyes glinted unpleasantly. The simple, unadorned box was open, and the apples sparkled in the morning sun.

Baldur, Thor, and Bragi closed in on me, shielding the young goddess from my reach.

"Go away, Loki," Baldur ordered. His hair glowed in the Well's light and his jaw was set. "There is nothing for you here."

"Breaking your own rules already, nephew? May not all the gods eat in turn?"

Everyone seemed to be watching me. No one answered my question. Even the songbirds stopped singing.

Bragi finally spoke up. His face was ravaged and his long beard was disheveled. I had never seen him angry before, but his melodic voice now trembled with raw fury.

"You handed my wife off to a *giant*, Loki! My own Idunn! She won't tell me anything about her time away, but I can see it was the sheerest agony!"

"I got her back, didn't I?"

He turned to Thor, his eyes haunted and imploring.

The Thunderer's hand was wrapped so tightly around Mjolnir's short handle that his knuckles had whitened from the strain. Thor and I had fought together many times and had traveled many lands, but his stormy eyes were truly frightening that morning. A rumble built in his chest, promising me great hurt.

"Go away, Loki," Baldur repeated. "Go, and suffer just as we did. You must pay for all your evil."

I glared at him, then looked over my shoulder to appeal to Odin. The All-Father was nowhere to be seen.

"No help there, God of Lies," my nephew told me.

"Thor?" I said, "Surely you see how this is really Baldur's fault? We shouldn't have to beg for what is rightfully ours!"

But he only growled into his auburn beard and hefted his hammer.

The gods jeered at me as I settled myself onto a sunlit stone. My knees were already feeling shaky and when the breeze caught my hair, I saw that gray strands peppered my ebony locks. Sigyn padded over, concerned, and Baldur trailed after her, his face a mask. She leaned in very close and started to offer me a bite from her apple.

My nephew uttered an unfamiliar word of magic. The fruit jerked out of her hand and spiraled away, dispersing into shards of light.

"Do not try that again, Sigyn. Justice must be done."

My love shook her head with ferocious intensity. Above us, the red-gold leaves rippled and bobbed on their stems like frothing waves, surging with all the life and power of Asgard—the exact same power we gods should have had for ourselves.

Baldur paced around my goddess, to my other side, and laid an immaculate hand on my shoulder. I would have struck him with fire then and there, but my flesh felt so wispy. My bones were cold and frail, as brittle as chalk.

"Fellow Aesir, look at the Mischief Maker now." My nephew's faultless blue eyes fixed on me, alight with a strange sort of compassion meant for me alone. He sighed heavily. "See how his hands turn to dry parchment and quiver? How his knees give out beneath him?"

The other gods shuffled nervously. Thor slipped his hammer back onto his belt with a troubled frown.

"There will be no further thefts," Baldur continued. "Our apples are safe." He paused reflectively, then raised his voice so it would carry throughout the grove. "*We* are safe! There will be no Ragnarok!"

"Tell it to Surt!" I snarled up at him. An instant later, I doubled over coughing.

My bastard of a nephew actually patted me reassuringly, his touch soothing me through the cloth of my tunic.

"It saddens me that you cannot share in our joy," he whispered. His light—the sense of his presence—flowed through me. I shuddered, thoroughly sickened and utterly comforted all at once.

Nanna glided forward to join her husband. "Who is like unto Baldur, the gentlest and fairest of all the gods?" she asked. The others lowered their heads.

"No one," murmured Bragi, wiping a single tear from his cheek. "No one at all. Baldur is the best of us."

Nanna favored him with a soft, satisfied smile. Sigyn's gray eyes were steel, but she kept silent.

Baldur ignored them and walked over to my goddess. "I am sorry for how you must feel, watching your beloved weaken. We will not let him die. You have my word on it."

She inclined her head, her mouth still pressed into a defiant line.

"You may go now, Sigyn. I know how you miss your forests."

Condescending wretch.

The goddess I had hoped to marry shook her head, trying to resist the command. But she seemed ill at ease, as if the gesture were costing her.

I took her hand and brushed her palm with my scratchy, weakened fingers. "Go for my sake, not his," I told her. "I can't stand for you to see me like this, my star. It will only get worse." I wanted to say more, but I started coughing again.

She bent down, kissed me lightly on the forehead, and spun away. Her small face was etched with pain.

Baldur was surveying the other gods as if he and not Odin were their ruler. I narrowed my eyes and scowled up at him from my rock.

"My one friend here is gone, nephew. Will you keep your promise?"

"Always. No lies ever taint my tongue, Trickster."

The other gods drifted away. Baldur remained with me and offered me his well-muscled arm. I could no longer stand without his help.

"We must find a place for you to rest," he said. "My own hall, Breidablik, will not have you, of course. No unclean thing may dwell there."

"I bathe more often than Thor does."

My nephew smiled dutifully at the joke, but without any true humor. I was reminded of the slick sheen of a mirror, of how its metallic reflection obscures whatever is hidden behind it.

"Come along, uncle. Perhaps the fires of Valhalla will comfort you."

"That's a long journey."

"It is. And yet we made it every day when Idunn languished with your friend Thiazi. We had only our staffs to lean upon, Loki. No one could help us when we were all thralls to old age."

Baldur was calm. So calm. The God of Light guided me along the path and helped me maneuver my trembling feet over a difficult root. His face was patient and his arm was steady.

Fury gnawed at my stomach. What a self-righteous, two-faced, manipulative piece of...

I felt a pulse then, like the first beat of a heart.

Baldur blinked and peered about in confusion. The trees went still, and all the birds stopped chirping.

I felt the surge again, even stronger than before. I halted and lifted my chin, inhaling deeply. The air was somehow different all of a sudden. Charged and fresh. Alive.

All at once, the sky exploded into song. A great wind rushed through the treetops, as wild as the roaring sea, as free as a pack of wolves loosened on the hunt.

There was a third pulse. With it, all my power flooded back into me.

I yanked my arm out of Baldur's grip. My nephew gasped, his face paling with shock. He spun on me, his mouth open with disbelief.

"Surely you couldn't have—"

I threw back my head and laughed at him.

"Not me, you fool! Didn't you wonder where the All-Father has been all this time?"

The other god stared at me, horrified. "But we had all agreed—no, he wouldn't...."

I was slapping my hand against my leg, caught up in the hilarity of it all.

"Oh, but he would! The Aesir are the Aesir again!" I exclaimed.

With an exuberant shout, I jumped into the air and flashed into the shape of a crow. I sped away over the trees, rolling and cawing, shedding black feathers in my wake.

The last sound I heard from below was Baldur's choked sob.

CHAPTER TWENTY

SKATHI

Asgard Past

Thiazi the giant was dead. With every god and goddess restored to wholeness, we turned our attention to the Jotun's rotting body. Thiazi had flown over Asgard's walls shifted into his favorite false form, that of a huge golden eagle. His corpse was substantial, and it was already beginning to stink.

"Doesn't he have a daughter?" Thor asked as he kicked one of the burnt eagle toes with his heavy boot.

"That wasn't something we discussed when he was dragging me about!" I responded, grinning despite myself. I was in the best of moods that day. "You spend more time in Jotunheim than I do, Mighty Thunderer."

"Yeah. And you spend more time with their women. I figured you'd know the genealogies by now."

I put a hand to my breast, pretending to take offense. But I quickly fell to chortling. My full Aesir strength was back, and my unbridled magic danced through my veins. All was right again in Asgard. Thor gave me a good-natured smile. He said nothing of the apples, but relief was plain on his face as well.

What could compare to being a god, resplendent and free, the complete master of his own power?

I tapped my foot against a curling talon that was as long as I was tall. The keratin was the dark color of granite. "Let's just light him on fire again," I suggested. Because I could, I called flickering yellow flame to my hand. It spread up my fingers as if they were wicks. I grinned again broadly.

"Fire. That's your damned solution to everything, Loki. No, with a giant this size, you'll scorch the grass so bad it will never grow back. We'd better dump him off somewhere."

I arched a cynical eyebrow at my companion. "Certainly, friend Thor. As long as you do the lifting."

He took stock of the gods on hand. "Heimdall and Tyr," he decided, "you two get the legs. Njord and Ullr on wings. I'll take the head."

"Careful of the beak, Lord Thunderer," Tyr said. I stepped aside to let him grasp the vast, scaly eagle toes with his golden hand. The warrior god braced his legs and found a solid grip after a few tries. He was sweating by the time he had wrestled the foot off the ground.

I watched with relaxed amusement while they fought to move the body. Thor was the strongest, and he hefted Thiazi's feathered head with little problem. But the others were not doing so well.

"Anytime you need a cheery blaze just give me a shout!" I told them with a lazy wave.

"Shut up, Loki!" rumbled Thor, his arms straining as he kept the head aloft.

"Good—idea—" Ullr puffed. "Fire—I—mean."

"Are we Aesir or are we mortals? Set your shoulders to it!" Thor ordered.

Odin approached us then. His single eye gleamed mysteriously, and he was clad in his usual blue-gray. He wore one of his wide-brimmed traveling hats and held his gnarled walking stick at his side.

"A fine day for sport, my friends, but I need you to assemble in Glitnir's fields. Thiazi's daughter has arrived, and she seeks recompense for her father's death."

Thor uttered a curse and dropped the eagle head. It struck the grass with a thud that shook earthworms from the soil. "What do we owe her?" he demanded loudly. "This monster stole Idunn and attacked Asgard! I'll pay her with Mjolnir if I pay her at all!"

"No. We have obligations," Odin said softly. "We will fulfill them." There was no arguing with him when he took that tone. Thor shook his head and fell in behind his father.

Skathi, the Jotun Thiazi's child, awaited us beside Forseti's rock. A slicing wind, frigid and forlorn, blew through her grayish blonde hair. She wore an austere dress of unbleached wool, and no jewels sparkled from her fingers or neck. Her eyes were red from tears, and her lips were cold and bloodless.

"Lord Odin," she said in greeting. Her voice was the winter, the falling of deadly stones from the heights.

"Skathi," he replied gently. He stepped forward and kissed her on each cheek. The others and I traded long looks. Something was up.

The giantess was very wealthy for all that she dressed so plainly. She would accept no wergeld from us. No, she wanted an Aesir husband and a bellyful of laughter for her pains. The All-Father, for some twisted reason of his own, seemed entirely too willing to give her these two things. He asked only that she pick her husband by his feet.

Technically, I was still single. I was more intelligent than the others and, catching a hint of where things were going, I soundlessly inched away from the group. I eyed the sheltering outcroppings of stone and the thick tussocks of spindly grass, seeking a place to conceal myself. I already had a wife in mind, and it was not that grim giantess.

I sang a rune under my breath, the beginnings of a spell that would transform me into a common sparrow. Odin's voice cut through my magic.

"Loki, get over here. You too, Baldur."

"I'm already wed!" the Hanged God's favorite son objected.

"A high-born man can have a number of wives, can he not?"

Baldur hung his head and made no answer. Skathi was favoring him with a pondering, possessive look. She knew exactly which god she wanted.

Grumbling, I removed my boots and took a spot beside Forseti. The God of Law met my gaze. His gray eyes were profoundly disturbed.

"Can he really do this?" I asked the younger Aesir.

"Odin's decrees carry," he whispered back. "Nonetheless, I feel like chattel right now."

"You and me both. You know who I'd have, if I must be married at all."

Forseti leveled me with a chilly little smile. "I am certain that Skathi, at least, will insist that you take your vows before Var. What would you do then, God of Fire? Var is quick to punish those who stray outside their marriage!"

I blanched at that. "The giantess had best pick you!" I hissed back. "You're both made of ice and ruthless to the core!"

"I serve the law and the law alone! I want no wife!"

We glared at each other. Fortunately, by then Skathi had made her choice based entirely upon our feet, and it wasn't me.

Njord was a handsome god. His slate-gray hair was the color of thunderclouds over the ocean, and his build was strong. Garbed in his velvet tunic trimmed with colorful pearls, he looked ready for a wedding. The kind god of prosperous winds, bountiful trade, and calm seas beamed welcomingly to Skathi, his bride. But his smile died as he saw her expression. Her eyes glittered with fury.

Skathi now had a husband, but she wanted her promised laugh as well. At the best of times, it would have been no easy thing to bring joy to those cold lips, but she had just failed to acquire Baldur for her very own.

Naturally, fulfilling the second part of Odin's deal fell to me. There are stories about the occasion. They may be true, or they may not be true. The entertainments of gods and giants are not always meant for mortal understanding.

In the end, our brumal visitor did indeed laugh. She laughed much less after nine days in Njord's hall. Soon, the two were separated, but Skathi was by then a full Aesir, a goddess in her own right.

Some time later, after Sigyn and I had celebrated our own wedding and I had returned from another trip to Midgard, I sat drinking in Valhalla. The night was a particularly cold one, but our servants had warmed the mead and mulled it with heady spices. Bragi was playing an elaborate tune on a flute while Thor's daughter, Thrud, kept his beat on a hide-skin drum. I watched the other gods come and go, not joining in on any particular conversation. The music was excellent and the fires were bright. It was a good evening to be in Odin's hall.

"May I sit with you?" asked a steady, dispassionate voice. It might have been Forseti's, except it was decidedly feminine. I found myself meeting Skathi's frosty gaze.

"Of course, lady," I replied graciously. I gestured expansively at the bench, and she took a place a polite distance away. Her colorless, narrow lips were curved down.

"No one here likes me much," she noted in a clinical tone.

"One can't like what one never sees. How often do you leave Thrymheim, goddess?"

She shrugged and pulled a soft cape trimmed with white fur closer about her shoulders. "Rarely," she admitted. "I make the councils at Vingolf."

"All work and no play?"

She sighed. "You made me laugh once when I thought I would never laugh again. I could use some more laughter now."

I smiled at her shrewdly, my raven-black hair falling past my cheek, hiding the hints of the mischief I was thinking up. "You could use a friend as well, Skathi," I told her.

"I could at that."

"A Goddess of Ice and a God of Fire. Who could think of a better pair? Have some mead with me and drink to it!"

She gave me a startled little laugh and accepted a crystal glass of Asgard's golden, honeyed wine.

"To friendship," I said, raising my drinking horn.

"To friendship," she agreed.

We talked of the wild forests and of the practicalities of journeying in mountain terrain. Geri shuffled up to beg a tidbit of boar off me, and I introduced him to my new ally. He panted happily as she scratched his pointy ears.

"Don't bother with Freki," I advised her. "He answers to no one but Odin and Frigg."

"I'll remember that," she said, her eyes dancing. They were beautiful in the way that light on frost is beautiful. I noticed another pair of eyes on us. Baldur was watching our every move.

"Mind you own business, hound!" I told him in a scathing voice. The handsomest of the gods had not apologized for his behavior at my betrothal, and he had brought a nearly identical frown to my wedding. My brows lowered, and angry fire danced across my fingertips. I wished he'd give me an excuse to use it.

"I said nothing, uncle."

"Your face speaks for you often enough!"

Skathi leaned in close to me. The invigorating scents of snow and pine needles followed her as a perfume. I inhaled deeply.

"Baldur is much respected," she said quietly. "I heard you do not get along, but I did not realize the extent of it." She blinked. "Am I his enemy now? Just for sitting here?"

"How should I know? But I doubt he'd ever warm to a giantess. He has very strict ideas. Best to take what you already have."

She considered that, then nodded.

"I must go home now," Skathi murmured after a bit. "The heat of this hall drains me. Come visit me sometime."

"I'll do that, goddess." I offered her a hand. Her fingers were even icier than her eyes, and a tingling cold spread up my arm at her touch. Still, I kissed her on the wrist. Her skin flushed angrily, but the mountain goddess allowed one corner of her mouth to twitch up, so subtly and quickly that I would have missed it if I weren't paying attention.

"Thank you for the mead and conversation, Loki." With that, she was gone.

I more sensed than heard the All-Father's presence as he came up behind me. Taller than any other god and cloaked in his own shadowy and unassailable penumbra of magic, he could be mistaken for no other. He wore his plain steel battle helmet that night.

"Well done," he said, as if my conversation with the wintry goddess had all been a part of some plan of his. Odin lifted his voice so everyone could hear him.

"I'd have Skathi welcomed in my hall and throughout all of Asgard." He sought out Baldur's gaze then. The God of Good inclined his head, but with visible reluctance.

I didn't like snow. Snow made traveling difficult and tested the strength of the best cloak. It blocked attackers from view and muffled the sounds of an approaching foe. Snow had little use, but it could bring much harm.

Skathi, however, seemed enamored with the stuff. Snow seethed down all around me. Only the horizon was clear. A pastel green patch of sky showed through the gloom. Off in the distance, amber rays lit up ice-capped mountains.

I'd planned ahead and brought a walking stick with me. I cursed under my breath as I approached the bleak walls of Thrymheim. Outside, nothing had changed. Thiazi was dead and Skathi was that hall's mistress now, but the place was as foreboding as ever. The sorrowful calls of wolves echoed from the mountain valleys, and pine trees swayed in the gales, casting swirling, dusty crystals from their boughs. I continued along the sleek trail, searching out each toehold. I did not see Skathi until she hailed me.

"Loki, welcome!" She wore thick furs pulled over her fair head. Her eyes were full of merriment.

"Hail, Skathi," I said, keeping my voice light. "I'm not yet frozen to the bone! You must be in a good mood today!"

"I am. Come, let me show you inside."

"I'll agree to that, mighty lady."

We found seats beside the hall's single, roaring hearth. Skathi poured us mead from a bottle of cut glass shimmering with frost. The drink was very tasty, but it slid down the throat like ice. I shivered and moved closer to the fire.

As I relaxed with the mead, I surveyed Skathi's hall. The walls and floors were polished stone. Tapestries in violet and green, and silver and every shade of blue, hung from the rafters. They were intricate, but they added no warmth to the chamber. Shelves of bone-like pine held painstakingly arranged goblets and the occasional Jotun heirloom. Everything was obsessively clean and precisely organized. It seemed that the goddess of the windswept slopes and the bubbling mountain springs had no tolerance for dirt. Her domain was spotless. Pristine.

I suddenly understood why she and Njord had parted ways. The Sea God's feet were well washed, but his hall was full of tracked-in sand and smelly racks of drying fish. Seafaring was hardly a tidy business.

The goddess was watching me with curious eyes. "Whatever are you thinking about?"

"Only that you keep a clean home, bright lady. And that your former husband does not."

The corner of her mouth tweaked up. "Quite so, God of Fire."

"It's a lovely hall," I continued. I lifted my glass to her. The mead glimmered in the flames. "Still, I see little entertainment here. Tell me, how do you pass your days?"

Skathi shrugged. "Outdoors, mostly," she said shortly.

I put down the frosty drink. Alcohol usually quickened the blood, but the mead she'd served me felt like liquid winter in my veins. I did not finish it. The goddess smirked at me and downed the last of her own mead.

We went for a walk. At her word, the clouds fell away and golden rays sparkled across the drifts and danced off the hoarfrost, creating a world of light and rainbows. We followed the course of a boiling stream. It smelled of minerals, and its waters were tinted a gentle turquoise. The rising steam comforted me and took some of the worst bite from the air.

Skathi stopped at the edge of a flat, open field. Stiff golden grasses poked out of the snow, and a lone wren hopped along a fallen log, digging for insects. A breeze whispered by, chilly against my neck.

"Let's play a game," she said.

I raised an eyebrow at her, thoroughly surprised by the suggestion.

"I know magic, Loki. See if you can keep up!"

Shaking my head, I took a step back from her. "A fine jest! I like you, Skathi. I don't wish to set you on fire!"

She answered with a close-lipped smile. A moment passed. "Ah, afraid, are you? Of a goddess in her own domain?"

I stiffened, my eyes flashing. "Don't be a fool."

"Then accept the challenge."

"Fine."

"You first." She held out her arms invitingly. In Thrymheim, she did not dress as severely as she did elsewhere. Her sleeves were woven of soft, vibrant blue wool, and her gown was trimmed with glittering furs.

I sighed remorsefully even as I drank in her loveliness. The whole thing was ridiculous. I was one of the creator gods and had shared blood with Odin himself. The goddess had absolutely no idea what she was getting into.

Still, a challenge was a challenge. I was an Aesir and couldn't turn it down. I kept my runes simple and tempered my flames as well as I could. Nonetheless, at my word, a rippling wall of fire sped toward her. I winced at its speed.

I did like Skathi, just as I'd said. She was independent, strong-willed, and smart—qualities I admired. It was a pity that she had decided to push the issue and seek out her own destruction.

As the fire roared over her, hiding her form, I sensed a change. Between one instant and a next, my spell began disintegrating back on itself, halted by magic as solid as the side of a glacier. I had the feeling that I was crashing against a mountain made of green ice, reflected light, and rock cliffs older than entire worlds. There was something of Jotunheim about her counter-spell, but also something more—an elemental presence, an ancient force.

I grinned to myself. Perhaps we were not so unevenly matched after all. With the wave of a hand, I increased the power of my runes.

"Is that all you have, Loki?"

Flame spun wildly, seeking fodder. Skathi's shielding spell kept my fire at bay, but could not extinguish it outright. The air around us grew humid, and new frost laced through the nearby pines, born of the conflict. With the instincts of the Aesir, we both let off at the same time. Skathi's face was alive with fierce triumph.

"A draw, mighty lady," I said as I inclined my head to her. "And against one of the creators, no less. Well done!"

She laughed, and the peals rang through the forest. "I told you I know magic!"

Many months later, I began to pick up on a change in Skathi's behavior toward me. She had become friends with my wife and they were often inseparable. The goddess of the mountains got on very well with the goddess of the Alfar forests. Sometimes, I'd come upon them snuggled together, whispering into each other's ears. They were as close as any sisters. Or perhaps closer still. I was not one to worry about such matters.

Nonetheless, Skathi sought out my company too. Arms linked, the two of us strolled together under a full moon, lonely sojourners in a motionless world of silvered shadows and glowing ice. Bands of stars blazed above us. The eyes of Skathi's dead father were up there, flung into the sky by Odin as another gift to the giantess. Thiazi would never be forgotten. By then, I had some inkling of what the All-Father had seen in her. We had been lacking a god or goddess like Skathi. Our family seemed more complete with her in it.

That night, her fingers gripped mine tighter than they ever had before, and her eyes lingered on my face. Her movements were more deliberate and relaxed, as if she had resolved some important question in her own mind. I had my suspicions. But I did not give them voice.

We came upon a precipice overlooking a frozen lake. A dim column appeared above, a delicate white glow that divided upon itself and spread into curtains of light, brightening to emerald and violet. Soon, a full aurora rippled across the northern sky. I laughed out loud, enjoying the feel of its magic. A gentle crackling, almost a hiss, sifted down to us. We were hearing the song of the northern lights.

The goddess beside me slipped her hand deeper into the crook of my elbow with something more than the touch of a friend. A tingling, numbing cold crawled up my arm. She spoke my name quietly. Invitingly. Her eyes were numinous, full of cool fire.

"We are very close, are we not?" she whispered.

"We are."

"And there is truly no jealousy in your marriage?"

"None, fair lady."

The corners of Skathi's mouth lifted up. She took my hand again and raised it her lips, her fingers closing around mine. I tried to smile back, but a heartbeat later, my expression turned into an outright grimace. Prickling frost shot through me, absolutely unbearable in its cruelty. Without thinking, I spoke a quick rune to warm myself.

Skathi's lovely eyes widened in shock, and she yanked her hand away. Her gaze became hurt and offended—and moist with tears that she was determined not to shed.

"I meant no harm!" I assured her. I rubbed my wrist vigorously as I made an apologetic face. "Your fingers are very cold indeed, dear lady." I kept my tone compassionate. The pain her touch had caused me had not been her fault.

"But I thought...." Skathi looked away, trying to keep her chin high. Stepping closer, I gently squeezed her shoulder through the fur cloak.

"Look at me," I ordered. She did.

I held her gaze for a long time. Black eyes burning with the worlds' first fires sought out the very soul of winter.

The goddess—my friend—was truly beautiful. Her blonde- and silver-streaked hair was radiant in the moonlight. Her cheeks were rosy, and her face was a reflection of her sharp wits and Jotun strength.

Skathi sighed softly as I finally removed my hand. We had just shared as much intimacy as we could ever hope to share.

We were very close.

We had much in common.

But we could never change our deepest natures.

chapter twenty one
the best of us

Asgard and Midgard Past

The twelve gods met again in Gladsheim. Sigyn had just borne me a son. Narvi's tiny smiles were sweeter than the first sunrise and his wondering laughs were now my entire universe. I longed to be home with my family, but Baldur had other ideas that morning.

"Father, I have been thinking. I would like to be more involved with Midgard." My nephew held his chin high, for he knew he was Odin's favorite child.

"Are you not content here, meting out wisdom to the gods?"

"I am. But you and Thor spend a great deal of time with the mortals. So does Freya, and her brother too. Even my Forseti guides them as they speak their laws. And yet... yet they are still tainted with much evil." Baldur did not look at me, but I caught the undertone of his words readily enough.

"That is their way," Odin responded mildly.

"It doesn't have to be," the handsome god countered at once. His voice thrummed with his fervor. "I can save them from their baser natures! They only need my light!"

I snorted, hardly believing what I was hearing.

"Still yourself, beloved son. Your place is here. Do not trouble yourself with the affairs of Midgard. Their fields are harsh and their truths are shrouded. Leave them be." Odin's one eye was very serious.

It was Forseti who brought the changes to my attention. One summer evening, we were all feasting in Vingolf. I stretched out on a cushioned seat, lying flat on my back and watching spiraling incense fill the chamber. Flowers decorated every beam and doorway. I heard my son giggling as he was passed around a circle of admiring goddesses. I smiled up at the twists of smoke, feeling very much at peace.

My reverie ended all too quickly.

"I don't understand it," the God of Law was saying to Thor. His voice was tinged with real frustration. "Open assemblies fall before kings and chiefs. One man speaks, and the rules change each day on his whim. Something is not right."

The Thunderer belched and helped himself to another of the frothy dark beers he'd snuck into the hall. My old friend had never had any use for wine.

"Don't look to me for answers. I kill giants and guard the mortals' travels. My daughter's a better one to talk to if you'd know of their politics."

I sat up abruptly, my dark eyes glinting. "Mortals are as changeable as the flame I gave them," I told the younger Aesir. "You've seen enough of them to know that."

"I have. But this is different. I... feel it."

"You, Forseti? Heed a feeling over a fact?" I grinned at him, and not in an entirely friendly way. Baldur's son returned a forbidding stare. He was in no mood for teasing. "Something is very wrong," he repeated, emphasizing each syllable.

I shrugged at him and downed some more of the heady wine. "Fine. I'll look into it. You'll owe me a favor, though."

"Agreed," the other god said immediately. That was an indication of just how disturbed he was, right there. "Thank you," he added after a brief pause. He finally drank some of his own wine, again thoroughly self-possessed.

"Think nothing of it, Forseti. I was getting bored anyways."

Thor rolled his eyes and huffed into his beard. "A year's worth of problems follows one minute of your boredom. I think I'll come with you this time."

I raised my glass in a mock salute. "Only if you can keep up, Thunderer!"

The two of us arrived at a fortified Midgard hold. It was built of tightly fitted granite and its high stone walls were scoured clean. Inside, polished swords hung mid-way between the vaulted ceiling and floor. They gleamed with iron spite. Mortals scurried to and fro, many in thrall to their lords. All unseen, we peered about, getting a sense of the place.

"No giants here," rumbled Thor, confirming my suspicions.

"Why is the God of Law so upset, then?"

A mortal man sat down on a gilded throne and began to speak. As soon as he opened his mouth, I knew why Forseti had been even more dour than usual. With a nimble jump back, I grabbed Thor's broad arm and frantically began tugging at his sleeve.

"We need to get out of here! Now!"

The Thunderer blinked at me, confused. "There's nothing going on here. What's the rush?"

"You're wrong! I'll leave without you if I must!"

My companion shifted Mjolnir into his right hand, but it neither flared nor crackled as he held it aloft. He waved it around a few times, then put the fearsome hammer back in his belt. "See? What did I tell you? Nothing. This must be an evil of their own making."

"No, it's not! Now, please—let's go!"

Once we were outside, I collapsed beneath an oak tree. Thor towered above me as I hunkered down and wrapped my arms around my knees.

"What was that all about?" he demanded.

"Hush. Let me think." I rested my chin on my pulled-up knees, trying to get a hold of myself. My skin felt gritty and my lungs seemed to be scratching at me from within my chest, as if they wished to escape the prison of my ribcage. An unpleasant crawling sensation still threaded its way through my blood, like knives in my veins.

Blood. That was the key. My friend wasn't one of the creators. He hadn't been able to pick up on the knowledge that had hit me almost instantly back in that fortress. There was a blessing over the son of Ask, a blessing that felt entirely Aesir: gold, unfaltering, and gloriously bright. I wrenched to one side, shaking and ill.

"You look like a corpse, Loki," Thor contributed helpfully.

"I said to hush. I'm still thinking."

"Well, hurry up."

I ignored him.

An Aesir's power flowed through the keep, but it was much different from any gift that Odin, Honir, or I had ever bestowed on a mortal. It had felt stark and lonesome, a light unto itself. Honir's second-guessing had been wiped out entirely, replaced with an unfaltering self-assurance. Odin's blessing of spirit was gone too. The mortal humbled himself before nothing. He was his own entire world, and the world was entirely his.

Only my fire remained, dulled and corrupted almost past my own recognition. Drowned in the other Aesir's sanctification, it churned and doubled back on itself, devolving into patterns I had never meant it to form.

I ran my hands through my hair, still shivering. I felt like I'd never be warm again even though the Midgard sun beat down on the fields around us and dappled the oak leaves. It was a very hot day, but my blood was ice.

Thor crouched down and offered me a hand. "Something's shaken you up badly, Loki. I think you need to get back to Asgard."

"We both do," I told him. "But this can't wait on your goats."

My companion grumbled a bit, but didn't argue with me. I muttered a spell and was off, hurtling through the spaces between realms.

Odin propped one mail-clad elbow against the armrest of his carved high seat. I was alone with him and his crows. I wished I'd curbed my impatience and had the Thunderer at my side. Too late now.

Huginn cocked his head to one side and opened his thorn-like beak to croak out a derisive opinion. Muninn, however, seemed more inclined to listen to me. Freki and Geri had nothing to add to the discussion.

"You are confused, Trickster. This could not be the doing of an Aesir."

"It is. I am sure of it." I looked away, examining the painted and studded shields hanging on a nearby wall.

"Which god or goddess might be responsible, then?"

I did not want to name the name. "It would be best if you saw things for yourself."

Odin slowly shook his head. The Mightiest of Gods was often very tired as of late. His skin was parched and his cheeks were sunken. I doubted he slept well any more. Not so long ago, he'd eagerly journeyed off to Midgard and other worlds. Now he always stayed home.

"Are you all right, brother?" I asked him.

His eye brooded over me. Its former blue was tarnished and filmy. "I owe you no answer," he told me.

I frowned. Something wasn't right. As the All-Father continued speaking, my feeling of unease grew.

"Now, tell me truly, Loki, if one such as you can. You have a suspect in mind, but you hoard your thoughts as a dwarf hoards gold. Speak, or waste no more of my time."

I took a nervous step back, already casting an eye on the closest of Valhalla's hundreds of doors.

"The blessing was that of your son, Great One. Baldur's presence is thick in Midgard."

Odin's lips pressed up in a nasty smile. "A fine joke. Flee here before I repay it by hanging your strung-out guts from my rafters."

"I'm not joking, lord."

He rose then, terrible and ferocious.

"Ask Forseti!" I yelled. "Your own grandson! He knows of this!"

"I shall. And when your lie is exposed, I'll nail you to Yggdrasil myself."

Again, his words seemed discordant to my ears. My blood-brother had threatened me with fates worse than death many times before. No, that was nothing new.

But there was no respect in his voice now. I heard nothing of the eternal bond between an Aesir and an Aesir. Nothing of the fierce joy of approaching combat, of strife and challenge. Contempt slithered through every word. An oath-breaking mortal might have hoped for a better reception.

As the God of Law had said, something was very wrong.

Thor was the last to reach Gladsheim; he settled heavily into his chair just as I began to speak. Small sparks danced around his booted feet. He could build up a charge when he rode between the worlds.

I placed my right hand on an oath-ring and told the gods everything I had learned below. Baldur watched me with a sorrowful expression.

Njord shook his head disbelievingly, and Ullr's eyes were wide and just a touch amused, as if I spoke of fables. Honir, of course, looked uncertain, and Freyr and Tyr both glared at their boots, fingering their belts for weapons left outside the grove. Heimdall's face was gray with anger, and Bragi had twisted around in his chair so that only his shoulder faced me.

Thor merely shrugged, as if he had nothing to do with anything. Forseti alone nodded as I told the others of what I had seen. His gray eyes were intense.

Despite all their unspoken hostility, no one interrupted me. Every god had a chance to say his piece in that sacred assembly.

When I was done, I took my seat again. An uneasy sensation wormed its way through my gut. The All-Father was not the only one who seemed to have lost something of himself as of late.

"You've all heard the Trickster's account." Odin's voice was soft with menace, like the ocean just before the first sails of the invading fleet are seen. "What say the Aesir?"

My nephew stood up, his movements solemn and heavy with grief. "Loki brings only confusion to this divine place. We give him every chance, and he throws our charity back in our faces. You all know my works, and his." Baldur bowed to the other gods, the very picture of unpresuming goodness. He sat down again.

Odin inclined his head. "Well said, my bright and beloved son."

In an instant, Forseti was on his feet. He usually moved with careful deliberation, but now he spoke hurriedly, as if he feared being shouted down. "Listen to the evidence! Loki speaks the truth!"

Baldur sighed, a sound like the softest breezes of spring and the first gentle dripping of melting ice. "Dear, dear son. The Trickster has misled you. No, my princes rule justly in Midgard. Their decrees create peace and prosperity. But what would the God of Chaos know of unity? What would the father of Fenrir know of love?" He gave me another one of those compassionate, pitying looks. "His nature is not as ours."

Gladsheim was the holiest of all holy places. There, the gleaming trees sang with their own power. The shimmering, misty light running through the fields was alive, and the blinding heart of our circle pulsed with forces older than the Cosmos. When a hush fell in Gladsheim, it ran deep.

A hush ruled then, after Baldur's confession. The sacred grove was shocked into silence.

Odin was the one who finally broke that silence, for he was the only one who could. "You admit that you have gone to Midgard, my son? Though I advised you against it?"

The God of Light nodded, then smiled a beatific smile. "I did. And I gladly tell of it, father. Loki always lies. He cannot help himself. But know that I have worked only wonders there."

The All-Father pondered this and made up his mind.

"Very well, Baldur. I trust your wisdom." Odin glanced away, and some troubled emotion seemed to flicker about him. "Loki, you must leave now. Gladsheim is not for you."

Forseti held up a hand, palm out. "Not so fast." The God of Law wore an oath-ring bound about his upper arm, and it now shone with its own zealous silver light. "None of the Twelve may be cast from Gladsheim. Not even by you, grandfather."

"He casts himself out, son," murmured Baldur in his warm voice. "You are a kind god to think of him, but he makes his own choice."

"I am neither a kind god nor an unkind god. I speak only of the law. You break ours now."

"No impure thing may remain here," intoned Odin. He leaned forward, his brow creasing. "Loki must go."

I leapt to my feet. The highest god's turn of phrase sounded all too familiar. Baldur often said the same thing about his hall, Breidablik.

There was a scuffling of soft boots as Forseti rose as well. He strode forward and leveled an accusing glare at his grandfather. "Then lose me too! I won't condone your error with my presence!"

He followed me out, his steps strong and furious, and his hair glaringly white in the unceasing radiance of the grove. The God of Law was trembling with rage. We set off down a clay trail, dry from a recent lack of rain. Clouds of dust puffed up behind us.

"My father's will prevails," the younger Aesir observed in a tight voice. "They're unable to resist him now."

"I don't understand. How does he hold such power over gods?"

"It's very simple. He is all perfection and goodness, light and grace." Forseti's expression was grim. "To say no to Baldur is to choose rejection over unity. Corrosion over beauty. Bloodshed over peace."

"Like the Vanir," I muttered darkly. "I thought we had won that war."

He raised an eyebrow at me, not quite following my meaning.

"Before your time," I told him. "But no, this is far worse. The All-Father himself is *not* himself."

"Yes. He is swayed just like the others."

"What do we do now?"

The silver-haired immortal paused beside a small, gnarled dogwood. He bowed his head, his wavy locks covering the sides of his face. "Perhaps we can do nothing. I admit that I am scared. Even now, I want to run back to Gladsheim. I want to bend my knee and ask my father for his forgiveness."

I just stared at him.

"I know him to be deeply wrong," whispered the other god. "But I also know he would welcome me. All would be right again between us."

I put a steadying hand on his arm. "Stay strong, Forseti." I sighed then. "I taught him his magic, you know. Ever the proper uncle." I made an ugly face, like I had tasted something foul.

He shivered.

"Is there truly nothing we can do?" I asked quietly. "Nothing at all?"

"I can think of only one possibility, Loki. Talk to Odin, someplace far from here. The further from Asgard, the better. Otherwise...."

He didn't finish the thought.

There was no need to.

chapter twenty two
murder

Baldur's influence grew with each sunrise and sunset. The immortal denizens of Asgard basked in his goodness, laughing and at total peace. Even my Sigyn gathered flowers to string through his flowing hair. Our son Narvi skipped along behind her, his dark brown curls catching the golden rays and his narrow, waiflike face lifted in praise.

Being faultless in all things, the God of Light welcomed my family into his presence. Sigyn only had to remain far from the borders of Alfheim, the realm she had once loved. My wife was lost to me, and with her my son. My own child peered up at me as if I were a stranger every time I came near. I learned to keep away.

One evening, as I wandered Asgard's paths alone, I chanced upon Bragi. The fair-haired bard with the lustrous, curling beard had balanced himself on a fallen log. His legs were stretched out comfortably in front of him.

"Hail, God of Song," I said.

"Hail," he muttered without any enthusiasm. He ran his long fingers over the strings of his gold-plated lyre, frowning with concern. The strings twanged unpleasantly, and the notes were flat and sour.

"What's wrong with your lyre?" I asked him.

"Nothing I can find. It should play as well as always. But all my instruments are the same as of late. I can coax no sweet chords or cheerful melodies from them."

"Let me see."

He chuckled wryly, the ringlets of his beard quivering. "You, Loki? You'll never succeed where I have failed!"

I held out a hand and made a curling motion with my fingers. "Just give me the lyre. I even promise I won't steal it."

"Always the gentleman, aren't you?" he murmured. With all the tenderness of a new mother handing off her baby, he slipped the instrument into my waiting hands.

I whispered a few warding runes over the lyre, then swiftly re-tuned the strings. When I was done, I struck up a rolling melody. My quick and shifting chords harmonized against the simpler and more evocative refrain I pulled from a memory.

Bragi's mouth fell open. "How did you—I mean, it's working!"

I bowed and gave the lyre back to him. Like someone who has finally discovered a feast after months living off stale bread, he eagerly began playing. His abilities were far greater than mine, of course. The music he created spiraled and soared through the woods to dance with the first stars gleaming against the purple cloak of twilight. I listened for a while. There was an old joy to the music. I could forget Baldur and all the trouble he had caused us while Bragi played.

The God of Song finally moved on to a slower piece.

"Take your time here," I told him softly. "Play as long as you can in this place. I don't think my tuning will survive much travel."

He nodded, his eyes shut and his head bent to one side as he listened to melodies only he could hear. The smile on his lips was honest and grateful.

I didn't tell him that the instrument would go flat again as soon as he brought it into Baldur's presence. He wouldn't have believed me if I had.

I still ate in Valhalla. Sigyn avoided our cabin, and its empty rooms only reminded me of everything we had once shared. Instead of torturing myself, I'd stop by Odin's hall to gulp down a quick horn of mead and pet Geri for a bit. I always left as soon as I was done.

Glitnir offered a little solace as well. Forseti's court was a bleak place in those days. Oath-rings hung from rough-hewn altars, unused, and the hearth fires were pale and subdued. Baldur's judgments carried throughout Asgard. His son's more temperate justice was forgotten.

The God of Law rarely spoke now. He drank mead with me and obsessively read through parchment after parchment, reviewing his jurisprudence as if it could somehow shelter him against what was happening to the other gods. I took to reading those papers too, pointing out loopholes and inconsistencies while Forseti's lips twitched down in acknowledgment. Every once in a while, he'd have enough. He'd pull himself to his feet, stalk over to my chair, and wordlessly retrieve his documents. I'd know that my welcome had run out and find other diversions.

That time was a nightmare and Baldur too had nightmares. The God of Good was tormented with visions of his own death. My blood-brother knew much of dreams and prophecies, and he feared for his son. He set off for Niflheim to raise a seeress from the dead and learn all he could of the danger.

I was waiting for Odin when he finally left my daughter's realm. The other god was hunkered down over the arching neck of Sleipnir. He reined in the eight-legged horse when he saw me.

"Get out of my way, Loki. I've just had the worst of news." His face was ravaged with grief.

"Speak with me a moment, Great One. Were we not blood-brothers once?"

"We were and we still are. Though lately I regret the choice."

My lip contorted up in a snarl. "Hear my rune, then go as you will."

I spoke a Word, a Word not unlike the one I had once spoken to cast down Ymir. It echoed along the serpentine root paths and flicked by dying universes, restoring their suns to short life. The mists carried the spell into forgotten crevices, and dripping waters bled the Word down to Yggdrasil's questing roots.

Odin blinked his one eye and shook out his steely locks.

"Your son charms you," I told him. "Can you see that now?"

The All-Father growled deep in his throat, a low, lethal noise. But it was not directed at me. "I see it now, my brother."

"You won't for long. The rune's song will fade quickly, even down here."

"Lend me some of your fire."

I stepped up and brushed my fingertips against his.

"Better," rumbled the God of the Slain. "I summoned the ghost of a mighty sorceress. I know that blind Hod will kill Baldur."

"Hod? His own brother?"

"The same. You must ensure this happens, come what may. Soon, I'll seek to prevent it by any means. You must be even more ruthless than me."

I actually whimpered at that and pulled away from him.

"I'll have your promise, Loki."

"To help murder your son?"

The Hanged God nodded once. "Give me your word on it," he repeated in that voice that could not be denied. The dreadful god's cloak fluttered about him, stirred by the underworld's dry and dusty breezes.

"Hod will take the blame?"

But the Wisest God did not answer my last question. Unmoving and inscrutable, he loomed over me, his face weathered and hard. The dim cries of the dead rattled up through the fog surrounding us.

Eventually, he spoke again. "A third and final time, Loki, I ask you for your promise."

The insights and premonitions that came of Aesir blood—of Odin's shared blood—were already winding their way through my spirit. The knowledge they brought settled upon me, as cruel and gray as a noose.

"I damn myself if I accept," I whispered.

There was no sympathy in my blood-brother's gaze. "You damn all the worlds if you don't."

I had to force out my next words. Barely audible, they broke upon themselves even as I uttered them. "You have my promise, my lord."

Baldur's father shook out Sleipnir's reins and rode off without saying a farewell. For a long time, I stood where he had left me, staring blankly into the void. Strange thoughts and impressions, half prophesy and half hallucination, drifted through my mind, dashing into blackness if I tried to focus on them too long.

After a while, I was as ready as I ever could hope to be. I set off for Asgard.

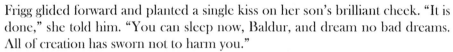

Frigg glided forward and planted a single kiss on her son's brilliant cheek. "It is done," she told him. "You can sleep now, Baldur, and dream no bad dreams. All of creation has sworn not to harm you."

We had gathered in the fields outside Gladsheim. Although the gods had banned me from the grove itself, they couldn't ask me to stay away from those sun-bathed meadows. I kept my face carefully impassive as I listened to her blessing. But internally, I fumed. Frigg was just making my oath that much harder. Meanwhile, Odin looked on, beaming with approval. The overly cheery expression was unnatural on him.

But what had been natural in Asgard as of late? The animals no longer roamed free or hunted their prey. No, they only desired to loll in the grass soaking up the God of Good's light. Songbirds abandoned their nests, leaving their eggs to grow cold and die. They too cared for nothing but Baldur.

The Aesir were hardly any better. Thor had set aside his frothy horns of dark ale and instead chatted gaily with the handsomest of the gods. Skathi giggled and frolicked in the warm fields, skipping and singing as she went by. Even Forseti now lazed at his father's feet, a strange smile lighting up his once-serious face. Baldur often reached down to caress his only son's cheek. The former God of Law watched him adoringly, his gray eyes shining with worshipful bliss. If at times they glistened more feverishly, only I noticed. A muted horror would suddenly appear in their depths, and his whole body would tense with absolute despair. Such episodes passed swiftly. My nephew's sway was nearly absolute.

By then, I was entangled in my own struggles. A new sort of fire, unfamiliar and compelling, now consumed me: I wanted to be a part of that joyous and untroubled group. I thought of kneeling before Baldur, of asking him to make me pure. He had that much goodness in him. He could change me if I but asked it of him. Every hour was a new fight against that impulse. My turmoil was all the worse when I had to join the other gods in the field.

After Frigg's pronouncement, the Aesir tested Baldur's strength. They were hesitant at first, for no one wished to see him suffer even the tiniest injury. But joy overtook them as they realized that their beloved ruler was indeed immune to all harm.

Soon, laughter rang, and axes and swords flew. Baldur lifted his hands with a surrendering, approving chuckle. His golden hair ruffled about his strong neck and his azure eyes sparkled. He was unhurt.

I stepped away from the others and crossed my arms over my chest. My fingers clenched painfully into my own flesh, and I muttered to myself, my mouth twisting with distaste. How was I to take him down? Odin, who had sworn me to ending Baldur's life, now flung his great spear at his invincible son, crowing with mirth.

Through shapechanging and through my own wits, I uncovered the answer from Frigg herself. The goddess had not exacted protection from one lone thing in all the Cosmos, a single fragile growth of mistletoe. She had thought it too small to ever harm her child.

The sun was hot and the air was still as I went off in search of the plant. Asgard was always calm and summery lately. There was no variety, no rumbling storms or low-hanging thunderbanks. I felt like the weather was a physical force, a suffocating blanket pressing in around me. I longed for a sharp breeze or wild gales that would drag at my cloak.

A stand of oaks grew above a stream bank. Their leaves did not rustle, and nothing lived among their curving boughs. Any creature that could find its way to Baldur had done so already. Those that could not had starved. I crouched down to nudge the bones of a rabbit kit with a twig. It had been too small to travel any distance and had paid the price.

After wandering about, I finally found what I was looking for. A tiny ball of mistletoe clung to one of the oaks. Its leaves were round and its berries were waxy and slick.

I did not wish to climb the tree. Instead, I sung a spell and transformed myself into a woodpecker. I clicked my powerful beak, then ruffled out my fire-red crest and vividly banded wings. Uttering the bird's primordial call, I lofted myself into the branches, my path dipping and rising in erratic swoops. My sharp talons easily latched into the bark. I tilted my head to one side and snapped up the frail sprig of mistletoe.

Once I was safely on the ground and back in my own form, I cradled the plant in my open palm. A heavy knot constricted my chest. No weapon could be made from such an insignificant little growth. No wonder Frigg had not bothered with it. Still, I wrapped the mistletoe in a square of cloth and hid it in my tunic. I walked between the sterile trees while hopelessness spiraled through my being. What was I to do with such a tiny, useless plant?

The forests my Sigyn had once loved would remain desolate. In time, all the worlds would succumb to Baldur's will just as Asgard had. There would be only unfailing light, peace, and stability. Only eternal, enraptured thralldom.

And then it hit me. My wife was the answer. She could make any cutting thrive. I had seen her rescue crumpling, dried stems and nurture them back into boldly blooming flowers. Rotting, yellow-leafed saplings had found new life in her care, growing into mighty trees. Perhaps she could save the brittle ball of mistletoe.

My goddess was in the fields outside Gladsheim, lying on her back. Her arms were spread out with contentment, and Narvi sat next to her, his oversized white linen tunic falling about him as he busily knotted strings of clover together. As soon as he saw me, he gasped, sprang to his feet, and ran off to where the gods were still making sport with Baldur and throwing every kind of missile at him.

My shadow fell over my wife. She blinked, and her brow creased with aversion.

"Loki," she said, without any warmth.

"I need your help."

She pulled herself into a sitting position and crossed her thin wrists over her bent knee. She didn't bother to stand up. "With what?" she asked darkly. Suspiciously.

"I have a plant in need of your care. See how its stems already break? You could make it strong again."

She sighed heavily. "Why? What do you care for plants?"

"Is not mistletoe holy? I thought to present it to Baldur."

My poor, innocent wife's entire face lit up like the dawn. "Well finally, Loki! Are you truly coming around? At last?"

"I am, wife. I've done a great deal of thinking lately."

She rose up, held the tiny sprig between her soft fingers, and murmured ancient magic over the failing plant. The smooth leaves began to fill out, and the twigs toughened and widened.

"This must be a gift to remember. Make it bigger."

My wife had known me through the sorts of eons only a god could comprehend. If she had not been lost under Baldur's spell, she would have figured out that my black eyes gleamed not with good will, but with a far more malicious fire. But all her good sense was gone. Obliviously, she sent more of her gentle magic into the mistletoe. Soon, the round spray was nearly as wide as her waist.

"Will this do?" she asked.

I stroked my chin, contemplating what I saw. It would be enough, I decided.

"It will, and nicely. I'll want to prepare it first, of course."

My goddess smiled at me. "I keep ribbons with my combs. Use them if you'd like."

"An excellent plan. Thank you for all your help. I know Baldur will appreciate it." I smirked at my own words as my wife leaned in to kiss me on the cheek. It was the only affection she had shown me in a long while.

I carried my prize away to a secluded spot beside a gurgling spring. With my own spells, I crafted the branch into a fierce wand, a dart that was almost a small spear. It was exceedingly well-balanced and was sharp as a thorn. Such a weapon could easily slice its way through a god's breast and pierce even an immortal's beating heart.

Ullr had once cast a rune back when he and I had hunted together in the

179

early wilds of Midgard. Its sound was like liquid on my lips. My deadly wand glowed with a fitful gold light. The sheen of magic soon melted away, and the mistletoe again looked like an ordinary wooden dart. My weapon now carried the blessing of Ullr, the god who always struck true. It would not miss its mark.

Kneeling beside the spring, I bowed my head and held the terrible dart, caressing it and trembling violently. None of us had ever slain a fellow god before. I knew, in my deepest being, that the murder had to be done. But the very thought of it felt like poison, as unnatural as the world Baldur had called into being.

No, I did not want to carry that pointed wand back to the Aesir. I did not want to speak wheedling, cunning words in blind Hod's ear and slip the killing mistletoe into his open palm.

And so, I procrastinated. I plumbed the depths of my own fear until the words of my promise to Odin sounded so loudly in my memory that they drove me to my feet.

Smoothing down my crimson tunic, I forced a smile onto my lips.

I approached the joyful throng. The gods were at play in the amber afternoon rays. Their laughter rang like bells while cruelly honed axes and polished swords flew across the field. The God of Light's bright hair still ruffled about his strong neck. His wondrous blue eyes still sparkled with joy.

I placed a hand on Hod's arm and murmured seductive words in his waiting ear.

His questing fingers closed around the dart.

With a single toss, Baldur's life was ended.

CHAPTER TWENTY THREE
PUNISHMENT

Asgard Past and Present

Baldur was dead. The fairest and wisest of the Aesir, the handsomest of all the immortals, beloved by all beings and all of creation, lay crumpled in the grass. A wood shaft stuck out from his chest, like the war banner of a victorious invader thrust into the hill above a ravaged village. Blood—coarse, sticky, vivid blood—drenched the god's formerly white tunic, spreading under his broken body in a darkening puddle.

Caught in the first wave of shock, most of the Aesir simply stared. They couldn't believe that what they were seeing was real. This had to be a joke, a prank of some sort. Their shining god would leap to his feet any minute now, laughing and full of high spirits.

He had to. Baldur could not die.

It was Frigg, his mother, who first grasped the truth. The goddess of high magic, who never spoke of her visions, now unleashed the most unearthly of wails. Her grief was keening and primal, the loss of all things given voice.

She knew. She knew, for she had not taken an oath from every last thing that dwelt within Yggdrasil's branches.

I moved away from Hod, and their wrath fell on him. He too died a bloody death that day. Weapons were not hard to come by on that field.

Frigg again traveled throughout all of creation. My daughter, Hel, decreed that she would return Baldur to us if every last thing in every last world wept for him. But my child was clever. She got word to me, and I took the form of a giantess.

Odin's wife was the wisest of the goddesses, and her presence was compelling. When she found me and asked if I would shed but one tear for her son, I almost felt something for him. He had truly been good, after all. But then I remembered the time young Baldur had called up every bird and animal to attack me. I recalled the way my flesh had been pulled apart and how he had laughed that day. I thought of my Sigyn walking through silent forests and of the son who was terrified of me.

I did not weep for Baldur.

As his burning funeral ship fell apart at sea, billowing orange flame and wreathed in tarry smoke, I finally relaxed.

It was done. All the worlds were saved.

But the Aesir were already whispering among themselves and casting dark looks in my direction. They knew of my enmity for Baldur. They knew I could change shapes. And they knew that only one giantess in all the realms had not cried for the God of Good. It was not difficult for them to put those pieces together.

The others dispersed from the beach, sobbing or lost in their own thoughts. I paced up the gray strand, listening to the cackles of gulls. Briny winds whipped at my shoulder-length hair. I felt very alone. There was no sense of satisfaction, of closure. I became more and more certain that that my part was not over, but only beginning. I was an Aesir, and I had sensed much outside Niflheim when Odin had given me my charge.

As if my thought had summoned him, my blood-brother suddenly strode up to me, powerful and tall, and full of his own deathly magic. "Well done, Loki," he said.

I lowered my head and gritted my teeth, not answering.

"You will speak of this to no one," he continued, brimming with grim cheer. "Not that they'd remember if you did! I alone carry the thought and the memory!"

I was silent.

"One last time, I'd have your promise, Loki."

I turned on him and struck at him with fists and fire. Both rained ineffectually against his wide, mailed chest, leaving me with scraped and bleeding knuckles, and scalding blisters conjured by my own flame. My blood-brother wrapped a heavy hand around my wrist. I finally gave up, and stood before him, quaking, my head bowed in submission.

"It is a terrible thing to kill a god," he said simply. His voice was deep with the roaring surge of battle, with the calling forces of forgotten magic. It was his voice again. And I heard understanding in it.

I nodded.

"I'll tell no one, my lord, unless you give the word."

"Good."

We walked further up the beach. Scuttling clouds fled by overhead. The day had been stormy and sunless, the coast black with chilly shadows. Waves frothed over spinning grains of sand. We moved away from the water, closer to a line of dense sea-grass. The tide was coming in.

"You did what needed to be done," Odin said at last. "But a murder is a murder. The gods will seek their vengeance on you."

I growled low in my throat. "So tell them the truth!"

"No. There may come a time for that. It is not now. Asgard must heal. The worlds must heal."

"And what of me?"

The God of the Slain raised his eyebrows, and his single eye gleamed like a dying universe.

"What of you, Loki?" he rumbled. "I fed my own son to the waves and flames today." He left me. His long cloak trailed behind him, tossing in the ocean winds.

None of the gods had a kind word for me. The months passed by, and Sigyn kept to her elven forests, avoiding me as much as she could. Narvi stayed with her. When he did see me, he immediately hid behind my wife, his dark eyes glinting with fear.

Asgard was as solemn as a tomb, full of sadness and softly spoken words. But even the immortal Aesir had to come to terms with what had happened. A glorious feast was planned; the shining Alfar were to be there, and all the gods too. There would be cauldrons of beer and bottomless casks of mead. Everyone would drink to the memory of Baldur.

Instinctively, they took their feasting away from Asgard. Our realm was heavy with memories and was also too fair. A gathering to honor a dead god required a more somber setting. Aegir the Sea Giant's hall was chosen for the occasion. He would gain much renown for hosting such mighty guests.

I overheard their plans, but no one invited me to Baldur's wake. Even without proof, they all suspected me of the murder.

My own visions haunted me as the evening of the feast grew closer. I knew I had to go, that I had to crash their festivities. And I knew that doing so would spell my doom. I couldn't see anything beyond that, but in my heart, I was sure that I'd only be flinging myself into some dreadful, waiting abyss. Murder was indeed murder.

I sulked as the other gods made their plans, downing horn after horn of mead. Finally, one of my fellow Aesir sat down beside me. Cold-eyed Skathi watched me at my drink.

"Burdened by a guilty conscience, Loki?" she asked in a frosty tone.

"Go away," I told her.

"No. You were my friend. I thought I could trust you. But you betrayed us all."

"You don't know what you're talking about," I replied, truthfully enough.

She stood back up, her slate-colored dress swishing and her cloak of white fur bright about her arms. Skathi flashed me a dreadful smile. "I dream dreams, Trickster. I think you're about to get what's coming to you."

I spun away from her. My hand clenched against my horn so hard that the beaten gold snapped, sloshing mead on the table. The winter goddess cackled at me cruelly.

Too soon, the evening of the feast arrived. I crouched on top of a barnacled rock, gazing down at an immense hall lapped by the ocean's seething waves. Aegir's home lay next to the ocean. It was built of heavy wood beams bolstered up on loose piles of gold. The treasure glowed with its own fire, and its subdued, watery light flickered along the walls like will-o-wisps.

I heard the cautious talking and laughter of the other Aesir carried on the wind. Nearly expressionless, I tried to listen in, but I was unable to pick out individual words or voices. I helped myself to another deep swig of the strong ale I'd brought with me, then tossed my emptied horn into the roiling waters.

I had started drinking before sunrise. My limbs felt numb and my chest was tight. My hate burned through me, stoked and fueled by the alcohol.

I'd meet my end that night, but before I did, the Aesir would hear much that they did not wish to hear.

The one truth that could save me was denied to me. By my own blood-brother's order, I could not let it pass my lips.

All the other truths—the nastiness and deceit that the Aesir tried to bury away—would come out. I'd be the one who spilled the gods' innermost secrets. All the worlds would soon know their deepest shames.

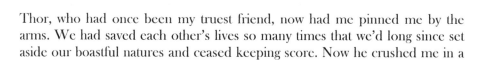

Thor, who had once been my truest friend, now had me pinned me by the arms. We had saved each other's lives so many times that we'd long since set aside our boastful natures and ceased keeping score. Now he crushed me in a grip I could not escape. The strong hands that had aided me in Jotunheim and Midgard held me fast.

I had tried to elude him and failed. Changing into a salmon had not worked. The Thunderer had caught me by the tail, and now the gods and goddesses screamed for my blood. I had pushed them past all endurance with the many insults I'd hurled at them.

I had ruined their memorial feast. Not a single word I had spoken had been untrue, and their rage was all the greater for that.

I tried wrenching about a few more times, but the battle was already lost. Nothing could break Thor's hold. I let myself fall still, then lifted my head with quiet dignity. My black hair stirred about my shoulders, tousled by the moist winds lifting off the nearby waterfall. Its frothy waters had not proven to be the sanctuary I'd hoped they would be.

"Three Aesir are dead because of you, Loki," Forseti pronounced. His tone was as distant as always, his words enunciated and sober. I had said nothing against him in Aegir's hall. The God of Law had never done anything untoward, anything that could be condemned.

Syn marched forward, bearing a sword and a round shield of wood and leather.

"Baldur, Nanna, and Hod are your victims," he continued. "You must answer for them all." The goddess of defendants smacked her sword against the shield, approving the charge.

The silver-haired immortal stepped back, and the other Aesir all began yelling at once, brandishing sharp weapons. I would have died at their hands like Hod if Odin hadn't shifted forward. His huge form blocked me from their swords and daggers.

"SILENCE!" he roared.

Every sound cut off. Even the pounding of the waterfall ceased. It did not dare keep making noise after the All-Father had spoken so.

The dreadful god's one eye burned. "It is my son who died. It will be I who decides his murderer's fate. Will any gainsay me?"

No one was that stupid.

"I know a rune, one that can undo any bond, set any prisoner free. I know its magic, and what must be done to reverse it." He angled around to face me, and I trembled under the fury in his gaze. "The magic is vicious. It cries out for innocent blood. But the Trickster will be bound—bound so that even he may not escape."

My thoughts were only half coherent by then. Lucky, I thought. I was getting off lucky, for I was not to be killed right there. But my stomach twisted upon itself, and my heart grew very cold.

No. There was more to this. Much more.

The highest god ordered my family to be brought before him. Sigyn had not gone to the hall. As usual, she preferred the trees and fields to the gatherings of the Aesir.

Odin stared at her a long time, his lips curved down in a severe, regretful scowl. Then he motioned her forward. The mightiest of gods put his wide hand behind her neck and bent down to whisper something in her ear.

No one heard what he said. My wife's face drained of all color. Her gray eyes widened and turned filmy with shock. But she nodded, slowly and grimly.

The All-Father's will would be done.

She went to Narvi, who wasn't any taller than her waist, and hugged him with ferocious intensity. And then she disappeared into the gloom, tears trickling down her cheeks. She didn't spare me a single glance.

I hadn't figured out what was about to happen, not even then. I was exhausted and spent, still suffering from the last haze of the alcohol.

Odin hefted his gleaming axe, and it all became so very clear.

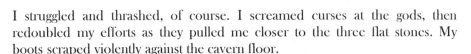

I struggled and thrashed, of course. I screamed curses at the gods, then redoubled my efforts as they pulled me closer to the three flat stones. My boots scraped violently against the cavern floor.

"It's over, Loki," rumbled Thor. His voice was as foreboding as the mounting tremors of an earthquake. "One more kick like that last one, and I'll knock you out cold!"

I panted heavily. They couldn't really be doing what they were doing, I thought wildly. Frantically. It was all some sort of sick hoax. It had to be. My mind spun and reeled, unable to grasp what was happening.

No, they were serious. Serious as only the Aesir could be. The gods carried enchanted bonds woven from my young son's intestines. Narvi had died before my eyes, bleeding out on the grass as I watched.

This was no joke. A deadly fever would show more sympathy and a killing blade more restraint than I could expect from them now.

The All-Father followed along behind the others. He said nothing, just as he had said nothing as he gutted Narvi. His single eye was inscrutable.

One final time, I sought out Forseti. Baldur's son was garbed in his white tunic, and his gray eyes were almost as impassive as Odin's.

"God of Law!" I shouted, "What of an open assembly? Sworn testimony and measured judgment? I've had none of these things!"

Thor lifted a heavy hand and whacked me across the jaw, tossing fresh blood onto the rock floor.

"Leave him alone!" the Thunderer bellowed.

But the younger Aesir actually came forward.

"The Trickster is right. He has a right to our due process before the High One's will is made final."

As Baldur's only son drew near, I saw that his eyes were red with sorrow and his skin was dry and bloodless. For a moment, I dared to hope against hope that the child of the god I had murdered might save me.

But the loss of his parents was too fresh. Nanna's heart had burst at the sight of her bright Baldur laid out for his final journey. The loyal goddess had died on the spot and she had burned alongside her husband. Their ashes had mingled together, released into the crying skies.

Forseti was an orphan. Revulsion flitted across his face as he looked at me. "He has the right," he said more quietly. "But this matter is too close to me. I recuse myself from it. Let someone else hear the appeal."

Nobody said a word.

"Then Odin's ruling stands." He inclined his head to his grandfather and moved away again.

"Enough stalling!" boomed Thor. "Baldur's murder is avenged today!"

Sigyn joined me some time later. She held up the iron bowl and watched as the poison pattered down into it, each drop foaming and noxious.

My wife was silent, more silent than the ageless stone walls closing in around us. Her grief was too deep for any words. Still, she remained at my side, ever dutiful, locked away in darkness far from the Alfar realm she loved.

My sentence was her sentence.

My punishment was her punishment.

"Well, there you go! Now you have the truth!" I finished in a scathing voice as

I glared at the other immortals huddled around the Yule bonfire. "Hail the Aesir!" I added sarcastically.

No one spoke. What could they say?

Sigyn was visibly trembling. Skathi hesitantly put an arm about my wife's shoulders. Her pale eyes were wide with shock.

"I... I can't believe this," whispered gentle Idunn. "Surely, we gods and goddesses could not have been so misled?"

Forseti stirred beside me. "We could, and we were. My father was not easily resisted. I remember it all now."

The assembled gods shifted uneasily. I wanted to gloat at them, to flaunt how I had saved them all. But I had passed too many hours of recounting things they had forgotten, and I had relived too many dark memories. Pain filled me, curdling through my blood. I had no fiery words for them, no barbs or taunts.

I scrambled to my feet. "A fine Yule this was!" I growled as I flung my emptied mead horn to the ground. Before it could even strike the dirt, I was already gone, off into the forest at a run. Dried leaves crunched beneath my boots and frigid air slammed against my face. I could move faster than any of them when I wished it.

I wished it then, with the fiercest desperation. I could no longer stand to be their presence. I needed to be alone.

Thrudheim was a large realm. I kept running until I exhausted myself. Finally, I pulled to a stop and leaned up against a vast oak. Naked branches scratched at the cloudless night sky, creaking and swaying mournfully.

I pressed my cheek against the tree. Memories of golden summers and deadly winters flowed through me. The oak was thousands of years old. Its delicate green buds had unfurled to Asgard's sun long before I had ever been cast into darkness and fettered down to rock slabs. Songbirds had nested in its heights and rains had sprinkled its leaves before venom ever eroded my immortal flesh. Its bark was cold and rough against my face.

Before I was even aware of what was happening, I started weeping. Sobs wracked through me as the grief I had never expressed tore through my body all at once. I clasped at the bark, hugging the tree. Somehow, the oak understood. Salty drops hit the dead grasses, and my muffled cries blended into the sounds of the forest.

I braced myself against the tree for a long time. Slowly, my anguished choking lessened. Shaking and weak, I wiped my crimson sleeve across my eyes, then buried my head in my arm. Another, less intense wave hit me, and fresh tears soaked through the cloth of my tunic.

Eventually, it was done. I ran my fingers down the side of the oak in quiet gratitude. The hard sorrows and dark secrets I had carried for so long had ebbed out of me, purged and washed away, shared only with the tree.

It had understood me. It had offered no words, for no words could ever have been sufficient. But its presence had been a balm. A balm to a god.

My hand was still resting against the towering oak when I lifted my gaze to the sky. An aurora was forming in the heights, illuminating the forest with its ethereal glow. A scattering of thin, green bands rippled above me. Then striations of purple appeared.

The aurora seemed normal enough. I began to turn away. Suddenly, it blazed anew, recapturing my attention. The colors changed in the space of a heartbeat. The purple brightened to the purest, most victorious shade of red I had ever seen, and the green shifted over to a brilliant, searing yellow.

Flaring curtains crossed the horizons. Living sheets of light burned past the stars, whispering powerful songs.

Fire danced through the skies of Asgard.

All the Aesir were doing me honor.

chapter twenty four
Death and Dreams

Asgard Present

For days after, I wandered the most isolated fields and forests of our realm. I kept to myself. My heart felt raw, and I had much to resolve in my own mind.

Eventually, I found Breidablik. I stood among the broken stones and frozen thistles, staring down at Baldur's former hall. I wore a long cloak of black wool, and snow fluttered through my hair. The wind droned mournfully, bitter with the stories of yore.

Breidablik lay abandoned. The hall where no unclean thing could dwell was thick with fallen leaves and layers of dirt. Many of its walls had long since fallen in on themselves, and its golden roof had collapsed under its own weight. Floors of perfect, clear crystal still glittered dully underneath the debris, but their surfaces were gritty and marred. Entire ecosystems thrived within the rubble, and a number of trees had forced themselves through the open space where the roof had caved in. One of these had grown directly into a broken wall, its living trunk fusing with stone and gold as if it were trying to gorge itself on Breidablik's remains.

I wasn't sure why my steps had taken me to those crumbling ruins. Curiosity, perhaps. Baldur would have never allowed me anywhere near the place when he had been alive. But there was more to it. The sight of the dilapidated hall fit my mood. I *wanted* to be standing under that gray sky with chilly flakes settling on my cloak like tiny, brittle stars.

"Well, nephew," I murmured. "I suppose it comes to this."

The tangled weeds and barren trees did not answer.

"Better you than us," I added. With a shrug, I leapt down onto the gold-paved road to the hall. I stooped to one knee, pocketed a loose chunk of the valuable metal, and sprang back to my feet.

When I reached the shattered doors, I halted abruptly. Some part of me still feared to enter Baldur's hall. Some part of me still felt unworthy. Unclean.

Grimacing to myself, I removed my newfound nugget from my pouch and hurled it off into the gray forest. It spun in its flight and flashed just once before it was lost among the thorny undergrowth.

"Hail, brother of my blood."

I shook out my bangs impatiently and didn't bother responding. I hadn't journeyed to fallen Breidablik seeking any sort of company. I wanted to be left alone.

The highest of the gods walked up to me, moving with a warrior's control. He was back in his usual mail tunic, and he traveled by himself. Huginn and Muninn soared over other worlds.

Odin said nothing further. I considered the open threshold for some time, then finally stepped inside the gutted hall. Wet leaves and moist dustings of snow made the footing treacherous.

The place looked as bad from the inside as it had from without. Roots had broken through the floor, and the few remaining walls were blackened, their gold turned porous by the merciless progression of the seasons.

My blood-brother followed me soundlessly.

"You see all things," I said darkly. "This is the fate of all the gods, if you think about it."

He sighed, a low rattling noise that reminded me of spears beating against shields. The All-Father caught my gaze, and his blue eye burned with unspoken disagreement.

"Hold out your hand," he commanded.

"Why?"

"It is my will, Loki." His voice shifted, taking on that note of authority that no Aesir could ignore.

I held out my right hand.

"The other," he ordered. "The one we swore on, you and I."

Almost tenderly, the God of War cradled my smaller hand in his calloused palm. He lowered his head. Silver and iron strands trailed over his brow as he slowly traced his finger along the single scar I still carried.

I was a god. I could heal any of my wounds—except that one, the one I'd gained from tearing a blade through my flesh to mingle my blood with Odin's.

At his touch, a gray flame coursed through me, seeping up into my limbs like killing frost. I shuddered and tried to pull away, but his grip tightened.

"My gift," he murmured in a softer voice. I bit back a retort, sensing that something far deeper was afoot. "Sleep here tonight," he told me. "See what dreams visit you."

I looked about the thistle-choked space without any enthusiasm. Odin nodded, then turned his back to me and left. The sun was sinking rapidly, the twilight murk giving way to the longer shadows of night.

Grumbling to myself, I found a sheltered corner, then settled down and called up a fire. I spread myself out beside it with uneven moss for a bed and only my cloak for a blanket. The flame was steady and warm, powered by my will.

No birds called from the forests and no bats flittered above on their hunt. Breidablik was as still as a grave. The place was as unnatural as its dead master.

My thoughts drifted. Eventually, I descended into sleep.

The first dream was a familiar one, both nightmare and prophecy. Billions of mortal years flew by, spiraling away toward the ultimate doom. Suns that had once lit flourishing worlds grew cold. Others exploded and collapsed back onto themselves, pulling everything around them into their insatiable embrace. The distances between the remaining stars increased. Darkness consumed the universe we called Midgard, flinging it into the profoundest sort of cold—a cold that only Odin, of all the gods, could truly comprehend. When the last scattered suns finally disintegrated into the blackness of entropy, Heimdall blew his horn. Its clarion call echoed through the realms, shuddering up Yggdrasil. Asgard trembled too.

The leaf we had protected for so long was ready to fall. It had to fall. It was already dead.

I moaned and struggled in my sleep.

I suddenly found myself in Valhalla, down on bended knee. My heart seemed to empty a little more with every beat.

Odin lifted his spear to me in a parting salute. "It is time," he said. His voice was the freezing void.

I knew that I had to fight against him, against all the Aesir. The bonds between us were as broken as everything else. Love was gone, as was hope. I felt nothing as I nodded back, got up, and left Asgard for the final time.

In the way of dreams, everything changed without warning. I stood at the prow of a mighty warship carrying the troops of the dead. My daughter, Hel, was at my side. One half of her body was pale, shining with sickly light, and the other half was as deep and dark as the night seas we crossed.

And then I was in the fields outside Gladsheim, waiting. The grass was brown and lifeless underneath my feet, and the sky—the gods' eternal sky—was pockmarked with deep, smoldering holes. Their edges burned like embers, eating the heavens.

I smiled at the sight, then raised my hand and summoned my own flame. Surt, the most dreadful of all the fire giants, rumbled behind me. His armies rushed in, and this time there was no stopping them. They tore through the crumpling fields and shaking halls of Asgard. A surge of heat reduced Glitnir to sludgy metals, and all her laws were forgotten. Vingolf collapsed into a billowing cloud of soot. Only Valhalla remained.

Its many doors crashed open and Odin's hosts flooded out to do battle. Ragnarok had come at last.

I whispered evil runes, calling forth a writhing, scorching sword made by Surt himself. A fiercer fire than any I had ever known was my weapon now. Heimdall threw himself at me with an incoherent shriek. His tunic gleamed pure and bright, and the very last rainbows of our realm shimmered about him. We were evenly matched. We fought long and hard, consumed by our hatred, oblivious to the other struggles raging around us.

All at once, agony speared through my chest. I was connected to Odin by blood, and my blood screamed out in response as he died.

Devoured by my pain and fury, I launched myself at my old foe, secretly—fervently—hoping that he'd finish me off. Heimdall's killing blow slashed into my flesh, and I grinned at him sardonically. I lifted my arm for the final time, and my flaming sword ripped his body apart.

There was darkness.

There was nothing.

There were no gods.

An eternity passed.

No time at all passed.

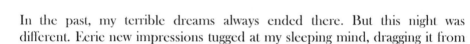

In the past, my terrible dreams always ended there. But this night was different. Eerie new impressions tugged at my sleeping mind, dragging it from those strange and hollow places. Forward, onward.

Light caressed the scar on my palm and poured through my being. For the first time ever, the dream continued.

"Father, wake up."

I blinked and opened my eyes. I could see only the horrifying, tingling blackness that had tormented me in the cave. But I felt no bonds. No rock tore into my back. No enchanted lashes dug into my wrists and legs. I touched my hand to my own face to make sure it was real. It was. I could feel the skin underneath my palm, smooth and subtle.

"Hel?" I whispered.

"I'm here." Dry fingers brushed across my brow, then gently stroked my hair. My sight returned.

I was on a dead field, looking down at my own corpse. Crushed ribs, jagged and white, stabbed through my torn side. My brown, crusty blood coated everything, including Heimdall's useless weapon. He was sprawled out nearby, his chest unmoving and his empty eyes fixed on some point far above.

I should have been appalled and afraid. But I only took in the details with a clinical dispassion. Slowly, I peered around. I saw no one but my daughter.

"This is death?" I asked her.

"It is yours. No two are the same."

I met her gaze. She was beautiful. So beautiful.

One side of her shone as brightly as Gladsheim once had. Her pink eye had changed. It was now clear, and it seemed to be graced with all the colors that had ever been. Her other side was the comforting deep stillness of a million summer nights, the kind of nights when the worlds retire into themselves, awash in mystery and magic. That second eye was as profound and wise as the Cosmos. It was soft and black, alive with some joyous secret.

"Daughter," I said, awed, "I've never seen you like this before."

Her delineated lips curved up in a gentle smile. "You always told me I was lovely."

"Indeed I have, sweet child."

"Come, we have much to do."

She held out her dark hand to me. I took it and followed her, for she ruled now. All authority, all power were hers.

Nestled in the knots and circling woods of Yggdrasil, two lives stir. They are hesitant at first, like young fledgling birds perched on the edge of their nest contemplating the sheer drop that faces them. They don't know what's going to happen. A next step awaits. It must be taken. But what is that step?

Honir, the only creator god who had survived Ragnarok, lifts a beckoning hand. He gestures encouragingly, reassuring them with a tentative smile. His blonde hair falls about his unscarred neck. His hazel eyes are compassionate.

"What happens now?" I ask Odin. I keep my voice down so I won't distract Honir. The Father of All places his weighty hand on my shoulder. The touch is familiar and yet not familiar.

We had died, he and I.

He doesn't answer, but when he turns to look at me, his two eyes flash brilliantly. They sparkle and dance with the infinite, full of song and light.

My attention returns to Honir. The other god is now speaking with the pair of spirits. Above us, the leaves of Yggdrasil rustle, carrying laughter and music. They glow with a blissful radiance, in all the hues of gold and green.

"Loki, what gifts will you give to the children of Ask and Embla?" Odin asks me. His young voice is steady and serene. The god's chestnut brown hair cascades down his back, and his sky-blue tunic moves in the breeze.

I start at the question. It's an old one, one I had answered before, long ago.

"I... I don't know yet, my lord. And you?"

He raises his head and chuckles. The sound of it is like the deep, rich earth in the woods—the call of new and glorious expanses, of adventure and rejoicing.

"Why, my brother, I don't know yet either!"

Honir looks back at us, beaming. His expression is inviting. We know it is time.

We step forward. Me, strangely calm, my red tunic shining. My black eyes are bright and just a touch amused. Odin, the Father of All who is wise beyond the measure of all realms and worlds, pauses for a moment to wink at me.

Solid and tall, he takes his place between us.

The highest of the gods bows his head to Honir. The three of us join our hands together, fingers interlocking.

An eternity passes.

No time at all passes.

All is reborn.

My fire had burned low. Orange cinders popped softly as I sat up. I stretched my arms to work out the kinks. Yawning, I looked about Breidablik. The dawn's amber light spilled over me and fresh air brushed against my cheek. I spoke a rune, and the last of the embers cooled. With another word of magic, the fire pit disappeared. My cloak was no longer necessary. I folded it over one arm and got to my feet. The twisting thistles were gone, and the clumps of dirt and weeds were nowhere to be seen.

White roses climbed the walls now, filling the vacant hall with their heady perfume. Restored golden panels gleamed like sun-drenched seas. The crystal floors sparkled again, and it was impossible to tell how deep they ran. They seemed to descend forever, to the very core of our realm.

When I reached the entrance, I stopped and placed a hand against the clean stone. I surveyed the transfigured hall.

I lowered my head, a god acknowledging the memory of a god. "Rest well, Baldur." I touched my fingers to my heart, in honor of the dead.

I joined the others in Valhalla that afternoon. Yule was ending in a few days, and I was finally in the mood to celebrate. The warlike hall was decorated festively. Ivy and holly wound up the thick spears supporting the roof, and pine branches garlanded the tables. Hundreds of long golden chains daggled from the ceiling of shields above, hung with bauble-like clusters of mistletoe.

I found a place beside Thor, who was giving me a searching look over his ale. He huffed into his beard uncomfortably. "So... um, we're all right, aren't we? You and me?"

"Never better, old friend."

He nodded, relief plain on his face. I rested my elbows on the surface of the long table, watching the others come and go with a good-natured smile. The mead was especially delicious, and the smoky scents of Valhalla seemed particularly bold and invigorating.

Bragi struck up a holiday tune on his lyre, and many of the gods and goddesses stood up to dance. Their steps were quick and graceful. Normally, I would have been among the first out on the floor, but that day, I relaxed at the table. The after-effects of the dream still lingered—healing, but fresh in their intensity. I was content to sit with my old companion.

Thor raised his shaggy red eyebrows at me. "You're a quiet one. For a change."

I shook my head and gave him an easy smile. "Don't get used to it."

He grinned back. "Well, good. You had me worried there for a minute." The Thunder God gulped down a mouthful of beer, then belched in a self-satisfied way. "Hey, I'm going to Midgard after the holidays. You interested?"

I gave it some thought, then nodded. "Giants again?"

"That, and I have something I want to show you." I tilted my head to one side and my dark eyes lit up with curiosity, but he didn't explain further.

We drank together, enjoying each other's company.

The festivities continued as the sun set and the snow fell. Though sharp winter gusts rattled the eaves, all was warmth and life in Odin's hall.

There was finally peace among the gods.

That was not to say that harsh words were not sometimes traded between us. We had disagreements which dragged out for months or even years. Tempers soared and settled, and alliances formed and dissolved, only to form anew. Sometimes divine treasures went missing and their former owners flew into pointless rages for a time.

But when we, the eternal Aesir, met together in Gladsheim, we set all our differences aside. We spoke with wisdom and with love—with patience and consideration—and our counsel was just.

We never again had a perfect peace.

But we had a true peace.

We were immortals, the gods and goddesses of the deepest joys and richest triumphs. Each of us was true to our own ways and each of us forged our own path. We lived, dreamed, and thrived, always in accordance with our highest natures.

But we were never truly apart.

We were friends.

We were family.

We were free.

EPILOGUE

Asgard and Midgard Present

Light streamed through the open doors of Glitnir, heavy and dewy with the dawn's promise. The rays illuminated the silver floors, and dust motes sparkled like minuscule, drifting suns.

The morning was peaceful. The dry scents of tomes and parchments mixed with the heartier odors of coffee, and warm breezes found their way inside the hall to gently ruffle the papers on Forseti's desk. The young God of Law looked very content. He sipped at his drink and made his way through one of his many volumes. I couldn't remember ever seeing him so at ease. He still moved with academic deliberation, but some of the reserve and most of the coldness were gone.

I felt very close to the other Aesir. We had shared much, he and I, and I truly did not wish to disturb him when he was clearly so happy. But I was bored. Very, very bored.

After cooling my heels for as long as I could bear, I finally gave into temptation and began entertaining myself with the ruby I'd stolen from Odin's hall. I spun the gem between my fingers, admiring the way it flashed and glinted in the early morning beams. I gave a subtle jerk of my hand, and it bounced into the air, scattering crimson brilliance across the desk. I made a clever movement with my wrist, and it danced along my knuckles, only to be snatched back up again.

Forseti lifted an eyebrow. "That's terribly distracting," he noted.

"I'm sorry, my friend. But you're taking forever and the day is lovely. I'm eager to be off."

With a martyred sigh, the God of Law finally closed his book. "Public intoxication is not illegal where you're going," he told me.

"Right. So... you're absolutely sure?"

The other Aesir returned my gaze levelly and kept silent, but the gray eyes evidenced the smile he was trying to hide.

I grinned at him, sprang to my feet, and shot him a flippant wave in parting as I dashed for the exit. A moment later, I was outside, flying past his silver fence with the roar of the river in my ears. A wispy fog still clung to the low areas near the rock where the God of Law had once promised to witness my marriage, but the sky itself was blue. The winds carried gentle mists off the churning waters, and these mingled with the sunshine, washing the field in rainbows.

The Yuletide was past, and it was a good time for a journey. I no longer avoided Heimdall. Bifrost was the quickest bridge between the realms, and I capered straight down it, laughing as the glowing particles of the spectrum surged around me. I was swifter than Thor's chariot; I was swifter than any other god.

It was evening in Midgard and the weather was unseasonably warm. Thor was waiting for me beside a dirt path, clutching an oak staff in his heavy hand. He wore his usual green tunic and a jerkin of brass-studded leather. Mjolnir gleamed sleepily at his side, as if it were getting in some well-earned rest before we found any giants.

I called up a dark-stained walking stick of my own and crowned it with my purloined ruby. I was in my favorite red tunic, and my new staff would go nicely with the rest of my look.

The other Aesir greeted me. Then he lifted his face to the trees and inhaled deeply, like a wolf getting the lay of the land. I watched him, my head angled to one side and my expression curious.

"Let's go east," he decided at last.

"Certainly, Mighty One," I said. "Any particular reason?"

The Thunder God snorted. "Be patient for once. You'll see soon enough."

We struck off down the trail with him in the lead. The other god's steps were bold and strong. I grinned and danced along after him, easily keeping pace. Sometimes my sure feet would find a stone to leap and whirl upon, or a fallen log to cavort along. The moon was rising, full and white, and it bleached the forest of all color. Only the browns and grays remained. Within these I could see every twirl of bark and each silvery, rattling leaf. The details became their own beauty.

Warm air teased my hair. I skipped once, then pounced into a night eddy, twirling in place as it spiraled dry leaves about me. Being in Midgard again was the purest joy. Thor looked back at me and shook his head, smiling into his beard.

"All right, I'll admit it," he said. "I missed this."

With a graceful jump, I was back at his side. I gave him an easy grin, and we were off, faster than before. I had no idea where we were going, and I didn't care. It was the most natural thing in all the realms to be out on some unknown adventure with the Thunder God.

The Midgard night hummed with its own magic. We crowned a rise and followed the moonlit trail past a lake. Ducks quacked sleepily, and a startled heron took off from the rushes below, huge, dark, and silent.

I noticed that Thor was actually slowing down. He frowned to himself thoughtfully, then stopped and held up a hand.

"Feel that?" he asked.

I paused. My tunic fluttered as I stood still, overlooking the lake and taking in Midgard with Aesir senses. "I'm not sure what—"

"Give it a moment," he instructed. I did.

The perception came upon me slowly at first, then broke over my mind all at once, like a pent-up river bursting through a confining tangle of mud and sticks. I blinked rapidly, bracing myself against my staff.

"You pick up on it more on a night like this," Thor said. His tone was almost aloof. I knew he was hiding great emotion. Normally, I would have teased him, would have tried to draw him out or goad him. But not then.

The thoughts wove in and out, some clearer than others. Some were steely and rigid, abristle with self-righteousness. Some were gray and nearly unformed. Others were strong and full of a wish to do good. But the thoughts were there. I could feel every single one, intertwined against the endless tapestry of mortal preoccupations and concerns.

"They truly remember us," I said softly. "I hear your name."

The other Aesir chuckled. "Keep listening then!"

Fainter, flickering under the surface like embers, was something else... something unexpected. My name. And the memory of it was not always combined with hostility, with fear or derision. I raised an eyebrow at Thor.

"So, there you have it," he said gruffly. "Doesn't change anything, of course. I'd kill their damned giants anyways." He scowled at the lake, as if daring it to disagree with him. "Midgard is Midgard."

"As you say, Lord Thunderer."

He started off again, humming a warrior's tune. As usual, he lost the key very quickly. Bragi would have been horrified. I followed along behind him, thinking hard. Perhaps he was right. We were who we were. Mortal thoughts would never change that. But I was gratified all the same.

We traveled many hours, we two gods—one in red and the other in green, and both well used to each other's company. Eventually, we happened upon a valley. The full moon was dipping low and the night was now still. The sun would rise soon. We stood up on a hilltop among brittle grasses, regarding the sparkling lights of a great city. The throat-tickling odors of car fumes reached us, along with the dull hisses and slaps of early traffic.

Underneath the drowsy mortal reflections lurked the evil, brooding presence of giants. I lifted my chin and caught Thor's eye. We were Aesir. We would not let our ancient enemies reign there unchallenged.

Our gait was confident and assured as we started down the rocky trail. Mjolnir now glowed with orange and white fire, crackling from my companion's belt.

I called up flame of my own. My laughter was light and free, as sweet as a child's. Thor hefted his hammer with practiced ease, and his deeper, booming guffaws echoed over the hills.

The Trickster and the Thunder God walked together once more. There would be a glorious battle that day and stories to tell in Valhalla long after.

Midgard is one of many worlds, but there are many worlds in Midgard.

Not all of these are places of unyielding, uninterrupted pavement—of piercing street lamps, noise and chaos, violence and despair. A pulse sounds beneath the cacophony, calming and steady.

That pulse can be heard in the laughter of a friend or seen in a smile freely given. The first dandelions of the spring dance to its song as they force their way through splits in the concrete. The warming air bears its cadence.

Its sound is louder in the woods. The trees sway with it, offering comfort to the weary. It drums softly over the velvet moss, among the ferns and over the remains of last year's leaves. Its song is not lost and can never be lost.

Sometimes, though, the pulse fades when it is closest. The trees are quiet and the ponderous clouds stalking the sky hang still. No tuft of grass stirs, no bird flaps its wings.

There is a space, a long pause between one breath and another. Time slows and then stops. The infinite is close. The eternal is but a touch of a hand away.

Something else is heard then, borne under the suspended rays of the sun. Gentle words. Words of solace and words of power.

Words of the spirit.

Words of the will.

Words of the heart's own blood.

Long ago, in times lost to memory, the gods created man and woman from the trees.

Among the trees, the gods still speak.

the end

author's notes

For more on Loki, Thor, and many of the other Aesir, the reader need look no further than Kevin Crossley-Holland's wonderful book, *The Norse Myths*. Most of the famous tales that are referenced in passing in this novel can be found in his indispensible volume. Crossley-Holland retells the myths beautifully and, as a bonus, provides a wealth of cultural and background information in his Introduction and Notes.

The curious reader may also wish to investigate the Lokka Tattur, a 95-stanza Faroesian ballad in which Odin, Honir, and Loki each attempt to save a man's son from a giant. The story portrays Loki very positively and gives another account of these three gods working together.

Finally, a note on Forseti. There is very little in the way of source material on this figure. However, a surviving Old Frisian legend mentions a divine stranger who brings law to the land while carrying a golden axe.

GLOSSARY OF NAMES AND PLACES

PLACES

ALFHEIM - The realm of the Light Elves. It shares a border with Asgard.

ASGARD - The realm of the Aesir gods.

BIFROST - The rainbow bridge that leads to Asgard.

BILSKIRNIR - Thor's hall.

BREIDABLIK - Baldur's former hall.

GLADSHEIM - The holy grove where the gods hold their councils.

GLITNIR - Forseti's hall.

HIMINBJORG - Heimdall's hall.

JOTUNHEIM - The realm of giants (the Jotuns) where Loki was born. It has grown considerably less hospitable over time.

MIDGARD - The place where the gods defeated the giant Ymir. "Midgard" may refer to the world created at the exact spot where the giant fell (also commonly known as "Earth") or to the larger universe containing that world.

MUSPELHEIM - The realm of fire giants.

NIDAVELLIR - The realm of dwarves.

NIFLHEIM - The realm of the dead where Loki's daughter, Hel, reigns.

THRUDHEIM - Thor's realm.

THRYMHEIM - Skathi's realm.

URD - A sacred well. The gods convene there each morning.

VANAHEIM - The realm of the Vanir gods.

VINGOLF - The hall where the goddesses hold their councils. It is known for the quality of its wines.

VALHALLA - One of Odin's halls.

VALSKALF - Another of Odin's halls. From Hliskalf, a chamber inside of it, he can see everything that ever happens in any realm.

YGGDRASIL - The Great Tree, the source of all being. All the worlds and realms are cradled in its branches. Its origins are unknown.

GODS

BALDUR - The former God of Good and Light. He was the son of Odin and was Loki's nephew. He was married to Nanna and had a hall named Breidablik where "no unclean thing could dwell."

BRAGI - The god of song. He is married to Idunn.

FORSETI - God of judgment, justice, and law. He is the only child of Baldur and Nanna. Forseti rules over Glitnir, the most modern hall in Asgard. He brews a mean cup of coffee.

FREYR - A god of nature, sunlight, and celebration. He lives in Alfheim and is married to Gerd. He is Freya's brother.

HEIMDALL - The god of boundaries who guards Asgard from its enemies. He is a former Vanir.

HOD - Baldur's blind brother.

HONIR - The god of uncertainty. He is one of the three creator gods.

LOKI - God of fire, mischief, magic, shapeshifting, and storytelling. A former giant, he is Odin's blood-brother and is married to Sigyn. Loki is the cleverest of all the gods. To hear him tell it, he also the handsomest.

ODIN - The most powerful of the gods and the ruler of the Aesir. He is the god of war, magic, and wisdom. He owns several halls, including Valhalla.

MIMIR - Odin's old friend. Mimir was killed by the Vanir.

NJORD - God of the sea. He is a former Vanir and the father of Freyr and Freya. Njord was married to Skathi for nine nights.

THOR - The god of storms and thunder. He is the son of Odin and protects

Midgard from giants. Thor rules over a realm called Thrudheim and has a hall named Bilskirnir. He *really* likes dark beer.

TYR - One of the oldest and wisest of the Aesir. A warrior god of order, as well as justice achieved through self-sacrifice.

ULLR - The god of joy, freedom, and victory. He is also the god of skiing.

GODDESSES

FREYA - An extremely powerful goddess of magic, battle, and love. Freya came to Asgard from Vanaheim and is the sister of Freyr. She can shapeshift.

FRIGG - Odin's wife and Baldur's mother. She is a goddess of magic and can see into the future.

GERD - A goddess of boundaries, protection, and earth. She is Freyr's wife. Gerd was a giantess before she joined the Aesir.

HEL - The daughter of Loki and Angrboda. She is the Queen of the Dead and rules over Niflheim.

IDUNN - Bragi's wife, known for her innocence.

LOFN - Goddess of love and forbidden marriages.

NANNA - Baldur's former wife. She died of a broken heart at her husband's funeral.

RAN - Goddess of the seas. She is married to a giant named Aegir.

RAUDFIFA - "Red Arrow," one of Loki's assumed forms.

SIF - A goddess of hospitality and fruitful fields. She is married to Thor, and her hair is made of spun gold.

SIGYN - Loki's wife, a goddess of nature and healing.

SKATHI - Goddess of winter, mountains, and magic. A former giantess who was briefly married to Njord.

SYN - A guardian goddess who witnesses refusals and helps defendants at trials.

THRUD - The goddess of strength. She is the daughter of Thor and Sif.

VAR - Goddess of vows and oath-taking.

OTHER CHARACTERS

AEGIR - A giant. He is married to the goddess Ran.

ANDVARI - A dwarf.

ANGRBODA - A giantess. She was the mother of three of Loki's children.

ASK - The first human male.

BOMBOR - A dwarf.

BROKK - One of two dwarf brothers. Loki lost a wager against them; they were supposed to get his head in payment, but they had to settle for sewing his lips shut instead. Loki has wanted revenge on them ever since.

BUTHLUNGR - One of Freya's two cats.

EITRI - Brokk's more intelligent brother.

EMBLA - The first human female.

FARBAUTI - A giant. Loki's father.

FENRIR - A huge and cunning wolf. He is the son of Loki and Angrboda.

FREKI - One of Odin's two wolves.

FULLA - A goddess who is also one of Frigg's handmaidens.

GERI - The second of Odin's wolves. Unlike Freki, he is actually friendly.

GULLINBURSTI - Freyr's golden boar, a magical creature made by dwarves.

HNOSS - Freya's daughter, a kindhearted goddess.

HUGINN - One of Odin's two crows.

JARI - A dwarf.

JORMUNGAND - A giant snake and the son of Loki and Angrboda. He encircles the universe containing Midgard.

LAUFEY - A giantess. Loki's mother.

LOTHURR - Another name for Loki.

LUTHER - Loki's mortal name.

MENNSKURTH - One of Freya's two cats.

MUNINN - The second of Odin's crows.

NARVI - Loki and Sigyn's son.

OTTER - A shapeshifting mortal. Loki killed him by accident during a hunt.

RICH - Heimdall's mortal name.

RIG - An old alias of Heimdall's.

SLEIPNIR - Odin's eight-legged warhorse. He is another of Loki's children.

SKOLL AND HATI - The wolves that chase the sun and moon.

SURT - The mightiest of the fire giants. He rules over a realm called Muspelheim.

THIAZI - A giant. Skathi's father.

THRYM - A giant who made the predictably fatal mistake of stealing Thor's hammer, Mjolnir.

YMIR - The very worst of all the giants. The gods killed him and created Midgard from his body.